THOSE
AMONG
US

Other books by Mike Taylor

Malama Ko Aloha

Double Cross

Rings of a Tree

Ten Bells

Eagle Bill

Those Among Us

by
Mike Taylor

Mike Taylor Publishing
Oceanview, Hawaii

Those Among Us

Copyright © 2026 Mike Taylor

Mike Taylor's books may be
ordered through booksellers or Amazon.com

Mike Taylor Publishing
PO Box 6958
Ocean View, HI 96737 USA

mt42953@gmail.com
Facebook and Instagram @authormiketaylor

ISBN (paperback): 979-8-9897244-5-1

Cover design by Mike Taylor

Cover design and layout by Jason Durham

Dedication

This work is for my wife, Marion, who keeps me going and to my family and friends who give me constant support. And to all of you who have purchased and read my other books... Thank you very much!

I also dedicate this story to my amazing granddaughter, Kaleiana. She's the one who requested me to write this because we both like scary movies. That is, until it's time to turn off the lights and go to bed...

So, if this story gives you chicken skin or makes you think you heard something moving around outside in the darkness... If you feel something cold touch the back of your neck and it startles you then I've done my job... you're welcome!

"WHEN THE FEAR HAS GONE THERE WILL BE NOTHING... ONLY I WILL REMAIN..."

-FRANK HERB-

CHAPTER 1

A young boy pushed himself off the floor, his head felt like it was going to explode. There was a light on in the upstairs hallway but, it's glow faded out halfway down the stairs, so the room was only gray shadows. He tried to stand but his head hurt so bad. Everything was out of focus.

When he was finally able to stand the room shifted slightly to the right before it settled. Laying at his feet was his father; he was lying on his back. His pajama shirt was torn and slit and there was blood... a lot of blood. He looked around the room for his mother but didn't see her, and he went completely numb.

Red and blue light flooded through the front windows casting dizzying strobes across the living room. Suddenly there was the sound of footsteps on the front porch stairs.

That's when he noticed that the front of his pajamas was also covered in blood, something was in his hand... The door was being battered open, he had something in his right hand... and... he could barely see it, so he held it closer to his face... it was a very ugly, sharp knife...

"Drop the knife!" Sheriff Dobbs flanked by Deputies, Green and Ellis pressed into the room, guns pointed at the boy. Sheriff Dobbs stayed with the boy while the other two quickly swept the house. "Drop it son," Sheriff Dobbs was slowly moving in. "We're here to help you," he stepped closer holding his hand out, he had holstered his gun keeping a close eye on the boy, who continued to stand there with a completely blank expression on his blood-soaked face. "Now, how 'bout you hand over that knife and we can have us a nice talk, okay?"

The boy handed him the knife, though he had absolutely no idea as to how he had it in the first place. His head really pounded.

He looked down upon the lifeless body on the floor and began to shake uncontrollably. Sheriff Dobbs examined the bloody knife in his gloved hand and was deeply troubled by it. Deputies, Green and Ellis searched the rest of the house and joined him back in the surreal flashing lights of the living room.

"Sheriff," Deputy Ellis motioned for Sheriff Dobbs to come over. "The boy's mother is upstairs..." he whispered, not taking his eyes off the young boy who looked like something out of a horror movie. "She was stabbed to death, like the father here... Phone was still in her hand... it's broken, so, I think she was able to get one good lick in before she..." he lowered his eyes and studied the floor.

"Search the yard and maybe..." Sheriff Dobbs released a frustrated breath. "I was gonna say, ask the neighbors but, shit, there are no neighbors out here. Least not near close enough to have heard or seen anything. Look around outside just the same."

"You got it Sheriff," Deputies Ellis and Green went back out the front door but, not without taking one last look at the carnage. The scene they stumbled into that night would haunt both men for many years to come.

Sheriff Dobbs bent down to address the boy, "You name's Sam, right?"

Sam nodded as tears fell in wet lines down his bloodstained cheeks.

"Well, Sam, let's us take a seat over here," he ushered Sam into a chair in the kitchen. He noticed that the back door was slightly ajar. "Have a seat there, Sam." He went over to find there were bloody fingerprints on the door handle and a bloody handprint on the wall next to it. "You wait here Sam, okay?

"Okay."

The Sheriff went outside.

"Sheriff? What are you doing out here?"

"Needed to take some air," he answered slightly startled. He closed the shed door and wiped his hands on his jeans as he walked toward the deputies. "I noticed the shed back there and took a look around it."

"We saw it too but it was locked," Deputy Ellis was watching the Sheriff.

"What about that boy?" Deputy Green wanted to know.

"He's sitting in the kitchen. You find anything out here?" He asked without turning around.

"Well, we did find some shoe prints 'round the side of the house. But nothin' else really. Gonna have to wait for morning to really see. Sheriff? You doing alright?"

"Yeah… Okay, better get Earl out of bed. This place needs to be processed pronto. Deputy Ellis, I want you to make the calls. Then I want you to man the phones, send Gladys home, she's had a long day as it is… Don't talk to anyone til we get this mess figured out."

"Deputy Green, I want you to stay parked out by the hi-way… but stay in the trees a bit. We need this sewn up tight, you boys got me?"

"Alright, Sheriff, we're on it." Both deputies left the house to the Sheriff and the boy. Deputy Ellis got in his patrol car. The first call he made was to, Earl Fact, the Coroner. He had gotten cranky in his old age and was none too pleased to have his sleep interrupted grumbling, 'why can't people die at a more decent hour.' He said he'd get there as soon as possible… Then he called Melissa, at the Jade County Emergency Station which boasted a small EMT team that took 12 hour shifts, it was about ten minutes away. The station served the whole of Jade County, which included somewhere around five-hundred souls including assorted; chickens, cows, horses, and old man Fitch's blue-ribbon hog named Ham. Melissa would get the ambulance rolling.

Sheriff Dobbs took out his handkerchief and grasped the doorknob, he was extremely distressed. He closed the back door and, as an afterthought, smudged the fingerprints on the wall, but not too much. He took off his rubber gloves and wrapped them in his handkerchief. He went to the sink and washed his hands. Then, he turned his attention back to Sam, who sat wringing his hands at the kitchen table.

"Sam? Sam." Sheriff Dobbs wanted to get Sam to focus his attention on him. "How old are you these days?" He was trying to remain calm, professional…. only, the truth of it was he felt sick, really nauseated. But he was the Sheriff, so he just had to gulp it back and make some sense of it all.

"10." Sam hadn't gotten his eyes to regain focus yet so everything was still real fuzzy.

"Do you know what happened here? Did you see anyone else here?" For the first time, in the stark light of the kitchen, he noticed that Sam had a nasty cut on his forehead. "Where did you get the knife?"

CHAPTER 2

The road was right where the guy at the cafe said it would be. He turned onto the narrow lane, his headlights illuminating the way with a column of light. Trees were fairly thick along the sides and threw long, rolling shadows out into the dark woods.

The road was in good shape for the most part and it didn't take long before a house appeared out of the gloom. He stopped to look at it, his old childhood home tucked far back into the woods. He sat there in his rental car trying to dredge up some memories of the place; there were so many blank spots, he remembered some things but, there was a huge block of his life that just wasn't there.

It was as if he were never a child... it hadn't ever bothered him until now, finding himself sitting in a car that didn't belong to him looking up at a house that held no familiarity, it made him feel very uneasy and kind of sick to his stomach.

There was movement off to his right side, he looked in that direction but saw nothing and figured it was some animal or a trick of the light, probably a squirrel. He started forward again until his car lights flooded the front of the house.

When he stepped out of the car it happened again. A shadow shot by him. This time he saw it, briefly, but, still, couldn't tell what it was, only that it was dark, really dark... and bigger than a squirrel.

Shrugging it off as fatigue from the long trip he unloaded his bags, fumbled briefly with the keys, and set his bags inside the front door, found the light switches and flipped on the porch light. He wasn't quite ready to explore the inside yet, not just yet.

Sam Henning sat on the top step of the front porch of his newly acquired house; evidently his parents had left it to him when they passed, a date and an event he was not aware of, but he felt it had been a long time ago, and again, he had no idea why. His face contorted with the effort to call forth any remembrance of either of his parents...

One day he gets a call from a very distressed sounding Mr. Perry, who said he was the executor of his parents' estate and had been trying to reach him for over a year. He told Sam that the previous executors of the estate had retired and that his firm had assumed the handling of the trust.

But Sam wasn't even in the country, hadn't been for a long time. He was pursuing a mediocre career in France and couldn't get away.

An electrical shock wave blast through his body upon receiving the news however, and he thought, maybe, he didn't want to get away... or couldn't. It didn't matter. He had little interest in having to go to a place he hadn't thought about since his younger brother was... he couldn't call anything to mind... nothing but shadowy, blurry images, no familiar voices from the past, nothing.

Now he found himself without a job, in a place that held no memory for him, and as such had grown strange to him, sitting on the front porch of a house that was bought and paid for with his parents lives.

There it was again... that shadow thing he had seen a couple times since his arrival. It was dark, darker than the night that loomed just outside the reach of the porch light. He caught it out of the corner of his eye but when he looked in that direction there was nothing.

Whatever it was had raced directly across his field of vision and was gone, definitely bigger than a squirrel. It made no sound, and it was very fast. The hairs on the back of his neck suddenly stood up as goosebumps raced over his body. Suddenly he felt prickly. In fact, for a brief second, he felt really cold, freezing cold...

The chimes at the end of the porch clunked and tinkled and he stood up, heart thumping between his ears. As he watched the chimes, they quickly settled down to a soft ringing but, something had to brush through them to make them do that. There wasn't even a faint breeze, the night was completely calm.

He was getting a little dizzy and decided to go inside. Once in the house he noticed a sort of stale smell, not repulsive that way, it was a smell like an old trunk freshly opened. He walked around making sure the doors and windows were all locked, curtains pulled tight.

When he was satisfied everything was secure, he settled into an over-stuffed chair and looked around the room. It wasn't a large room, but it was comfortable. There was a fireplace with a stack of wood beside it and Sam made a nice little fire creating a warm, flickering light that filled the room with a little more cheeriness.

It was odd that even though it seemed that a house which appeared and smelled like it hadn't been occupied for a long time was... clean, as far as any dust or spiderwebs looming in the ceiling corners. He switched on the reading light sitting at a table next to his chair.

He got up and went over to the bookcase, which was crammed with books. He plucked one off the shelf, at random, then settled back to relax and read. As he read, he slowly forgot about; His life in France, that awful hospital... the things that happened inside, the long trip, even the fact that he was back in his parents' house. It all had given him an uneasy feeling, even though he felt safer inside.

After a few pages he couldn't keep his eyes open any longer. He saw that the fire was just about out so he found a piece of paper to mark his place in the book he was reading, set it down on the little table by his chair and headed upstairs.

The first door he opened revealed that it had been transformed into a sewing room and why not? Supposedly he hadn't lived in this house for more years than he could hope to think of. Maybe since he was... no... it was one of those frustrating blank spots in his memory, he was young, that he knew. Where had they gone, the years? Time was moving right along but, he wasn't so much.

He opened the door to another room and found it was still a bedroom, for which he was grateful. He dropped his bags at the foot of the bed and hit the shower. He stood under the hot water, bracing his hands on the tile wall and let the water wash away his anxiety helping him to finally relax.

When he got out of the shower, he wrapped a towel around his waist and walked back into the bedroom. He slipped into his pj's and into bed. He slept like he'd never slept before until a bright morning sun pushed through the window creating a box of light that slowly crept across the floor and onto his bed.

Sam rubbed his eyes and sat up. It was a beautiful morning outside, he dressed, went downstairs, and made himself a cup of coffee before going out onto the front porch. The smell of pine was strengthening as the suns' warmth penetrated the surrounding forest.

He sipped on his coffee and wondered at the sudden change of direction his life had taken. Twenty hours ago, he was engulfed in a city full of light and sound and now... and now he was sitting on a sun warmed porch with a cup of coffee steaming at his side.

Birds flitting among the trees were singing as a light breeze played through the treetops causing them to sway just a little bit. Sam took a long deep breath, inhaling the tangy pine smell as he tried to adjust to the peacefulness of the place.

It was all interrupted by the sound of someone coming up the road. Sam wondered who would be out at this time of day? Whatever time of day it was. He had no idea at all who it could be... he hadn't told anyone he was going to be here... he hadn't been in touch with anybody... who was he to keep in touch with anyway? It was a truck; a very old truck and it was definitely coming to his house as he didn't think there were any other houses on this road. He stood as the truck came to a halt next to his rental.

"Can I help you with something?" Sam waited for a reply from the occupant who was slowly removing himself from the front seat. The man finally stood and slammed the truck door shut. He looked to be as old and beat up as the truck he was driving.

"Why," the old man took a second to light a cigarette. "You must be the long-lost son come to claim his mommy an' daddy's house."

"I," Sam was taken by surprise to say the least. "I... yes, I'm Sam. This is my, was my parents' house... until..."

"Names Martin, I been takin' care o' this place for more'n fifyeen years I guess."

"I didn't know."

"Well, I just come by ta see if ya need anything. I'll be 'round from time ta time ta... look after things.

"What kind of things?" Sam sat down on the top step setting his cooling coffee down next to him.

"Well, I... see to it the grass is mowed when it needs ta be... I make sure the pipes don't freeze in the winter months. Anything needs paintin' or repair... that sort'a thing."

"And, if you don't mind my asking? Who pays you to do these things?" Thinking he had no job or any prospects for that matter. He wasn't sure how he was going to feed himself, much less pay for a handyman.

"Oh, that's all taken care of," he was wiping off his driver side mirror. "It's all taken care of in some kind'a trust, my pay is, that is."

"I see."

"Anyway, so?"

"Oh," Sam realized he was waiting for him to answer his first question.

"Well, I just got here so I don't know what to say."

"There's plenty a time ta get yerself settled in," he finished messing with his side mirror. "I'll be on my way then, nothin' needs tendin' to right at this moment. You just take yer time, I'll be comin' back by in a week or so, 'less ya need somethin' from me in the mean time."

"But, how do I get a hold of you? Do you have a number I can reach you at?"

"Don't own a phone, find 'em ta be a nuisance ma'self." He reached for the door handle and climbed back into his truck.

Sam stood up, "but..."

"It's a small town. I'll be 'round." With that said he started up the truck and simply drove off back down the road leaving a filmy blue line of smoke behind.

Sam stood on the top step, his coffee all but forgotten, as he watched the truck disappear around the bend. As he listened to the retreating motor he wondered about the handyman and how he knew that he was there. And, about this trust deal... Maybe it was just a coincidence.

But it did remind him that Mr. Perry told him he had set up a bank account in town and that he could access it whenever he needed to. The bank President was apparently instructed to help him with the paperwork.

He remembered his coffee cup and bent to pick it up and when he did, he heard something moving through the bushes at the edge of the forest. It sounded big and when he tried to locate where the sound was coming from it stopped, there was nothing.

All of a sudden, he felt like someone was watching him but, he couldn't see anyone. Hard as he peered into the woods where he thought he heard the sound... he still came up with nothing... He stared into the brush a moment longer then went back inside to get a fresh cup of coffee.

While he was waiting for the water to get hot, he had that same sinking feeling of being watched. He looked over his shoulder and there, framed in the front window, was the dark shape of a person standing outside. His breath hitched in his throat.

"Hello? Who's there?" He called out, his voice choked with apprehension. No answer... "Can I help you with something?" Still nothing...

Sam opened the front door and flung the screen door open, a little more forceful than he intended, and it banged against the outside wall. When he glanced around the front porch, he found there was nothing... nobody there. He heard his water boiling over on the stove and raced back inside to pull it off the heat causing a great hissing and popping as the bubbling water splashed on the hot coils. He looked back at a window that only revealed the forest beyond. Nobody was standing there...

After coffee and a hearty breakfast consisting of a can of pork and beans, he found in the pantry he grabbed his car keys and headed outside locking the front door behind him.

Once he made it to the hi-way he paused listening to the car motor idling away as he wondered which way town was, it bothered him that he couldn't remember if he turned left or right last night when he found the road leading to the house. He panicked for a second before realizing it was a left turn that brought him to this road, so right will take him to town.

He breathed a sigh of relief as the first buildings came into view. The bank wasn't hard to find as the main street of town wasn't very long. He parked right in front and pushed through the front doors. The bank was small, like the town, and the few people inside gave him a quick glance which didn't surprise him as he was a new face around here. He stepped up to the desk where a teller was just finishing up with another customer.

"How may I help you?" She shuffled a few papers and waited.

"Ah, yes, my name is Sam Henning. I'm here to open an account that was set up by my family trust?"

"Did you say your name is, Henning?" The bank teller made a strange face.

"Yes, that's correct," the change of her expression was not lost on Sam who was becoming uncomfortable. He glanced around and noticed that the three people inside the bank were staring his way. That is until they saw him look their way and quickly turned back to their business.

"I'm supposed to set up an appointment with your bank President?" He figured that he should announce his purpose.

"Oh, why yes, of course," the teller gathered herself assuming a more professional attitude. "Please excuse me, Mr. ah, Mr. Henning." She rose from her desk, ventured one last glance at Sam and went to the other side of the bank, knocked on a door and disappeared. She returned a short time later to inform Sam that, Mr. Goble, would see him now.

"Oh, that was fast," he smiled at the teller, and she forced a smile in return.

"You can go right in."

"Thank you." Sam entered the office of the bank President and was offered a handshake and a chair.

"Please, make yourself comfortable, my name is Mr. Goble."

"I'm Sam, Sam Henning, pleased to meet you."

"Well now, Mr. Henning, I did receive word from a Mr. Perry that you would be coming by," He got up and opened one of the cabinet drawers pulling out a small stack of official looking paperwork. "Here we are, let's see," He looked over several pages before turning his attention back to Sam. "I'm sorry to hear about your folks, they were a nice couple and much loved in our community. I must say you were quite a while in returning."

"Oh? What do you mean?"

"I'm sorry, it's really none of my business, it's just that your... they have been gone for quite a while."

"I've been out of the country."

"Again, it's none of my business," he shuffled the papers once more to get everything organized. "Alright let's get to it."

"You mentioned my parents... what happened to them?"

The bank President looked up into the completely blank face of someone confused, an expression pained for knowledge. He had no idea how he should proceed or if he should proceed at all... "I'm sorry...I really don't know what to say..."

"You seem to know something about my parents... I don't remember... much..."

"I'm not sure I'm the one to be telling you about this." He took a deep breath and wiped his lips with the back of his hand. There was a moment of uneasiness as he looked into the face of the young man seated across from him.

'Please, I would really like to know what, if anything, you know. a What happened to them..."

The bank President thought for a moment then said, "Susan... Susan White?" He watched Sam's face for any sign that he recognized the name. But it was immediately evident, that the young man did not.

Sam made a face and shook his head.

"You two, when you were young... Why you were inseparable. We all knew you both were destined to marry," he stopped in mid-sentence. "Susan White. You should talk to her."

"I wouldn't know where to find her much less recognize her if I did."

"She's not hard to find, she works at McKandless Emporium. It's on the corner, next block over." His attention returned to the papers in front of him. "Now, uh, Mr. Henning... if we could get back to the matter for your visit?" He pushed the papers, five in all, across his desk and slid a pen out of his neat pen holder setting it next to the papers.

"Please, look them over. I assure you they are all in order. Your parents were very straight forward and to the point. You will find the document before you will reflect that. Take all the time you need. I have a few things to attend to in the front but, I will be back to answer any questions you might have," he paused for a thought. "That is pertaining to the matter of the will before you." He closed the door to his office and was gone.

Sam didn't take much time looking them over as Mr. Perry had briefly explained each one, in a letter, in advance. So, when the bank President came back the process was completed, both men stood, shook hands and Sam headed for the door. Before he opened it the bank President spoke.

"If there's anything else we can do for you to make your visit less stressful just let us know."

"Visiting? Oh," Sam turned around, "I'm not visiting, I'm here to stay."

"Well then, If there's anything…"

"Thank you, Mr. Goble, is it?"

"Yes."

"Well, Mr. Goble have a good day."

"You too, Mr. Henning."

After stopping at the local grocery store, and enduring another round of side glances, he carried his bags out to his car and was soon back on the hi-way and home. When he got there, he unloaded his purchases, grabbed a cold beer and went outside to relax in the only chair on the front porch.

He sipped his beer and, for the first time since his arrival, he gazed out at the scenery, really breathing it in. After a bit his eyes focused in on an unusual aspect of the landscape. Just through the trees he could make out a clearing of some size. He was drawn to it, but he had no idea why he should be, other than it looked like a nice sunny break in the woods.

As he came through the trees and stood on the edge of the clearing, he took a moment to survey the whole thing from his viewpoint. He started to feel funny like his body was tingling, on the verge of breaking a sweat even though the short trail leading to the open space wasn't far at all and the day was cool.

Then he noticed what looked like a short, planked platform, sitting on pilings. He saw that the ground in the open area was lower, much lower than the surrounding landscape as if the clearing had sunk about twenty feet.

A picture formed in front of him showing a beautiful lake with a small dock and even an occasional fish breaking the surface creating a series of rings that spread out in ever growing circles. A boy appeared from the trees and ran by him, laughing.

Sam called to him, but the boy kept running, only he had stopped laughing. Sam ran after him, all the way down to the dock... That's where the boy... vanished. Immediately, Sam was assailed with a tremendous headache, so bad he dropped to his hands and knees to keep from doing a face plant in the grass.

The ground shook beneath him and he thought he would be sick. And then, it all stopped, even his headache, which had been almost blinding a moment ago, subsided until it was gone altogether.

Slowly, he made it to his feet and saw that the clearing was just that... a clearing. No lake where a second ago fish were jumping, and a boy was running... just a field of grass...

When he felt secure enough on his feet he headed back to the house and another beer, the one he held was empty. As he started up the steps, he stopped cold. There was a set of wet footprints leading up the wooden steps, like someone had been there only seconds before he got there. His eyes traced their path until he realized he wasn't breathing and gasped.

The footprints ended on the top step where whoever left them, stood. He studied the prints and realized two disturbing things; the first thing was the size of the feet, they were small, child size. The second and even more troublesome was the fact that they ended right on the top step, they didn't turn around and leave they just… ended… as if whoever made them had simply vanished into thin air.

Curious, Sam bent down and touched one of the prints and to his amazement, they were dry not wet… The prints were more like a negative photograph image stamped on the steps.

He was so mesmerized by the sight of the prints that he was completely unaware of the car that had come to a stop in the front yard. Only when the car door opened and closed did he turn his attention that way. A man, to be about his age, stood looking up at him.

"Sam?" He smiled. "I heard you came back," he waited for some acknowledgment but all he received was a puzzled expression. "Don't you remember me? Sam, it's me… Glen Harris?"

"I guess I don't," he shrugged. "Sorry."

"Well, it was a long time ago," he found a spot on the hood of his car that he tried to wipe off in a nervous stall for time. "We went to school together… we were just little kids."

They stood for a moment, neither had anything else to say until Glen broke the silence.

"Hey, I brought some beers! Figure we could catch up," when he received no response he continued. "Hang on I got 'em in my car." He retrieved a twenty-four pack of beer and some chips from the backseat and slammed the door. Then he stood there, twenty-four pack in one hand, bag of chips in the other but, he had yet to be asked to come on up.

"I'm sorry," Sam recovered, "please, c'mon up. I have another chair I can bring out."

"Great!" Glen was relieved and climbed the stairs.

Sam watched to see if his new arrival noticed the footprints but, if he did, he gave no indication that he had so Sam went in to get another chair and joined his guest back out on the porch.

"So, I'm sorry, Glen is it? Well, I just got here... how did you know I was here?"

"It's a small town," he extended his hand and Sam shook it. "Oh, here ya go," Glen broke open the box of beers and handed Sam one.

"Thanks," Sam popped the top and took a big, long drink.

"Do you remember when we were kids, we used to swim in the small lake over there?" Glen took a swig of his beer and smiled. "Loved swimming in that lake..."

"I don't remember anything of that," he looked in the direction Glen was looking but, he could only see an open field that was definitely lower than the surrounding area.

"Yeah, when your brother, Pete, drowned they..."

"They what?" Sam studied Glen's face; his expression was one of indecision. "They what?"

Glen stared hard at Sam picking his next words carefully. Sam appeared to be kind of tired and a little confused he didn't want to dredge up any bad memories, not on his first day back.

"Hey," Glen grabbed two more beers handing one to Sam. "It's good to see you again, it's been a long time," he tapped Sam's beer with his own. "Welcome home."

Welcome home. The words resounded in Sam's, head as he drank his cold beer. What an odd thing to say to someone who has absolutely no recollection of living in this place...

They sat out on the porch drinking and making small talk until the beer was gone and the day had slipped into evening.

"Well, I guess I should be getting home," Glen stood, a little wobbly, and stretched.

"Hey, Glen, do you know a Susan White?"

"Of course I do," he smiled up at Sam who was leaning on the front railing. "It's a small town, buddy. See ya!" He got back into his car and drove away.

Sam watched him drive down the road as he picked up the empty cans. He thought, as the car disappeared down the road, maybe he would seek this Susan White out tomorrow. How hard could she be to find? It's a small town.

CHAPTER 3

After dinner Sam went out and sat on the front porch to watch the last of the sunset colors drain from the sky. He thought about his visitor, and more importantly, what he said, or didn't say. So, there was a lake out there in the clearing... apparently, he swam a lot, his brain refused to recall anything of a lake and why was it, now, just a dried-up old field? Where the heck did the lake go? Lakes don't just disappear... do they? Everything was, now, cast in shadows and he had little interest, as far as furthering any examination, at the moment.

He went back into the house, *his* house, but not before one last look around the gloomy forest that surrounded him. He flicked on the living room light and went about cleaning up his dinner dishes. As he was cleaning up the kitchen there was a knock at the front door, and it made him pause; who could that be at this hour? It was just after seven o'clock and he sure enough didn't expect to have company.

There it was again, just a light knocking. It made the hairs on his arms stand up but why would it? He dried his hands as he walked to the door, the closer he got to the door the louder the knocks got until whoever it was at the door really got to banging on it. When he reached the door, he saw that it was shaking with the force of the knocks. He hesitated for a second, his hand hovering over the knob.

Then, just as he grasped it the knocking, stopped. Sam eased the door open, slowly, wishing he had grabbed a knife from the drawer but, what would he do if he had to use it? The thought made his stomach do a flip-flop. He turned the knob and pulled the front door open, only to discover no one was there...

He pushed through the screen door and stepped out onto the porch to take a better look. When he peeked around the corner of the house the chimes, behind him, began clanging in earnest. They swung back and forth, violently, as if someone was running their hand, back and forth, through them. He swung around to catch whoever it was, and the screen door slammed shut... As abruptly as they started, the chimes came to a tinkling halt. Now Sam was scared, really scared.

He had no idea how long he stood there, frozen to the spot, staring at those damn chimes. It was disheartening to say the least. He focused his attention on taking one leaden step at a time... each step was a step closer... left, right, left right... take door handle in hand and turn... He was shocked at the difference in temperature inside the house it was extremely cold...

Sam went into the study; the first room he hung out in and built a fire. It was about as big a fire as you could build in the space provided but, he needed a big fire. He started to sit and decided he just had to have something to protect himself with. He went into the kitchen and grabbed a knife from the drawer.

As soon as he held it, he was assailed with flashing images of himself, his father, darkness and screaming... nameless faces in masks and white gowns, hovering and bright light... Then it was gone. He was shaking so bad he put the knife back in the drawer and found a mallet, a nice wooden mallet. He guessed it was for tenderizing meat, or something.

It felt good in his hand, so he returned to the warmth of the study and moved his chair closer to the fire. He tried to relax himself by concentrating on the flames that were now, devouring the logs in leaping oranges and reds. Their warmth soon spread out through the small room easing Sam's nerves a bit.

He got up and went back into the kitchen where he opened a bottle of red wine. He poured himself a full glass and went back to his comfortable chair by the crackling fire. No more sounds were heard, only the sound of the fire, popping and sizzling. That and the tumbler of wine and Sam was gone to the world.

CHAPTER 4

A low rumbling sound wormed its way into the dark corners of Sam's muddled dream world. He pried his eyes open and studied the book filled room with sleep blurred vision until objects became clearer. He winced at the gray light of a new day that was sneaking through the window to his left, illuminating the floor and slowly making its way up the walls. Whoever it was, was coming up the road. Of course, and why not, he reasoned, visitors were the very last thing he had on his mind. But, hey, it's a small town, who knows?

He groaned out of the chair he'd slept in and found he was the lucky recipient of a stiff neck. Outside the car had come to a stop so he hurried to the door but, opened it slowly... he didn't want to appear too anxious. When he heard a car door close, he opened the front door in time to see a very pretty woman, with auburn hair, come to a halt at the bottom step.

"Well, Samson... can't you say hello to an old friend?" She waited, hands on her hips, smiling up at him.

"Hello," holy-moly, she *is* beautiful! Sam thought to himself, not too loud he hoped. He stood there like an idiot, holding onto the door knob.

"Wow," she laughed. "You sure know how to make a girl feel welcome." Her laughter subsided then, "you have no idea who I am do you? Nothing? Not a glimmer of recognition?"

Sam was at a loss and embarrassed, there was no hiding the fact.

"I'm Susan? Susan White?" Her face scrunched up and she shook her head, taking a more defiant stance.

"I'm sorry," Sam was overcome with a feeling of total frustration. Why couldn't he remember this woman? She was right in front of him standing right there... and yet... he couldn't pry anything loose.

"Well, it was a long time ago... I heard you were back and well, on a whim I thought I'd surprise you with a visit. Some surprise huh?" She smiled up at Sam while she tapped her foot on the bottom step. "It's a-"

"Yeah, I know...it's a small town." He couldn't resist smiling down at her. "Would you like to come on up and sit? I only have beer or, or red wine. Guess it's a little early for that."

"I'm fine, I don't need anything to drink. But I would take a rain check... if you're asking.

"Okay," a little unsure of himself he added, "yeah, that would be nice, I guess."

"Well, buster you don't sound very excited." She marched up the steps, took a chair and sat down frowning. "You really, honestly, don't remember me, at all. I mean; to be fair, we were just little kids. But we always talked about getting married when we grew up," she looked at Sam trying to catch a glimpse of something... anything. "The whole town knew we were going to be together when we got older, we were always together, me and you."

Susan wasn't sure how she should proceed. She knew, through the grapevine, that he had been sent away by his uncle. There was only speculation as to where he had been sent and, even that conversation dulled and faded after time. She knew him as a boy but not as the man he had grown to be. She often wondered what it would be like if he ever came back.

She was drawn into the distant past and all the horrible things that happened to his family... and him, now, that she was right here, on the porch, sitting next to him she couldn't grab at anything to talk about. Not a single word. But it was nice just sitting there... like sitting next to a dream person... only he was real, very real... and handsome too. The moment, such as it was, was shattered when her phone started going off.

"Oh boy, that's my phone," she went down the stairs with the grace of an angel and retrieved it off the front seat. "Hello? Oh, hey Frank. Yes, I am. No. No... Frank you- Yes, I am. That was the plan, right? Okay. Okay. Ohhhkay, Frank! Don't make such a big deal about it. I'll see you over there. Yes. No, I'm taking my own car, no what... I'm coming in my own car and that's it. Yeah, bye...bye."

"Well, that was Frank," she made a face and shrugged her shoulders, as if the whole thing were out of her control.

"I gathered that."

"Yeah, well, there's a BBQ party over at the Shannons tonight and everybody's going..." she caught herself, "there'll be a lot of people there."

"Sounds like fun..." Sam remained in his chair feeling the effects of last night's wine start to tap him on the back of the head.

"That Frank he's...It's complicated," she took a deep breath.

"Yeah...I'm sure it is."

"It sure is great to see you again, Samson," She smiled up at Sam. "About that rain check? I-I look forward to it."

"Yeah, me too. Have a great day, Susan White."

"You do the same," She offered a little wave before ducking back into her car and heading down the road.

CHAPTER 5

Samson huh? He thought to himself, long after the dust from her departure had settled, funny. He'd never been called that, as far as he knew. Jeez, so many things to think about, so many things to remember…

The wine was knocking again, and he decided he'd better find something to eat, and fast. He got up and the world lurched to the left for a brief moment.

He was able to negotiate his way into the kitchen without incident and cooked himself a couple over easy eggs that turned out to be more over hard. He buttered his toast put it on his plate and sat down to enjoy his first breakfast… at home.

After he ate, he felt much better, so he decided to clean house. But once he got started, he realized it really wasn't in need of cleaning, so he figured on a nice walk around the property.

He stepped off the porch and halted, unsure of which way he should explore first. He walked to the right of the road and after a short while he was into a pretty deep forest. The trees were bunched a lot closer together. When he looked back he couldn't see the house.

As he slowly wandered through the forest he forgot about the weird events, the sightings, or perceived sightings… all of it. He was immersed in the sounds and smells, and just the life he felt around him; The sun was warm, the air pungent with pine sap and warm grass. The sky, cloudless and brilliant. He felt like he could wander around in the forest forever, that is until a blaring car horn shattered the moment into a million pieces.

Another blast on the horn set Sam in motion. He headed back to his house to see what all the commotion was about. He was not, however, having good thoughts about whoever it was.

When the front yard came into view Sam could see a couple of guys standing around a truck with ridiculously big tires. When he entered the clearing, and the guys spotted him they both straightened.

"Help you with anything?" Sam walked up to the two but kept his distance, they were both wearing smug faces and it made Sam uncomfortable.

"Hear that, Leroy? Sam here wants to know if he can help us with anything." He stepped closer to Sam who took a half step back.

"Yeah," Leroy circled. "Maybe you can tell us why you did it." He almost bit his bottom lip when his face went into contortions.

"I don't know what you're talking about," his heart was pounding. "I think it would be better if you leave." Sam stepped up to Leroy who shrunk back looking for support from the other one.

"You know who I am?"

"I couldn't begin to guess."

"Oh, you're a smart one aren't ya."

"I honestly have no idea," Sam wasn't smiling anymore.

"Once I tell you, you would be wise to remember."

Sam waited, his patience but was wearing thin.

"I'm… Frank… Frank Dobbs," he stood there expecting awe and maybe a little reverence. All he received was a look of total, nothing.

"Well, Frank Dobbs, I really think now would be a good time for you and, Leroy there, to get back in your truck and get off my property."

Frank smiled, "Well, how long you plannin' on visitin' our nice *peaceful* community?" The peaceful part was especially punctuated for effect. And to his frustration, again, he did not receive the desired response. He kicked a clod of dirt and faced Sam, "We'll visit some other time. Don't leave before we get that chance now," it was more like a challenge than a simple statement.

"Oh, I'm not going anywhere," Sam smiled. "I'm planning on living here for a good long time."

"Guess we'll be seeing you around then." Frank got in his truck while Leroy decided he'd take one last shot at Sam.

"Murderer," Leroy whispered as he walked around to the passenger side seat.

"What's that you said?"

Leroy gave Sam the finger to punctuate his little jab and slammed the truck door. They sped away leaving a dust choked cloud behind.

CHAPTER 6

Sam made a face and shook his head as he watched the Frank and Leroy show rattle back down his road. With a great sigh and a hope for no more visitors he went inside and grabbed himself a beer. It was still early in the day so he decided to explore some more.

He headed back into the forest, this time, from a different direction. He walked around to the back of the house and entered the woods from behind the garage, or shop he hadn't been in there yet, he wanted to see the woods around him first.

In this part of the woods the trees were a little bit closer and thinner around the trunk. It really smelled good in the trees. He stopped to examine a track on the ground; looked like a deer print pressed into the soft ground, so he followed its trail.

As he traced the movement of the animal through its sign, he began to hear what, at first, sounded like wind in the trees but, as he walked on he soon realized that what he was hearing was, in fact, voices. He stopped to listen, and it sounded like some sort of chanting. It definitely wasn't in any language that he knew.

He continued on, but slowly, listening to the voices and soon the voices and the tracks lead him to a small clearing. He stood at the edge, keeping out of sight. In front of him, on the opposite side of the clearing, were three women they were about forty yards across the way, he could see them pretty well. The women were dressed in, what looked to be, summer dresses, light colors with flower prints. They were swaying back and forth with the rhythm of their chant. They were so engrossed in their chant they had no idea he was there.

A strong smell of sage drifted in his direction, then laughter erupted off to his right. He looked in that direction and saw nothing, the laughter had stopped. When he turned back to the women they were standing and staring in his direction which unsettled Sam a bit. Something, or someone ran through the trees directly behind him, he jumped and twisted around to see what it was but, whatever it was gone. When he looked back across the clearing the women were also gone...

CHAPTER 7

Susan was a complete basket case by the time she pulled into her driveway. All the way home she couldn't shake the thoughts and feelings that were slamming through her body. She was almost, except for a very tiny glimmer of hope, sure she would never, ever see Sam again, after... what happened, and then him being sent away...

All these years she hadn't really been a dater, so to speak. She liked to go out with friends and hang out but, nothing really serious, except the near relentless hounding from Frank. She just wasn't interested and that's the way it went... until today...

When she entered her house, she dropped her car keys on the little table in the entryway and tossed her coat over the back of the couch in the living room. She kicked off her shoes and opened the refrigerator where she stood, staring at nothing in particular but, taking in the cool air hoping to clear her head a little. Her phone started ringing, it startled her out of her stare down with the fridge. She punched answer and grimaced when Frank's gravely voice invaded her ear.

"Still comin' to the party right?"

"Uh, yeah."

"Okay, I guess I'll see you there."

"It's not a date you know, Frank."

"Who said it was a date?" Frank's voice deflated slightly.

"I just want to be clear is all."

"I bet if it was Sam Henning, you'd think it was a date," the edge returned to his voice.

"Good-bye Frank," she hit end and just like that he was gone... too bad that doesn't happen in real life. She caught herself, knowing that it happens exactly like that in real life.

After she showered and got dressed, she took a seat on her front porch with a glass of red wine. She watched as the sky slowly caught fire in a blaze of brilliant reds, molten golds, and a bruising of soft purples. She was excited to go to the party but then again, she wasn't.

She had this crazy idea of capping her bottle of wine and paying Samson another visit, sort of push the rain check up a bit. Ah, but after a couple more sips she came to her senses and decided against the idea. She tipped back the last drop of wine and went back inside to collect her car keys and coat then she was off to see her friends.

The Shannon house was at the very end of a long, tree lined, drive. It was a nice place at the edge of town with meadows and a pond full of trout. The party was in full swing out back on a large, well-manicured lawn. There were a couple kegs of beer stationed at convenient locations and music was playing from a stereo by the BBQ area.

People were in clusters all talking at once, drinking and laughing. Then she saw him, but it was too late to change course, he was walking straight toward her. She grabbed a plastic cup and headed for the keg, hoping to buy a little time, and to have something in her hand.

"You made it," Frank was all smiles.

"Yeah, I'm here…" Her answer straightened Frank's smile some, but he quickly recovered.

"Did you see who's here?"

"I just got here. I haven't seen anybody yet," she aimed that last statement directly at Frank who looked away and frowned.

"The witches…" he whispered. "They're here. Isn't that kind'a weird?"

"First of all, Frank," she finished filling her glass and stood. "They aren't 'witches', Frank."

"Well, what are they then? I heard that they talk to ghosts," he kept his voice low, conspiratorial.

"Margrett Adams claims to talk to the ghost of her dear departed husband. Is she a 'witch'? Frank?"

"Well, I guess-"

"Hey, Susan," Thankfully one of her best friends, Joan, called squeezing out of the crowd. She was smiling and waving. She was coming to Susan's rescue. Susan heaved a big sigh of relief and took a good long swig of her beer.

"Hey you!" Joan gave her a big hug. Joan was a famous huger and almost squeezed the air out of Susan before pushing her back. "I'm glad you came. Hey, Randy Wilson, is here and so is his brother Bruce." She held her hand to her heart as if she would faint.

And then as if noticing him for the first time, "Oh... Hi, Frank," she made a face at Susan. "I didn't see you standing there," she gave him no more attention than she gave the flurry of moths beating themselves against the yard light over by the barn. She grabbed Susan by the elbow and ushered her into the noisy crowd.

Frank watched them disappear; he was pissed. And it was all because that psycho came back. Yeah, that must be it, why else would Susan suddenly give him the cold shoulder?

As the night went on it didn't get much better for good ole' Frank. Well, Leroy, finally showed up so at least he had someone to talk to. As if he *needed* anyone to talk to…

"Hey, Frank, you see over there? In the corner over there?" He turned Frank by the shoulders, so he wasn't watching Susan anymore. She was like a damn bucket of cold water, and he wanted to party! "See?"

"Yeah, I see 'em, what about 'em." Frank was having one of those bad thoughts that sometimes snuck into his head. It was an old feeling, long buried but, not forgotten.

"Hello," Leroy's face was shifting all over the place. "Frank? Where are you, Frank?"

"I see 'em, Leroy, I see those damn 'witches'."

"Frank, what are you doing," Leroy called after his friend who was pushing his way through the party. He called again but, his voice was swallowed up by the loud music, so he followed. When he came through the other side of the gathering he spotted Frank, he was getting another beer.

"Frank, what's-"

"Now, why would you think, *anyone* in their right mind, would invite a bunch a *scraggly* 'witches' to their party?" Frank was beginning to feel the effects of the five beers he had already consumed.

"Frank?"

"Unless," he glowered at Leroy, who shrunk back just a little. "Unless... nobody invited them... And if nobody invited them, they must be party crashers. Probably, they're looking to put some kind a weird hex on somebody."

"C'mon, Frank-"

"Maybe they came here to put a hex on you," Frank laughed at his own joke. But Leroy was not amused. Frank tended to show his mean side when he was into his drinking, which was, now, the case.

"C'mon Frank, cut it out," he looked nervously over at the women grouped in the corner, not at all sure that Frank could be right. But what if he was... he shook his head to clear his thoughts and went to the keg for another refill of beer.

When he had filled his considerable cup, he walked back to where Frank was still watching the 'witches'. "Hey, c'mon, let's go find us some girls to talk to. C'mon Frank." Leroy punched his friend in the arm and walked away melting into the crowd.

Frank couldn't shake the bad thoughts that were swirling around in is head. He decided to get a refill on his beer and maybe a change of scenery. Yeah, that's exactly what he needed.

"Hey, have you seen him yet." Joan took a drink of her beer waiting anxiously for an answer. "Susan?"

"Huh, sorry, my mind was somewhere else."

"I said, have you seen him yet?"

"Who? What are you talking about?" It was kind of hard to hear since they were standing next to one of the speakers.

"Sam," Joan blurted out loud causing a few heads to swivel her way.

"Yes, keep your voice down," Susan stared at the few people close enough to have heard until they went back to their own conversations. "I went over to his house."

"Are you kidding me right now? You went to the... his house?"

"Yes, I-I mean no... I'm not kidding... Yes, I went to his house

"What did he say?" Joan was starting to hyperventilate. "What does he look like, I mean," She took Susan by the arm and pulled her away from the speaker and away from curious ears. "You have to absolutely tell me everything," Joan caught her breath and waited.

"Well, he had no idea who I was..."

"Yeah, well, it has been what, fifteen years? So yeah, that's not so bad. And?"

"He's very handsome..."

"Geeze, Susan, you're killin' me here. Out with it."

"He's just getting used to being back... he seems... really confused. But he invited me up and we talked for a second. Then my 'ranch phone'," she made a face. "I... you know my dad put that thing in my car almost the second I brought it home. All the ranch hands have them in their trucks..."

"Anywayyy..."

"It was Frank, he wanted to know if I was still coming here tonight. I told him I was and that it definitely did not mean we were on a date."

"You're funny."

"And that was it from there. I think he needs time is all."

"Did he say anything? Did you talk about anything? You know, about what happened?"

"No, he said he doesn't remember hardly anything about his childhood. Even me. He had no clue who I was."

"Boy, I can't imagine what head trips he's going through." Joan clapped her hands to wake Susan out of her trance, "I'm gonna have one more for the road, how 'bout you?"

"Naw, I think I've had enough. Think I'll sneak out'a here," she could see Frank and his sidekick staring at the 'witches'. "I'll see you tomorrow, Joan."

"Yeah, okay, Susan," she leaned in close. "pretty exciting though huh?"

"What?"

"Sam being back and all? Don't you find the least bit exciting?"

"I'm not sure yet. Could be complicated," with that Susan made her way out. When she got in her car she sat there for a moment in the quiet. Then turned the key, the engine roared to life which startled her because she hadn't realized as she had her foot on the gas. She eased off on the peddle and headed home.

Frank and Leroy were getting pretty drunk so they decided to hatch a drunk plan. They waited for the 'witches' to leave, then they would follow them… see where they go and what they're doing. There was a half-moon lounging in the night sky. Plenty bright too, for sneaking around.

When the time came and the 'witches' were leaving Frank and Leroy hot-footed it out to Frank's truck. Leroy anxiously watched them drive away as Frank couldn't find his keys.

"Are ya sure you had 'em in your pocket?"

"I'm sure," Frank swore as the 'witches' were slowly getting away. "Maybe I dropped 'em and there 'uder the truck." Frank fell to the ground, but they weren't under there. He had a very hard time getting back up and once up he had to grab the door handle to keep upright.

"Damn it, Frank," Leroy had his face plastered to the window on the passenger side. "Yer damn keys are in the ignition. Get in and less go." And off they went.

Once they closed the gap they settled down at a safe distance.

"Think they know we're followin' 'em, Frank?"

"How should I know?"

"Wishes have crazy powers you, they can sense stuff."

"How 'bout you sense I could use one a those beers there."

"I didn'd even see those beers... you wand one?"

"Sure, Leroy. Wait," the truck hopped to the left and Frank over corrected causing the truck to sway back and forth till he got it back on the road. "Maybe I bedder hol' off for now, case I gotta drive."

"Shit, Frank pull over for ya get us killed-"

"Shhh, they're turnin' ov the road." They both got quiet and sat up, watching.

"Hey, Frang, Idn't that the road... back road to old man Quinlin's old place?"

"I think so... if I remem... rem... think it goes along the fence line of the Henning place..."

"Wonder why they're goin' out there? Nothin' out there but an old broke down house and stuff..."

When the three women parked at their secret spot, they got out breathing deep of the cool night air. They smiled at each other, clasped hands and walked down a small side trail, barely a trail at all, and they kept it that way by walking very carefully. Once they reached the small, moon saturated, clearing they laid out their blanket and started a small fire.

Frank and Leroy were trying to put together what few brain cells they had left and not really getting anywhere.

"Less just keep flollowin' 'em," Leroy had a hand on the dash for support.

"We've come this far..." Frank ground the gears a couple of times before he found the right one and off they went, no lights, very sneaky. They rolled into a dark part of the forest and killed the engine. It was made even darker as a cloud had momentarily blotted out the moon.

Then, just about thirty yards or so away they spotted a flicker of light. The 'witches' had a small fire going and were huddled around it. As Frank and Leroy watched they started chanting and swaying, they looked at each other then back at the scene across the way which was now accentuated by the moon's soft glow.

Frank eased his door open very carefully as not to make any noise, Leroy did the same, only, his door made the faintest squeak, they both stopped still, listening and watching. It seemed not to disturb the 'witches' by the fire so Leroy left his door the way it was, and they both snuck up for a closer look.

The chanting was meaningless to Frank and Leroy, but it did have a captivating quality to it that held the two men's attention. Abruptly, there was movement behind them and they quickly turned in that direction.

They couldn't see anything, even though the lighting was relatively good, something was definitely moving out there and it wasn't that far away. Then it stopped. Frank and Leroy gave the whole affair a second listen before they went back to watching the 'witches'. Between the flames of the fire, the chanting and the swaying Frank and Leroy were suddenly not feeling so hot.

"Hey, Leroy. Knock it off," Frank whispered.

"Shhhh, knock what off?"

"Shhhhh, quit doing that to the back of my neck."

"Damn it, Frank. I'm not doin' nothin' to yer neck," Leroy whispered back. He was incensed that he would be accused of something he didn't do. And by his best friend…

"Shhh, Leroy. Just keep yor hans' where I can see 'em."

Leroy grumbled something and they looked over at the 'witches'

"Hey, Frank, they're not movin'… are they?"

"No, they're just sitting there," Frank shifted position to clear a rock from under his stomach. "Maybe they're in some kind a trance… or something."

"Yeah, that could be…" Leroy stopped mid thought. "Hey, Frank? Frank?"

"Be quiet, Leroy," he raised a finger to his lips and hissed.

"But, Frank, one of 'em is lookin' straight at us… Frank?"

"Don't move, maybe she doesn't see us."

"Yeah, maybe she's just lookin' in are direct'n as a sort a coincidence."

Neither man moved, or even dared take more than half a breath at a time for fear of being discovered. They were scared which was starting to sober them up some.

"Aaahhh, that's it Leroy!" Frank rolled up to his knees rubbing the back of his neck.

"Jeezus Frank! Shit! What are you yelling for? Now they'll see us for sure."

"You didn't just scratch me on the back of my neck?" He lowered his voice to a growling whisper.

"There ya go again, Frank." Leroy kept his eyes on the 'witches'. "I haven't laid a finger on you but, that doesn't mean I won't if you don't stop actin' crazy."

"Look at my neck, Leroy. Is it scratched?"

"Let's see," he focused his attention on Frank's neck. "Oh, uh, yeah you got a real nice scratch there Franko." Leroy's facial muscles were causing a riot of movement.

"Well, what's it look like? Is it bad?"

"Boy, Frank, it's not bad but, it's not good either."

"Leroy," Frank was fighting to keep his voice down. "Just tell me what the hell it looks like."

"It's, well, it's three red scratches." He looked across the way and his heart stopped.

"Leroy? What is it. Leroy?"

Leroy was speechless. His addled mind was trying it's best to identify something that was completely unrecognizable. He had no words to describe the thing that was making its way across the field toward them. It was a shadow or something and it moved in jagged stops and starts like an old-time movie.

"Leroy?"

"Frank, we gotta go," Leroy shot to is feet, arms out for greater balance. "Frank and I mean right the hell now! Look!"

Frank was still on his knees trying to steady himself but, the thing inching toward them was so absolutely frightening... He felt his body start to go slack. It took him a second to get the full adrenaline punch which turned him nearly stone cold sober.

"Okay, I've seen enough!" Frank declared getting quickly to his feet. He wobbled there for a second before he started running. Leroy was right on his heels, both men were huffing it double time back to the truck where they jumped in and locked the doors. They were sucking air like a couple fish out of water.

"Frank, start the damn truck will ya?" Leroy looked frantically around for that shadowy thing.

"Yeah," he fumbled with the simple act of inserting key into ignition and turning it... It took a couple agonizing tries before the good ol' Ford engine roared to life.

Frank jammed her into gear and off they went in a hail of dust and flying rocks. They fish-tailed back down that road way faster than reason should allow. They skidded onto the hi-way where Frank cranked the wheel for home.

Sam was not having much luck sleeping. When he heard yelling and the sound of a vehicle racing around well, he figured it was time to get up and make some coffee. It wasn't until he had his cup in his hand and was comfortably seated on the front porch that he realized the sky was still glittering with stars... He went back into the house and checked his watch, sure enough it was early, two forty-five in the morning early... Sam took a deep breath of the fresh, early, morning air with its crisp touch and decided that since he had the coffee, and he was up might as well wait. He went back inside and grabbed his sweater before finally readying himself for the first moments of a new day.

The sun was just beginning to throw the slightest bit of light when Sam took his third coffee out onto the front porch and sat down. Birds could, now, be seen flying around the forest branches, their song having begun well before first light. Sam had a contented smile plastered across his face. For the first time in his memory, which wasn't much, he felt content. No worries, plans... no plans?

———————————

Frank and Leroy were able to make it home in one piece. They swerved into the main road that ran down the middle of the Lindsey Mobile Home Park. It was located at the very edge of town and was littered with all the recognizable ornaments, from flamingos, windmills and garden gnomes to brilliant bouquets of flowers cast in plastic. Their trailer was on lot 33 and that's where Frank aimed his truck.

The next morning Leroy was already up making breakfast.

"God, Leroy, for once I'd like to wake up in the mornin' where I didn't have to smell burnt bacon," Frank tugged his jeans on and pulled a shirt over what used to be a heavily muscled body. Now though, too little exercise and too much drinking had taken its toll.

His head was throbbing but that wasn't the worst. Not even the bacon burning on the stove was the worst. No, it was whatever it was that they saw in that meadow last night... that was the worst. It still sent icy shivers down his spine to think about it.

"I like it crispy," Leroy called from the kitchen which was slowly filling with smoke.

"What?"

"Crispy, that's how I like my bacon."

"Crispy? I like my bacon crispy too," Frank fanned the air as he entered the kitchen. "But that is burnt." He pointed to the dark shriveled strips that sizzled in the smoking pan.

"It's a fine line," Leroy retrieved the bacon and laid it on a paper towel.

"Well, Leroy, from here that line don't look too awful fine," Frank snatched a piece and shoved it in his mouth.

"Well, for somebody who don't like burnt bacon you sure don' mind helpin' yourself."

"That one was less burnt," Frank crunched his bacon while he made a pot of coffee.

"Hey, Frank want some eggs?" Leroy had a carton of eggs and was getting ready to crack a couple right into the bacon grease.

"Uhh, you're not gonna put those eggs in all that grease. I like mine cooked in a lot less bacon grease.

"Okay, Frank," Leroy took the frying pan and dumped some of the grease on the ground by the back steps. "This okay for you, Frank?" He held the pan so Frank could see.

"Yeah, only you're dripping on the floor."

"Oh, geeze," Leroy quickly wiped off the side of the pan and set it back over the fire.

When breakfast was done and the coffee percolated, Frank and Leroy sat down to eat. They each took a couple of bites of their eggs and a sip of coffee then they just sat there staring at their respective plates and not saying anything. Each man was making a valiant, though, feeble attempt at finding the right words, or any words for that matter, to describe what they both clearly saw.

CHAPTER 8

After a satisfying breakfast consisting of, two beautiful over-easy eggs, well, one broke, toast and a sausage patty accompanied by a strong cup of coffee, his fourth, he was ready to go. He walked out onto the front porch took in a deep breath of pine scented air, still morning fresh, and a thought struck him.

It had all the makings of a monumental revelation if only his thought process wasn't slightly hampered and a little muddled by the accumulated effect of the coffee and not that much sleep. The combination was making it very difficult to remember the name of the place where Susan White said she worked. He decided it would be much easier to drive into town and find it. After all it's a small town...

McKandless Emporium wasn't hard to find as it was one of the tallest buildings in town at three stories. He parked his rental car and went inside to find the place was huge. There was a woman working on a cheek full of gum at the cash register and he approached her.

"Hi, I'm looking for Susan White?" The woman, whose name tag revealed her name was Daphne, gave him a funny look as she chewed away. Finally, a light bulb flashed on and she came around from behind the register to point the way.

"She's in fishing supply." Daphne was really eyeing Sam up as if he were some exotic circus animal. "Go up those stairs over there," she pointed again. "Fishing supply is on the second floor."

"Thanks," Sam smiled but she wasn't smiling back. "This way?"

"Yeah the stairs are just over there, by the weight equipment."

"Okay, thanks again."

"Sure."

Sam turned but didn't get too far when Daphne called to him.

"You're him, aren't you."

"Him?" Sam had no idea how to respond so he waited for clarification.

"Sam, right? Sam Henning?"

"Yeah, that's me," he was confused by her question. "I'm Sam Henning, do you know me?"

"I know about you," a sheepish grin etched across her face. "Everybody knows about you."

"Okay, well, have a good day," Sam found the stairs and jogged up to the second floor.

"Wow," he was amazed at all the fishing equipment, the place was stuffed. He stopped another employee and asked.

"Susan White?"

"Two isles over, at the end."

"Thanks," he headed off in the direction indicated. Just before he went down the aisle he looked back and, surprise, the dude was staring at him. He shrugged it off and walked up the aisle bristling with fishing poles of assorted colors and saw Susan hanging supplies on pegs.

"Hey, Susan, Hi."

"Hi yourself, Samp...Sam," the look of surprise on her face kind of had the opposite effect that he was expecting, it made him a little uncomfortable. "Planning on doing some fishing?"

"Uh, no, at least not in the near future, as far as I know," He felt a pang in his chest. She was very beautiful. "No, I just stopped by to say hi is all."

"Oh, I'm glad you did."

"The woman downstairs, the one at the cash register?"

"That's Daphne."

"Yeah, well, she said she knew me, actually she said she knew about me and then she said my name. I've never seen her before."

"She said she knew you?"

"No," he took a breath. "She said she knew about me."

"How far back do you remember?"

Sam thought for a second.

"I remember being in a school... in France... and I remember getting a call from a man representing my parents estate... and sometimes..."

"What? What else do you remember?"

"Nothing else that makes any sense." Sam shook his head and frowned. "Why do the people of this town look at me like I'm some sort of freak?"

"Okay, Sam, settle down buddy," she took him by the shoulders. "How 'bout I take you up on that drink rain check. Will you be home later? Say around five?"

"Yeah, I don't know where else to go. I don't need groceries, I've been to the bank... Yeah, I'll be home."

"Okay, well, I better get back to work."

"I'll see you later then." He smiled and walked away. He felt a little better, maybe Susan can shed some light on why people stare at him the way they do. She has this thing about her, he struggled for the word..., this self-assurance thing about her that makes him feel, comfortable. Like he can trust her.

Why can't he dredge up even a tiny morsel... just enough to nibble on... to understand who she was, is. It was aggravating that she should know him so well... or at least remember him, them so damn well.

As Sam walked out the front door of the McKandless Emporium a truck pulled up in front of his car and stopped, effectively blocking him in. Much to Sam's surprise two men got out and walked toward him.

"Hey, Sam, I thought we'd run into you again," Frank leaned against the passenger side door of Sam's rental while Leroy circled around behind him.

"Help you guys with something?"

"You know," Frank pushed off the car and stepped up to Sam. "Leroy don't you think it's kind'a funny every time we see this guy he asks us if we need anything."

"Yeah, like we're helpless or somethin'," Leroy moved in closer and tapped Sam on the shoulder. "You think we're helpless nutcase?"

"I don't know what you are but you're blocking my car."

"Oh, I hadn't noticed," Frank smiled showing some teeth.

"It's an easy mistake," Sam backed up a step. He needed to put some distance between himself and Frank who was way too close. "So, if you could move, I'll be on my way."

"What are you doin' here anyway?"

"That's my business."

"Boy, you sure have yourself a smart ass mouth," Leroy bumped Sam with his shoulder. Sam didn't react to Leroy's poor attempt at intimidation.

"Are you going to move your truck?" Sam kept his voice calm as taught by the strict school masters. A place of harsh punishments... a place where fear is your constant companion.

"Maybe," Frank gave Sam a little push.

"I don't want any trouble," Sam was starting to get irritated, an old feeling crept up his spine and he caught it like a catcher catches a fastball. He couldn't let that 'old feeling' loose... he just couldn't. He had been severely punished many times for unleashing the darkness within him. In fact, he was sure it had been punished out of him... until now, in this moment.

"Oh, we don't want any trouble either," Frank kept up with that phony smile.

"Then would you please move your truck so I can go," Sam's heart rate was starting to crank up a few notches. He could hear his pulse thumping between his ears.

"Best way for you to stay out of trouble is to stay out of this store. For that matter be better for all of us if you would just disappear," he made a gesture with his hands like magicians do when they make things disappear then crossed his arms over his chest.

"Yeah, as in leave our town or else," Leroy was getting bolder.

"Well, that's not going to happen," he could feel his muscles tightening. "I don't particularly like to be threatened," Sam looked Leroy square in the eyes and predictably, Leroy flinched. It was just a little flinch, but it was enough to give Sam the information he needed. "Look I don't know what your problem is and I don't really care but, I need you to move your truck, now."

"Ooooo, he's getting feisty idn't he, Frank?" Leroy stated from a safe distance.

"Yeah, Leroy, he's almost scary huh?"

"Yeah, for sure," Leroy's face was contorting uncontrollably, it was hard to look at.

By this time, they had attracted a small crowd of onlookers who had gathered behind the Emporium windows. Then, fortunately, the person owning the car behind Sam's rental came out and drove away. Sam seeing his chance took it. He got in his rental and headed for home leaving Frank, Leroy and the onlookers to watch his exit.

By the time Sam pulled onto his road he had settled down somewhat. He got out of his car and went inside to grab a cold beer out of the fridge. He went back out and sat on the porch holding the beer to his forehead. He took a couple deep breaths and a good long swig.

The blurry images that swirled in his head on the drive home were unrecognizable to him. There were only flashes of clarity, glaring lights and wavy images washed in red hues. It all just led him toward a corner, the same corner; a corner completely devoid of light, the kind of darkness that makes your eyes jump when they try to focus.

It made him feel anxious. He knew there was something lurking in the abyss of that corner the thought of which, especially since he came back, shot ripples of anger through his body to the point where he would start to shake. But it wasn't just the anger... it was also the fear. A deeply intense fear. The very thought of going into the darkness sent icy cold fingers tracing down his spine.

He had no idea where these, sometimes bombarding, thoughts and images came from except he was pretty sure that to find out would be to peer into that corner. I mean really push your face into it, maybe it would expose some answers, sure... but, at what cost? What would it cost to do that? To stick your face into the darkness and see... you'd have to be damn ready for the outcome. First, he had to find a light powerful enough to penetrate the darkness. 'Course, in the end he wasn't so sure he was that brave, 'cause you'd have to be brave.

Gray jays chased each other through the trees while smaller birds chirped and whistled deeper in the forest. The treetops swished softly as a light evening breeze pushed through them. Somewhere a bird screeched. Sounded like a big one. Sam stood and stretched working his body this way and that to try and relieve the tensions of the day. He downed his beer and smiled though he had no idea why.

Sam went inside to grab another beer. The clock on the kitchen wall said it was four-thirty, and he was getting a little bit nervous. While he was inside the porch chimes started tinkling which startled him some.

He grabbed his beer and slowly opened the front screen door as if expecting to find someone and wasn't surprised that no one was there. He looked over at the chimes and they abruptly stopped, like an invisible hand held them. Then, he heard it, the unmistakable sound of a beater truck rumbling down his road. He dreaded what he already knew, trouble was coming he could feel his pulse ratchet up as the blood in his veins started pumping for real. He set his beer down on the railing and waited. And sure enough, here they came... Stopping in front of the house the truck was momentarily washed over by the dust cloud they created. Sam stood on the porch frowning at the unwanted company.

"Hey, we was drivin' by and thought we'd stop and say hello," Frank wore a big grin, he looked a little tipsy and his sidekick, Leroy, didn't seem to be in much better shape.

"What do you want?" Sam was in no mood to be bothered especially since he was expecting company.

"Is that any way to greet company?" Frank's smile turned downward as he surveyed the area like a wolf surveys it's prey. His eyes roamed all over the front of the house and each side, as far as he could see. Frank was acting excessively nosy even though he hadn't yet taken more than a dozen steps from his truck.

"Yeah, not very neighborly, are ya?" Leroy was not to be left out of the conversation.

Sam made no reply, just stood on the top step frowning down at the two irritants in his yard. He wasn't about to be drawn into their little bullshit game.

"Well, Leroy, Guess we'd better get along," Frank sighed. Head swiveling for one last look around. "We still got a few more things to do before *our* day is done." He gave Sam a long, almost bloodthirsty look, "You didn't by any chance see anything in the woods last night?"

"I have no idea what you're talking about," Sam rolled his shoulders. Not two hours ago these two threatened him in front of the McKandless Emporium.

"You know, you probably don't at that, c'mon, Leroy," Frank called before returning to his truck and just like that they were off in a cloud of smoke and dust down his road.

Sam stood on the top step taking deep long breaths as he tried to calm himself down. He didn't know why those two were targeting him, he'd never seen them before, until two days ago.

Susan went to her locker and changed out of her work vest. She paused before she closed her locker door, she was having feelings... feelings she hadn't known existed... ever. She smiled and closed the locker door only to have to reopen it because she forgot her car keys.

"Okay settle down," she scolded herself. It's no big deal. Just a couple of old friends having a couple of drinks to old times, right? She was aware it was something way more than that only she didn't have a clue what it could be. He'd been gone and out of her life for many years.

They were just little kids. She was living her own life now and she *was* happy... That's an easy summation but not necessarily true. There were events in their lives that would forever link them together. Some of those events were of the unspeakable nature, some were harmless childhood remembrances.

Anyway, she brushed those thoughts aside as she had to concentrate on parking at the Wine Mart. Once inside she was again assailed by the same vexing thoughts and was having a hell of a time deciding which wine to get.

"May I help you?"

Susan was startled out of her thoughts by a young man with flaming red hair, she recognized him from around town. "Oh, hi, I was just trying to pick something out. And I'm afraid I'm having a ridiculously hard time." Susan was assailed with a near panic attack. She was nervous and... she was nervous.

"Mind if I ask if there is food involved?"

"Yes, you may," she caught herself, "I really have no idea… probably not, just some wine. I like red."

"Okay, well, let's mosey on over to the red wines for starters." The young man was kind enough not to give her a hard time for being in the white wine section. "Alright here we are. We have some real nice sipping wines here in this section," he spread out his arms to include the section he was referring to. "If you need anything else?"

"No, thank you," she peered at his name tag, "Todd."

"Hey, how did you… oh geeze, gets me every time," he blushed and walked away to help another customer.

Susan located a nice Merlot and headed for the check out where the same young man waited.

"Okay here ya go, all set," the clerk handed over her bagged wine.

"Thanks, have a great evening," Susan turned for the automatic doors.

"Hold on. Ah, you forgot your change," he rounded the counter and handed her the change and receipt. Then he smiled.

On the ride out to Sam's place her mind was a desert. Her thoughts had momentarily shut down, and she was glad. She thought as she walked back to her car that maybe she was just to wound up and maybe they could do it another time. But can you do a rain check on a rain check?

Sam plucked his warm beer off the railing and frowned at the thin layer of dust on the top. He was done with beer maybe some wine… "Maybe I should just wait and see what Susan brings," he told himself as he returned to the solitude of the front porch.

It wasn't long before he heard the faint sound of a car coming up the road and his heart damn near burst out of his chest it was pounding so hard. He had to calm down. He told himself over and over until it became a mantra. He was still chanting to himself when a red car came into view and stopped in his front yard... then his heart stopped, and a funny feeling came over him. It would keep him awake that night thinking about it.

"Hey, there he is!" Susan climbed out of her car and waved. She reached in and produced a brown bag. "Hope you don't mind brown bagging it?" She laughed. She had a great laugh Sam thought.

"Not at all, c'mon up, Susan, have a sit on the porch."

"Why, don't mind if I do. You got anything to open this with?" She pulled the bottle free of the bag.

"I think I have just the thing," Sam took the bottle. "Make yourself comfy I'll be right back," Sam stopped at the door. "Styrofoam okay, I haven't had a chance to get glasses. Actually, I did have the time I just forgot," He shrugged his shoulders and silently scolded himself for rambling on so.

"Here we go," Sam returned all smiles and holding two cups full of deep red wine.

"Oh, I see, you're a kidder. Okay." She lifted her cup to examine it and Sam, on impulse, clunked his cup to hers, and she smiled caught slightly off guard.

"So, you approve of the wine choice?" Susan asked as she looked out into the surrounding forest.

"It's perfect," Sam smiled. "I was wondering..."

"Yes?"

"Well, how long have you worked at the Emporium?"

"That's it?" Susan frowned in a playful way. "That's the first question you have after all this time? After all that's happened?"

"Yeah," he made a face. "I don't know what to ask and even if I did, I'm not so sure I want to know the answers."

"You know what Sam?" She signaled for a freshen up on her wine and Sam topped it off. "You are absolutely right. Let's just take it slow, okay?" She could see Sam relax immediately and she felt better. "No sense barging in right away let's get to know each other again. I kind a like that idea."

"Me too," Sam was starting to feel more and more relaxed as they talked. Was it the wine or chemistry, or was it just plain ol' curiosity? Sam was easing into the concept of getting to know someone who was apparently prominent in his forgotten life. An old childhood friend, who, according to the man over at the bank, everyone thought would someday be husband and wife. If anyone could complete the puzzle of his early years maybe she could…

"Earth to Sam," Susan pressed her foot on top of Sam's. "Where did you go?"

"You know what we should do, Leroy?"

"What's that ol' buddy?"

Frank inwardly resented his 'buddy', Leroy. To Frank, Leroy, an old childhood friend he eventually roomed with at the school for troubled boys, was the embodiment of what Frank never wanted to be. He was going to play in the NFL for crying out loud! He had it all; money, girls… then he was sidelined forever, comeback story a shambles, along with everything that went along with it. Maybe bitter was a better word but then again, Frank wasn't blessed with a large vocabulary. He wasn't blessed with a large number of friends either. In fact, Leroy made the sum total of his friends…

"Frank? You were sayin?"

"Wha- oh, uh, pass me another one a them bruskies. Thanks, yeah, I think," he leaned in closer so no one else would be privy to the conversation. "I think…we keep a close eye on our new arrival and when he leaves his house we sneak over there and scope the place really good."

"Ahuh..."

"I think we should figure out a way to scare the shit out of him. I mean scare him so bad he takes off, back to wherever he came."

"But, Frank, isn't he from here? Like in the same house, here?"

"Dammit, Leroy, I mean away from here don't you get it?" By the way Leroy's face started to contort he was pretty sure he wasn't following at all. "We gotta come up with something I'm telling you. Sam Henning has to go he's ruining my chances with Susan. Again."

"Did you say, again?"

"You heard me. When we were kids, he was always in our way! I, well, me and Susan we were supposed to be together. But that damn Sam Henning ruined everything! And I mean everything!"

"Okay, Frank, I know. I got you, I was there too. Just settle down some. We'll figure something out, no problem."

CHAPTER 9

By the time Sam and Susan were talked out the first stars were pale lanterns in a darkening sky. They were able to get by the initial nervous banter but stayed on the easy path of conversation.

It was okay for both parties, there was just a bit too much emotion swirling around them as they sat there drinking wine and enjoying each other's company on Sam's porch.

"Oh, geeze!" Susan set her empty wine glass on the floor next to her. "What the heck time is anyway? I should be going I have to work in the morning!" She stood as did Sam. There was a brief moment of comfortableness but, when they smiled at each other that all went away. After all, there were no expectations. Nothing written in the stone of their history that demanded anything from either. So, they shook hands.

"I had a great time, Sam," she located her sweater and put it on. "It was really nice to talk to you. I mean it's been what... fifteen years?"

"Something like that. It was good for me too." He was feeling the wine and didn't want to risk saying more. "Let's do this again sometime, only, next time I'll throw something on the BBQ," he caught himself, "wait, I'm not sure I have a BBQ." They laughed and Sam walked Susan to her car even though she said it wasn't necessary.

On the drive home Susan was numb, not a thought of anything one way or another entered her muddled head. She was like one of those zombies except, she wasn't particularly interested in human flesh. Just the thought sent an army of goose bumps racing over her body.

She hadn't realized it earlier but now that she was home and there were no more distractions… not that Sam was a distraction… "Who am I kidding?" She scolded herself. Sam was a *big* distraction, a *huge* distraction! She slipped out of her work clothes and into her pajamas then went into the kitchen, snapped on the light, and went about making herself a cup of chamomile tea. She put a heaping spoon of honey in her cup and set it to steep on the little table by her favorite chair which she snuggled into. She smiled to herself as she re-played the evening's conversations. She felt happy, happier than she's felt in a long, long time and it felt good.

Her tea cooled and finally became cold as she dozed off with her thoughts.

After some time, Sam went inside and got into his pajamas but, instead of going to bed or reading… he decided to go back outside and sit on the porch. The moon, which was waning, was slowly rising through the trees, creating shadows within the forest. As he watched the shadows creep across the forest floor something caught his eye. It was just to his right.

What drew his attention to it was the fact it was so very dark. An anomaly in shadow. Like what he saw when he first came down the road to his house. Dark like that. Now, it was beside a tree not forty yards away, standing completely still. He watched in fascination for a good ten minutes before a sound diverted his attention just long enough for whoever, or whatever, was standing by the tree to vanish.

He felt like getting up and calling it a day, but he also felt compelled to stay put in his chair on the porch. There it was again. The… person or… whatever it was had reappeared in the forest. It had retreated farther away but still dark, really dark. It was without distinctness as far as a face or any defining features. It appeared as a shadow within a shadow.

Then he wondered, was it the same one as before? Or were there a gang of shadows lurking just out of the throw of the porch light. As he watched it... he didn't even know what to call it... so yeah, *it*, for the time being and, *it* remained completely still. The funny part, if you could call it funny, was the fact he didn't feel threatened by *its* presence. There was no feeling of fear at all.

He remained in his chair waiting for the *it* to do something. He couldn't really go to bed knowing there was something standing out in the woods. But, after another ten minutes of watching, his eyes started to get buggy, he began to lose focus.

He felt so wonderfully relaxed and must've nodded out for a second because when he opened his eyes, he discovered he was lying on top of his bed covers and wondering how he got there. He didn't remember getting up from his chair outside. Sam rolled out of bed to sneak a peek out his bedroom window only to find a beautiful morning sun throwing its soft light into the surrounding trees, the dark shape had gone. He watched birds waking in song and flight.

Sam stepped out onto the front porch with a fresh cup of coffee and inhaled the crisp morning of a new day. The warming pine sap subtle on the air would be stronger as the sun warms.

As he sipped his coffee, he smiled thinking about last night. He wanted to stop by the McKandless Emporium but, decided against the idea, last thing he wanted was to seem too anxious, they both agreed to take their time. So, he opted for a ride in the countryside sort of get his bearings. Find out what's around him.

Sam slung his pack over one shoulder and locked the front door. He tossed the pack in the passenger seat and twisted the key. His rental, a mustang, dark blue, roared to life and he headed down the road toward adventure.

"Frank! Frank!" Leroy was tapping on the window of the Pine Tree Stop and Go. He could see Frank at the checkout then watched anxiously as he pushed through the door and walked toward him.

"Leroy... What are you banging on the damn window for?" He frowned down at his friend.

"I just saw Henning, he drove that way," Leroy pointed, his face twitching some.

"Well, shit, Leroy the hell didn' ya say somethin? Alright let's go he's heading up north."

When Leroy and Frank turned down the road to Sam's place, they were like a couple high school kids looking for trouble knowing full well there wouldn't be any. They rolled up to the front of the house and Frank killed the engine. They sat there for a second while their eyes darted all over the place. When they were absolutely sure the coast was clear, they got out of the truck and walked up the front porch steps.

"What are ya thinkin', Frank?" Leroy climbed the steps to the front door, he tried the doorknob and found it to be locked, no surprise there. He went to the front window cupped his hands around his face and peered into the dark interior of the house.

"I'm gonna check around back," Frank called up to Leroy who still had his face pressed to the window. He walked around the side of the house slowly inspecting the layout for potential hideouts and escape routes as he planned his little scare stunt.

He found a wood pile stacked against an old shed about thirty feet from the side of the house, it was perfect. They could come in by way of the back road... 'what was that?' Frank muttered to himself as something ran behind him. "Leroy? Leroy you better not be screwin' around." He waited a moment and all was still and very quiet. Frank didn't really like quiet much, his mind tended to wander to dark places when it was quiet.

He walked through the trees behind the wood pile and found a nice little meadow with wildflowers. As he continued his walk, he discovered that the back road was a lot closer than he originally thought when he and Leroy found the 'witches' and that other thing... Frank was getting spooked. He swung around in a slow circle but, only the forest and a few birds appeared in his line of sight. Just the same he felt weird like he was being watched.

Leroy continued to inspect the inside of the house he could make out, what looked like the living room. It was hard to see much inside. Suddenly, a black form loomed up behind of him its image a reflection in the glass. Leroy back peddled until his butt slammed into the railing. That's when the chimes went crazy. They swung violently back and forth clanging into each other creating a loud discordant rattle.

"Leroy, what are you doin'?" Frank made his way back to the wood pile where he could hear a clinking sound and remembered there were chimes hanging at the far end of the porch. When he rounded the corner of the house he found Leroy standing there looking at the chimes which were now, only, lightly tinkling against each other. It was odd since there wasn't even a hint of a breeze. When Frank came around to stand at the foot of the steps the chimes abruptly stopped. "Leroy?" He called in a voice not quite his own. "Leroy! Hey Man! Leroy!"

"Whoa, what the hell's going on?" Leroy sat down in on one of the porch chairs and put his head in his hands.

"Leroy, what's the matter? Why were you just standing there like that?" Frank took the stairs two at a time and pulled the other chair over to where Leroy was sitting.

"Holy crap, man I got the worst headache," Leroy groaned as he rubbed his head.

Frank got out of his chair and went over to inspect the chimes. He studied them closely expecting them to start up again but they didn't, so he ran his hand through them out of frustration. Frank was not one to be on the other side of his scare stunt, fact he didn't appreciate being scared at all.

"C'mon Leroy, I found a place where we can hide and it's not that far from the old road so we can come in that way."

CHAPTER 10

"So, you're going to honestly sit there and tell me that all you talked about was... what the weather? Your favorite football team?"

"I don't watch football," Susan corrected good naturedly. "And no, it didn't go as boring as you might think."

"Well," Joan eyed her friend the way she always did with a wrinkled brow and a crooked smile.

"Don't look at me like that," Susan reached over and swatted Joan on the shoulder.

"You're hiding something, what is it?" Joan folded her arms in mock defiance and waited. "I've got all afternoon and so do you," she challenged. "Chris we could use a couple of cold ones next time you come this way. Now, there's a looker, huh?"

"Huh?"

"Oh boy, you know what? I think I'll just go on over there to that wall and have a conversation. I bet I'd be a lot more interesting."

"C'mon Joan, sit down you goofy woman. There's more in what we didn't say... a lot more."

"So, c'mon, Susan, spill it. It's me, Joan? Remember? Your old buddy from since forever?"

"It's hard," Susan leaned into her beer and watched the tiny bubbles float to the surface. "He... He seems so lost. Like there's a huge chunk of his life that's blocked or should I say locked out of his memory. I mean, I don't want to be the one to pick that lock. But, at the same time, I'm curious. Does that make sense?"

"Uh, yes and, no. But more yes, I think. Well, just, give me an example."

"Okay," Susan reached for her beer and took a big gulp. "Let's see, he has no clue about us… how we were, which isn't really earth shaking, it was a long time ago and we were just kids. He doesn't remember the lake and how we used to swim all the time… He doesn't remember anything about his brothers' death, and, for that matter I'm pretty sure it's the same with his parents as well." She took another sip of her beer.

"Wow. I mean, how does that make you feel knowing these things? I mean, shoot what are you going to do?"

"Well, for one thing I'm not going to just blurt out these past events to him. I think it would be better to let Sam sort it out. I could help but I have no idea what to say."

"How about starting out with a simple remember when," Joan downed the last of her beer and pushed her glass aside. "You know, remember when we used to go swimming? Just keep it simple. That's what I think anyways."

"No, you're absolutely right," Susan finished her beer and leaned in closer. "I'm going to do that next time we see each other."

"And when is that?"

"We didn't make any plans other than Sam said, next time he wants to throw something on the BBQ."

"Man wants to cook for you, I'd say that's a pretty good start."

"Yeah well, like I said we didn't make any plans."

"Oh shit," Joan's breath caught in her throat. "Chris load us up with one more round, will ya?" Beers landed on the table and Joan took a couple big swigs causing a coughing fit.

"Geeze, Joan what the hell…" Her words trailed away as she saw Frank and his sidekick, Leroy walk in. "Shit."

Susan turned away looking at Joan's' face to gauge their movement. By the way Joan's eyes narrowed she knew they had spotted them and were heading in their direction.

"Here they come," Joan groaned into her next sip of beer.

"Hey girls, what are you two doing?"

"Us two, 'girls' are having a beer. What are you two boys doing out so late?"

Leroy laughed; Frank ignored the comment. Frank slid in next to Susan while Leroy cozied up to Joan.

"What do you two say we go get us a 12 pack and head over to Gibson Lookout?" Frank leered at Joan daring her to say a word.

"Yeah, it's almost a full moon tonight," Leroy added as his face started doing acrobatics.

"It sounds like fun, boys, but I have to work in the morning, early?"

"Yeah, me too," Joan frowned into the remaining sip of beer and pushed the glass aside. The moment had been interrupted. "I gotta go. It's getting past my bedtime," Joan stood shouldering away from Leroy while providing a block for Susan's exit.

"Well, maybe next time then," Leroy sat back down and motioned for Chris to bring a couple cold ones.

"Yeah, next time." Frank tried to hide the fact that he was extremely pissed and having bad dreams… but he wasn't exactly successful in his attempt.

"Okay, c'mon Susan let's head on down the road," She smiled at Frank and Leroy, took Susan by the elbow and off they went to their respective cars. "Nice, relatively clean exit wouldn't you say?"

"I don't know… I wish he never came back here." Susan unlocked her car door and said good night. Both of them drove off into the cool quiet night.

CHAPTER 11

The sun was slowly completing its ark across the sky by the time Sam turned off the hi-way. He noticed shadows were growing in the forest on either side of his road. He felt both relaxed and excited about his little excursion, although, if he was being honest with himself, I mean truly... honest? Sam had to deal with his underlying feeling, deep down inside, that he wasn't entirely alone at his house... He was also tired and glad he grabbed a burger at, Judy's Burger Barn.

When he pulled up in front of his house he sat in his car for a second, looking at the house as if under a microscope. His burger and fries permeated the air inside his car. *'There must be something here that can help me sort things out,'* his inner voice, always a constant companion whispered. *'Sooner the better.'* his conscious mind was trying very hard. His conclusions, so far, had always ended the same; it was just a house... and it belonged to him now.

Back in town Frank and Leroy were having their usual Friday night hurrah over at the Howling Rooster Bar and Pool Hall. The only reason they get away with the pool hall part is they do have *a* pool table. Frank and Leroy began their evening parked at the bar then migrated to a table in the shadows.

"Alright, Leroy, tomorrow night's the full moon."

"Why, Frank, it's been full the last couple nights," Leroy's jaw started to work back and forth. "You'd have to be damn near blind to not have noticed how bright it's been the last coupl'a nights. See the moon-"

"I mean tomorrow night. That's when it's gonna be its fullest," Frank pulled on his beer and wiped his forehead. "Now, can we stop with the astrology and get back to what we were talking about?"

"I lifted a mask from the five an' dime. I think it's perfect," Leroy was getting excited which caused a chain reaction with his facial muscles.

"Alright, Leroy." Frank motioned for another round as he leaned in close. "Leroy, we pull this off... you know really scare this freak?" Frank was hyperventilating, the euphoria he was experiencing almost made him giddy. "Why, I tell you this, Leroy, we pull this off... We'll be heroes," Frank gasped at his own delusional thought process.

"Frank?" Leroy got his emotions under control which made him a whole lot easier to look at. "I'm not exactly sure what you mean by that. I mean heroes? Frank?"

Frank took a good long breath letting it out slowly, calming himself as the shock waves of revelation coursed through his body. "Leroy, you're not lookin' at this the right way-"

"Okay."

"We get rid of mister, Sam Henning, we get rid of a psycho murderer... we get rid of-"

"He wasn't ever convicted... was he, Frank?"

"Will you quite interrupting me? Damn." Frank took a moment to regather himself, downed the rest of his beer and got real close to Leroy's face, which was never that easy. "It don't madder shit if he was convicted or not. Everybody around here knows he did it. Everybody, Leroy."

"A'right Frank not so loud, buddy."

The beers landed on the table and Frank sat back in his chair rolling the cold, sweating bottle between his hands. He was deep in thought, immersing himself in the make-believe world of the town hero. It was something he'd dreamed of for a long, long time...

"Frank?" Leroy waved his hand in front of his friend. "You really think we'll be heroes? I mean... I never, in all my wildest dreams, thought I'd be a hero." He took a swig of beer and smiled, a rare thing for Leroy.

Neither man said anything for a while, they just sat and drank their beers, one after another.

"I gotta hit the bathroom," Frank announced to no one in particular and stumbled in that direction.

Leroy, he wondered a lot. It didn't take much of a subject to arouse his wondering mind and at that moment he was really wondering about tomorrow night and the plans they had to scare off, Sam Henning. Though, Leroy's first and second impression of him was, he didn't seem like the type to scare easily. But then again, he thought to himself, Frank had a definite way about him that made people afraid. He'd witnessed it firsthand when they were in the reformatory together. Frank could be a very scary dude. He didn't especially like it when Frank got scary.

Kyle Heckler walked in and surveyed the room with a sparkling eye. He was one of the old timers. The kind of person that knows absolutely everyone in the surrounding area and they know him. He was pushing through his seventies with a fierceness born of hard work and determination. A man of pioneer spirit with bushy beard and flashing eyes that sparkled under a ball cap that had to be at least 30 years old. Its emblem advertising, Lou's Gas 'N' Go, in dirty faded red letters. Lou's Gas 'N' Go was as gone as last winter's snow. It burned down when the Sheriff Office caught fire taking the town Sheriff and Lou's place with it.

"Well, look what the cat drug in," Leroy's upper lip curled, his eyebrows began to twitch. He didn't like the crotchety old man. The 'crotchety old man' didn't care much for Leroy either.

Kyle ignored Leroy which is what he mostly did and, took the stool at the far end of the bar where he always sat. Him and the other old farts like to sit there, drink coffee, and swap lies with each other. Only, today, he sat alone, and Leroy wisely left it that way.

"Leroy," Frank strode back into the room like one who expected some recognition, Etta, at the bar was busy washing glasses and Kyle was staring straight ahead. It was another deflating moment, Frank would tuck it in his mental file labeled, Sam Henning...

The next day Susan was straight-arming it through the front doors of the Emporium when someone called.

"Hey, Susan?" It was Daphne a co-worker at McKandless Emporium. "Hey, you are one difficult person to get a hold of," she broke from the small knot of co-workers assembled around her register and raced to catch up with Susan who was already half way down the front steps on her way to get a double cheese burger at Judy's Burger Barn, sit under her favorite elm tree, on her nice peaceful bench, and devour it... with double-fried fries of course.

"Oh, hey, Daphne," Susan smiled over her shoulder but kept her stride causing Daphne to reach out and take hold of her elbow. "I'm on lunch, Daphne what is it you want?"

"Are you heading over to Judy's?"

"I think we both know the answer to that one," she slowed to let her co-worker catch up.

"I'm going there as well," she was finally able to match Susan's stride. "I just dearly love their veggie burger with that dreamy sauce she makes... You know Judy makes her own."

"This I am aware of."

"What are you getting? I bet you're gonna have the fish sandwich with that crazy dreamy tartar. Wait! Don't tell me... I bet you're going to get that outrageous BBQ chicken sandwich... what does she call that?"

"Actually, no, Daphne... Today I'm feasting on a double cheese burger with twice fried, fries."

"Oh," Daphne was caught slightly off guard but quickly recovered with a nervous laugh. "Hey, to each his own I always say."

"You are absolutely right Daphne," she was still walking only now, her pace quickened as Judy's bright yellow sign, with that giant burger floating above it, appeared just up ahead.

They were out of things to say at the moment as they concentrated on their respective orders. There was a young couple in front of them. They were definitely passing through, talking about how quaint the little town was and how absolutely cozy their room was at the only hotel in town, The Wander Inn.

Forty-nine fifty a night plus cable which hasn't really made its way into their little valley yet. But there was internet. Susan stepped up to the counter and placed her order topping it off with a vanilla shake. She stepped aside to let Daphne do the same. While they waited, they both busied themselves with the task of reading the complete menu, written in a neat hand, behind the counter. Or just looking absently around the dining area.

Their orders arrived within seconds of each other. They each paid, leaving a nice tip, and exited the air-conditioned cafe. Once outside Susan headed for her lunch place.

"Okay, Daphne, have a good lunch," she called over her shoulder.

"I will, thanks, Susan. Hey, where do you eat? I usually go back to my desk and eat…"

Susan stopped and faced Daphne. She knew what was coming, might as well get it over with so she could eat her mouthwatering burger.

"I have a place over there you're welcome to join me if you like."

"Okay, Great."

"It's right over there," Susan nodded in the direction. When she reached her destination, she sat down on her bench busily arranging her meal.

"This is nice," Daphne carefully laid out her meal consisting of her veggie burger and blueberry smoothy. "It's much better than eating at my desk. I always manage to spill something- oh geeze," a small piece of her burger escaped its bun and nestled in Daphne's lap, leaving a thin mustard trail behind. "I told you. That's why I don't wear light colors," She gave a little laugh and plucked the wayward piece off her lap and into her mouth before busily wiping at the mustard track.

Susan just nodded and ate.

"Boy, you sure have a healthy appetite," Daphne wiped a smudge of mayo from the corner of her mouth. She stopped mid bite and marveled at how Susan was devouring her burger. "You should take a breath every now and again, we still have another twenty minutes of lunch time left.

Susan put down the last few bites of her burger and twisted some fries in her ketchup and mustard dip. She chewed them like they were the last double fried fries on earth.

"What do you think about Sam Henning being back?" The question came flying in out of the blue taking Susan completely by surprise.

"I haven't given it much thought," she answered in between bites. She finished her burger and the last of her fries then slurped down her vanilla shake and sat back content and full.

"I mean, why... you used to be an item back in the day. You and Sam."

"That was a long time ago."

"Do you think he did it?"

"Huh?"

"You know. Do you think... he really killed his parents?"

"How should I know, Daphne? I wasn't there and he was gone shortly after."

"That was the weird part. I mean, didn't his uncle send him away to some asylum or something in a foreign country. The family was very rich, I heard," she finished her veggie burger wiped her mouth, wadded the rapper up in a neat ball and tossed it in the trash can.

"Okay, well, that's lunch," Susan stood and deposited her trash. "I'll see you around, Daphne."

"Hey, thanks for sharing your secret lunch spot with me. I see why you chose this spot. It's nice. See you at work, Susan," Daphne waved and strolled back at her own pace enjoying the last few minutes of her lunch break.

Susan slowly made her way back to the Emporium. She scolded herself for being so defensive about the subject of Sam Henning. She should've expected that question because it was a fact that she and Sam were childhood sweethearts, everybody knew that. It was a natural question for anyone to ask, after all, Springville was just like any other small town she guessed, people tended to know each other's business like it or not.

She finally pushed through the front doors of the massive sporting goods store where she has worked since high school. She smiled at customers and waved to a couple of her co-workers, ignoring their stares, before taking to the stairs which would place her back in the fish and tackle department where she took up restocking the shelves and pegs with every fishing gadget imaginable.

As she went about her work, she couldn't shake the thoughts that kept seeping into her brain; Sam Henning was back after a long absence it made her feel both excited and uncomfortable. It was a problem that she would have to figure out, sooner the better. She knew there would be more of the same questions. She had to be less defensive and more accepting of whatever the outcome might be. It wasn't any body's fault, people were just naturally curious. Especially in a small town…

CHAPTER 12

Sam turned off the hi-way and found a parking space right in front of the Emporium. He got out of his car, stretched, and pushed through the front doors. Once inside he surveyed the vastness of the sporting goods world. Three stories full of anything you can imagine and some I bet you couldn't. He was approached a young man who's name tag identified him as, Elbert. He was a tall lanky kid with a crooked smile and even crookeder glasses that sat sideways on his nose.

"May I help you find something, sir?"

"Yes, is Susan working today?"

The young man with the crooked glasses smiled his crooked smile and pointed up. "She's on the third floor today."

"Isn't that where she always works?"

"She's one of the ol' timers, so she works wherever."

"I see, thanks," Sam took the stairs to the third floor while the young man watched him. He looked over at the cashier and she mouthed an exaggerated, "I know."

Sam reached the third floor and stopped to get his bearings. Susan rounded the corner with an armload of boxes and almost dropped her load when she spotted him standing over by isle 7. Sam saw her and waved as he walked toward her.

"Hey, what are you doing? Looking for anything in particular?" Susan set her boxes down on an empty shelf and stretched her back.

"I… was looking for a BBQ. I looked around my house and found an old rusted out one behind the tool shed. It was in pretty bad shape."

"Well, you might have a hard time finding one here."

"I'm sorry?" Sam was confused. "Isn't this a sporting goods," he looked around the huge store then back at Susan. "Correction, huge sporting goods store?"

"Yes, Sam, The McKandless Emporium is one of the largest in the state," she was smiling.

"So, you're saying… what exactly are you saying?"

"You're standing on the camping floor. No BBQ's," She was trying not to laugh, she could see he was embarrassed.

"Oh," he scanned the isles and shelves and realized his mistake. "Yeah, I see. Tents and cots… no BBQ," he made a face and smiled.

"Okay mystery man. What's your plan?"

"Nothing," he shrugged his shoulders. "Just need to get a BBQ."

"Well, they're down there… on the first floor," she waited smiling at his discomfort.

"Okay," Sam looked around rubbing his hands together. "Guess it's back down to the first floor, have a great day."

"Thanks, you too. Oh, ask for Elbert, he will help you pick out a BBQ."

"Okay, yeah, I already met him. Thanks, see you around."

"It's possible, you will."

Damn, she's forward… and beautiful Sam thought to himself as he descended the stairs in search of Elbert.

Elbert proved to be somewhat of an expert on BBQ's and after a lengthy examination coupled with Elbert's prodding Sam picked the perfect one and out the door they went. Elbert helped Sam lift the box into his trunk and tied a rope on the trunk lid so it wouldn't bounce.

"Thanks, Elbert. You've been a big help."

"You're welcome, Mister Henning."

"Please, call me Sam," He made his way around to the drivers' side and climbed in.

"Okay, Sam," Elbert leaned down and waved through the passenger window. "Have a good Day."

You too," with that Sam was off with his new BBQ.

Daphne could hardly contain herself as she climbed the stairs to the third floor. She had seen Sam walk in and watched him talking to Susan. She reached the third floor and found Susan opening boxes of sleeping bags for a display.

Daphne cleared her throat, "Hey, Susan. How's it going in camping?"

"Good," Susan tucked an errant lock of hair behind her ear. "What's up, Daphne?"

"Oh, nothing. I'm down on two... camping apparel."

"Hey, can you hand me that box behind you?"

"Sure," Daphne handed the box over and watched as Susan went about freeing its contents. "I saw Sam come in earlier," she waited.

"Yeah, he's looking for a BBQ."

"Oh, a BBQ, huh?"

"I sent him back down to Elbert."

"Ah, good choice. Elbert knows his BBQ's, that's for sure."

"Anyway, well," Susan held her hands out palms up. It's an ancient gesture signaling the end of a conversation.

"Yeah, I better get back to folding hunting shirts. See ya later, maybe for lunch?"

"Okay, later," Susan went back to her unpacking, but she had to shake her head. She knew damn well why Daphne had come to her department. Lunch... she might take a late one.

———————————

When Sam got home, he went about untying the trunk and the spider web that Elbert had made because he was concerned the box would fall out if Sam were to hit a bump. He was fumbling with the last knot when he heard a car coming down his road. The knot would not give up its hold and Sam didn't have anything to cut it with. He gave up on the knot and waited for whoever was coming down his road. It sure sounded like a truck and he hoped, at once it would not be bringing the Frank and Leroy show back. To his relief it was the caretaker, what was his name? Sam struggled and as soon as he saw that old truck roll into his yard the name, Simms, popped into is head and he relaxed.

"Hey there young man," he called out his window.

Sam watched as he kicked open his door and sort of rolled out while lighting a cigarette.

"Mister Simms, what brings you out this way?"

"Well, I seen you was at the Emporium ya had this big box stickin'-

"You saw me? Where where you? I mean…"

"I was getting' a haircut 'cross the street," he answered somewhat annoyed for the interruption. "Thought ya might could use a hand unloadin' whatever it is ya got there."

"Well, that's real nice, Mister Simms-"

"Call me, Marten. Everybody does."

"Okay, Marten. Thanks."

Marten took a long leisurely pull on his cigarette as he assessed the situation.

"Looks like, Elbert, tied this knot," he reached for his knife pulling it free of its case and unfolded it. "Elbert never tied a knot a good sharp knife couldn' undo."

"Great," Sam and Marten took hold of the box and lifted it to the ground.

"Damn, you sure got the top a the line here," Marten's eyes lit up like a kid on Christmas. "Let's get this beauty out o' the box!"

"Hey, I was told he was the got-to-guy for BBQ's and…"

"Yeah, the kid knows BBQ's."

They cut the box open and Marten went to his toolbox together he and Sam assembled the Q. They were carrying it over to the spot Sam thought would be the best place when they heard someone coming down the road.

Frank's truck rumbled in next to Marten's and sat there. Frank, Sam realized, had a flare for dramatics.

"Damn show-off," Marten grumbled under his breath.

"What's going on Frank?" Sam called. It was his yard and he'd be damned if he'd let Frank think otherwise. It took a second before Frank made his entrance, Leroy slunk around from the passenger side. Frank leaned against his truck and lit a cigarette.

"Just passin' by," he took an exaggerated pull off his cigarette letting the smoke out slowly, big show.

"Is there something I can do for you? Frank?" Sam and Marten set the BBQ down and waited.

"We seen you at the Emporium," Leroy was the first to find his voice.

"And..."

Marten snubbed his butt on the heel of his boot and fired up another.

"Thought we had an understanding," Frank pushed off his truck and struck a somewhat menacing pose which was completely lost on Sam or Marten.

"An understanding? Frank?" Sam faced Frank.

"Thought we agreed you weren't to go into the Emporium."

"Well, Frank, I needed a BBQ. Where you figure I could get one if I didn't go to the Emporium?"

Marten smiled and puffed on his cigarette.

"How the hell should I know, Sam." Frank took a step closer and Leroy, face starting to contort, circled the other way. It's an old hunting tactic; split up and surround, cause your prey to make a decision whether to fight or take flight... or choose which one is the best choice to take out?

Sam was not amused. He just wanted to get his BBQ set up and maybe throw a couple steaks on to break it in.

"Look, Frank, I really don't want any trouble from you or your side-kick Leroy there. I'd like you both to climb back in your truck and leave me alone."

Frank laughed at that one.

Leroy parroted Frank which was what he normally did in these situations.

"He's funny," Frank took an exceptionally long pull on his cigarette and blew it out in one puff of smoke. "You think he's funny? Leroy?"

"Yeah, he's kind a funny," Leroy took up a position between Sam and his new BBQ.

"You think he's funny? Mister Simms?" Frank stared hard at the old man standing next to Sam.

"I think it'd be a good idea if you two hard cases hit the road and left this young man alone," he stared back just as hard at Frank who flinched ever so slightly which made Marten smile.

"You better watch your tone with me old man," Frank moved toward Marten who openly faced him.

"Like I said," Sam stepped up to Frank which didn't set well with Frank. "I want you both to get back in your truck and get the hell off my property. And I will go anywhere in this damn town I please and you, Frank, better not threaten me again," Sam got up real close to Frank and stayed that way till Frank backed down.

"C'mon, Leroy, let's get out'a here," Frank opened his door and turned for one last shot. "Someday that smart ass mouth of yours is gonna cause you problems," he slid in behind the wheel and slammed his door. Leroy got in but not without one last menacing look at Sam.

"Good, that's real good," Marten was waving. "You boys just run along and find someone else to pester, bye now."

Sam shook his head and walked over to his new BBQ.

"Don't let those idiots bother ya son," Marten fired up another smoke. "Let's get yer new Q set up."

CHAPTER 13

Just as evening claimed its place and shadows were stretching across the forest, three young women made their way to their spot in the woods. They walked quietly without speaking until they reached a small clearing with a fire ring in the middle.

The moon was slowly creeping up into the darkening sky and somewhere in the distance a night bird issued its lonely call. Deeper in the woods a larger animal moved, sniffing the air as it ambled along into the night.

"Clare, did you remember the sage?" Jorden, a dark-haired woman with haunting light blue eyes wanted to know.

"Of course, I wouldn't leave home without it," Clare ran her long fingers through her red hair and pulled a stick out of her pack.

Veronica, the third member of the party was a striking young woman with long sandy blonde hair and green eyes. She was the tallest of the three. They were the town witches according to those who thought they knew them, although they liked to refer to themselves as Spirit Talkers.

They had come to this particular part of the forest because it was their power spot, a place where they called upon the spirits. Some people in town might call them witches though they looked anything but. They dressed in summer dresses of light colors and wore no; hats, black capes, or carried brooms.

They were about the unwitchiest looking witches you would ever find and yet they remained an oddity and pretty much kept to themselves. They lived together in a log cabin at the far end of town not far from Sam Hennings' place.

"Okay, Leroy, you know the plan?" Frank put on his mask and studied himself in the bathroom mirror.

"Damn, Frank, you look bad ass," Leroy pulled his own mask over his head and faced Frank. "What do ya think of mine?"

"It looks good, Leroy. Now do you remember where we're gonna go in at?"

"Yeah, back road, park and walk in behind the old storage shed."

"Good. It's just about time to get going."

"I could use a beer," Leroy lifted his mask until it sat on top of his head and went to the fridge. "You want one?"

"Sure, beer sounds good about now."

"Ask me a beer sounds good anytime," Leroy tossed a can to Frank and popped his own. "Frank?"

"Yeah, Leroy."

"Do you really think we can scare Sam? I mean what happens if he sees us?"

"Quit your worrying, Leroy. We'll have masks on and besides, he won't see us unless we screw up. We're not going to screw it up are we, Leroy?"

"Well, I sure do hope not. If he finds out about what we're doing it could be really bad."

"Leroy, damn it, finish your beer and let's get on the road."

"Okay, Frank," Leroy upended his beer and tanked the rest letting out a very loud burp. "Now, that tasted awful good," he pitched the can underhand and missed the trash can by a couple of feet.

"Are you about ready?" Frank was heading out the door and Leroy quickly followed.

Sam was kicking back on his porch with a nice cup of red wine. He was waiting for his new BBQ to heat up and burn of the newness. He had a nice thick steak on the counter all seasoned and ready.

The sun had dipped below the horizon setting the forest in a blaze of color. He got up and went down to check on the progress of the burn off and couldn't smell the newness anymore. He climbed back up the stairs and went inside to retrieve his first offering to the BBQ.

Ahh, the sizzle of the steak on the hot grill was a satisfying sound which made Sam's stomach gurgle. Once it had achieved the proper cook, perfect medium rare, Sam took it off the fire and into the house where he poured a fresh cup of wine and sat down at the kitchen table to devour it. Halfway through his delicious steak he paused. He thought he heard something outside and went to the front window to check.

The sky had bruised over into deep purples and the forest was steeped in shadow. He couldn't see anything out of the ordinary. Sam returned to his meal and finished. He washed his plate, grabbed some more wine then decided to bring the bottle out onto the front porch where he sat with his feet propped up on the railing.

Sam was full and very happy with his new BBQ. He thought of Susan and decided to invite her over for some burgers this weekend... or whenever she was off work. He took a deep breath and smiled into his wine glass. He felt great, better than he'd felt since arriving back at his childhood home.

The three young women started a small fire and laid out their spirit calling paraphernalia which included a book of incantations and sage, a small bird feather, and three stones.

They joined hands and swayed back and forth as they recited their incantation. It wasn't long before they heard the sound of a vehicle and they stopped to listen.

It stopped somewhere out in the woods. They waited for a moment longer and didn't hear anything so they resumed their calling of spirits. Soon they were lost in the rhythm of their chant and the burning sage.

"C'mon, Leroy, what's the hold up?"

"I can't see very good out of my mask."

"I told you, you should've found one with bigger eye holes."

"Okay, that's a little better," Leroy pulled his mask down lower and aligned the eye holes to see better. "Frank?"

"What is it, Leroy?"

"You see that glow way out there in the trees?"

"No, oh yeah, I do see it," Frank studied the glow for a second. "Those witches are at it again."

"Yeah, what happens if they see us and put some kind a whammy on us?"

"Leroy..." Frank took a moment to compose himself. "Will you please quit your worryin'. They won't see us from way out there."

"I hope not."

"Damn it, Leroy," Frank pushed onward mumbling under his breath. "C'mon."

When they reached their hiding spot Frank had to pull Leroy into the darkness behind the storage shed when Sam came out onto the front porch.

That was close Frank thought holding Leroy by the shoulders until Sam had settled back in his chair. Frank found the string that he had tied to the wind chimes on the porch and slowly unwound it from the nail he had pounded into the side of the shed. He pulled it gently causing the chimes to tinkle ever so slightly. It was enough to catch Sam's attention he turned to look in that direction. Both Frank and Leroy had to cover their mouths as they smiled under their now sweaty masks.

The three, Spirit Callers continued their chanting and swaying until Veronica stopped.

"Hey, Veronica?" Clare watched the change in Veronica's face. "What is it? What's wrong?"

"Behind you," Veronica pointed with her chin. "There's a young boy standing right.... behind... you," Veronica kept her voice low but there was a slight tremble to it. Clare and Jorden, both, looked over their shoulders and their breath stopped. There it was the very thing they had been trying to contact, they hoped. The boy stood just outside their firelight, but he was plainly visible.

"Hey, who are you?" Veronica was the first to speak. They waited holding hands, fearful of breaking their circle. The boy was wearing swim trunks he was or appeared to be wet, like he just got out of the water. He was standing half in shadow so it was hard to tell who it was.

"Can you tell us your name?" Clare asked.

No response.

"My name's Clare, this is Veronica and that's Jorden." Clare waited a moment and still no response.

"Can you tell us where you were swimming?" Jorden wanted to know. Nothing... Then, the boy slowly backed away, out of their firelight and dissipated into the cool night air.

Clare got to her feet and went to the place the boy had stood a second ago. She bent down and gasped.

"What is it, Clare?" Both Veronica and Jorden wanted to know.

"It looks wet, where he was standing, but it's not, it's dry," Clare, touched the ground, shaking her head.

"Are you sure?" Veronica and Jorden joined her each touching the ground confirming what Clare had discovered.

Frank gave another, light, tug on the string setting the chimes in motion, catching Sam's attention. Leroy was beside himself with excitement until Frank gave him an elbow in the ribs.

"Geeze, Frank."

"Shhh, dammit, Leroy you're gonna get us caught," he hissed at his partner in crime.

Sam got out of his chair and went over to the chimes which had gone silent. He studied them for a moment he didn't see the string, as that end of the porch was out of range of the light. He gazed out into the darkness as if he might have seen something out there.

Frank and Leroy slunk back a bit watching him, hoping he wouldn't discover their little trick.

Sam gave a big sigh and returned to his chair and his cup of wine. He was full of steak and wine and feeling pretty relaxed. He sank back into his chair on the porch but wasn't really thinking of any one thing in particular, just snippets of thought.

And then it happened a voice from long ago spoke; *"You were supposed to be watching your little brother! It was your one and only job this summer..."* The voice sounded raspy with age.

Sam shot out of his chair as if it had been electrified. He was shaking all the sudden. Completely rocked. Tears burned in his eyes as they ran freely down his cheeks blurring everything... The chimes started in again, only this time more aggressively.

"Hey, what's wrong with him?" Leroy had noticed Sam's change.

"Leroy, go easy on the string, shit," Frank was getting mad, plus, truth be told, he was starting to get spooked.

"Frank, I'm not touching the damn string," Leroy looked at his friend whose masked face was hideous in the gloom.

There was the soft sound of a foot crunching a dry leaf behind them and they turned as one to see what it was. There, barely visible in the distance, was what appeared to be a small boy. He stood there staring at the two men in the scary masks.

"Frank?" Leroy whispered, voice shaking.

"I see it, Leroy, keep yer voice down," Frank studied the figure standing not ten feet away and his heart stopped.

"Wha-" Leroy lost his voice. It was getting hard to breath inside his mask.

"I don't know," Frank's voice was muffled behind *his* mask.

Sam stood and walked to the railing, *what was that?* He wondered squinting into the darkness outside the porch light. He stood there for quite a while which made Frank and Leroy even more nervous.

Still the figure of the boy stood silently by… Staring…

"Frank let's get out'a here," Leroy was quickly losing his nerve, he was gasping for air.

Frank couldn't take his eyes off the figure who was now standing so close, too close.

"Frank?" Leroy was ready to bolt which would draw Sam's attention and put an end to their little scheme.

Sam, seeing nothing, pushed off the porch railing and went into the house. That's when Leroy finally lost it and ran off through the woods like a wild man. Frank had no choice but to follow. As they ran, they tore off their masks leaving them behind. Once they located Frank's truck they jumped inside, locking the doors as they did.

Sam heard the commotion and went back out but could see nothing in the darkness. He could definitely hear somebody or somebodies running out there but had no idea who they were or what they were up to until the chimes went off again startling him. Sam froze for a second before he went over and grabbed them, tightly, in his hand to stop them.

That's when he felt the string. He gave it a light tug, paused for a moment, then went back inside to retrieve the flashlight he bought at the Emporium. Returning to the chimes he felt for the string again and followed it with the beam of his flashlight.

He went down the steps and around to the side of the house where he again found the thin sliver line running off his porch shining in his flashlight beam and followed it until he found himself standing behind the old shed. He shined his light on the ground and discovered tracks, two sets of tracks. He could make out that they were bunched up there behind the shed but who could it be?

On further inspection he could see they headed off through the trees but, he wasn't eager to follow, not in the dark. He decided it would be a lot smarter if he waited till morning, and that's what he did. He returned to the porch, gave the area around the shed and surrounding forest one last sweep of his flashlight beam and went inside.

Clare, Jorden, and Veronica heard two people running, they heard a truck start and peel off into the night.

"Who do you think they were?" Clare was trying to pierce the darkness with her eyes.

"Sounded like they were in a big hurry," Veronica stood by Clare's side.

"Wonder who that boy was?" Jorden's question brought Veronica and Clare back to the moment.

"You don't think..." Clare looked at her two friends and her words trailed off.

"What, Clare? What are you thinking?" Jorden asked.

"Okay, wait," Veronica held her hand up. "Clare? Are you thinking about the boy we saw? Or wondering who those people were that took off in the truck?"

"I think I have a pretty good idea who it was in the truck... It's that boy, Veronica? Didn't you find something about a boy drowning?"

"Yeah, I did," Veronica paused to think. "It... It was Sam's younger brother..."

1

CHAPTER 14

A box of morning sunlight crept across the floor in Sam's room. He was already awake staring at the open beam ceiling. The voice… It sent chills down his spine just thinking about it. What did it mean?

He rolled out of bed and padded downstairs to the kitchen where he filled the tea kettle with water and set it on the stove. *Okay,* he thought, *now what.* He was so distracted his mind was a jumble. He climbed back upstairs and got himself dressed.

"You knew he wasn't a good swimmer! How could you let this happen?!

Sam had to grab onto the door handle to keep from toppling over. His head was in a tailspin he felt sick to his stomach. It took him a while before he trusted himself to stand on his own. The high-pitched scream of the kettle snapped him out of it, he raced downstairs before it boiled over.

He grabbed a towel and lifted the kettle off the fire thankful when the scream settled into a low whine then stopped hissing altogether. He took the jar of instant coffee off the shelf and put two heaping spoonful's in his coffee cup, poured in the steaming water and set the pot back on the stove, turning the fire off.

Sam stepped out onto the front porch and took a big deep breath of the cold morning air. The pines wouldn't fully scent the forest until they were warmed by the sun. He raised his cup for that first sip and burnt the crap out of tongue and upper lip. *Okay, let's start over* he told himself. He took in another deep breath of the morning air and settled into his chair, pulling it up so he could rest his feet on the top of the porch railing. He rolled his warm cup in his hands and remembered something. He got up, setting his coffee cup on the railing, and walked over to where the chimes hung silent at the end of the porch.

He studied those chimes for a few minutes before he noticed saw the fine line attached to the upper ring where all the other lines are tied to the long metal tubes. He leaned on the railing and followed the line with his eyes until it was lost in the backdrop. It did appear the line was headed toward the locked shed just inside the trees. Walking back, he scooped his coffee off the rail and headed down the front steps. When he rounded the corner he got a chill all the sudden and it stopped him in his tracks.

Reaching up he felt for the line and followed it to the corner of the shed. There was an eyebolt for the line to pass without getting snagged on the sheds rough wood. Sam came around to the back of the shed and realized whoever it was making those chimes rattle also had a clear view of the front porch. He studied the ground and found it to be trampled with boot prints. They came and went the same direction. Sam gave the line a sharp tug and it popped off the chimes making them ring like crazy for a second before stopping.

Well, hell, Sam thought, might as well get dressed and see where they go... He headed back inside. Within five minutes he was dressed and standing back out on the front porch. The instant coffee was buzzing through his system aided by a touch of adrenaline.

He had no idea or reason why he should feel so intimidated by the locked shed, but he did. One thing at a time. Sam followed the tracks leading away from the shed into the forest. It was interesting though, the closer he looked, he could see the tracks going back the way he came were flat, like they were walking. The set of prints he was following away from his place were kicked up, they were running. Yep, they were definitely running. He stood up and stretched his back, he had to laugh because they, whoever they were must've spooked themselves.

He noticed something ahead on the path. When he got to it he just stood there staring at it, puzzled by it. He bent down and picked it up, holding it at arm's length. It was a Halloween mask. He spotted another one a few feet ahead on the trail... Long way til Halloween. Then it hit him right between the eyes. *Whoever they were at his house, must've been wearing these masks... Why would anybody want to try to scare me anyway?* He wondered.

Sam picked up the masks, both with gruesome expressions frozen in time; he located a tree, jumped as high as he could and impaled them on a dead, broken branch just a little inside the trees.

He kept going, curiosity getting the better of him. The tracks lead him to a narrow side road where he saw plain as day, the evidence of someone putting the peddle to the floor. They kicked up a whole bunch of dirt leaving two rough furrows behind.

The wind changed and he caught a whiff of smoke, camp-fire smoke. He searched the area within his sight range and headed in the direction of the smell. It wasn't long before the smell of smoke got stronger and he found an old campfire place, with a circle around it... Halloween masks? Fire pit with a circle around it? He turned heading back the way he came until he was by the shed again and having those same weird thoughts. If he were to try and pin it down he would say it felt like he was being pulled toward it, but he had absolutely no idea why he should. At the same time if he felt something wasn't quite right or a little off he tended to keep his distance from it.

A young boy ran past him into the woods. Scared the hell out of him it happened so fast. *"Okay,"* he said to the emptiness around him, *"better get something to eat."*

He was at the stove trying his hardest to achieve the perfect over easy eggs when he decided to just scramble the darn things and be done with it. When he was finished he took his breakfast out onto the front porch to enjoy. He took a seat and sniffed the pine scented air before he dug into his food. As he was eating he looked over at his brand-new awesome BBQ and thought of taking a drive over to the Emporium to see if Susan would like to come over later.

Yeah, the thought of Frank wormed its way into his thoughts but, he wasn't about to be intimidated by him, no way! He finished his breakfast almost dropping his plate when he stood. Something was out in the forest, it was dark, darker than shadow and it made Sam's skin ripple with goosebumps. He watched it for who knows how long before it vanished even then he kept his eyes glued to the spot where it was. The chimes started going off and he went over to inspect them. The line was gone. He reached out to wave his hand over them and they came to a tinkling stop. He took one last look at the trees and, finding nothing, went back inside to clean up the kitchen.

Sam got into his car and headed to town. When he got there he turned right and, as always was able to park in front of the Emporium. Town was relatively quiet. It was mid-morning. He went through the big front doors and was awestruck, as always. He couldn't believe such a place could exist in such a small town.

He noticed the girl at the cash register was staring at him and he smiled, he mouthed the question, and she pointed up. Sam took the stairs and found Susan unpacking boxes of boots.

"Hey good morning," Sam smiled and walked over.

"Hey yourself," Susan tucked a lock of hair behind her ear and stood. "What brings you to our humble small town hardware store?"

"Well," he stalled, "I have this new BBQ..."

"I heard," Susan was trying to keep the smile from her face.

"I mean, sometime if you'd like to come over and help me break it in…"

"Sometime huh? That could be now or sometime later… Or maybe even next year," She had a tinge of guilt for working him so but…

"Well, what are you doing after work?" Sam took a boot off the shelf and worked it in his hands.

"Hmm, I'm feeling like eating a big juicy… burger."

"Okay then," Sam took a smelled the leather infused air and looked around.

"So, I'll see you later? Sam?"

"Oh, sorry. Yes, I'll stop by the grocery store and pick up some supplies."

"I'll bring the wine."

And they stood there with these goofy expressions plastered to their faces.

"Okay," Susan was first to snap out of it. "So, I gotta get back to work… and you have to…"

"I'll see you… later."

"You said that already."

Sam spun around and took to the stairs. When he reached the bottom all eyes were on him. He walked out the front door and ran smack into Leroy who recoiled as if he were snake bit.

"Leroy," Sam smiled at him and walked by.

"Thought you were told not to come 'round here."

"Not used to seeing you without your handler," Sam stopped and faced Leroy.

"Yeah, well, I gotta be goin'," he pushed through the front doors without another word.

Sam drove over to the next block where he found the Springville Grocery Store. He loved the smell of the place. It was the picture of a small-town store; packed tight with everything you could ever want to cook or bake, or ready-made. If you went there around seven in the morning Alma would just be pulling out a tray or three of biscuits and sweet rolls. It had an old cash register and old pictures of the town on the wall behind. Alma, a spirited woman of seventy or so. Always smiled and acknowledged you when you came through the door. Small town...

On the way home he thought about what they would talk about. He quickly dismissed it. Go with the flow. As soon as he turned into his road he was stopped by a roadblock of sorts... He stopped and got out of his car.

"Frank," Sam closed the distance but left room. "You're blocking my driveway."

"Oh, sorry we was just takin' some shade," he lit a cigarette while Leroy shuffled in the background.

"Well, suppose you take it over somewhere besides my driveway."

Frank made a face while he took a big, long drag of his cigarette, blowing smoke into the sky.

"Do you have a problem with short term memory... Sam?"

"Actually, I can recall things very well," he got a jolt that shook him because there were complete blanks that he couldn't recall. "Why don't you boys get back in your truck, Frank, and move off my road. Now, Frank," the furthest thing from Sam's mind was to get into a fight with Frank. The dude was huge, but he did limp slightly which indicates a weak spot. No, he scolded himself. "Frank, I won't ask again," Sam stared hard at Frank who did the same until his gaze broke and he looked over his shoulder at Leroy who was already standing by the passenger door.

"We'll have to settle this some other time," he scowled at Sam and drove off in a cloud of dust.

"*I've got nothing to settle with you, Frank.*"

When Sam stopped in front of his house he sat there for a second while he tried to will away the dark thoughts that swirled in his head. Once he turned his thoughts to the here and now he got out of his car and went into the house with a full bag of goodness to prep for big night... *no*, his inner voice whispered, *don't make it anything more than it will be.*

Setting the grocery bag on the counter he pulled out its contents spreading them out. He put the lettuce and tomato in the fridge and got out a bowl to mix the hamburger meat with his special seasonings. When he was finished, he put the meat in the fridge and washed his hands.

He headed out the door and placed his hands on the sun warmed top rail. He took deep breaths of the rich pine scented air, as deep as he could, letting his breath out slowly. He looked over at the silent chimes and wondered if he should tell Susan about it. Again, his inner voice, or one of them at least, scolded him, *go with the flow.* He went down the steps and into the yard where he admired his new BBQ, waiting to taste juicy burgers from its' flame hot teeth. Sam took the cloth he had hanging on a hook on the side and wiped it clean.

———————————

Susan was distracted. She was a machine as she went about unpacking the boots and arranging them on the shelves. She hardly even realized she was on to jackets when her new lunch partner, Daphne, called to her from the first floor.

"Hey, that's lunch," Daphne hung her apron on the hook behind her and straightened her hair.

Susan purposefully hung up a couple more jackets before she responded with a shrug.

They didn't get too much past company talk until they were comfortably seated at Susan's once private lunch spot. Susan unwrapped her beautiful double cheeseburger and dove in.

"So, did he ask you?" Daphne was wiping a non-existent smudge from the corner of her mouth.

"Susan fought to swallow instead of choke on her first bite. Thankfully it turned out to be swallow but, it took second before she could speak.

CHAPTER 15

Before Sam finished prepping for his burger fest, he took a break and grabbed a beer from the fridge. He headed outside to look around and gather himself. His heartbeat faster as the time for his dinner guest to arrive grew closer. He took several breaths and had to take a seat until the stars quit floating around his head. He stood again, took a nice refreshing drink of his beer, and went to gather some wood for the fire pit. As he approached the shed, he started to feel bad. Not so much sick, but heavy... and a little sick.

He had no idea why but, he always had a funny feeling, in the pit of his stomach, whenever he approached that darn shed. Especially in light of the resent discovery of unwelcome visitors. He grabbed an armload of wood and took it over to the pit where he stacked it ready to light, he stood back to admire his work, perfect. Nice outdoor fire... burgers sizzling on the BBQ... *nothing to get all worked up about.*

Well, everything was pretty much set, not much else to do but... The sound of a car wormed its way into his thoughts and he wondered who it could be. Too early to be Susan. Shortly, a very old Volkswagen, the color of robin's eggs, appeared in his front yard. He had no clue who it was, so he waited. A striking young woman with jet black hair climbed out and smiled.

"Hi."

"Hi."

"My name's, Veronica?" She closed her door and walked over to Sam with her hand extended. "I live over that way."

"Okay," Her eyes were very pale blue, almost white which gave her a haunting, alluring appeal. "I'm Sam," he shook her hand.

"I know who you are and who you are not, Sam," her smile never diminished.

"What can I do for you?"

"My sisters and I call spirits."

"Okay," a chill entered his body making him shudder slightly.

"There are unsettled spirits here," She walked in a circle with her arms outstretched as if she could actually feel the spirits.

"Did you say unsettled… spirits?" Sam thought he might not have heard her correctly, he was some distracted but, decided to go along with the conversation, as out of the blue as it was.

"We can help clear this place and let the spirits pass on."

"And how do you do that? Clear an area."

"I call on the spirits and talk to them. I communicate through seance. Clare? She's the same as me, she can talk to them, too, but she sees them also. Jorden my ither sister is into herbology."

"Well, that's… good to know," Sam smiled at the striking young woman in her summer dress. "I'll certainly keep that in mind."

Just then the chimes started to tinkle, lightly at first, then they went wild before stopping altogether.

"Yes, Sam," she was still smiling. "The sooner we clear these spirits the better," she whirled around, got back into her car without another word, and drove off. Sam took a seat on the bottom step. Then shot up when he saw a young boy walk out of the trees and wave at the retreating car. Sam watched transfixed as the boy turned his way and vanished.

"Shit! Shit shit shit! What the hell was that all about?" He looked into the trees and of course there was nothing… *"Okay, Sam, ol' buddy, we have to get ourselves together. We have a visitor coming here in…* "What time is it anyway?" he wondered aloud, before rushing up the stairs to see. Yep, he had exactly thirty minutes to get everything ready and he spent that thirty in a whirlwind of motion.

Finally, he stepped back to admire his handy work; two chairs with a small table between them, *flowers, oh geeze!* He scolded himself and ran into the house to retrieve the bouquet of wildflowers he'd picked earlier.

Okay, flowers and pot in hand. Sam set the flowers in the middle of the table then stood back again... *Plates!* He went back in to get two plates and the condiments. Okay, he was finally ready.

Moments later a car swung into his front yard and a face that could melt the ice packs of the North Pole, smiled up at him.

"Hey, you!" Susan reached in and grabbed two brown bags. She was wearing blue jeans with a long-sleeved plaid shirt, "Great afternoon huh?" She floated up the stairs holding the brown bags out for him to take.

Holy moly, she looks stunning! She smells good too.

"Hello?"

"Yes, yes, it is," Sam took the bagged bottles of wine into the kitchen, when he got there, he realized, to his horror, he hadn't changed his shirt, oh boy. "I'll be right ou-

"Hope you don't mind," she walked into the kitchen just then. "I got two different kinds."

"Oh, no, that's... yeah good idea. I-I'll be right down," he tugged on his t-shirt. "I need to change my shirt."

"I'll open the wine while you find something to wear," she couldn't help staring after him. *He has a very muscular body. Not a bodybuilder's body but, one formed with hard work.* she thought. "Don't be long, I'm thirsty,"

She was a kidder. That was good.

Sam returned wearing a bright Hawaiian print shirt.

"Here you go, Sam," She handed him a glass of wine. "Good to see you've made the big move and bought some real glasses."

"I was one of the bigger moves of my life. Thanks, let's go out on the porch," Sam held the door. "Are you hungry? Should I fire up the BBQ?"

"Think I'd like to unwind a little from stocking hunting boots." Susan sat in one of the chairs and Sam in the other.

"Sounds good to me, course, I'm not the one that has to go to work in the morning."

"Me either. Nice flowers," Susan smiled at Sam who's heart was jack-hammering in his chest, he wasn't so sure she couldn't hear it.

"Okay, no hurry then," Sam scooted his chair up enough to prop his feet up on the railing. Susan did the same.

"You know we sure had some good times in those woods," she took a sip of wine and stared off into space.

"I'm sorry, what did you say?"

"Huh? Oh, Me and you. That was our playground," She swept the air with her arm. "Sam? Don't you really remember... anything?"

"Remember things I'd rather not." He took a second and a sip of wine. "I don't remember... being young... who my family was... you..." Sam stood and gripped the railing. "As hard as I try I..."

"It's okay, Sam," Susan stood next to him gripping his shoulder.

"Is it? I mean is it okay?"

"I think it's okay if you just take your time. That's what I think. C'mon, let's sit back down and relax."

"People look at me as if... I don't know," Sam took his seat and relaxed, as much as he could in the company of such a forward, beautiful woman. It was more than her looks so much though or the way she spoke... there was something else about her that created a strong attraction, one he'd never...

"People don't know the real story; they only know gossip. That, unfortunately has become their truth."

"*Their truth*?" Sam sat up in his chair. "What is *their* truth? Do you know, Susan?"

"I believe the only person who truly knew the truth was the Sheriff, Sheriff Dobbs? He was the first through the door when your… He died in the fire that took his office. It was reported as a suicide. There's a small number of older men who think it was too," Susan paused to take a sip that turned into a gulp, sending her into a coughing fit. When she recovered, she continued. "Anyway… Shortly before that he sent his son away. Some say he was sent to a school for troubled kids. Others say he just went to live with his aunt back east. People have compiled so many theories over the years it's hard to sort them all out."

"What have you sorted out? You say you knew me, that we were young together. More wine?"

"Yes, please," Susan's head was absolutely swimming!

"Here ya go," Sam carefully filled her glass, then his and placed the bottle close. "So, who was this, Sheriff Dobbs' son? Did he… did he ever come back? I don't know why he should, I have no know idea who he is or what he would do," he caught himself rambling and stopped.

"Sam," Susan took his hand in hers. "Can we just enjoy each other's company tonight? There is so much I want to tell you but, tonight… tonight, I'd like to just drink wine, scarf down a couple of juicy burgers and drink more wine."

"Okay, I can handle that," as an afterthought he asked, "I think I should get a phone put in."

"That would be nice."

"Who does that? Do you know of a telephone company?"

"As luck would have it, I do," She reached over for more wine. "His names' Hank."

"Okay."

"He's the phone guy around these parts. He's also a locksmith. He lives down the valley," Susan breathed in the evening air. "If you want, I can set it up for you."

"That would be great… If it's not too much trouble."

"No trouble at all. He's… an interesting old man."

"Oh, boy. More interesting old men," he kidded.

"Hey, how's about we light that fire pit. It's getting dark enough."

"I'm on it," Sam got up and before long had a nice fire going. "You getting hungry? I feel like I better eat something before I get drunk."

"I'm ready!" Susan went down to hold her hands over the warm fire while Sam fired up the BBQ.

They sat and ate their burgers in silence, except for the occasional expressions of satisfaction one experiences when diving into a delicious burger. Stars were starting to punch through the darkening dome of sky. An owl announced itself somewhere off in the darkness of the forest.

Two old friends settled into each other's company, bathed in a soft glow of fire light, with easy talk and, an almost, mutual feeling of familiarity…

CHAPTER 16

Sam was full, half drunk and elated by the evening, hit the bed like a ton of bricks, and was out pretty much on contact. It wasn't long before he heard his name being called.

There was someone knocking on the front door… then he flinched when he heard the unmistakable sound of the front door slowly swinging open…

"Sam, Sam, c'mon! Let's go swimming! C'mon!

Sam rose from his bed and noticed the room was changed… slightly out of balance. He felt different… nothing was familiar… even the air had a heavy, stale, sort of essence to it… Sam made his way carefully downstairs and came to an abrupt halt.

"Sam, c'mon, let's go already." A young boy stood on the front porch already in his swimsuit, he was calling through the open front door.

"Okay, hold on let me get my swimsuit on." Sam felt it was his voice… he heard himself say it, but it wasn't… he didn't say it… He went back up to his room in a body not his own. When he came back downstairs he saw his younger brother, Pete, still standing just outside the door. The forest behind him was lit up with the summer sun.

Sam and his brother ran through the woods laughing and teasing each other as they zigzagged through the trees.

Just ahead, just out of the trees, was a plank dock. Sam hit that dock at a dead run pounding over its warped, sun-bleached boards and dove into the sparkling cool water. The shock of cold water electrified his body, bubbles flew by his ears as he knifed through the water. When his momentum slowed, he rose to the surface to find his brother standing at the end of the dock.

"What are you doing? You're the one that wanted to go swimming, so, jump in." Sam churned the water with his arms to stay afloat. "What are you waiting for? No, no don't do that," Sam watched Pete sit down and dip his toes into the water. "You're just making it worse on yourself. Dive in like I did," Sam was growing impatient. "Go back to the trees and run and dive in. It's the best way. Now, c'mon, already."

"I'm gonna just jump in," Pete stood and looked down at the water, took a deep breath and jumped. They splashed each other swimming swam back, forth splashing and laughing. Sam challenged Pete to a race and let him win at the last second. Sam dove under and grabbed him by the ankles pulling him under then pushing him back up to the surface where he sputtered and coughed, rubbing the water from his eyes. Then, Pete went under and was gone...

Sam splashed and ducked under the water searching for his brother in the blurry half-light but, he couldn't find him... He kept searching until he grew too tired. He pulled himself up onto the dock where he lay panting and crying.

And that's how he woke up. He struggled to free himself from the bed sheets which were wrapped around his legs.

Once freed he stood, shaking, and ran to the bathroom where he threw up. When he had nothing left, he stood in front of the mirror and stared into a face that didn't much resemble his own. He splashed his face in cold water which sent shivers over his body. He toweled off and padded downstairs to start a pot of coffee. When he poured himself a cup he stepped out onto the front porch to enjoy the coming of a new day. Halfway through his cup he heard a vehicle coming down his road and he stood placing his cup on the porch rail.

It wasn't long before a very old pickup truck roared into his yard and chugged to a stop. A man who looked as old as the truck he was driving rolled out and promptly closed the door on a corner of his coat causing him to fall back against the truck. A string of cuss words emitted from him as he opened the door and grabbed his coat out of the way. He was still swearing when he walked up to the porch.

"Good morning!" Sam called.

"Mornin' yourself young man!" He called back still muttering under his breath.

"What can I do for you?"

"Nothin', it's what I can do for you. Susan said that you wanted to get your phone installed."

"Oh, yes, you're the phone guy."

"That and other things. Name's Hank," he looked around and noticed the wire going to the cabin. "Looks like the phone line is still hooked up. Should be able to fix you up, no problem. Just need to take a look at what you have inside."

"I'm Sam."

"I know."

"Alright, well, come on in," Sam held the door while Hank shuffled inside. "I think the phone jack is right over there," Sam led Hank into the living room to a jack by the bookcase.

"Oh yeah, I see it," Hank bent down and bumped his head on the corner of the shelf which unleashed a whole new string of swearing. "Sorry, my wife keeps getting after me to control my swearing."

"Oh, I think you're doing a good job of that."

"Thanks, *it's* a work in progress." Yep, just what I figured," he stood and scratched his stubbly chin. "Just need to pick out what kind of phone you want."

"Okay."

"Come on out to my truck and take a look at some of the models I brought with me."

They walked back out to Hank's truck and Sam noticed the writing on the door; *Hank's Fix it* in faded letters was almost too far gone to read. It turns out Hank did indeed have some phones to look at. He said if Sam didn't see anything of interest, he had a catalog he could look through.

"I like this one," Sam pointed out a simple old school black phone.

"You sure? I mean I have some more... modern ones here. Would you like the wall mount or table model?"

"No, I like that one."

"Well, suit yourself. Basic black table model it is," he seemed almost disappointed. "I'll have you hooked up in a jiffy."

"Great, thanks."

"I'll be right in," Hank rummaged around the clutter behind his seat and grabbed a box which he brought into the house. It wasn't long before he stood to admire his work. "Thought a young man such as yourself would've gone for one of my more modern phones. But, hey, if it's basic black you want, basic black is what you have."

"I appreciate that, thanks."

"Well, you're welcome. Anything else I can do for you today?" He busied himself with putting his tools away.

"There is one thing..."

"Well, I'm no mind reader son."

"Susan said you were also a locksmith?"

"That's true enough, just one of my specialties. You got a lock needs opening?"

"Yeah, how did you know?"

"Hell fire, son, you mentioned a locksmith. Usually that means a person needs a lock opened."

"I supposed you're right."

"A course I am. Now where's this lock needs opening?"

"It's right over there," Sam led the way.

"Well, you could'a busted this little thing off with a hammer."

"Yeah, I don't have a hammer."

"Well, you're in luck, I'll be right back," Hank shuffled back to his truck and, after some more rummaging around he was finally able to locate his hammer, but, not without a lot of swearing.

"You sure that hammer will break it?"

"I'm a locksmith, son, now stand back aways, give me some room."

"No problem," Sam gladly took a step back.

It took one well aimed whack and that old lock gave itself up to tumble to the ground. Hank did the honors of pulling the shed doors open and they let out a squeal of protest as rusty metal ground against rusty metal. Hank stepped, back covering his face with his hand.

"Whew," he rubbed his nose while making a face. "Don't figure that's been opened in a long time."

"I wouldn't have any idea," Sam moved closer and peered into the shadows of a past that he couldn't recall... he did notice a smell. It wasn't offensive but, it wasn't entirely pleasant either. And it was cold... colder than he thought it should be.

"Well," Hank lit a cigarette and continued to stare into the darkness of the open shed. "Is there anything else I can do for you this fine morning?"

"I believe that's all that I can think of for now," He smiled at Hank but, lost it when he looked toward the open shed.

"I'll be on my way then, Sam?"

"Yeah," Sam was jolted out of his thoughts. "I'm sorry mind went somewhere else for a second there."

"It's understandable, son," Hank gave Sam a sort of, *I know what's going on around here*, look. "Have a good day, then."

"I will, thanks, you do the same."

Sam watched Hank crawl back into his beat-up old truck and promptly close the seat belt in the door. He yanked and yanked all the while swearing like Sam had never heard before. Then he stopped opened his door and pulled the belt out of harm's way.

He looked up at Sam and smiled a sheepish smile and closed the door on his coat. Sam wasn't about to warn him and possibly go through another round of obscenities. He just waved and watched him drive off down his road, corner of a coat flapping away.

CHAPTER 17

"Well, Frank," Leroy opened a beer, even though it was only nine o'clock in the morning. "You think we should go back out there and find our masks?"

"If you didn't lose yours, we wouldn't have to," Frank was in a bad mood.

"Hey, Frank, you lost yours too!"

"Yeah, I lost it. You took yours off and left it."

"I took mine off 'cause I couldn't see. You lost yours. We both lost our masks, Frank."

"Yeah, okay," Frank got up and fished a beer out of the fridge and sat down on his well-used couch. "We gotta go back and try to find 'em before someone else does."

"Hey, Frank," Leroy gulped down the rest of his beer and under-handed it at the trash can which he missed by a couple feet, the beer can clanking onto the pile already started a week ago by the looks of the shiny tin mountain. "Maybe we should go back out there tonight and see if we can find 'em."

"Hell, I'm not goin' out there in the dark!" Frank added his empty beer can to the growing pile in the corner. "Them damn witches are out there at night doin' who knows what all… could put a spell on us and we wouldn't even know it."

"Yeah, I guess you're right about that," Leroy got up and shuffled over to the fridge to grab another beer. "You want another one, Frank?"

"Why the hell not." Leroy tossed him a beer and took one of his own.

"I think it would be a good idea if we went out there in the daytime," Frank took a big swig of his beer and balanced it on the arm of the couch. "I don't think witches have power in the daytime."

"How do you know that, Frank?"

"I read it somewhere," he said as if challenging Leroy to dispute it.

"Well, sounds right to me, Frank. But if anybody finds those masks…"

"They won't!" Frank literally sucked the beer out of its can and crushed in his meaty fist. "We'll find those damn masks right where we left 'em, you'll see, Leroy. Now, turn on the game will ya?" Frank settled back feeling the two beers he virtually inhaled relax his body. The couch such as it was, was something anyone else would have tossed out long ago. Leather that was severally cracked in places, one corner of the arm had been chewed on and was leaking stuffing. It was used.

It took one more round of beers before the dynamic duo was ready to, once again, head into the creepy woods, where witches and killers reside. Once they veered off the hi-way Frank downshifted when he did the dust caught up with them and they quickly closed their windows.

"Geeze, Frank," Leroy let go of the dashboard. "You tryin' to put me through the damn windshield?"

"Shhh, I thought I saw something. Right over there," he pointed in the direction, and they watched to see whatever it was.

"I don't see nothin' but trees, Frank." Leroy looked at his partner for signs of witchcraft and could not find anything obvious.

"Yeah, probably just the wind," Frank ground his truck into gear and off they went, but slowly.

When they reached the spot, they thought they were the other night Frank cut the engine and they sat there, in the truck as if expecting something to happen.

"Frank? Frank," Leroy was not much for sitting in the woods for very long. Leroy was no nature lover, he preferred the wilds of a bar to the wilds of a forest. "Frank!"

"What? Damnit Leroy quit yellin'"

"I was just wondering if you're plannin' on us sittin' here all morning?"

"I'm listening."

"What do you hear? I don't hear nothin'"

"Shh, just be quiet for a second, will ya?"

"Okay, geeze. No need to get yourself all worked up, Frank."

"Leroy… just shut the hell up for a second, will ya? There it is!"

"Frank, cut it out you're startin' to scare me. And I don't much like bein' scared."

"Goddamnit, Leroy." Frank snarled. "Just…" Frank sucked in a big breath trying to control his temper which was a little frayed at the moment.

"Do… you see something… Frank?"

"No… thought I did… let's get those masks and get the hell out of here."

"I'm with ya there, Frank. Sooner we get out of here the better. All I wanna do is sit in the Dusty Rose and drink beer. It's Saturday after all and drinks are half price."

"Yeah, let's git this done and do just that."

With that they exited the truck like, two weary, slightly skittish, schoolboys. They started on the trail they hoped would lead them to their discarded masks. With two sets of eyes darting everywhere they searched and searched… with no luck and with nerves beginning to fray slightly they searched on and on… Just as they were about to give up hope Leroy jumped and bumped into Frank who pushed him away.

"Damn, Leroy, what now?"

"Look!"

There, up in a tree, were their masks. There was a branch sticking out of their foreheads. It was a frightening sight.

"How do ya suppose they got way up there?" Leroy wanted to know.

"How should I know," Frank was trying to figure out just how they were supposed to get them down from there… "Shit!"

"I don't climb trees, Frank," Leroy wanted to make that perfectly clear from the start.

"Well, I ain't no monkey either," Frank was walking around the tree, shaking his head.

"You ask me... I think it was those witches who put our masks up in that tree."

"Nobody asked you," Frank snapped. He was more than frustrated at the turn of events.

"Well, if you were to ask..."

"Well, I won't."

"Alright, Frank, alright. Take it easy."

"Take it easy? Take it easy? Is that what you said?"

"Frank..."

"You expect me to take it easy when our masks are ten feet up in that tree? Hell Leroy. Whoever put our masks up there knows..."

"What, Frank? What do *they* know?"

"Hell, I don't know. I think, whoever they are, hung them up there as some sort of message."

"Shit. That means *he* knows."

"Dammit Leroy. That's what I've been saying."

"*He* knows for sure, Frank. I mean he could set a trap for us. Or, who knows... he's a cold-blooded killer... he... he could slip into our trailer at night and slit our throats."

"Geeze, Leroy... you gotta stop watchin' those mystery shows."

"I like to watch mystery shows," Leroy was a little defensive when it came to his mystery shows.

"I'm just sayin' that it's giving you strange thoughts, that's all I'm sayin'."

"Well, I have no idea what you're sayin'."

"Let's drop it for cryin' out loud," Frank took another visual survey of the tree and came up with a plan. "C'mon over here Leroy. I'm gonna boost you up so you can reach our masks."

"I don't know, Frank."

"Alright, you boost *me* up, then, Leroy," Frank didn't have his happy face on.

"You know damn well I can't lift you up, Frank."

"Well then, get over here so I can lift your scrawny ass up and get our masks. Hurry up! I gotta date with a cold beer over at the Dusty Rose, now, c'mon."

"Alright, Frank. Alright."

Frank hoisted Leroy up far enough to get the masks but he had to pull like hell to get them off that broken branch.

"Okay, Frank, you can put me down now. Frank?"

"What the hell was that?"

"Frank you're cutting off the circulation in my legs. Put me down."

"I don't know what that was but," he dropped Leroy and scanned the area.

"Thanks a lot, buddy."

"Okay," Frank had that wild look Leroy was very familiar with the possible repercussions such a look had to offer. "We got our damn masks, let's get the hell out'a here," Frank's eyes were everywhere.

"What did you see, Frank?"

"I don't know… and I don't wanna know either now, let's amscray."

"I'm with you, Frank."

They walked back to the truck and hauled ass out'a there, making a beeline for the Dusty Rose.

CHAPTER 18

The road down to the 'witch's' place was a long windy affair with a couple large rocks in places to keep the unwary visitor on their toes. When Veronica reached the little gingerbread house nestled in the afternoon sun, she gave a huge sigh of relief.

She always felt a calming sense when she was home and maybe more specifically, the surrounding forest which she firmly believed that ancient forces of energy still permeated. If you asked her, she would tell you it was past residue.

She was gifted with being able to see things... things like shadow figures. And disembodied voices. But it's not always an easy or pleasant experience. More often than not it could be quit unsettling.

After his visitor left Sam sat out on the porch and contemplated his next move. It had been an interesting morning so far. Maybe an adventure is in order he thought. But, where? What? He stood and stretched then went down the steps and around the side of the cabin where he found himself standing in front of the shed with its doors flung wide open. He didn't try to focus on anything in particular, just stood there peering into the shadowy confines.

He was frozen to the spot as the doors, one by one, slowly closed. He took a step back and rubbed his eyes thinking that would help, but it didn't. That's when he made his decision about what to do. He walked back around the cabin and went inside to get his coat and a bottle of water.

When he got into his car, he sat there with his hands on the steering wheel staring out over the hood. Sam turned the key and the engine roared to life startling him, he had accidentally stomped on the gas pedal then quickly took his foot off. He took a fresh grip of the steering wheel and scolded himself. He drove out his road and hit the hi-way. He headed north hoping he would be able to remember where his turn was.

As he reached the other end of the valley, he spotted a dirt road that looked to be the one, although he had no idea for sure. That's what adventures are all about, discovery.

The road was narrow and hemmed in on either side with thick forest. Once he wasn't paying attention and had to swerve to avoid ramming a particularly huge boulder on the edge of the road.

A short way in he stopped to look at some mobiles hanging from the trees. The more he looked around the more he saw. In fact, the trees were literally cluttered with them. Sam felt compelled to get out and give them a closer look. They were made of driftwood and forest debris and tied with rough string.

They were a little spooky, he thought as he walked in a short circle. He couldn't believe how many were out in the trees. They were interesting, that's for sure.

He climbed back into his car and continued along until he spotted a house through the trees on his right and when he came around the last bend in the road there it was. He slowed down as he entered the front yard so he could study the house in more detail.

It was a gingerbread house. The main body of the house was different colors light blue on the front porch area, green on one side and he couldn't see the other side. The trim is what caught his attention. It was so ornate in its detail. Red with different shades of blue.

And coming down from the peak of the roof were shingles that were layered like fish scales running down to about the middle of the front wall. He was very impressed with how ornate it all was. He was shaken out of his reverie when there was a knock on the passenger side window. He gathered himself and got out of the car.

"Hi," He was a little embarrassed for the intrusion and struggled with what to say next.

"Hi yourself. Is there something I can help you with?"

"Yeah, Hi," Sam walked around the car. "My name's Sam."

"I know who you are."

"You do?" He found himself looking at a striking young woman in a light-colored summer dress.

"Yes, I do," she looked up at him. "What can I help you with, Sam?"

"I-I'm not sure..." he stumbled.

"Well, it's kind of hard to know what I can do for you if you're not sure yourself."

"Good point." Sam smiled a nervous smile. "I guess... I'm here because someone came by, I can't remember her name, she stopped by to talk to me about...spirits. I think she mentioned restless... spirits?" He felt funny saying that but that is exactly what he came to talk about.

"That would be Veronica. She's out in the forest gathering herbs. I'm Jorden. Clare, the third member of our little party is out meditating somewhere."

"Okay, well, nice to meet you, Jorden. Do you know when she'll be back?"

"Could be in an hour," she shrugged her shoulders. "Or it could be after dark. We never know when she'll come back. Would you like to come in for some tea?"

"Sure, that sounds good."

"Hope you like rose hip? It's all we have right now."

"Rose hip it is, thanks."

"Well, are you going to stand out here gawking? C'mon inside, that's where the tea is," she reached the front door and waited for Sam to catch up before they went onside.

The inside of the house was just as spectacular.

"Do you take honey?"

"I'm sorry?"

"Honey? Do you take honey."

"Yes, thank you," Sam felt his face warm. He had never seen or even imagined witches as pretty and scolded himself for not paying closer attention. "You have quite an interesting place here," Sam took the offered tea, warm in his hands. "Thank you."

"Thanks, would you like to sit out back? It's nice out there."

"Sure," Sam followed her out through a cozy kitchen with an old wood stove tiled floors heavy wooden dining table; lace curtains on the windows... then out through the back door and into the bright afternoon sun drenched yard. There was a table out under a giant pine tree, one of those wrought iron sets with for ornate chairs, white. And that's where they ended up.

"You're right. It is very nice out here," Sam took a deep breath of the pine scented air and felt his whole body relax.

"Hope you enjoy the tea, Sam."

"Yes, it's really good. Hot but good, thanks."

"So, Sam," Jorden set her tea on the table and leaned back in her chair. "What brings you down our road?"

"I have seen things... at my house."

"Have these 'things' been inside your house?"

"I'm not exactly sure..."

"Well, Sam," she took a sip of her rose hip tea then set it back down. "Either they have been in your house, or they haven't."

"I don't know."

"What are you seeing, exactly."

"A dark, very fast something. It's out in the woods…" Sam took another sip of his tea, it went down before he could swallow which sent him into a coughing fit.

"Are you okay?"

"Yes, thanks," Sam got himself under control and set his tea on the table. "Think I'll let that cool a little."

"You said… Dark things…"

"Yes, and they're fast," Sam turned his teacup in his hands. "But sometimes I see them just standing, or whatever, out there in the woods… just at the edge of where you can see."

"Do these… dark things seem aggressive in any way?"

"What do you mean?" Sam scanned the woods, he was feeling a little nervous.

"Do… have they ever attacked you in any way? Scratches? Pushing? Throwing things at you?"

"No… none of that," None of those things sounded the *least* bit fun.

"Well, maybe these entities are trying to contact you. Have you given that any thought?"

"No, I haven't. I don't know why they would try to contact me."

"Something in your past, perhaps? Something unresolved?"

"I don't remember any of my past life. Not even people who claim to have been my closest friends."

"You don't remember-

"Nothing, I don't remember a darn thing…"

CHAPTER 19

Susan finished stocking the last hiking boot out of the last box and wheeled the empties into the back room where there was a crusher. She pulled open the door and shoved her boxes in. She shut the door and punched the button. The machine grumbled into motion.

Susan walked away to her locker where she slipped out of her work coat changing it for her sweater. She headed for the door and fresh evening air when she heard her name being called.

It was Daphne. She was hurrying toward Susan waving and smiling. And Susan slowed to wait for her.

"What is it, Daphne?"

"Oh, nothing, really," She surveyed the first floor of the emporium as if seeing it for the first time.

"You seem to be in an awful hurry for nothing…"

"Yeah, well, I was wondering if you and Sam are still… together."

"Together?"

"Yeah. An item?"

"I'm not sure I'm following you."

"Really?" Daphne took an exasperating deep breath and took another, more direct approach. "Do you and Sam still have the hots for each other?"

"Oh, that's what this is all about," Susan smiled, though inside she was fuming, and said, "He doesn't even remember me from those days. He's just trying to figure things out."

"That doesn't really answer my question."

"No."

"Okay, why didn't you say so in the first place?"

"I don't know Daphne," Susan threw up her hands in defeat.

"Okay, well, no big deal. I was just wondering is all."

"Well… I guess I'll see you in the morning then."

"Huh? Yes, see you in the morning, Susan."

Susan made it to her car without further interruption. When she slid in behind the wheel she sat there. She had a strong urge to get a bottle of wine and drop in on Sam.

She went into the wine store and picked out a bottle, well, she picked out three before she settled on the one. Once out in her car she again sat behind the wheel wondering to herself; *What am I doing? I should at least call him first. He has a phone. I should call him… I have no idea what his number is…* Susan turned the key and off she went, to drop in on Sam. The day was slowly slipping away as she drove down the hi-way. But when she reached the road she was looking for she hesitated. *What is wrong with me?!* She asked of the empty seat beside her and was even more upset by the silence.

Susan dropped the stick shift into gear and turned in. It wasn't long after she pulled up in front of the cabin that reality smacked her right in the face. Sam, wasn't home. Her heart skipped a beat but, what did she expect anyway? She sat there for a second fighting the memories, not because she was afraid or, dreaded them… she was more confused than anything.

Here was someone, who meant something to her many years ago, that just happened to walk back into her life… and her past. Only that very special someone, has no idea who she is… or what they were, confusing. She didn't realize that she had gotten out of her car until she heard something… it sounded like something was over by the shed on the back side of the house.

She took a couple tentative steps in that direction. She stopped to listen and there it was again… a sort of rustling sound and it was definitely over by the shed. Susan started in that direction again but only got a few steps when a big raccoon went ambling off into the threes.

She noticed that the shed doors were open. Now she questioned herself, were they open before? Or closed. She stared into the darkness of the old shed a moment longer until she started to feel uncomfortable. Besides it was getting late.

Susan got in her car and headed back out to the hi-way. Trees were passing by on each side of the road and Susan was lost in thought. She came around the last turn and a flood of headlights illuminated the inside of her car. She swerved to the side and stomped on the breaks.

Sam saw the car in front of him only a brief second before being blinded by the oncoming lights. He swerved to the side of the road and stepped on the brakes rolling up his window against the plume of dust.

When everything settled down, he started laughing because he saw Susan's face in the glare of his headlights and wondered if the same surprised look was plastered on his own face.

He got out of his car and walked over to Susan who was rolling down her window and laughing.

"Hey, why don't you watch where you're going?"

"I was on my side of the road pal," Susan smiled. "I got a bottle of wine here…"

"Yeah?" Sam tried to make a straight face. "What do you plan on doing with that bottle of wine?"

"I… was looking for someone to help me drink it."

"Huh, and did you find this someone yet?"

"I'm not sure," Susan rolled up her window and pretended to drive away.

"Hey, wait!" Sam ran after her, knocked on her window and she stopped.

"Yes? What is it?"

"Well, I was going to say if you don't find anyone to help with the wine… Come back and I will… help you drink it. I-if you don't have any luck that is."

"It *would* save me a lot of driving around, if we drank it at your place."

"Okay, turn around and I'll meet you there."

"Sounds like a plan."

By the time Susan pulled into the yard Sam was on the front porch with two glasses and a wine opener.

"Hey, you don't waste any time there, fella," Susan teased as she climbed out of her car. And you even got real glasses? Wow. I came to the right place."

"C'mon up and let's pop that cork," Sam sucked in a breath and hoped that didn't sound too anxious, or anything.

"Yes," Susan joined Sam on the porch and handed over the wine bottle.

"Okay, here we go," Sam set the bottle on the table and handed Susan a glass of wine. "What are we drinking to this evening?"

"Let's drink to you getting a phone," Susan tipped her glass to Sam's. "By the way, would you mind giving me your number?"

"I don't know," Sam frowned into his glass. "I'm not in the habit of handing out my number to just anyone."

"I don't exactly consider myself to be just anyone."

"Oh, Well, I don't consider you just anyone either."

"That's a start," Susan smiled and took a sip of her wine.

"I noticed, earlier, that you got the old, shed doors opened."

"I thought I closed those doors when I left," Sam stood and went to the end of the porch to see for himself. "Yeah closed, just like I left them."

"Wait, what?" Susan joined Sam at the end of the porch and sure enough... the doors were closed. "Huh, I could've sworn they were open just a little bit ago..."

"I closed them as soon as I left," Sam recalled the funny feeling he had when those old doors yawned open. "Truth is I closed them because Me and, even, Hank got this weird... I don't know. I do know that I closed them... and latched them so they wouldn't come open in the wind or something."

"I'm mistaken, I guess." She made a face and took another sip of wine.

"Could'a been a trick of the light," Sam was wondering himself. But he was very sure he closed those doors.

"Here, let me freshen up your wine," Sam topped her glass off and did the same with his before returning the bottle to the little table.

"Thanks," Susan held her glass in salute and settled back in her chair. "Nice wine don't you think?"

"Yeah, I like it a lot," Sam was still bothered by the shed door thing. "You know your wine, that's for sure."

"Sam..."

"Susan?"

"Do you ever... have you ever wondered about your past?"

"Not really..."

"Hmmm."

"Least not until I came back here."

As stars started to sprinkle across the darkening sky Sam and Susan sat quietly together, alone with their thoughts.

CHAPTER 20

"You know what I think, Leroy?" Frank took a big swig of his beer and slammed it down on the bar.

"Easy, Frank," Leroy scanned the near empty bar then, turned to face Frank as his face started doing acrobatics.

"What is it you think?"

"You absolutely, cross yer heart, salute the flag, swear to all mighty God..." he took in a breath and another gulp of beer. "You saw that nut case drive in the witches' road."

"With my own two eyes, Frank. Plain as I see you sittin' in front of me now."

"Well, well."

"So, Frank, what were you thinkin' a second ago?"

"I don't really know what I was thinkin' actually... but, I don't like it. I know that for a fact. Jim, can we get some more beers down this way?"

"I have a good idea he's up to no good. Thanks Jim. Him going to see the witches, doesn't make any sense."

"Maybe they got him in some... I don't know, maybe they put some kind'a spell on 'im."

"You could be right, Leroy, you might just have something there," Frank gulped his third beer like he'd been out for days in a sun parched desert. "Yo, Jim, one more beer here?"

"So, what do you s'pose we should do?"

"Stealth recon, that's what we do. Thanks Jim, just keep 'em coming okay... We might have to split up-"

"No sir!"

"Keep your voice down, Leroy!"

"I'm not splitin' up, Frank. That's final."

"What the," Frank moved in closer to Leroy and lowered his voice. "The hell's wrong with you?"

"I'm not gonna do whatever it is your thinkin' of doin'... alone, period... ennnd," and he held that N. "Of discussion." Leroy downed his beer and flattened the can on the bar. "Jim, I'm ready for another beer when your comin' this way."

"Alright you big chicken," another beer gone. "We'll do this together."

"So, what exactly are we gonna do, Frank?"

"I don't know yet, but I'll damn sure figure something out."

Sam woke up with a slight headache. The sun was ridiculously bright in his bedroom window, he turned away from it, with a pillow over his head. It didn't take long for him to give up and roll out of bed but, when he was putting on his pants, he heard someone running down the hall... then down the stairs.

Darkness washed over everything like a cloak. To Sam's horror he realized it wasn't someone running ... He was running down the stairs, he was in the living room in the darkness... his head hurt, he felt sticky... he... he saw...

In a flash it was over, and Sam was left panting on his knees in the middle of the living room floor with no idea how he got there. When the room stopped spinning he got to his feet and lurched for the couch. He was sweating and it was a cool morning. He got up from the couch, slowly, and went out onto the porch. He sat down in one of the chairs and quickly started feeling better.

The chimes tinkled to life, but softly. There wasn't even a puff of air moving. Suddenly, Sam got to his feet and went down the front steps thinking that whoever set up that line has come back. When he rounded the corner, he stopped in his tracks. The shed doors were wide open. He stared into the shadowy gloom like he was hypnotized.

He felt a great sadness wash over him as he moved on wooden legs, toward the shed. Gritting his teeth against the emotions stampeding through his body he closed the doors and replaced the hasp, once he located it next to a tree a few feet away. He was too shaken to wonder how the hasp ended up over by the tree. He just picked it up and snapped it through the ring on the doors.

When the doors were safely closed and secure, he stepped back trying, to still his pounding heart. The sadness was completely gone, replaced by extreme confusion. He had to call Susan. The thought hit him like a ton of bricks, Sam ran back into the cabin and had the receiver in his hand when he realized he didn't know where he left her number. His heart was hammering in his head making it almost impossible to think straight. He was hyperventilating and had to sit down again.

Sam took deep breaths and tried to concentrate on the beauty around him. It took a while but, he was finally able to get himself under control. Once he settled down, he felt foolish for wanting to bother Susan, she was at work anyway. When he went back inside, he spotted the paper with Susan's number right away, it was right there on the kitchen table.

He got a drink of water, then he splashed his face in the sink. When he looked up there was someone standing there, he groped around for a towel to get the water out of his eyes and when he did there was nothing there. But the front door was open...

Susan was already busy at work, a slight tinge of a headache reminded her how close she had gotten to him, to Sam. It wasn't the right time and they both knew it. Thing is it might not ever be the right time.

"Hey Susan," Daphne came around the corner with a couple boxes on a hand-truck. "Where do you want this stuff?"

"Oh, set it over there, thanks."

"You're welcome."

"Is there something else?"

"No, see you at lunch?"

"I don't know when I'm going to go to lunch today, Daphne. I have all this stuff to put out."

"Okay whenever I'll be ready to chow down another one of those crazy veggie burgers at Judy's."

"Alright, well…"

"Okay I better get back to the wonderful world of socks and underwear."

"See ya," Susan went back to sports equipment. She thought, as she was busy trying to concentrate on her job and not her heart. It was a real tug-of-war, and her concentration on the job was slowly losing ground.

———————————————

Sam, having, almost, completely regained his composure, was able to clean up the kitchen. He even went so far as stocking some wood by the fireplace. He was still rattled but it wasn't anything he couldn't handle, he'd been rattled before; *'Alright, who's crying in here? If you don't stop that crying… everyone of you are going to the quiet place. Do you want to go to the quiet place?'* It always got quiet after that.

He did get a slight jolt when he remembered he had taken the line off the chimes so, when he thought about maybe catching someone he had to laugh. The not so funny part was that the possibility of someone pulling the line was a lot easier to accept than what just happened, where the chimes moved on their own. *Maybe Veronica knew something he didn't, course that wouldn't be difficult since he didn't know much of anything,* he wondered to himself.

Sam was trying to come up with an excuse to go to the Emporium and see Susan. He had to have a good reason; problem was he couldn't think of one... Then, he decided didn't really need any excuse after all, he was just going to jump in his car and go. He figured he could always use charcoal, yeah that was it. He plucked his keys off the peg by the door and before he knew it, he was pulling up to the Emporium. He marveled at the size of it compared to any of the other buildings in town. He was getting out of his car when a guy walked up to him.

"'Scuse me," the guy was blocking his way. "I help you with something?" Sam asked.

"Nope."

"Well then you wanna step aside and let me pass?" Sam was starting to feel his pulse ratchet up.

"Nope."

"Look, what problem do you have with me, because I've never seen you before."

"My problem?" he puffed up some gritting his teeth for effect. "My problem is you," he poked Sam in the chest with his finger.

"I don't know what you're trying to do here but I need to get by."

"Maybe I don't want you to," he folded his arms across his chest in a clear display of defiance.

At that moment a primal signal, born of ancient origin, tapped Sam on the shoulder and set into motion a fight or flight response. Shortly after the guy grabbed Sam by his shirt, Sam snapped, making his response perfectly clear.

When Sam stood up, he found he was surrounded by wide-eyed onlookers. He looked from them to the object of his violent reaction who now lay unconscious at his feet. A siren sounded in the distance alerting Sam to another possible danger. A commotion erupted in the growing crowd.

"Sam? Sam!" Susan pried herself out of the people and took Sam by the arm. "Are you alright? What happened here?"

"Suppose you hand over that knife now so we can have us a talk."

"Sam?" Susan looked into Sam's face he was different she couldn't explain how but the look in his eyes... it was cold.

"Now, can you tell me what happened here? Where did you get this knife...."

"Sam talk to me."

"I don't know... what happened."

The siren got loud then it stopped. Sam looked over at the crowd of people, he was in a daze though he was unharmed.

"Okay, everybody step back a bit so I can figure out what's going on here. Step back Fred, please." The sheriff got on his radio, when he saw that a person was down, and called for an ambulance. He quickly handcuffed Sam and led him over to the back of his cruiser. Susan watched helplessly with the rest of the crowd.

Later, when it was determined that Sam acted in self-defense, as reported by several witnesses from across the street at the Silver Scissors Barbershop. Sam was released and when the tough guy came to in the ambulance, and the EMT's determined he suffered no life-threatening injuries other than a broken nose and a cut lip, he was patched up and delivered to the sheriff's office where he was placed in jail until he cooled down.

"Sam," Susan went to him when he was released, "What happened? Are you okay?"

"I'd be a lot better if I could get the hell out'a here."

"Okay, let's go," Susan led the way so Sam could get to his car. "I'll just grab some things and meet you at your place. You gonna be okay, Sam?"

"Yeah, thanks."

"Okay you're clear to go," She looked hard into his face and didn't recognize the person in front of her. "Okay, I'll be right behind you," she had to raise her voice to be heard over the crowd noise.

Susan worked her way through the people who were starting to disperse. She went back into the Emporium and smack into Daphne.

"What was going on out there?"

"I'm not sure, Daphne."

"You were out there, what did you see?" Daphne was almost pleading for information.

"I saw an asshole get the crap knocked out of him," Susan kept moving while Daphne kept stride with her, in an effort to fill in the blanks. "Other than that, I have no idea what exactly happened out there."

"Well, who was it? The a-hole I mean."

"It was Charlie, Frank's cousin."

"Oh, my."

"Yeah, hey I have to go," Susan had her car keys and was heading for the front door of the Emporium. "I'll see you tomorrow, Daphne," and she was out heading toward her car. There was still a hand-full of people milling around discussing the latest event. Not much really happens in Springville so this would provide the town with plenty of gossip.

When Susan pulled into the front yard at Sam's she found him standing on the front porch grasping the railing.

"Hey buddy," she called up to him as she got out of her car. "You doing, okay?"

"Yeah, I'm okay," he didn't believe it and was sure she didn't either.

———————————

Frank and Leroy were sitting in their stuffy trailer, at the Lindsey Mobile Home Park, playing five card stud and drinking beer when, Randy Cortney, from up the street came banging on their door.

"What the hell!" Frank almost dropped his beer Leroy's face was all over the place. "Who's that banging on my door?"

"Open up, Frank," he quit knocking and waited.

When the door flew open, he stepped back and accidentally swallowed his gum.

"What's all the fuss, Cort?"

"I-it's your cousin, Charlie."

"Well, damn, Cort spill it. The hell's the big deal about my cousin?"

"He's been in a fight, that's what."

"A fight?" Leroy squeezed in beside Frank.

"Damnit, Leroy, back up you're crowding me."

"Now, what's this about, a fight?"

"Well, I was at the Emporium buying some new socks. They have a lot of socks there."

"Will you get on with it, Cort."

"Okay, yeah, sure. Well, like I said-

"For crying out loud, Cort."

"Okay, okay. Take it easy, Frank."

"I will as long as you get to it."

"So, I was coming out and I seen, that psycho dude, you know, Sam Henning? He punched your cousin, Charlie a good one. Knocked him clean out. I was just comin" out and I seen it! Then the sheriff came. He put Sam in handcuffs at first then he took 'em off when the ambulance came-"

"Ambulance?"

"Yeah, the ambulance came and your cousin, he finally came around but, his face looked like it exploded, I mean it was a mess. Anyway, the sheriff he talked to Melissa then he put the handcuffs on your cousin then Melissa got into the ambulance and drove off. I thought, at first, that your cousin was dead way he was layin' there so still like he was."

"Where did they take 'im?"

"I don't know they just drove off. I expect they'll keep him at the Jade County Emergency Station until the city ambulance comes to pick him up, if he's hurt that bad. Otherwise, I b'lieve they'll keep him at the Emergency Station."

"C'mon, Leroy, let's get going!"

"Why, where we off to? We don't even know where he is."

"We'll go check out the Emergency Station first. C'mon, Dammit, Leroy."

"I'm comin', hang on, Frank," Leroy gulped down the last of his beer, grabbed his coat and was out the door. Frank was waiting impatiently in his truck, revving the engine.

"Sam?" Susan went up the steps and stood behind him not knowing what to do… she knew what she felt she should do and that's what she did she griped his shoulders. "Sam." She squeezed him and felt him relax into her. "Sam, what happened?"

"I don't know," he was trying to gather his thoughts. "I pulled up to the Emporium and this guy comes out of nowhere and stands in my way," Sam was breathing easier. "I asked him to move, twice, and he refused. Then, he grabbed my shirt I don't remember much except the Sheriff had me in handcuffs at one point which I didn't understand since I was the one under attack."

"Holy crap, buddy, you had a rough morning."

"It started earlier, this morning…"

"What? C'mon, Sam let's sit down, c'mon," she guided him into a chair, and she took the other one. "What do you mean it started earlier this morning?"

"I was getting dressed and all the sudden I heard what sounded like someone running down the hallway and down the stairs."

"Wh- who was it? Sam? Sam?"

"It was me…"

"Okay, wait a minute… say that again? You thought you heard someone running down the hall… then down the stairs… why do you have the idea it was you?"

"I ended up on my hands and knees in the middle of the living room and I… I…"

"It's okay, Sam."

"I honestly have no idea how I got from my bedroom to the living room. It was like I was dreaming. Or something… I don't know."

"Geeze," Susan sucked in some air through her teeth.

"I came out here and sat down and felt much better. Then the chimes started moving and I thought that… I went around to the side of the cabin and the shed doors were open. I closed them the other day. I even put a hasp through the ring. When I got closer to the shed…"

"Let me get you a drink of water, hang on," Susan went inside and reemerged with a glass of water which she handed to Sam.

"Thanks, I was getting a little dry."

"You were saying you went to the shed…"

"Yeah, it was just a weird morning. Then I ran into that guy, whoever he was."

"You've never seen him before?"

"No, but that's not saying much."

CHAPTER 21

Jorden came home with a basket full of flowers and medicinal plants. She walked up the front steps and went inside where she set her findings on the kitchen counter. Clare and Veronica were at the kitchen table deep in conversation.

"Am I interrupting anything?"

"Oh, hey Jorden," both women looked up.

"I didn't even hear you come in."

"What are you guys talking about?" She took a seat at the table and took off her rubber boots.

"We were just discussing Sam Henning."

"Oh? What about him?" Jorden tied her hair back in a ponytail.

"I went to his house the other day," Veronica took a sip of her tea. "I told him about the spirits. He didn't take it too well, I think."

"What did he have to say about it, if anything?" Clare wanted to know.

"He didn't say much, actually," Veronica got up, rinsed her cup in the sink then set in the strainer to dry. "He doesn't know much."

"What do you mean?" Clair got up from the table and put her teacup in the sink.

"I mean, he doesn't seem to know much about anything. I feel he's lost. He has no past to guide him in the present."

"Are you saying he has no recollection of his past life in that house? Or in this town?"

"That's exactly what I'm saying. It's like his past has been erased," Veronica went to the sink and washed her hands then, busied herself with tying the stems of the medicinal plants she found so she can hang them in the pantry to slowly dry.

"I think someone is trying to contact him from the other side," Clair sat back down at the table playing with tarot cards.

"I felt that same thing too. As soon as Sam came out of the house, I felt a presence close by."

Jorden sat in a chair over by the window.

"He needs our help," Clair announced.

"Yeah, but we can only help him if he asks, you know the rules," Veronica joined Clare at the table.

"I doubt he will be doing that any time soon."

"What makes you say that, Veronica?"

"He seems to be blocked from accepting our kind of help," Veronica stood. "I'm going for a walk you guys want to come along?"

"I'm going to work in the garden," Clair also got up and went for the front door.

"What about you, Jorden?"

"I think I'm going to read for a while, but you go ahead Veronica."

"I will." And out the door she went.

"I'll be in the garden, Jorden."

"Okay, have fun," Jorden went to retrieve her book from the table in the living room. She stretched out on the couch and got about three pages read before she fell asleep.

———————————

It was peaceful in the garden. The sun was warm, pine scent permeated the afternoon air. Clair was busy digging potatoes in the warm earth when she caught movement out the corner of her eye. She looked in that direction but saw nothing. So, she resumed her digging. There it was again just outside her periphery vision. This time she ignored it and after a short while it came closer.

She could feel the coolness of it... felt sadness and a great weight on her heart. She stopped digging and turned slowly, what stood not fifteen feet away was a small boy, in a bathing suit. He was wet as if had just gotten out of the water but, there was no water except for Coogan Creek, but that was a mile away at least.

Clair got to her feet to face the boy, and he backed away farther into the forest. She was fascinated by him. His face was blurred which gave him a sort of sinister look though Clair felt no threat from him at all.

"Who are you?" She asked him but, he didn't answer. "It's okay where were you swimming?"

He pointed in the direction of Sam's place but there was nowhere to swim there. Or at least there hadn't been for a very long time. Not since his father drained the small lake.

"Were you swimming in the lake?"

He nodded, yes.

"What are you doing here?"

He looked over his shoulder, in the direction of Sam's place, again. Then, he simply vanished into thin air, leaving Clair wondering. She quickly walked over to where the boy stood seconds before and could still feel the coldness. In fact, it caused goosebumps to race over her body and she shivered against the cold spot.

When she stepped back, she was, again, warmed by the afternoon sun beaming down through the trees. She took a deep breath and raised her face to meet the sun's radiance.

It was still there... close by but unseen. Clair could still feel it's presence, she tried to summon it but she was unsuccessful in her attempt. She wasn't properly prepared, who would be? Veronica would be...

CHAPTER 22

"So, what you're tellin' us is... what exactly?" Frank leaned on the sheriff's desk, planting his hands flat looking him right in the eye.

"First off, son, you'll want to get yourself off my desk," Sheriff Thompson had been sworn in three weeks after the tragic events that led up to the death of the former sheriff. It took a month and a lot of hard work to rebuild the new sheriff's office where they now were. "Second of all you don't come into my office and start demanding I do whatever you say."

"You don't know who the hell I am," Frank challenged, after stepping back from the desk. "My father was sheriff here, way before they gave your city ass the job."

"I was sorry to hear about your dad, son, we went to school together."

"Yeah, well... what is my cousin doing in your jail when he was clearly the victim."

"Your cousin is a victim all right, that's why he's in my jail," Sheriff Thompson leaned back in his chair.

"If you agree that he's a victim then... why... is...he...sittin'... in jail?"

"Your cousin is a victim of something you're getting yourself close to, son. He was trying to bully a citizen of this town. I will not tolerate such behavior, apparently the other person who rearranged your cousin's nose didn't tolerate it either," Now, the Sheriff stood and leaned on his desk, palms flat. "Do I make myself clear to you?"

"Oh, you make yourself clear alright."

"Your sidekick there has a voice after all."

"I'm nobody's sidekick, Sheriff," Leroy protested.

"Whatever you say, now suppose the two of you go find something else to do, something constructive."

"You know wh-"

"Get the hell out of my office, Frank, unless you want to sit in there with your cousin."

Frank leered his best leer at the Sheriff. When he realized it wasn't having the desired effect, he stormed out the door. Leroy gave it a good slam for effect.

Once outside Frank took a deep breath and shook his head which was never a good sign.

"Frank?"

"You know what, Leroy?"

"What, Frank."

"I'm starting to put together a shit list, and I already have so many names on it that I should start writing 'em down."

"I need a beer," Leroy declared to no one in particular.

"Do you know who's at the top of my shit list, Leroy? Do you?"

"Why if I was to take a guess..." he made a big deal thinking on the question, because any attention thrown his way was a big deal. "Would it be... hmmm..."

"Dammit, Leroy," Frank was about to implode. "You know as well as I do that, that damn Sam Henning is at the top... Hell he's higher than the top he's...'

"Sky high, Frank?"

"Wh- sky high? What in the hell are you talking about, Leroy? For cryin' out loud, Leroy."

"Okay, Frank... why don't you tell me what he's higher than, Frank," Leroy was getting agitated. He was never a fan of being talked down to. Even though he wasn't mush over five feet tall.

"You know what, Leroy? Never mind, let's go get us some beers and go home. I've had enough irritation for one day," without another word Frank walked over to his truck and drove away.

"Frank!" Leroy yelled as loud as he could, but Frank continued along until he stopped at Clover Street, there's no stop sign on Clover Street. Leroy waited he was hopeful. He watched with a growing sense of relief as the truck made a U-turn and came back.

"Leroy," Frank called rolling down his window. "Sorry buddy, my mind was a million miles away."

"Geeze, Frank," Leroy's face was doing acrobatics as he slid in the passenger seat. "Okay, Frank?"

"Yeah."

"Well, let's go get them beers then," Leroy buckled up, a thing he rarely did.

The dynamic duo took off in blaze of blue smoke and a backfire when Frank shifted into third.

"Sam, you feeling better?"

"Oh, I feel way better, thanks for having my back," Sam smiled and Susan smiled back.

"I always had your back... and you always had mine."

"Had?" He looked over at Susan and his heart skipped a beat. "I wish I knew what it is you know."

"Oh Sam, that's what we can do together. We'll just take it a little at a time, okay?"

"Yes, I feel so left out of my own life... if that's possible."

"I'm just glad you're okay. That Charlie, he's a scary one."

"You don't know *anything* about scary... and that's a good thing."

"I'm hungry. Wanna get something to eat?" Susan's stomach was rumbling.

"Ahh, I don't feel like going anywhere."

"Well, Judy's is just down the road a ways... I'll get us a couple of juicy burgers, what do you say?"

"I'd say that's too tempting to say no. Yeah that sounds good. I'll get some money, hang on."

"I got it," Susan was already down the steps.

"Wait let me-"

"I'll be back by the time you get your money," she called over her shoulder.

Sam was smiling at his good fortune to run into such a friend as Susan.

It wasn't long before he heard her coming back up the road.

"See, told you I'd be right back," Susan got out of her car with two bags and met Sam at the top of the stairs.

"Wow, that looks like a lot of food you have there. What do we need?"

"Just these two chairs, I have napkins, salt and pepper."

"Okay, we're all set then," Sam sat down as Susan was laying out their feast. "Sure smells good."

"Judy's is the best," Susan dove into her burger until she realized she was eating like a madwoman and stopped with a sheepish, special sauce, grin. "Do I have anything on my face?"

"Nope... you're good," Sam resumed devouring his burger. They shared an order of fries which they consumed with great enthusiasm.

"Wow, I didn't realize I was that hungry," Susan reached for a new napkin and wiped her mouth. "I could eat those burgers every day!"

"Yeah, I could definitely become a regular customer," Sam wiped his mouth and took a sip of his beer.

"How's your beer? Can I get you another one?"

"I would love another kind sir, thanks."

When Sam went inside to retrieve two more beers the first thing he noticed, after feeling the intense cold, was that his breath was coming out in foggy plumes. The living room was eerily dark, even though it was still early afternoon. He could smell a faint odor... and it made him extremely uncomfortable.

"Sam?" Susan called from outside. "It's getting real thirsty out here."

Sam heard her voice but, it sounded like she was calling from far away. He was aware of something in his hand and held it up to see...

"Oh, Sam, are you alright in there?" When she received no reply, she got up and went to the door.

She saw Sam standing in the middle of the room, he was just standing there like he forgot something. "Sam?" She went to stand beside him. "Sam," she gently shook his shoulder. "Sam, what's the matter?"

"Huh? Oh, ahh…" Sam reacted as if he'd been asleep.

"What are you doing standing here?"

"What?"

"Sam, you were just standing here... like a statue."

"I-I don't know. What was I doing?"

"You were going to get us some more beers, don't you remember?"

"Wow," Sam shook his head to clear the cobwebs. "I have no idea…"

"Well, let's get those beers and go back outside, okay?"

"Yeah, okay," Sam felt a little dazed but was able to go to the fridge and locate the beers with no other problems.

"Okay, here we go," Sam handed Susan a beer and set his on the table while he took his seat. "Sorry about that. I have no idea what happened."

"You feel okay?"

"Yes, I feel great," he took a sip of beer and set it back on the table.

"You scared me for a second there, buddy," She took a good long drink of her beer and wiped her mouth. "Sure tastes good on a warm evening."

"Yes, it does."

"You sure you're doing okay?" She looked at Sam searching for any sign.

"Yes, I'm doing fine," Sam studied his feet. "A lot on my mind I guess."

"I don't doubt that for a second. If there's anything you want to talk about... you know I'm a pretty good listener."

Sam had to give that suggestion a little thought. There was so much he felt like he needed to figure out... but, where to begin? He was still processing the experience he remembered from the school he was sent to. A place of fear and pain with a good mixture of darkness thrown in for grins.

Try as hard as he might he still couldn't remember anything before that. Like why was he there in the first place? He remembered he was in a room, a small room, with only one window and a heavy door that was locked most of the time...

"Sam? Sam," Susan was staring hard at him.

When his thoughts returned to the front porch and the beautiful woman who had a worried look on her face he smiled as his face warmed with embarrassment.

"You did it again," Susan downed the rest of her beer and set it on the table.

"Sorry," Sam made a feeble attempt at a smile. "I've been having all these random thoughts jump into my head the last couple a days. Only problem is I'm having a hard time sorting out what, if anything, they mean."

"Like what kind of random thoughts? Can you talk about them?"

"Oh boy," He could feel his face warming as he tried to sort out something, anything.

"I can tell this is really hard for you but, maybe I can help."

"How? I mean I don't even know where to start..."

"Okay..." Susan was wracking her brain as to where a good place to start would be. Had to be something safe, light... "When we were kids, we used to play in these woods..." She looked at Sam to see if he was getting anything.

"Yeah, okay," Sam searched for a fragment of recognition but came up with nothing.

"We'd pretend that we were the only ones left in the world... and that your father was..."

"What, Susan? My father was what?"

"Oh, maybe I shouldn't have started there..."

"No, it's okay." Sam took Susan's hand in his and gave it a reassuring squeeze. "Go on... continue."

"Your father...," Susan looked down at her feet for a second. "Sam? Your father was..."

"C'mon."

"He was a very angry man. Ever since your brother..." her words trailed off. "We were scared of him, a lot of people around here were. That's why we used to hide in the forest," there it was. Susan waited for Sam to say something.

"I don't understand."

"Your father, he had a very bad temper, he...he used to take it out on you."

"Damn it, Sam. When I ask you to do something I'm not asking you to do it tomorrow, I mean now!"

Sam looked at Susan like a man completely at odds with the information.

"Sam?" Susan noticed the faraway look in Sam's eyes. "Sam... I'm sorry."

"Why would you be sorry?"

"I don't know... maybe it's because...," she gazed out into the darkening woods.

"Could we talk about... us? I mean, when we were in... friends?"

"We were more than friends, Sam."

"Okay, I want to talk about that. Would you like to switch to some very nice red wine?"

"I would."

They talked, and even had a few laughs, until the wine was gone as well as the day, which had turned to night without being noticed by either Sam or Susan until Sam looked out into the now dark forest.

"Wow, I didn't even notice how late it got."

"Is it that late?"

"I don't know, it's pretty dark."

"I should be going," Susan stood, stretched, and smiled down at Sam who stood collecting the glasses and plates.

"I'll put this stuff away and be right back," Sam went into the house. He paused for a brief second in the living room before heading into the kitchen. He placed the dishes in the sink and went back out onto the porch where Susan was slipping on her sweater.

"I had a real nice time Sam, again," she smiled at Sam. "I'm glad you came back. Sam… I missed you."

"I'm glad I came back too," Sam got shy all the sudden. "I just wish…"

"What? What do you wish, Sam?"

"Oh, I don't know why I said that. It's gonna take a little time for me to adjust I guess."

"We have plenty of time," She moved closer to Sam and surprised him with a quick kiss on the cheek.

Sam recoiled slightly.

"I'm sorry, I shouldn't have done that."

"No, it's okay, I liked it."

"Alright pal, time for me to hit the road," she lingered a moment then started down the stairs.

"Susan," Sam called when she reached the bottom step. "I had a good time too. I'm glad I have you as a friend."

"Me too, Sam. Good night.

"Good night, Susan."

Sam smiled as he watched her drive away. He took a seat on the porch and replayed their conversation. He was happy, he felt he was slowly getting some information to finally begin to understand.

He knew it wasn't going to be an easy thing to get through but, it was a necessary process if he wanted to get on with his new life.

He came to the decision that he needed to get himself a truck and turn in his rental Mustang.

Tomorrow, he would stop by the bank and see about financing one. First though he needed to find out where a car dealership is.

The night had grown cool, so Sam went into the house to retrieve his sweater off the peg by the door. He went back outside and settled into his chair. He took a deep breath and yawned. He stared off into the inky darkness of the surrounding woods.

His mind was blank which was a good thing, he wasn't thinking about anything, just sitting out content with the world. At that moment he had two things on his mind; one being the incredible evening he just had with Susan. The other was anticipating the ownership of a new truck, his new truck. He liked the Mustang fine enough it's just that you couldn't put much in it. Yep, tomorrow he will find the perfect truck.

CHAPTER 23

Sam awoke with a start. It was dark, he had no idea what time it was, but he thought it must be very early in the morning. He blinked his eyes open rubbing the sleep from them as he reached for the little night light on the stand by his bed.

When he snapped the light on his heart froze. At the foot of his bed was a dark shape... very dark. It was a shape without recognizable form. It felt like it was sucking the air out of the room making it hard for Sam to catch his breath. He pushed himself up to a sitting position and the last thing he saw before he blacked out was the little boy whose face was a blur.

A warmth fell over Sam he felt good, he felt relaxed. The warmth was suddenly alarming though, and he snapped awake blinking up at the sun overhead. When he reached out his hands he felt the ground which made his head swim, rotating the sun for a sickening moment. He sat up and to his complete shock he found himself staring at the shed doors. He had no idea how he got there... Just like the other morning when he found himself... Sam quickly got to his feet and lurched for the nearest tree before he toppled over. When his head cleared, he went back up to his room and got dressed.

He decided to turn his rental car in and get himself a truck. He needed to go to the bank and see about making a loan. Once dressed he was in the kitchen with two beautiful eggs frying in the pan waiting for the perfectly executed flip of the wrist that would create the perfect over easy goodness. Settling for scrambled eggs and toast he grumbled through his breakfast and was out the door.

Once on the hi-way Sam's anxiety about the morning's events slowly faded until he was pulling up to a stop in front of the Springville Savings and Loan.

"Mr. Henning, it's good to see you," Mr. Goble, the bank President motioned for Sam to take a seat. "What can I do for you today?"

"I'm turning my rental car in. I want to buy a truck," Sam took the offered chair. "Something a little more practical."

"Oh, I understand completely I don't know what I'd do without my old truck."

Silence pushed its way in just then as both men sat contemplating.

"So, what is it I can help you with?"

"I want to make a loan... so I can buy a truck."

"Why, Mr. Henning. You don't need to make a loan."

"I don't?"

"No, No," Mr. Goble smiled across his desk. "You can use the credit card I issued to you."

"I'd like to pay in cash. Unless that's a problem."

"It's no problem at all. Do you have a specific truck in mind?"

"Not yet, but I'll know it when I see it."

"Go over to Lorrain's it's just down the road about ten minutes."

"Lorrain's?"

"Lorrain's New and Used Cars. They have a good selection and good prices."

"Okay, Lorrain's..."

"You pick out the truck that suits you and have Ed call me here at the bank. I'll take care of everything from here."

"I just realized... how will I get my rental car back. Wait, maybe..."

"I can arrange for your rental to be returned."

"But, really," Sam was amazed at how helpful Mr. Goble was.

"Yes really, it's no problem, no problem at all."

"I mean, that's just great, Mr. Goble. I really appreciate it," Sam shook his hand and left.

Lorraine's New and Used Cars was just up ahead according to the large green and red sign that would be hard to miss. He pulled into the lot and found a place to park. He got out of his rental and scanned the lot filled with cars of every shape and color absorbing the morning sun. It's glare reflected off the windows as he walked by. He spotted an old truck standing alone on the corner of the lot and walked over to it.

"It was my grandpa's truck," a young man walked up to Sam and stood beside him.

"What year is it?" Sam wondered as he looked in the window.

"It's a sixty-two. My grandpa loved this truck. He only used it to get parts, he hardly ever drove it the last ten years or so."

"What color is that anyway?"

"It's butterscotch. He loved butterscotch," the young man seemed almost embarrassed.

"I like it," Sam was admiring the truck.

"If you're interested in a new car..." He straightened his tie ready to make a sale.

"I'm looking for a dependable truck."

"Well, we have lots of those over there, let me show you," he started to head in that direction but stopped when he realized he wasn't being followed. "Over here this is where the trucks are," he started off again.

"What about this truck?" Sam couldn't take his eyes off it.

"Well, that's not exactly for sale. We just park it in the garage at night and roll it out to the corner during the day."

"It runs right?"

"Oh, yes, it runs great. My grandpa took real good care of this truck," he returned to stand by Sam. "It's a very dependable truck. I bet it will outlast us," he put his hand on the hood as if he was touching something special to him.

"I'd like to buy it," Sam smiled at the now nervous, young man. "What are you asking for it?"

"I, I never thought of selling it," he scratched his head. "I really don't know. We really have some nice, newer trucks over there I could show you."

"C'mon, this truck suites me. Can we take it for a test drive?"

"Sure, I guess, but I really don't know about selling it. I'll get the keys and be right back."

Sam peeked in the window again and was impressed how clean it was. Original bench seat, good ol' metal dash that won't ever crack from the sun... it was perfect. All he had to do is convince the young man to sell it to him.

"I'll give you a good, fair offer of twenty thousand, cash. Right now."

"Well, gee, I..." the young man stammered as he weighed his options.

Sam looked in the window again.

"I see your grandpa switched the shifting from the steering column to the floor."

"Y-yeah, he took the transmission out of an old grain truck," the young man answered with pride.

"My name's Sam Henning. Whats yours?"

"Hi, I'm Ed, nice to meet you, Sam."

"So, is there a Lorraine?"

"Oh, Lorraine," Ed smiled. "Lorraine was... is my aunt. She was taking a fell'a on a test drive in a nice Buick and she never came back."

"What? You mean she was kidnapped?"

"Oh, no," Ed gave a nervous laugh. "She sent me a letter about two weeks after. Said she fell in love and married the fell'a. Said the car dealership was mine to do with what I wanted."

"That's quite a story, Ed."

"Yeah," he was a little out of breath. "Fell'a bought the Buick," he added as an afterthought.

"Wow."

"Hey, did you say your name was…"

"Sam. Sam Henning," Sam watched as the color drained from Ed's face. "You okay, Ed?"

"Yeah, sorry. What were we talking about?"

"We were talking about this butterscotch truck right over here. I offered you twenty thousand cash," he smiled though he was some concerned with Ed's reaction to his name.

"Oh yeah," his face scrunched up as he gave the proposition some deep thought.

Sam waited patiently while Ed worked it out.

"Okay. You know what? Okay," Ed nodded to himself. "My grandpa told me about you. I just moved here about eight years ago, steady that is. He told me…" Ed stopped his line of thought.

"Yes? What did he tell you?"

"Nothin', never mind I was just rambling on," he took a breath and got back on the subject at hand. "Why don't you come in and we'll get this deal done, what do you say?"

"I'd say that sounds great, Ed."

They went into a small, air-conditioned office. There were pictures of people and cars all over the walls along with his business license and diploma from Macklin Cross College. Sam took a seat as Ed sat behind his desk.

"We don't really have papers on that truck as far as contracts."

"That's okay with me."

"I mean we could draw something up I s'pose…"

"No need, Ed. All you have to do is agree on the price, we shake hands and it's done. Except for calling Mr. Goble over at the bank. He will make the arrangements," as an afterthought, "You could call him now, if you like."

"Oh, okay let me just... Hi, hi could I speak to Mr. Goble please, yes it's Ed. Thanks."

Ed winked at Sam and smiled.

"Yes, Mr. Goble H- Yes, my wife is fine, thank you. I know we'll definitely have to do that again. Absolutely. I have Sam Henning here and- Okay sounds great... yes that works for me... right... Okay... You too, Mr. Goble... yes have a good day yourself... okay goodbye."

"Everything good, Ed?"

"Yes, all good, Mr. Henning. All good."

"You can call me, Sam. It sounds less formal."

"Alright... Sam. Let me get you those keys," Ed opened his top desk drawer and fished out a set of keys. "Here you go, Sam. I think my grandpa would be happy you have it."

"Thanks, Ed. Thanks a lot."

Sam left the air conditioning for the heat of a new day. He walked slowly toward his new, old, truck, taking in every beautiful line of it. He got in and sat there for a moment smelling the clean leather smell of the interior.

It was everything he wanted. He inserted the key into the ignition and the truck rumbled to life surprising Sam. He turned it off and opened the hood. He saw Ed heading his way with a big smile crossing his face.

"Why, Ed, you didn't tell me your grandpa was a wild one."

"Yeah, well, he did have a wild streak at that. Think that's why my aunt took off with that fell'a and his new Buick. She was wild too."

"So, what do we have in here anyway, Ed?"

"Yeah, what you have there is a three twenty-seven Chevy engine. It has a lot of get up and go that's for sure."

"Nice, totally unexpected but, nice. Thanks again, Ed."

"We'll see you around, Sam," Ed waved and walked over to his next potential sale.

CHAPTER 24

Sheriff Thompson put the key into the cell door lock but didn't turn it.

"Listen to me close, Charlie. I don't want any trouble in my town, you understand?" He eyed his prisoner sternly. "I like peace and quiet, most folks around here feel the same." He turned the key and stepped back while Charlie walked by.

"What about my things?"

"I have your things in my desk, hang on," the Sheriff pulled out a wallet and a set of car keys and handed them over. "Be a good idea if you remember what I said."

Charlie exited the Sheriff's office and stretched in the morning sun. He looked back in the Sheriff's window and spit contemptuously on the sidewalk before strolling away to find his truck and a cold beer.

It wasn't long before he was headed for the Dusty Rose and that long anticipated cold beer. He parked his truck out front and pushed through the doors where he landed at the bar and hollered for a beer. When it arrived, he held it in his hands like it was something reverent.

Over at the far end of the bar, Marten Simms and Kyle Heckler were drinking coffee and talking.

"What do ya think about the Henning son bein' back in town?" Kyle took a sip of his coffee and pulled on his cigarette.

"Well, I guess I don't think about it too much. He seems like a nice young man. I don't get any, out of the ordinary, feelings about him. In a way he's my boss now that he's back in his house."

"Say, Marten, isn't that Charlie down at the end of the bar?"

"Yeah, guess the Sheriff let him out. He sure looks busted up," Kyle smiled into his cup of coffee.

Marten glanced in that direction and was amused by the busted-up face of one of the towns so called bad boys.

"You starin' at old man?" Charlie caught Marten looking his way and took exception to that fact.

Marten just made a face and looked away which didn't set too well with Charlie who had already downed three beers in rapid succession. He was feeling the buzz.

"Bob, get me another beer will ya?" Charlie slammed his empty beer bottle down on the bar.

"Kid's got quite a flare, don't he?" Kyle shook his head at the feeble display.

"Downright scary if ya ask me," Martin chuckled puffing on the last of his cigarette.

Charlie was starting to feel like those two old men were making fun of him. His face throbbed and he couldn't breathe through his nose so, he wasn't in the best of moods. He turned away from his reflection in the mirror, he took great exception to the mangled face staring back at him. He swore into his beer before gulping it down.

"Another, Bob. Bring me another beer."

"Look, Charlie... I think you had enough for now. Why don't you go down to Judy's and get yourself something to eat," Bob nervously wiped the bar.

"Why don't you mid your own business, Bob."

"It is my business, Charlie," Bob blinked back. "I-I mean, look at you. You don't look so good Charlie... your face is-" Quicker than Bob could react Charlie had him by the front of his shirt and was pulling him over the bar.

"He sucker-punched me," Charlie hissed.

"T-that's not the way I heard it."

"I just told you what happened he came up behind me!"

"Go easy there, Charlie," Kyle called from the other end of the bar. He stubbed out his cigarette and slid off his stool as did Martin, only he kept his cigarette tucked in the corner of his mouth.

"Okay, Charlie, whatever you say. Now, let go of my shirt," Bob had his hand on the handle of his bat but, Charlie came to his senses and turned him loose.

"And you two, ol' coots, better damn sure mind your coffee. I don't want any trouble with you," He glowered down at the two men but, it didn't have the desired effect because his face was so swollen it just came off as what it was, a busted-up face. *"Damn that Henning son of a bitch!"* He swore under his breath. "To hell with all of you losers," Charlie declared through swollen lips. "I'm getting' the hell out a here!" And he stormed out the door.

Charlie stumbled out to his truck, opened the door and fell in. Once he was sitting upright, he made a couple failed attempts at getting the keys in the ignition. When he finally managed to get it started, he stomped on the gas leaving the bar in a haze of rubber and exhaust smoke. In his haste he almost side-swiped a mailbox on the corner of Almond and Crescent.

The idea came to him as he raced down the RR44 to stop in on his cousin, Frank. When he saw the sign announcing the Lindsey Mobile Home Park, he swerved into the main road taking out a flamingo and two gnomes. He slid to a halt right behind Frank's truck and spilled out of the door landing in the gravel driveway. Swearing to himself he stood and stumbled up the front steps where he banged on the door.

"Son of a- who the hell could that be at this hour?" Frank protested as he tossed his empty beer can onto the ever-growing pile in the corner and went to the door. "What the hell do- Charlie? What are you doing here?"

"Is that any way to greet your cousin?" Charlie stood weaving slightly on the tiny doorstep.

"Damn, Charlie, he really busted you up," Frank stepped back while Charlie slipped by him.

Frank closed the door and took his seat.

"Shit, Charlie," Leroy looked up from the baseball game. "Can you see, okay?" Leroy wanted to know.

"I see fine," Charlie growled. "Got anymore a those beers?" He collapsed on the couch.

"Yeah, I was just getting myself one."

"Get me one too, huh, Frank?"

"Get your own, Leroy."

"I just figured if you were there anyway..."

"You figured wrong, Leroy. So, when did you get out?"

"Coupl'a hours ago," he popped his beer and grumbled as he touched its' cold rim to his swollen lips. "I jus' get out'a prison and some hard-ass Sheriff throws me in his jail. I was the one attacked," He protested between painful sips. "Was having a couple a cold ones over at the Rose til those pain in the ass old farts ruined it."

"What old farts are you talking about, Charlie?" Leroy plucked a beer off the shelf and closed the refrigerator door with his knee. He sat down on the opposite end of the couch and popped his beer.

"Leroy, do you mind?" Frank took a gulp of his beer and looked over at the horror that was his cousin's face. "He sure pasted you cuz," Frank shook his head and took another swig of beer.

"He sucker-punched me!" Charlie was just a little sensitive on the subject of the actual punch.

"That's what I thought," Leroy smiled as if he was a man who had more than just a couple of things figured out.

"Yeah, he's a chicken shit, for sure," Charlie gingerly sipped his beer. "I'll get him for this, that's a damn promise," Charlie declared.

"Yeah, a real chicken shit, huh?"

"Leroy..." Frank cautioned, shaking his beer can in his direction.

"Okay, Frank, geeze," Leroy turned his attention to his beer.

"Anyway, that new Sheriff..." Charlie's line of thought dwindled when he saw the pile of beer cans in the corner. "Where does he get off actin' so high an' mighty?"

"Well, he's not a new Sheriff, Charlie," Leroy fancied himself town historian all the sudden. "He's been here a long time. Since the old one burned up in the fire."

"Careful, Leroy, that was my dad you're talking about."

"I know that, Frank, I'm just sayin'."

"Well, don't, Leroy."

"Okay, Frank, okay. Take it easy."

"Don't tell me to take it easy, Leroy."

"Okay, Frank, geeze," Leroy went back the game.

"I'm gonna pay that Sam Henning back for what he did to me!" Charlie heaved his empty beer can at the stack in the corner and went to grab another.

CHAPTER 25

Sam drove away from the car dealership and onto RR44 which took him out of the trees and onto the flats where the road stretched out like a shimmering ribbon nice and strait. He gently applied more pressure to the gas pedal and was pressed back into his seat by the speed of acceleration. The powerful drone of the engine as it flew down the road was exhilarating. He rolled down his window so the wind could whip through his hair. He was happy.

He let off the gas and glided to the side of the road where he got out and stood there listening to the engine rumble. A car passed and he felt funny just standing there on the side of the road so he climbed back in and made a U-turn for home. He drove the rest of the way under the speed limit.

When his road came up he turned in and drove slowly over his dirt road. Not that it was rough, he just didn't want to get it all dusty the first day. As he came around the last bend in the road, he saw a car parked in front of his cabin. He pulled up beside it and got out. There was a woman standing on his porch and she moved up to the railing, smiling.

"Hi," she called.

"Hello, can I help you with something?" Sam stood at the bottom of the steps. He'd seen her before but couldn't remember where.

"That depends," she remained standing on the front porch, she was holding something in her hands that she was balancing on the top rail. The morning sun set her red hair on fire.

"I see," Sam said, but he didn't. "My name's, Sam," he climbed the stairs to meet his… guest.

"Oh, I know who you are, Sam Henning," she reached out to shake his hand.

"Well, that puts me at a slight disadvantage," when he shook her hand, she held his a moment longer which made him a little uncomfortable.

"I'm Daphne? I work at the Emporium?"

"Yeah, I think I've seen you there. You must know, Susan... what am I saying everybody knows everybody here," *she's stunning standing there,* Sam thought. He had the feeling she knew exactly how she looked and the effect she had. She definitely made Sam feel awkward but, not in the sense she was hoping. She was actually having the exact opposite effect, it was a little irritating.

"It' a small town, Sam."

"I'll say. So?"

"Oh! I just dropped by to say hi. I made some cookies to sort of welcome you to our funny little town."

"Thanks, Daphne... that's nice of you..."

"Well, I guess I better get a move on..." she waited...

"Okay, well, Daphne... It was good to meet you, thanks for the cookies." Sam stepped aside and still she waited.

"Oh," as if she just realized the meeting was over. "Okay, I'll probably be seeing you around."

"It's a small town," Sam smiled as she floated down the stairs.

She waved, slid into her car and was down the road.

That was... interesting... Sam thought. He went inside and grabbed a beer from the fridge then came back out to sit on the porch. He couldn't take his eyes off his beautiful new/old truck. *Butterscotch... who ever thought of such a thing...*

Sam sipped his beer and stared until he heard a noise coming from the shed area... He sat there for a second longer until it sounded like the shed doors were opening. When he got up, there was a crashing sound from in the house. Like a window had broken. Torn about which way to go first he went into the house.

Once he was inside, he looked around frantically but could see nothing out of place or broken. He went into the kitchen. That's where he stopped to catch his breath. Broken glass was scattered on the counter over the sink, more shards sparkled on the floor.

He was stunned. On further inspection he found the lock to the shed doors in the corner by the stove, he would have missed seeing it had it not been for the sun coming through the window by the kitchen table. Like a man in a dream, he saw his hand reaching down to pick up the lock he felt disconnected in some way.

He picked up the lock and held it in his hand where he studied it as if it were some rare stone, it was still locked, but the locking mechanism was bent over the lock body. It was useless... Sam walked over to the broken window, crunching on glass as he went, and looked out. Through the hole in the window, he had a clear, beeline, view of the shed. The doors were wide open. Sam stood there mesmerized by the sight which made him feel a little dizzy.

Then, he heard it... it was very faint. At first, he thought his ears were playing tricks with him, then he heard it again... it was the faint sound of a child crying... it was coming from inside the shed. As soon as he realized it the doors slammed shut with such force Sam fell back against the kitchen table hurting his shoulder. He slumped to the cool tile floor and sat there panting like a dog on a hot day.

The sound of someone driving up his road brought him around. He shook his head trying to clear the haze between his ears. *What the heck time is it?* He wondered to himself as a truck came to a stop in his front yard.

"Son-of-a-bitch!"

"Hey, Hank," Sam came out onto the front porch rubbing his head.

"You okay, Sam?" Hank slammed his door and forgot his cigarettes which sent him into another frenzy of swear words.

"I see you're still working on your swearing," Sam came down the stairs.

"It's a work in progress," he said and swore when he couldn't get his lighter to light.

"What brings you out this way?"

"I don't know. Thought I'd check in on ya," when he noticed Sam's new ride, he swore all the way over to it, whistled and swore some more.

"Yeah, I just got it today."

"I thought something was different when I drove by Lorrain's. So, you got the old man's truck," he noticed Sam was holding something in his hand. "Whatch'ya got in yer hand there, Sam?"

"Oh," Sam only just realized he was still holding the twisted lock.

"How'd ya do that?" Hank was still looking at the lock in Sam's hand.

"I-I don't know," and he didn't. "I do have a broken window… in the kitchen."

"Oh?"

"It's just one of the panes. I can fix it myself."

"Okay, whatever *you* say. Heard you had a new BBQ," he fished out a fresh cigarette. "How's that workin' out?"

"Great," Sam waited.

"Well, if ya have no need of my services…"

"Thanks for stopping by Hank."

"You bet," He got back in his truck but was having trouble getting the door shut which elicited a whole new string of cussing.

Sam waved as his guest finally got turned around and was headed back down his road.

CHAPTER 26

When Daphne rounded the last bend in the road out of Sam's place, she pulled over by a truck that was pulled off to the side of the road. She stopped and smiled, then got out of her car.

"Hey Daph, Whatch'ya doin'?"

"Hi, L'roy," She snatched the cigarette out of Leroy's hand and took a good long puff. "I'm just welcoming the newest member of our quaint little town," she gave him a stern face and smiled at Hank when he drove by, "What are you doing out here?"

"Me? I'm just takin' some shade," Leroy stared after the old truck until it rounded the bend.

"Shade huh, L'roy? It's cool out today. Why would you be needing shade?"

"Well now, what about you?" Leroy fumbled with his cigarette pack trying to shake a fresh one out without spilling them all onto the ground. He was able to get it done, light one and return it to the corner of his mouth.

"What's that supposed to mean, L'roy?"

He liked the way she said his name…

"Oh nothin," Her red hair was bursting into flame as the sun cleared the treetops.

"Are you sure it's nothin', L'roy?" She batted her green eyes and smiled when she saw Leroy's face start to quiver. "I don't think it's nothin', L'roy," she stepped closer and twisted her finger in the collar of his t-shirt causing a riot of movement on his face.

"Well," Leroy stammered. "I would like it if we could go get us a beer sometime over at the Rose."

"Just a beer, L'roy?" She pulled him closer. "Girl likes to eat once in a while, L'roy," Daphne was in full flirt mode. "What about…" she twisted his shirt tighter. "What about… dinner sometime?"

"Y-yeah, sure." Leroy gulped hard. "Dinner sounds like a good idea, Daph."

"Well, you know where to find me, L'roy," Daphne released him.

Before Leroy could recover, she was waving out her window as she took to the hi-way and was gone.

He smoked his cigarette down to the nub before snubbing it out on the sole of his boot, looked around and slid behind the wheel. He sat there for a second gathering his thoughts while lighting another cigarette. He wondered what she was really doing at Sam's. The thought made him both nervous and a little bit pissed.

Leroy has had a thing for Daphne for a long time. Since he moved geminately up to Springville with Frank, about five years ago. He was captivated by her red hair and, her slight accent which he didn't quite understand. She claimed to be from Springville, as in born in. *If that damn Sam Henning is trying to make a move on my girl…*

Leroy started the truck, he and Frank bought together, and sped off in a cloud of dust. He was headed to the Rose to meet up with Frank and Charlie. As he drove down Route 44, he began to wonder, more intently, about the fact that Daphne had actually turned down Henning's road in the first place.

He had followed her from when she left her trailer, where he had hoped to meet her, until she turned off the hi-way. He had just pulled in when she came out. *God, how she makes me feel!* He thought to himself as he barreled down the hi-way.

Judy's Burger Barn sign loomed up in the distance, just down the street was the Dusty Rose Bar. Leroy cranked the wheel and skidded to a halt in front of The Rose. He kicked open the truck door and coughed against the cloud of dust he had dragged behind him.

Frank and Charlie were inside working on their fifth beer. Frank growled when he saw Leroy pull in.

"Damn it, Leroy!" Frank shook his head. "You in some kind'a race or somethin'?"

Leroy surveyed the room before his eyes landed on Frank who sat leaning on the bar puffing on a cigarette. "I'm not racin'."

"You took long enough," for the first time, since Leroy came in, Frank turned. "What were you doin' anyway?"

"Things, Frank. Things."

Frank made a face and went back to his beer.

"Hey, Charlie," Leroy nodded and took a seat next to Frank which put Frank between him and Charlie which relaxed him some.

"Leroy, how you doin'?"

"I'm good," he shook Charlie's hand then waved at the bartender. "Can I get a cold one down this way?" It didn't take long before one slid his way and he grabbed it.

"Boy, Charlie..." Leroy was trying to pick his words carefully as he knew Charlie was still riled up on the subject of his busted-up face. "Looks like your face went down some," he smiled like a fox caught in the hen house.

"Leroy," Frank leaned in so he could see his aggravating friend better. "I told you to leave off."

"It's okay, Frank," Charlie motioned for another round. "He don't bother me."

"I just saw Daphne Dunkin drivin' out'a Sam Henning's place," he took a swig of beer and waited for the reaction from Frank.

"Daphne was at...," Frank choked on his beer which took him a second to recover from. "What do you suppose she was doin' there?"

"Well," Leroy took a nice slow gulp of beer delaying the moment. He set his beer down carefully...

"C'mon, Leroy for crissake! Get on with it," Frank had no patience for Leroy's drama moments.

"Okay, Frank," Leroy rolled his beer between his hands.

"Leroy, I swear!"

"Take it easy Frank. She said she was there to welcome... to welcome... That damn Sam Henning to town! Shit!" Leroy downed his beer and called for another.

"That's good news, Leroy," Frank smiled.

"Why? What do you mean that's good news?"

"Means that psycho is interested in, Daphne."

"Well, Frank, that is not good news," Leroy's face was a riot of spasms. "Daphne's my girl, Frank."

So, Frank," Charlie had had enough of the conversation and wanted to change the subject. "What's your plan as far as that Henning son-of-a-bitch?"

Frank leaned in on his elbows. Charlie and Leroy did the same; three conspirators plotting no good...

CHAPTER 27

After the excitement of getting his new, old, truck and finding a surprise visitor standing on his porch, followed by the broken window deal, he was about done for one day. He went inside and sat by his phone holding the paper, with Susan's number on it, in his hand. He dialed her number and waited only to get a message saying she wasn't near her phone. He replaced the handset in its cradle without leaving a message.

Sam got up and went to get another beer out of the fridge. He was just kneeing the door shut when he heard an approaching vehicle. He went out onto the front porch and was, again, surprised by another visitor. There was a sheriff's cruiser coming to a stop in his front yard. He watched the sheriff get out and stretch.

"Hello, Sheriff," Sam called from the porch. "What brings you out this way?"

"Hello, Sam. Mind if I come on up for a visit?"

"Not at all, c'mon up."

"I'm Sheriff Thompson," he offered his hand.

"You already know who I am," Sam shook his hand and offered him a seat.

"It's a-"

"Small town, I know," Sam finished his sentence. "Can I get you some water? Or…"

"I'd take one of those beers if you have another."

"I'll be right back."

"You sure have a nice place here," Sheriff Thompson called.

"What's that?" Sam came back out with two fresh beers.

"I said, you sure have a nice place here. Oh thanks," Sheriff Thompson took a sip of his beer and balanced it on his knee.

"Thanks, I'm still getting used to the place."

"How do you like our little town, so far?"

"So far… everyone has been really nice with a few exceptions."

"About that… Sam, you know I had to make contact with you."

"No, I don't know that. Why would you *have* to contact me? I didn't start that fight."

"No, but you sure finished it. Sam," he set his half-finished beer on the top rail. "You really have no idea why I'm here?"

"Nope, none. If it's not about the fight…"

"Well, Sam… there was a double homicide perpetrated in this house. It was fifteen years ago."

Sam was dumbfounded but made no reply.

"Actually, technically, it still remains an unsolved case," Sheriff Thompson waited for some reaction from Sam but, all he got in return was a blank stare. "Sam, I have read the files as it was a federal crime. Do you understand?"

"I'm afraid I don't, no."

"What do you remember? I know it was a long time ago, Sam."

"I remember doctors. Lots of doctors."

"Yes, according to documents I found your uncle, he took you away claiming you needed psychiatric help, and the court agreed as you were unfit and underage to stand trial."

"I don't know…" Sam took a long swig of his beer and set it on the little table next to him.

"Honestly, I was surprised that the records didn't burn up in the fire. Luckily, they were kept in another room in a metal cabinet."

Sam stared out into the shadowy forest not really keeping up with the conversation. His mind was off in another direction.

"Sam? I have also read the medical reports as they were ordered by the courts to turn over."

"Okay... You know, Sheriff Thompson? I really have no idea what you're leading up to, but I don't like it. I've had a rough couple of days, and I just want to get to know where I am for a while if you don't mind."

"You know, Sheriff Dobbs was a good friend of mine," he lifted his beer for another drink but, set it back on his knee instead. "There were a few things that I found that just don't seem to match up."

"Like what?" Sam was getting irritated by the line of conversation; it made him feel uncomfortable for reasons he didn't know.

"Well, like when Sheriff Dobbs took you into the kitchen that night. He wrote in his report that the kitchen door, leading to the backyard, was closed. But, according to both Deputies, Ellis, and Green it was open when they first cleared the house."

Sam made a face and shrugged his shoulders.

"Also, there was a perfect bloody handprint on the wall to the right of the door. This was also confirmed by Deputies Ellis and Green. Only in Green's report he noted that while the print was pristine the fingers were smudged and they were unable to lift any usable prints," Sheriff Thompson picked up his beer and this time he drank. "Why do you think the handprint would be good and the fingertips smudged?"

"I really wouldn't know, Sheriff. I have absolutely no idea what you're getting at."

"A psychologist's report I read rated your intelligence very high."

"And?"

"I'm just saying they found you to be very smart. I find that interesting."

"There are a lot of smart people in this world, I imagine," Sam could feel his pulse start to ratchet up a few notches.

"Yes, I suppose you're right," Sheriff Thompson finished his beer and stood. "Well, Sam, it was good to meet you. I hope we can talk again sometime."

"Stop by anytime Sheriff," he heard his voice say it, but it was actually the very *last* thing he wanted.

"You have yourself a good day, Sam," he extended his hand.

"You do the same, Sheriff," Sam took his hand and shook it.

Sheriff Thompson went back to his cruiser but, before he got in, he looked back up at Sam.

"Try to stay clear of Charlie, that young man's trouble with a capital T."

"I'll do my best, Sheriff."

"That's good, that's really good," he smiled up at Sam but, before he got in his cruiser he said off-handedly, "You know, they never found the murder weapon..."

Sam stared down at the Sheriff who had one leg in the car.

"It's funny," he paused as he looked up at Sam. "Both Deputies Green and Ellis mentioned a knife in their reports... Have a good day," Sheriff Thompson tipped his hat, climbed in behind the wheel and headed back down the road leaving Sam confused and wondering...

He went inside to grab another beer then came back out to sit on the porch. He sat there for a moment before he decided to try to get a hold of Susan again. He went back inside and sat by the phone, staring at it. His mind was completely muddled, he had no idea what to do. What the Sheriff said really disturbed him. He wanted to call her but, he wouldn't know what to say even if she *did* answer the phone.

CHAPTER 28

Sam decided the best thing to do was get into his fine new/old truck and go cruising. He had no actual destination in mind he just turned onto RR44 and drove. He turned onto the main street of town and couldn't help but notice the casual looks and outright stares he was getting. If he figured it was because of his truck he would be right.

Before long, after a left turn onto a side street, he found himself parked in front of a store called, The Mystic Door. It boasted concoctions, crystals, herbal teas. He got out and pushed through the front door where he was assailed with the smell of incense and other things he couldn't imagine. The chimes over the door announcing his entry startled him, and that fact was not lost on the young woman standing behind the counter smiling at his discomfort.

"Well, good day, Sam Henning," Jorden smiled as she straightened her paperwork. "Is there something I can help you find?"

"I was wondering if you had any of that tea... I can't think of the name of it right now."

"Rose hip, like we had at our house the other day. Is that the one?"

"Yes, that's it, rose hip."

"I have it over here," Jorden went to the shelves in the back.

Sam let his eyes wander around the little store. There were crystals of every shape and color, the things he saw hanging in the trees the other day... all kinds of books and candles and things, he had no idea what they were.

"Here we are," Jorden set a bag on the counter. "How much would you like?"

"Oh, I don't know. A medium bag I guess?"

"Medium bag it is," she proceeded to fill a bag. "Do you have something to put this in to steep?"

"Steep?" Sam hadn't heard that word before. He wasn't much of a tea drinker.

"Yes, you put your tea in this," she placed a silver ball, with tiny holes in it, on the counter. "You put your tea in this then dunk it in your cup of hot water. That's how you steep it."

"Huh... and how long do I keep this... ball thing in my cup?"

"A couple minutes should do the trick. Depends on how strong you like it."

"Okay, I guess I'll take one of those too," Sam smiled down at the young woman finding it hard to believe people in town referred to her and her sisters as witches.

"Okay, Sam, will there be anything else for you today?"

"I think that will do me for today, thanks."

Jorden put the tea and steeping ball in a bag and rang up the purchase on an old cash register. "That'll be ten dollars and twenty cents."

"Okay, thanks a lot, Jorden. You have a great day."

"You do the same, Sam. Oh, Sam?

"Jorden?"

"Someone is trying to contact you... Do you have any idea who it might be?"

"I've had a lot of people trying to contact me since I got here."

"Okay, Sam. You have an awesome day."

"I will do my best, you too."

Sam went out through the door, trying to ignore the chimes, and got back in his truck. Just when he was about to start it up there was a knock on his window. Sam rolled it down and found an old man standing there smiling at him.

"Can I help you with something?"

"My names' Cleat, Cleat Morgan?"

"Okay, Cleat, I'm-"

"I know who you are, Sam Henning. I went to school with your father. We were in the same grade."

"I see," Sam waited to see if there was more.

"I… that was a really bad thing that happened to your parents. And to Sheriff Dobbs…"

"Oh?"

"Yeah, well, I saw you come out of *that* store and figured I'd come by and say hello"

"I'm glad you did."

"Well, you have yourself a good day, Sam. Oh, a friendly piece of advice? I'd steer clear of *those* people."

"*Those* people?"

"I guess every back hills town has their oddities… if you get my meanin'." He stepped back and simply walked away.

Sam fired up his truck and headed for home.

When his road came into view he turned in and relaxed as he drove down his tree-shadowed lane. When he reached his house, he sat in his truck for a second, with the engine idling, and looked around his yard. He wasn't looking for anything in particular, just looking. Finally, he shut the truck off and grabbed his purchases.

When he reached the stairs, the chimes started to sound. Not loud, but lightly, like the sound fine China makes when you flick it with your finger? He looked around at the forest and all was still, not a puff of wind. He slowly climbed the stairs never taking his eyes off those chimes and went inside. He set his bag of tea and his keys on the counter and went for a drink of water. As he was filling his glass the chimes really started going off.

Sam stormed out the front door and down to the chimes that were flickering all over the place and yanked them off the eye bolt. His mind was racing as he flew down the stairs and pulled on the shed doors… they were locked, and he didn't have the key. Chimes firmly grasped in his hand he ran back up the stairs and into the house scooping his set of keys off the counter.

Back down to the shed he fumbled with them until he found the right one and opened the lock. He pulled one of the doors open with such force it crashed against the side of the shed startling him a little. He took a second to gaze into the dark hole that was the inside of the shed then tossed the chimes inside and locked the door. He stood there for a second as if he had something to say but had forgotten what it was.

CHAPTER 29

Sam dropped his keys back on the counter, put away his purchases, and went about the task of making a sandwich for lunch.

Sandwich done he grabbed a beer and went out onto the porch. Once he was settled in his chair he took a few bites, had a sip of beer, and just sat there staring out into the woods. He thought about the old man, Cleat, who had approached him at his truck. He said he went to school with his father... it bothered him because he didn't even know his own father, couldn't remember anything particular about him at all... His mother, either, for that matter.

What happened? That's the big mystery. One that bothered him very much, especially since he came back. He was in a house he had never known but, supposedly had grown up in. A house filled with memories, locked away with no key to be found. There was a large void in his early life where he had absolutely no clue. The part that bothered him most was the fact that the people who lived in town knew something... more than he knew. He hoped Susan could help him figure it all out. But he also wondered to himself, 'do I really want to know? I mean really?'

Once the sun went down and the air grew cool Sam went out to gather some wood to make a fire. After changing into his pajamas, he poured himself a glass of wine and went into the living room where the fire was cheerfully crackling away. He set his wine down on the table beside him and picked up the book he had been trying to read.

The room was warm, and Sam's wine glass sat empty at his elbow. It wasn't long before he was asleep with his book in his lap. Somewhere around three in the morning he was awakened by a noise in the kitchen. He stared at the glow of the last of the fire and waited.

There it was again... Sam's heart rate quickened. At first, he thought it could be the house transitioning from a warm day into a cool night. No, it was coming from the kitchen... It sounded like someone was walking around in there. Slowly, he set the book on the table and got out of his chair. As he silently made his way to the kitchen, he heard the back door open, and he stopped.

One of the kitchen chairs made a noise and Sam moved faster. He flicked on the kitchen light and blinked against the sudden brightness. Immediately he felt wet and sticky... He looked down and to his horror discovered he was covered in blood. He looked over at the back door and his heart stopped. The door was slightly open and to the right, by the light switch, was a bloody handprint.

The walls began to pulse in and out. In and out. Sam's head ached. The ceiling was buckling with a sickening up and down, up and down motion while the floor rippled under his feet... It felt like the whole house was about to come apart. Sam stumbled for the chair at the kitchen table and plopped down hard burying his face in his folded arms. The whirlwind roar in his head was deafening and he gritted his teeth against pain of it. He lifted his head shouting at the mayhem happening around him.

———————————

Veronica awoke with a start with a deafening ringing in her ears. Clair heard her and sat up in her bed. Jorden slipped out of bed and went into check on Veronica.

"Hey, what woke you so suddenly?"

"I'm not sure," She rubbed her eyes and waited a moment for the ringing to stop. "I guess I was having a dream... It felt so real."

"What was it about, do you remember?" Clair came into the room stretching.

"All I remember is someone shouting... or, or, screaming very loudly... Then I woke up."

Sam's mind was racing; the images flying by too fast to make sense of, try has he might.

"Drop the knife! Drop it son..."

"Where are we going?"

"Away."

"But why?"

"I have to take you away from here, far away."

"But why? I'm scared!"

"Do you know what happened here? Did you see anyone else here?"

"Alright bring him in here we must do this quickly. Nurse?"

"I'm here Doctor Hanson; we're bringing him in now..."

He must've lost consciousness at some point because when he finally was able to stop the voices and the pounding in his head he looked up and noticed it was just getting light outside. He inspected himself and found his pajamas to be clean. He saw that the back door was closed and there was no handprint on the wall next to it, for which he was grateful.

He eased himself out of the kitchen chair and shuffled outside. He felt tired and sore. The morning sun was creeping onto the front porch. He pulled his chair over, so he was sitting in a warm pool of light.

Sam laid his head back and closed his eyes trying to still his throbbing head. The chimes began to tinkle scaring Sam so bad he leaped out of his seat as the air sparkled with static electricity.

He stared, stunned at the chimes, which had miraculously returned to the hook at the end of the porch, happily tinkled away. At least, Sam reasoned, there was a slight breeze. It offered a very unsatisfying comfort but, he couldn't take any more. In his exhaustion he started to wonder if he was truly losing his mind...

CHAPTER 30

"Are you feeling better Veronica?"

"Yes, Claire, thanks. The tea is helping."

"I sure would like to know what you were dreaming about this morning," Claire was putting jam on a couple slices of bread.

"Me too," Veronica got up to put her cup in the sink. "Where's Jorden?"

"She went out for a walk. She'll be back soon."

"I have to open the store pretty soon," Claire swept through the house putting things away and grabbing her keys. "You gonna be in later?"

"Yeah, I'll be there just have to do a couple of things around here first."

"Okay, see ya later," Claire waved and went out the door.

"Good morning, Veronica," Jorden burst through the front door with a handful of wild mint. "Look what I found down along the river," She placed the mint in the sink to wash before putting it in the refrigerator.

"Nice," Veronica grabbed her keys by the door. "Okay, Jorden, I'm off to work."

"Okay, Veronica, have a great day!"

"I will, you do the same. Later!" And Veronica was out the door.

Claire was busy setting up the displays in the store when the door burst open. A big man with dark glasses and a piece of tape across the bridge of his nose stood surveying the place. Right behind him another man pushed through the front door.

"Good morning!" Claire called. "Is there something you're looking for?"

"Uh, yeah," Frank stepped up to the counter while Charlie stayed planted where he was.

"I'd have an easier time helping you if you told me what it is you're looking for."

Frank looked back at Charlie and smiled a wolf's grin.

"We're lookin' for witches," he moved some things out of the way and placed his hands flat on the counter. He stared hard at Claire who wasn't about to be intimidated. "There are no 'witches' here."

The chimes signaled and Veronica swept into the room. She took one look at the two men, both of which she was semi familiar with, and knew they were trouble.

"Have you men been helped?" Veronica took up a position next to Frank who turned her way leaning an elbow on the counter.

"Oh yeah, we've been helped," He turned a frown on Veronica and was disappointed when it didn't achieve the desired effect. "We, are here lookin' for witches."

"Uh, there are no 'witches' here," she shook her head. "Whatever gave you that idea?"

"Do we look like 'witches'?" Claire smiled at Frank which infuriated him and pleased Veroica.

"How should I know what the hell witches look like. For all we know you can change your looks."

Both Claire and Veronica erupted in laughter at the notion.

The chimes announced another arrival, it was Leroy.

"Hey, what are you doin' in here?" Leroy was looking around the store with a mixture of curiosity and disgust. "When Arron Walsh down at the Seed and Feed told me he seen you guys come in here I couldn't believe it. What the hell's goin' on Frank?"

"Leroy," Frank took a deep breath. "Leroy we are here engagin' these two… fine lookin' women. Ain't that right." He addressed Claire who was not very amused.

"You know, come to think of it," Claire was warming to the subject. "I read somewhere that they can change shapes," she had to really concentrate on keeping a straight face.

"I told you, Frank," Leroy's face started to light up some. "Didn't I tell you, Frank? Witches *can* change shapes," Leroy was beside himself with vindication.

"Leroy if you don't mind…" Frank was losing patience.

"Now, suppose we all quite dancin' around the subject here." Frank directed the attention back to himself.

"Well, Frank, what exactly is the subject of this visit?" Veronica moved Franks' hand and put the items he moved back in their place. "Why are you guys here, Frank?"

"I wanna know, what you were doin' at Sam Henning's place the other day?"

"Well, Frank, first off what I do is certainly not any of your business. Now, if you have not come in our store to purchase anything, and, since you've had your look around, I think it's time you left."

"Wait, what are these things?" Leroy was picking up sticks and smelling them.

"Those things," Claire moved over to him. "Those are incense sticks."

"What do they do?"

"They smell."

"Alright c'mon, Leroy. Le's get out'a here."

"I want this one, it smells nice."

"That'll be a quarter, Leroy."

"Okay, here, thanks."

"You're welcome, Leroy," Claire smiled while Leroy's face turned a nice shade of red then it started doing crazy gymnastics.

"Okay, Leroy?" Frank had had it. "Is there anything else you see here that you can't live without?"

Leroy took a quick look around as he ran the incense stick under his nose. "Nope, Frank. I think I've got everything."

"Then let's get out'a here," Frank glowered at the two women before storming out the door followed closely by Charlie and Leroy who lagged behind for a second smiling back at Claire. He thought she wasn't half bad... for a 'witch'.

"Bye, Leroy," Claire batted her eyes at him, and he stumbled over the door jamb as he exited.

————————————

Sam, having regained his senses, for the most part, stood and walked to the end of the porch. He inspected the chimes with a stunned curiosity then leaned over the railing to peek back at the shed. He was shocked to find that the lock was on the ground and the shed doors were open...

The air around him turned cold prickling the hair on the back of his neck causing goosebumps to race over his body. Someone was standing right behind him. He took a short breath and turned slowly, what he saw stopped his heart for a second. There, leading away from him, were wet footprints. When he was able to will his legs to move, he followed them along the porch and down to the bottom step where they vanished.

Further into the woods he saw a boy in his bathing suit standing by a tree. Sam couldn't make out any features of his face as it seemed to be out of focus.

————————————

"You shouldn't do that Claire," Veronica came around to the back of the counter and placed her things on a shelf.

"Do what, Veronica?" Claire went back to pricing the new items.

"You know very well what I'm talking about."

"I was just messing with Leroy.

CHAPTER 31

"Well, you still shouldn't do that," Veronica and Claire burst into the house, deep in discussion.

"I didn't do anything." Claire tossed her things on the entry hall table and heading for the source of the smell of baked bread.

"You know very well..." Veronica set her things on the already crowded little table.

"C'mon, Veronica... You saw how they were acting..."

"Still," Veronica followed Claire, closely.

"Still nothing," Claire kept walking.

"Those boys are dangerous. Didn't you hear what they said?"

"I heard."

"They were looking for... 'Witches'. Well, did they find any? Of course not."

"All the same I would appreciate it if you didn't tease them anymore."

"Wow, something sure smells good,"

"What are you making in here, Jorden?"

"Oh, I just threw together some lentil soup and I baked a couple loaves of bread."

"I love lentil soup," Clair went to the kitchen drawer and plucked out a spoon where she proceeded to sweep by Jorden to dunk her spoon in the pot for a taste.

"Hey, Claire," Jorden swatted Claire with her wooden spoon. "It's not ready to eat yet,".

"You should have seen who came into the store this morning," Claire was baiting Veronica.

"Oh? Anybody I know?" She went back to her lentils on the stove.

"Maybe..." Claire smiled at Veronica who was in the process of pouring herself a glass of wine.

Veronica sipped her wine and made a face at Claire.

"Well? Who came into our store this morning?"

Claire offered one last challenge to Veronica, to add her two cents but, she looked away.

"Only Frank… and his cousin, Charlie, and later, Leroy." She waited for Jorden's reaction.

"Okay," She turned the loaves of fresh bread on their sides to cool properly. "Well, did they buy anything?"

"No… oh wait, Leroy bought a stick of incense."

"Yeah," Veronica walked over to smell the bread. "He spent a whole quarter."

"Wow," Jorden added a couple of shakes of Marjoram to the pot of bubbling lentils. "He must've found himself a job," she laughed at her own joke as did Claire and Jorden.

Veronica sat down at the kitchen table and cupped her wine glass in her hands.

"I'm worried about, Sam Henning."

"What about him?" Jorden brought one of the loaves to the table. The aroma caused Veronica's mouth to water.

"They wanted to know why I was at his place," She took the knife from Jorden, cut herself a piece and devoured it.

"Geeze, Veronica…"

"This is so good," Veronica shoved the last bite in her mouth and smiled up at Jorden.

"So, what was the big discussion you two were having when you came in?"

"Oh, Veronica thought I was teasing the boys…"

"She was," Veronica cut another slice of bread, this time buttering it.

"Oh, c'mon. I doubt if they'd even know they were being teased."

"It's still not a good idea, Claire."

"Alright you two dinners almost ready, if you're still hungry after eating all that bread, Veronica."

"I always have room for lentil soup," Veronica finished her last bite of bread.

"So, what else did they want?" Jorden set the bowl of soup on the table while Claire brought the spoons and bowls.

"They were just looking for trouble as always," Claire took her seat and dished up a bowl of soup.

"That's why you shouldn't tease them, Claire," Veronica ladled herself some soup and cut another slice of bread.

"Veronica's right, Claire," Jorden cut herself a slice of bread. "I don't think it's a good idea to mess with them at all."

"Oh geeze, I was just having a little fun is all."

"That kind of fun could cause trouble for us."

"How so, Jorden?" Claire blew on her spoon full before taking a bite.

"I don't know, with those boys one can never tell."

"Alright you two worry warts. I will try to contain myself from now on."

"Don't be so dramatic, Claire," Veronica said between bites.

"What the hell's that awful smell?" Frank came out of the bathroom and grabbed a beer from the fridge.

"Hey, it's not awful," Leroy took offense to Frank's statement. "It's incense, Frank."

"Aw, leave him alone, Frank," Charlie pulled his own beer out of the fridge and plopped down on the couch. "This place smells of stale beer and dirty dishes anyway. That stick improves the aroma around here."

"See, Frank?" Leroy sipped on his beer and gloated to himself.

"Be careful, Leroy," Frank cautioned.

"What? I didn't say anything."

"It's what yer thinkin', Leroy. And you know it."

"Okay, Frank, okay."

"You really think those pretty ladies in that weird store are witches, Frank?"

"We know they are," Leroy burst out louder than he intended earning him another stern look from, Frank.

"I mean... they don't exactly strike me as being witches."

"They're witches, Charlie," Frank got up and fetched himself another beer.

"I'll take another one, Frank," Leroy tossed his empty can onto the ever-growing pile in the kitchen corner.

"Get your own, Leroy," Frank dropped into his chair causing his beer to foam up. "Dammit, Leroy, now look what you did." Frank pawed at his wet shirt.

"I'm all the way over here, Frank. I didn't do nothin'."

"You two sound like an old married couple," Charlie made a face and tossed his empty onto the pile.

"Charlie, you wanna watch what you say in my house," Frank frowned at his cousin.

"It's my house too, Frank," Leroy scolded.

"See, my point exactly," Charlie helped himself to another beer.

"Next time you buy the beer, Charley."

"Okay, Frank, don't get yourself all worked up."

"Don't tell me what to do, Charlie."

"He's right, Frank, take it easy."

"Leroy."

"Let's go on over to, Judy's and get us a burger."

"I am kind a hungry," Charlie got up and stretched.

"That does sound good, Leroy. Let's go get us some burgers and on the way back we can stop by the grocery store so Charlie here can buy some more bruskies."

"Let's get going!" Leroy shot off the couch and headed for the door.

———————————

"It sure was a good idea coming to Judy's for burgers, Joan," Susan wiped her mouth and smiled at the remaining couple of bites she held in her hand.

"Yeah, every once in a while, I get the burger bug."

"I think I get the burger bug about three times a week," She stuffed the last bite in her mouth and washed it down with a root beer.

"Damn, Susan," Joan set her last half of burger down and took a drink. "People would think you're starving the way you put that burger away," She laughed and shook her head.

The bell over the front door at Judy's clanged in the new arrivals.

"Oh shit, look who just walked in. No, don't look, maybe they won't notice us."

"You're a burger hog," then, after seeing who it was that had entered Judy's Joan leaned in close. "But I'm not done yet."

"Hey, there's no hurry. I'll be darned if I let the likes of them run us out of anywhere," Susan declared in between sips of her root beer.

They were loud as always, Frank, Charlie, and Leroy, especially when they've been drinking, which was pretty much all the time, lately.

"Oh hey, Frank," Leroy stopped in his tracks. "Look who's here."

"Hey, Girls," Leroy waved at Susan and Joan, much to their disappointment.

"Well, well, well," you'd think Frank had just discovered the Hope diamond. A rough smile creased his face as he walked over to their table.

'Oh... Hi Frank," Susan was less than thrilled.

"What are you boys doing out of your cage?" Joan was no fan.

"Funny, Joan," Leroy sneered at her, and she shrugged her shoulders.

"Wow, Charlie, is it? Looks like somebody did a number on your face," Joan ate the last bite of her burger, wiped her mouth, and smiled up at Charlie who was definitely not amused.

"Well, Susan, shall we hit the road?" Joan stood.

"Yep, I've done all the damage I can do here," she laid her napkin over her empty plate and stood. "Enjoy your burgers... Boys."

The trio watched Susan and Joan exit before they took their seats at the counter.

"Where does she get off bein' sa snooty?" Charlie grabbed the menu and opened it so hard it almost ripped in half.

"I mean, Charlie..." Leroy leaned in to see by Frank. "Yer face is... well, Charlie ya still look pretty bad, you both do."

"Dammit, Leroy will you quit with that," Frank took a menu and started pouring over the possibilities while his stomach growled.

"Man, oh man," Leroy studied the menu with awe. "I always have a hard time decidin' what kind a burger I want."

"You always say that and end up orderin' the same one," Frank was hungry and drunk, not a good combo.

"Yeah, well, I like that one."

"Then why do you always say you have a hard time choosin'?"

"Man can choose whatever kind a burger he wants," Leroy turned his attention back to the menu.

"I know what I'm havin'," Charlie announced to the room at large.

Judy walked out of the kitchen with an order of burgers and told the boys she'd be right with them.

"Damn, those burgers looked good!" Leroy's face was twitching a little.

"Okay, fellas, what can I get'chya?"

"I'll have the Mexi Burger with extra jalapenos," Charlie put his menu back, satisfied with his order.

"I'm gonna try the Double Bbq'd Bacon Burger," Frank licked his lips.

"What'll it be for you hon?"

Leroy took one last longing look at his menu and ordered. "I'll have Valley Burger."

"Dammit, Leroy... I told you you'd get the same one. Every time you pour over that menu and order the same damn thing. Why do you even bother lookin' at the damn menu?"

"Geeze, Susan, your boyfriend sure messed up Charlie's face," She came to a halt in front of Susan's house and turned off the motor.

"He's not my boyfriend, Joan," Susan smiled at her friend a little self-consciously.

"C'mon, Susan. He's been your boyfriend as long as I can remember."

"No... there's been too much time passed."

"You really believe that? I mean do you even hear yourself?"

Susan just shook her head.

"Really?"

"I'm fine with being friends," with that Susan got out of the car.

"You are so delusional."

"Good-night, Joan. We definitely have to go on another burger binge again."

"Count on it. Good-night, Susan."

"See you tomorrow at work," Susan waved to the retreating car lights and went inside.

"Damn, that was a good burger!" Charlie wiped his mouth and dropped his napkin on his plate.

"I think I have found my dream burger," Frank leaned back and let out a big, satisfied breath. "Man, Leroy, you sure are nursin' that burger," Charlie gulped the rest of his coke and belched.

"I like to enjoy my burger," he hunched protectively over his plate. "Not like you guys."

"I'm goin' out for a smoke. You comin', Charlie?"

"Yeah, I'd rather not have to watch Leroy eat."

"The hell with you, Charlie."

Charlie ruffled Leroy's hair and exited Judy's.

Judy came over and dropped the check in front of Leroy. "How is your burger hun?"

"Good... Really good," Leroy was caught with a full mouth.

"My cashier is on her break," Judy smiled, she sure liked to watch people eat. "I'll take care of it when you're ready."

"Okay," Leroy was still fighting to swallow. He grabbed his coke and downed it making things worse and he lowered his head till he was sure he wouldn't choke. Then he realized he'd been left with the bill...

After paying he shuffled out. "Hey, you cheap asses," he found them standing over by the truck.

"You know what I think?" Charlie exhaled a great plume of blue smoke.

"What's that Charlie? What do you think," Frank scowled at his cousin.

"Think... I was thinkin'... why don't we pay those witches a visit?"

"No, nope. Not me. No sir," Leroy was definitely not having it and let it be known right off the top.

"What's a matter, Leroy? You scared?"

"Hell yeah, I'm scared," He lit his own cigarette taking the smoke deep into his lungs. "Me an' Frank tried th-"

"Leroy!" Frank flicked his cigarette at Leroy sending a rain of embers sparkling over his shirt.

"Damn, Frank what the..."

"Don't say another word," He struck a menacing pose, and Leroy shrank back from the subject.

"What's he talkin' about, Frank?"

"Nothin', never mind him he tends to ramble."

"Whatever, Frank," Leroy smoked his cigarette.

"Charlie? Are you nuts?"

"Why? What could happen?" He threw his cigarette butt into the dirt. "They'll never even know we're there."

"I don't know, Charlie. What happens if they use their... you know... their witchy powers?"

"Are you serious, Frank?" Charlie started laughing until he lost his breath and started coughing.

"You laughin' at me, Charlie?" Frank turned on him. "You want me to finish bustin' up your face, Charlie?"

"Whoa, Frank, take it down a notch," Charlie wasn't one to back down. "I wasn't laughing at you."

"Well, what were you laughing at?"

"The notion of... 'witchy powers. It just sounds funny is all."

Frank backed off a little, but not all the way. Frank was never known for having a long fuse.

"So, what do you say, Boys? Up for a little adventure?"

"What tonight?" Leroy wanted to know.

"Charlie?" Frank was frowning.

"What" C'mon, let's get us a bottle an' just park at the end of their road and see what there is to see."

"That's it? We just park at the end of their driveway?" Leroy shook his head.

"Yeah, that's it. We just sit an' listen."

"I guess that wouldn't hurt," Frank was warming to the idea. "It's almost full moon."

"Shit, Frank," Leroy wasn't convinced. "Sittin' out... at the end of a witches' road at night...in a full moon?"

"I said almost full, Leroy."

"Just the same. I don't like it."

"You don't have to come with us, Leroy," Charlie was ready to go.

"Well, what else do I have to do anyway?"

"That's it, Leroy," Frank smiled at Leroy.

"What are we waitin' around for? Let's get us a bottle and hit the road," Frank was already in the truck, firing up the engine.

CHAPTER 32

As they pulled into the road leading to the 'witches' place Frank turned off the motor and the three men sat absorbed in the silence that surrounded them.

"Well," Leroy was getting anxious. "What's the plan, now?"

Frank looked over at Charlie who was studying the dark woods around them.

"Frank?"

"Leroy, just wait a second, will ya?"

"I think we should go out and scout around," Charlie got out of the truck and lit a cigarette.

Frank did the same leaving Leroy momentarily alone. Leroy sat there in the truck, his eyes darting all over the darkness as if he truly expected something to jump out at him.

"Hey, Leroy," Charlie leaned into the window and grabbed Leroy by the shoulder. "You too scared to come out?"

"N-no!"

"Well, come on out then," Charlie opened the truck door. "Nothing to be scared of out here."

"That's what you say, Charlie."

"Oh, c'mon, Leroy, let's get a move on," frank lit another cigarette and frowned at his friend.

"Alright," Leroy climbed out and stood nervously by.

"Leroy, did you remember to bring the flashlight?"

"I got it right here," Leroy retrieved the flashlight and turned it on.

"Dammit, Leroy don't shine the damn thing in my face," Frank took a swat at it, but Leroy pulled it away.

"Sorry, Frank, geeze I didn't do it on purpose."

"Okay, you two lovebirds keep your voices down," Charlie came around to the other side of the truck. "We don't want to wake the witches," he whispered.

"N-no," Leroy was visibly nervous.

"Alright let's go," Charlie started to walk into the darkness.

"Hey, wait for us," Frank and Leroy caught up with Charlie and they slowly made their way into the darkness of the forest guided by the small round beam of light.

"Hey, Claire, will you pass me that wine bottle?"

"Sure," Claire slid the wine to Veronica who refilled her glass.

"So, tomorrow night is the full moon," Jorden was putting the food away. She returned to the table and sat down pouring herself a glass of wine. "Think I'm going to drink this out on the front porch.

"That sounds like a great idea," Veronica grabbed the wine bottle and the three of them went out to sit on the porch.

"It sure is nice out, huh?" Veronica stretched in her chair.

"Yeah, I love this time of night," Jorden stood and gazed out into the darkness.

"What's that?" Claire got up and joined Jorden.

"What?" Veronica got up. "What do you see?"

"There," she pointed. "Do you see it?"

"Someone's out in the forest," Jorden took a sip of her wine.

"Wonder who it could be?" Claire wondered.

The three women watched transfixed on the beam of light that was dancing around out there.

"Think we should call the Sheriff?" Claire mentioned after they had watched whoever it was walking through the forest, for about five minutes.

"They are getting kind a close," Veronica didn't like not knowing who was lurking around on their place, especially in the dark.

"I'm calling the Sheriff," Claire announced and went inside to make the call. She returned to the front porch after a couple minutes and informed Veronica and Jorden that the Sheriff would take a drive over here and check it out.

Sheriff Thompson, having already sent Deputy Riggs home, arrived at the road to the girl's place and saw Frank's truck parked part way in, so it wasn't easily seen from the road. He switched off his cruiser and got out shinning his flashlight around the area. At first, he didn't see anything then, a light in the trees caught his attention. He started walking in the direction of the bouncing light and it didn't take long before he heard voices in the darkness ahead.

"I think we should head on back now," Leroy was really getting spooked.

"Ahh, give me that flashlight," Frank was getting a little freaked out but would never admit it. He took the flashlight from Leroy and shinned it into the woods. Just then he stopped and looked at the others. "You guys hear that?" He looked around nervously playing the light everywhere, in an effort to locate the source of the sound.

"Wha'd you hear, Frank?" Leroy wanted to know.

"Thought I heard somebody behind us."

"Frank don't play around," Leroy wasn't one to mess around when it came to scary stuff. He did not like to be scared, by anyone.

"Take it easy Leroy," Charlie stood still, trying to hear what Frank heard.

"There you heard that right?" Frank turned his flashlight off, and the three men waited and watched as a circle of light bobbed around in the trees not too far away from where they were.

"Who do you think it is, Frank?" Leroy stood close.

"Shh, I don't know," Frank's heart was jackhammering in his chest, but his wasn't the only one.

"Stay still, maybe whoever it is won't see us." Charlie squinted into the darkness but couldn't make out much.

And they waited, the sound of footsteps got closer, and a beam of light passed around them but they remained still even crouching down some. Then, after what seemed forever, the footsteps retreated in the other direction.

"Whoever that was is leavin'," Frank whispered as he stood back up. The others stood too and listened to the footsteps recede back to where they came from which, Frank observed, was where they had left the truck.

"What do we do?" Leroy wanted to know.

"We stay put," Frank's eyes were wild as he searched the darkness. "We wait til whoever that was gets gone from here."

"I'm with you, Frank," Charlie held his breath, listening to the night.

"I don't see any more lights out there," Jorden looked at the other two.

"Me either," Claire shook her head. "Hopefully who ever that was is long gone."

Veronica's attention was diverted to a dark shape in the woods. It was just at the edge of the trees, and it was dark, really dark.

"Do you guys see that?"

"What, Veronica? What do you see?"

"Out there," she pointed in the direction. "Over by that tree with the crooked branch."

Claire saw it right before Jorden's eyes locked onto it.

"What is it?"

"I've seen it before," Veronica said studying the dark shape.

"I-is it a bad thing?" Claire wanted to know.

"I'm not sure, Claire."

As they watched and tried to speculate it sped off. It was big and very fast, and dark, darker than the shadows of the night.

As soon as they thought it was safe to move Frank, Charlie and Leroy headed back to the truck. On their way something made Leroy look over his shoulder. Call it a premonition or sixth sense but he did and when he did, he started to shake with fear.

"You guys?"

"What is it now L..." Franks voice dropped off.

"What's the matter," Charlie looked where the others were looking and felt the blood drain from his body. "W-what the livin' hell's that?"

Nobody said a word they were riveted by the sight of the dark shape that was not thirty feet away. They were momentarily paralyzed with fear and indecision. They watched the dark form, which resembled black smoke more than anything, until panic finally took hold, and they ran. They ran as fast as they could until the truck was in sight then they really poured it on. Huffing and puffing as their lungs fought for air.

Once they made it to the truck they jumped in, and Frank tore out of there leaving a thick cloud of dust in his wake. It wasn't until they had driven a ways that Charlie noticed something on the windshield wiper blade.

"Hey, Frank, pull over a second will ya, there's something on your wiper there."

Frank cranked the wheel and came to a sliding halt while Charlie got out to retrieve what looked to be a card.

"What is it, Charlie?" Frank pulled back onto the road and floored it.

"Why, it's a card. Turn on the inside light so I can see it. It's a card from Sheriff Thompson," Charlie examined it and turned it over. "Hmm..."

"What the hell does it say, Charlie?"

"It says, 'I'll catch you boys later.'"

"What?"

"It says "'I'll catch you boys later.'"

CHAPTER 33

"Hey, Frank, stop by the store and I'll get us some beers."

"Good idea," Frank pulled into the parking lot and Charlie got out and went inside.

When Charlie returned with two cold twelve packs the trio of explorers headed home to consume it. They drove in silence, neither one was capable of comment as to what they had seen back in the witches' forest.

Their world at that moment was captured within the circle of the truck's headlights. The shadowy scenery passing on either side of the road was a blur. The steady drone of the engine lulled them into a state of hypnosis as they barreled down Route 44 toward home and a nice cold beer to help them forget the thing they all saw out in the forest.

It wasn't long before the slightly dilapidated sign announcing, Lindsey Mobile Home Park, came into view. Frank cranked the wheel and slid onto the gravel drive taking out a flamingo and part of a small picket fence. When their trailer loomed up ahead Frank turned in and killed the engine. The three explorers piled out and stumbled for the front door. They fell into their respective chairs and panted from the ordeal. Slowly they returned to their normal selves…

"Okay," Charlie got up and headed for the fridge with the beers. "Who wants one?" He stuffed the boxes into the fridge and brought three out, tossing them to Frank and Leroy before plopping down on his end of the couch.

———————————

Sheriff Thompson sat at his desk with the same nagging feeling; Why did his friend take his life shortly after the Henning murders? What did he see that would make him do such a thing? He got up and went to the file cabinet. He retrieved the report of the murders and thought it was funny that the smell of the fire still permeated the papers even though they were spared from the flames by their metal cabinet.

He dropped the folder on his desk, flicked his desk light on and slid into is chair. He stared at that folder for a long while, it's not easy to read about the details of a friends' death. With a deep sigh he turned the lonely lamp toward the folder and opened it.

There were the assortment of pictures and print evidence, but he turned those pages until he found the reports submitted by Deputies Ellis and Green. He spread them out then he took out the report submitted by his friend, Sheriff Dobbs. It was getting late in a long day, but he couldn't get over the fact that two reports were matching and one, Sheriff Dobbs didn't add up.

How could the Deputies see one set of evidence and the Sheriff missed it? Too many questions that would be better off answered with a fresher mind. Sheriff Thompson gathered up the papers and put them back in the folder. He scooped it up and was just going to slide it back into its place in the file cabinet when he thought of something, a key piece of evidence.

Where was the knife?

CHAPTER 34

Sam was awakened, from a deep sleep, by the sound of knocking. At first, he rolled over and tried to ignore it. The knocking grew more and more insistent, and he gave up, swung out of bed and flicked on the light. He found his flashlight and put his house coat on, following the ring of his flashlight as he descended the stairs.

About half-way down he stopped… The knocking stopped. He stood there in the semi-darkness listening to his heartbeat while his ears hummed with the effort to find just where the knocking had occurred. Then it started again, someone was at the back door. Sam headed that way flicking on lights as he went. When he hit the kitchen light switch the knocking stopped. He shined his flashlight at the door window, and for a brief moment, he thought he saw a face looking in.

Sam went to the door and opened it only to find a dark void. He caught movement off to the far side of his vision. When he went down the back stairs and shined his light around outside, he saw nothing.

He took one last look around before heading back up the stairs. As he was reaching for the door a fierce banging erupted in the front of the house causing him to drop his flashlight which went tumbling down the steps and going out when it hit the grass. He was left in nearly complete darkness except for the little light bleeding out through the kitchen windows.

He carefully went down the steps to retrieve his flashlight, his heart pounded as he stood in the chilly darkness hitting it against the palm of his hand. Finally, it came back to life, its beam hitting him square in the eyes. He was blinded for a second and waited for the bright circles to dissipate from his sight.

Once his eyes cleared, he stumbled back into the house where the banging was very loud and disorienting. When he reached the living room it stopped and again Sam caught movement out of the corner of his eye but, when he looked in that direction there was nothing. He was out of breath, his heart was really thumping in his chest, he needed to sit down for a second to gather himself. That's when the scratching started...

He rubbed his tired eyes and shined his light in the direction of the scratching sound. His head was throbbing, his ears were ringing but he couldn't see anything that would ease his mind. He was staring into the black abyss out the window. He got up, a little dizzy, and walked over to the front window cupping his hands to the cold glass to block out his own reflection and nothing. He couldn't even make out the trees twenty feet away, it was pitch dark out there.

Suddenly a pale face appeared in the window bumping the glass and just as suddenly it was gone. Sam stumbled backward tumbling over the little table at the end of the couch. He quickly scrambled to his feet and looked back at the window... nothing but a dark square in the wall...

The scratching moved to what sounded like the kitchen window and Sam was starting to get pissed off. He was beginning to think someone was messing with him... but who? It was the middle of the night.

"Veronica? Veronica!" Claire heard her sister somewhere outside crying. "Jorden," She called, "Do you-
"Yes, I'm up what's going on?"

"It's Veronica, she's outside," Claire grabbed her house coat, a flashlight, and went for the door with Jorden close behind. When they came out to the backyard, they saw Veronica sitting in the oak tree and she sounded like she was crying. Claire and Jorden rushed out to comfort her and something ran off, it was dark, very dark and they only saw it for a blink of an eye.

"Veronica?" Claire spoke softly as she approached. She pointed the beam of her light up at her sister.

"Veronica?" Jorden caught up.

"What's the matter?"

"What are you doing out here?" Jorden pulled her house coat close against the coolness. "Are you okay, what's wrong?"

Veronica wiped her eyes and looked down at her sisters as if she was seeing them for the first time. When her head cleared, she smiled self-consciously.

"I don't know what got into me…" she took a breath to compose herself. "One minute I was sleeping in my bed and the next I'm…" She suddenly realized where she was, and it shocked her. "Here…"

CHAPTER 35

As the morning sun slowly lit the Lindsey Mobile Home Park Frank, and the gang were grumbling under their covers. A knock at the door got their attention and each waited for the other to see who the hell was at their door at this hour. When nobody got up and the knocking got louder Frank pushed out of bed swearing.

"Hang on dammit!" he pulled on a t-shirt and threw open the door. "Miss Lindsey?" He tried on a smile, but last night's smoking and drinking didn't allow too much that was smile worthy.

"Frank Dobbs," She eyed him with contempt, a small wiry woman who chain smoked and watched soap operas. She took a long drag on her cigarette before she spoke. "You run over ma picket fence!" Her voice was too loud for the morning plus it was very raspy from a lifetime of cigarette smoking. From behind her back, she produced the destroyed little fence holding it up so Frank could see.

"Are you sure?"

"Frank, might I remind you that in the last six months you have run over six," another long drag and a cough. "No... make that seven of my flamingos? Seven flamingos!" She went into a coughing fit while Frank fidgeted at the door. "I put that, this picket fence up so's you wouldn't run over anymore of my flamingos," she thought and smoked. "You run over Toby."

"Toby?" Frank was rapidly losing interest in the conversation.

"Toby... My good luck gnome? He was standing next to the last flamingo you run over."

"Well, he wasn't all that lucky if he got his self run over," Frank was done listening.

"You listen to me, now, mister smarty pants," she took another long pull, the ash was about an inch long. "You don't stop cuttin' that corner I'll have ta terminate our contract."

"Whadaya mean terminate our contract?"

"What that means is you will have to move your trailer out of, the Lindsey Mobile Home Park," She stared defiantly up at Frank as if daring to him say otherwise.

"I will try not to cut the corner again."

"I appreciate that, Frank," she knocked the ash off the end of her cigarette and jammed it in the corner of her mouth. She gathered up her busted white picket fence and stalked of muttering to herself.

"What was that all about, Frank?" Leroy wanted to know as he pushed his way into the door jam in time to see their landlord walking down the road.

"Oh, she was all bent out'a shape because she said I hit her flamingo."

"Did ya cut that corner again, Frank?"

"I might have… but I'm not gonna tell her that."

"How about just takin' the corner a little wider from now on, Frank."

Frank didn't answer he just walked into the kitchen and stared into the refrigerator like a hungry wolf.

Another knock on the door produced a snarl from Frank who charged back to the door.

"Now Misses- Sheriff?"

"Mornin', Frank," Sheriff Thompson smiled at Frank.

"Somethin' I can do for you, Sheriff?"

"Matter a fact there is," Sheriff Thompson rested his forearm on the handle of his revolver. "If you and your buddies, want to keep nosing around at the Reynolds place we're gonna have ourselves a problem. You wouldn't want to find yourselves sittin' in my jail, would you."

"You drive all the way out here to the Lindsey Mobile Home Park just to threaten me, Sheriff?"

"I want you to stop by my office tomorrow… Whenever it's convenient for you."

"Now, why would you want me to stop by your office, Sheriff?"

"I'll tell you when you come to my office."

"Mystery man," Frank sneered at the aggravation standing at the bottom of his steps.

"See you tomorrow, Frank," without another word he got back in his cruiser and was down the road.

"We got nothin' to eat, Charlie," Leroy watched Charlie do the same thing Frank did not two minutes ago. "If that's what you're thinkin'."

"Guess it's time to make a store run," Frank declared slamming the door.

"Yep," Leroy nodded, half awake.

"Charlie get your head out a the fridge! We're goin' to the store!"

"What the hell'd the Sheriff want anyway?" Charlie wanted to know as he slammed the refrigerator door. Leroy was mumbling about something on the couch.

"Yeah, Frank what did that Sheriff want? What the hell time is it, anyway?" Leroy was stretched out on the couch.

"Time to get up, Leroy, we need to go shoppin'… That's what time it is. Now, get yourself dressed."

"I am dressed," Leroy sat up rubbing his eyes.

"Well, let's get goin' then."

"Geeze, Frank what the hell'd that Sheriff say to make you so fired up?"

"Forget it. Let's go, Charlie's buyin,'" and Frank was out the door into the blinding light of a new day.

"Are you feeling better, Veronica?" Clare looked a little confused. "It's okay now. Do you want some more tea?"

"No thanks, I'm fine…"

"What did you see? Why were you sitting up in the tree?" Jorden always had to make sense of everything even, though, sometimes things just didn't work out that way.

"Don't know for sure," Veronica took a sip of her tea and set the cup down carefully, her hands shook slightly.

"You must've seen something... I mean what would make you come outside in the middle of the night and sit in a tree?" Jorden poured herself a cup of tea and sat next to Veronica.

"Really don't know how to explain it..." Veronica lifted her cup to her lips but didn't drink. "It was dark... darker than the night... It pulled me and lifted me up on that branch... I don't even... I'm pretty sure my feet..."

"C'mon Veronica," Clare joined them at the table with half a loaf of bread. "Tell us what happened."

"Like I said I had the sensation of being pulled and when I found myself standing... in the dark... I... I was lifted... into the tree."

"That's crazy, Veronica," Clare took a bite of bread. "So, that's it?"

"It was cold... The dark... entity was cold, it scared me. Then, then I saw him."

"Him? Who?" Jorden reached for the bread. "You saw this black, entity... what did it look like?"

"It was very dark, like I said."

"And you said you saw... him. What do you mean, Veronica? Who is him?"

"The boy... the boy with no face."

CHAPTER 36

Morning found Sam sprawled out on the chair in the living room. One by one he opened his eyes and stared out the front window. The forest was still wrapped in morning shadow and Sam groaned as he pushed himself up out of the chair. He had slept in a weird position and his body was letting him know about it.

He shuffled into the kitchen and put some water on the stove. He was reaching into the cupboard for a coffee cup when he realized he was out of coffee. He spotted the rosehip tea which would have been good but this morning he needed something a little bit stronger.

He took one more pass in the cupboard and there it was a brand new one pound bag of coffee. He pulled it out, filled the coffee pot, and fired up the coffee maker. He stood anxiously by as the water started to bubble and punched the button when it said ready to brew.

He stepped out onto the front porch and settled back in his chair to watch the morning light filter down through the trees. He let his mind go blank, a thing he could do very well, and enjoyed his coffee. His body felt like someone beat him with a bat, his head wasn't exactly tranquil either.

When he finished his coffee, he went back in and cracked a couple eggs in the frying pan. Today was his day to pull off the *perfect* over easy eggs... It didn't take long before he had to admit that scrambled was how it was going to be...

After breakfast he decided to take a drive into town, he needed a few things at the store. Sam grabbed his keys off the peg by the front door and scooted into his beautiful new/old truck. He turned the key, and it rumbled to life which put a big smile on his face.

When he pulled up in front of the Springville Grocery Store his mood took a dark turn. Three trucks away from where he parked, he noticed Frank's truck and that is not a good thing, especially after the night he just went through. He hoped his cousin Charlie wasn't with him, but it was a very good chance he was.

Oh well, he thought, *can't try to hide from people in such a small town.* He got out of his truck and pushed through the front doors. He spotted Frank and Charlie right away over by the beer section as they towered above the isles. He didn't see Leroy because he was too short although Sam was sure he was lurking around there somewhere.

Sam went in the opposite direction and put his mind on the task at hand. Once he got everything he needed, he headed for checkout where he ended up two customers behind the three amigos. At first, they didn't notice him but then Leroy forgot something and when he turned, he saw Sam standing quietly at the back of the line. He quickly turned back and whispered his discovery to Frank and Charlie who glowered in Sam's direction.

The three finished paying for their beer and left the store but, not without shooting Sam one more hard look. When Sam walked out the front door, he was met with a terrible blow that cracked loudly in his head. He stumbled but managed to hold on to his grocery bag. Before his vision could clear another blow smashed into him causing him to wince in pain as he felt like his whole right side had shattered.

A crowd of onlookers had assembled, and Sam was struggling to catch his breath. He dropped his bag and faced the blurry image of Frank who was winding up for another strike. Sam caught Frank's arm under his elbow causing him extreme pain. He quickly tucked his elbow trapping Frank's arm and struck him with a quick series of devastating blows to his face finishing with a punch to his ample stomach which proved too much for Frank who slumped down the wall in front of the store.

Before Sam could react, Charlie was on him pounding him until he made a mistake of letting up for a second to catch his breath, that's when Sam smashed him hard in his already bruised face sending him down in an unconscious heap. By now a large crowd had assembled including Susan who had come around the corner just as Charlie was going down. She stopped frozen by the scene of violence.

Sam was bleeding from a cut over his eye and had a cut lip. Frank's face looked like hamburger as he sat propped against the wall and Charlie was out. He didn't look much better.

Sam ignored the spectators, picked up his grocery bag and went over to Frank who put his hands up defensively. He grabbed him by the front of his shirt and lifted him.

"I don't know what your problem is with me," Sam whispered menacingly. "But you ever come at me again I will kill you." He pushed Frank back down. "Out of my way, Leroy." Sam walked to his truck, got in and drove away. Those people standing close by stood in silent shock. They all heard what Sam said, and a murmur spread through the rest of the crowd.

Susan stood in her own state of awe. The look on Sam's bloody face was nothing she had seen in him before, or anyone for that matter. She saw a face that was void of emotion, a face with the look of cold violence... and pain, and it scared her. The thoughts that swirled in her head at that moment were, she was sure, the same thoughts everyone else standing there was having.

Susan felt a sense of dread as her stomach did flop-flops. She made her way out of the thinning crowd and went back to her car. She wasn't even thinking of checking on Sam... No, that expression on his face scared her, made uncomfortable thoughts sneak into her head, that scared her also... *'He disappeared right after... 15 years... where did they take him?'* By the time she reached her car she heard the sirens.

The Sheriff arrived to find two of his favorite people severely beaten. One thing was sure there was no shortage of witnesses. He called for medical and interviewed the bystanders while the paramedics worked on getting Frank and Charlie stabilized. He was not surprised by the consensus of the crowd who described what he already believed to be the case but, when some of the people told him about what Sam had said to Frank, Sheriff Thompson became concerned.

CHAPTER 37

The drive home was painful. Sam had zero adrenaline running through him when he was attacked so there was nothing to take the edge off the punches. His right eye was watering, blood was drying on his face. His right side was bad. He had no doubt he had a couple broken ribs. He pressed on the gas and the truck shot down the hi way the speed felt so good he had to brake hard when his road passed. Finaly in his driveway sitting in front of his house he let out a deep breath and turned the truck off.

Sam slowly opened his door and just as gingerly slipped to the ground. He took a second while stars danced before his eyes. He made it to the porch and took a chair. His head was pounding, and he could feel his face swelling.

"You know," Sheriff Thompson took a step back as watched Charlie get bandaged up. Frank was next and he looked like he could use a couple stitches.   "You'd think you boys were smarter than to mess with Mister Henning. I mean I would'a thought after he gave Charlie there that sound beatin' that well, that would a been the end of it."

Frank made a face but didn't say anything.

Deputy Riggs entered the doctor's office and made a low whistle when he saw the carnage visited on Frank and Charlie.

"Ah, Deputy, I want you to take these two... gentlemen to the jail and make them comfy till I get back. I'm going to go out and check on Mr. Henning. Shouldn't be too late."

"Be glad to Sheriff," he smiled at the two banged up tough guys. "I'll see you back at the office."

"Alright, you boys be good now. Hey, Frank, at least now you'll be able to keep our appointment tomorrow." He left Charlie and Frank to their bandages and stitches and walked out the door to his cruiser. He drove down the hi-way wondering what he was going to find. Frank and Charlie were pretty messed up he hoped Sam was in a little better condition since, according to all accounts he was attacked.

He pulled up in front of Sam's house and got out. Sam was sitting out on the front porch and stood when he saw the Sheriff get out of his car.

"Well, young man, looks like you had another run in with your friend."

"He's no friend of mine Sheriff," Sam answered simply. He was holding a towel with ice to his face.

"I just left Frank and Charlie at the doc's."

Sam shrugged but didn't say anything.

"I have several statements and all of them said pretty much the same thing. That Charlie and Frank attacked you when you exited the store. Would you like to add anything?"

"No."

"Do you want to press charges?"

"No."

"Do you need medical attention? I can have Melissa come out to check on you."

"Don't trouble yourself, Sheriff."

"Oh, it's no trouble."

"No thanks. I can take care of myself."

"That I have no doubt about but, looks like you have a nasty cut over your eye."

"It's nothing."

"Okay, well…"

"I just want to be left alone."

"That is entirely up to you, Sam," Sheriff went back to his cruiser but before he got in, he turned back. "There were quite a few people that heard what you said to Frank," he waited for a reply and got none. "Just to be clear, did you tell Frank that you would kill him?"

"I don't remember, maybe."

"Well, I'm here to tell you I won't tolerate threats like that... from anyone. Do you understand me?"

Sam sat back down. At that moment he didn't give a shit what the Sheriff had to say.

"As you probably have already heard I'm reopening the murder case involving your parents," when he got no reply he continued. "I would like you to stop by my office in a couple days, I would like to discuss some things with you. It's not a request, Sam."

"Okay, Sheriff but," an electrical current swirled through Sam's body and he gripped the arms of his chair. "I don't know what help I could be." His voice was calm, almost calculated.

"I'm sure we can find something," Sheriff Thompson smiled up at Sam then got in his car and drove away.

Sam watched him drive down the road then he got up and went inside. He leaned over the sink and took the towel away. Drops of blood dotted the white porcelain and spread out...

"Tell me what you see, Sam," a doctor was sitting across the desk. He was holding up a card, with ink splotches.

"I don't see anything."

The doctor put the card on his desk and raised another one.

"What do you see now, Sam."

"Nothing."

The images dissipated and Sam ran some water to clean the cut he had over his right eye. He was hurting and he was mad, not a good combination.

When Sheriff Thompson returned to his office, he was greeted by Deputy Riggs who informed him that Frank and Charlie haven't caused any more trouble. Sheriff Thompson hung his hat on its peg and sat down at his desk.

"Your shift's almost through, Ken. Why don't you knock off early."

"Sure Sheriff, I might just take my wife out for dinner."

"You do that," then as an afterthought. "One last thing before you call it a night..."

"What is it, Sheriff?"

"Would you mind dropping Charlie off at his trailer?" Sheriff Thompson reached into his desk for the cell keys.

"No problem, Sheriff," Deputy released Charlie and walked him out to his cruiser. Neither spoke a word on the drive out to the Lindsey Mobile Home Park. Deputy Riggs let him out and watched him until he entered the trailer. He drove out but, on his way, he was stopped by the manager who ran out waving her arms. She was wearing a blue bath robe fuzzy slippers and a shower cap. She was puffing on a cigarette.

"They run over my gnomes again," She leaned in as his window came down.

"I'm sorry what did you say?"

"They, Frank, he run over one of my gnomes again and I want you to do something about it," She demanded lighting a cigarette with the reminder of the one she was working on.

"Well, I... I certainly will mention it to Sheriff Thompson... first thing in the morning."

"Alright then," she seemed satisfied and stepped back taking a long pull on her cigarette. "See that you do, Deputy."

"Yes ma'am," he rolled up his window and drove away, turning his thoughts to a date with his wife.

When Susan arrived home, she was shaking. She went into the house, threw her keys on the kitchen table, and went straight for the wine bottle. She poured herself a glass without spilling any and went into the living room where she plopped down in her favorite chair by the front window.

Today, though, she wasn't interested in the scenery outside, she was thinking of Sam and how violent the whole event was outside the grocery store. The look on Sam's face... he walked right passed her, but he didn't see her. It scared her to see that look. It scared her bad. So bad she was afraid to drive over to his house to check if he was alright, which is what a friend would do... should do. She was afraid of him... afraid of what she was thinking now... Afraid of what the town must be thinking...

CHAPTER 38

"Why, what the hell, Charlie?"

Charlie stumbled into the room and collapsed on the couch. He didn't answer Leroy, just put his hand to his face gingerly exploring the damage.

"Damn, Charlie… y-you don't look sa' good."

Charlie responded with a low growl.

"W-wanna beer?"

"Yeah."

"Here ya go," Leroy handed Charlie a beer but stood staring which didn't go over well with Charlie who dismissed him with a stern look. Not that it held much of a threat, being as beat up as his face was.

"How come they let you out? I mean, how come Frank has to stay in jail and you don't?"

"Sheriff wants to have a talk with Frank tomorrow," He took a swig of beer and grimaced.

"Oh," Leroy went back to his baseball game.

After a while Charlie stumbled to his feet and grabbed another beer, but he didn't sit back down. Instead, he paced.

"Charlie? You alright?"

"Hell no! I'm not alright! I'm Pissed," he declared as he downed his second beer.

"Alright, Charlie," Leroy gulped nervously. "Just take it easy."

"Take it easy? Take it easy?" Charlie looked out the living room window, it was getting dark outside. "I'm gonna make him pay…"

"Now, Charlie," Leroy grabbed another beer and tossed one to Charlie hoping maybe it would cool him down. "Don't start talkin' all crazy. Okay? Charlie?"

Charlie gulped his beer down and threw the can, hard, against the wall. He went to the fridge for another and almost pulled the door off getting it open.

"Okay, Charlie, let's j-just settle down some, okay? Charlie?"

"You tell me that one more time and... and... I need another beer, my damn head's pounding."

"I'll get it for you, Charlie. Sit down watch the game."

Charlie wobbled over to the couch and collapsed. It wasn't but a few seconds before he was snoring, and that made Leroy feel a whole lot better. Now he can watch his game in peace. He plopped down in the over-stuffed chair, and he too was out before the 9th inning.

———————————

Sam was at his new BBQ, bathed in the yard light, focused on tending a sizzling steak. The world around him was quiet except for the occasional cricket or a light breeze that rocked the treetops. For the first time today he was feeling relaxed, sore...but safe. The smell of the steak was making Sam's mouth water. When it was done, he took it off the fire to rest while he dished up his potatoes and green beans.

Sam set his feast down on the kitchen table and dug in. When he finished with the dishes, he poured himself a glass of wine and went outside. He listened to the crickets and the occasional creak of trees rubbing together, and then, everything got quiet. Too quiet... It snapped him out of his thoughts, and he went to stand at the railing. He tried to pierce the darkness with his eyes but could only make out the vague shadows of the evening forest.

Somewhere in the darkness there was movement. It was very faint. Could be a small animal. Sam's ears were ringing with the effort to locate the sound which, now, seemed to be getting closer. The chimes tinkled ever so softly, and it startled him. He went into the house to retrieve his flashlight when he heard what sounded like the shed doors crashing open.

CHAPTER 39

Somewhere in the wee hours of the night Charlie slowly got up and washed his face in the sink. In the gloomy light inside the trailer, he could see Leroy sleeping soundly on the couch. He was feeling his way toward the door when he stepped on a beer can.

Leroy stirred and reached for the light washing the room in a bright white light.

"Hey, Charlie," he struggled to stand. "Havin' a hard time sleepin'?

"Where's the damn truck keys?"

"W-why would ya need the truck keys, Charlie?"

"Wanna go for a drive."

"A drive? Why it's… what the hell time is it anyway?" He went into the kitchen to look at the clock. "Charlie it's one in the mornin'. Where you gonna drive at one in the mornin'?" He scratched his head trying to reason it out.

"Tell me where the damn truck keys are!" Charlie demanded.

"I don't think it's a good idea to take Frank's truck," Leroy was nervous.

"I didn't ask you what you thought," Charlie was searching for the truck keys and not having much luck. He was getting angry and Leroy noticed.

"Take it easy, Charlie."

"Don't tell me what to do!" He snapped. "Just give me the damn keys, Leroy."

"N-no, Charlie," Leroy's face was doing acrobatics.

Charlie finally spotted the keys hanging on a peg by the door and he ripped them off the wall.

"Charlie, wait!" Leroy tried to block his exit and was thrown across the room. He quickly got up and rushed Charlie in a last-ditch effort to stop him. Charlie smashed Leroy against the wall so hard he slumped to the floor, unconscious.

Charlie was breathing hard from the ordeal and left slamming the door behind him. He started the truck and threw gravel as he raced away. As he rounded the corner of the trailer park, he took out Miss Lindsey's white picket fence, a flamingo, and two gnomes. He raced into the darkness fighting to keep the truck between the lines.

When he flew past the road, he was looking for he stomped on the breaks. He barely managed to make a successful U-turn and came to a stop against a tree in the cover of the forest. He sat for a second panting, his mind racing, truck motor rumbling. He turned off the truck, reached for the flashlight and headed into the woods. His first few steps were shaky until he got his feet under him.

His flashlight beam danced around as each new forest sound made him jump. After a short time, his flashlight winked out and he pounded it against his palm but had no luck with its revival. He was suddenly emersed in the half-light of a nearly full moon.

He stood leaning against a tree and tried to figure out where he was. While he continued to work his way through the forest, he sobered some and began to question his own mind. He didn't like being in the woods, never had.

Suddenly, he heard laughter. It was faint at first then, after a while, it got louder... closer. At one point the laughter was coming from all directions, Charlie was getting spooked. He tried to get his flashlight working again achieving the same aggravating result, so he threw it against a nearby tree where it shattered into pieces. Now, he waited in the gloomy light contemplating his next move.

The air around him grew cool causing him to shiver. Laughter erupted close to his right and he stumbled against a tree. The sudden cold dried the sweat on his body leaving him sticky and irritable. He was seriously getting scared, and he really didn't like that feeling.

The laughter stopped as an eerie silence settled over the forest. Charlie felt sick and held onto the tree for support. His head was throbbing, he had to sit down.

He heard movement behind him and struggled to stand back up. Cold wrapped around him like a death cloak and he shivered against it. Someone or something was laughing again, close by and Charlie flinched.

A dark form appeared out of the semi-darkness. It had no shape that he could make out. It was more like smoke... or fog but, Charlie had the terrible feeling it was neither. The thing was stationary at first, billowing and floating in the distance. Then, it started moving toward him, growing and spreading out into a frightening apparition.

As the darkness neared Charlie could feel the weight of it, the tremendous force it created. He felt his body snap causing him extreme pain. He screamed and screamed... until he couldn't...

CHAPTER 40

Sam shot out of bed when he heard a blood-curdling scream somewhere out in the woods. He took a second to still his fluttering heart. Whatever that was it didn't sound good.

He slipped into his jeans, pulled on his sweater and went downstairs to the porch. The night was chilly raising goosebumps on his arms. He scanned the trees and, even though the light wasn't great it wasn't bad either. He saw no sign of anything out there.

Hard as he tried, he couldn't see anything out of the ordinary. Then, laughing... to his left over by his truck. He heard it clearly before it stopped, and he shivered a little. The chimes tinkled lightly at the end of the porch causing Sam to jump. He swore to himself as he looked in that direction.

"What the hell was that that was screaming?" Sam wondered. He took one last look around but saw nothing, so he decided to try to go back to bed. Before he headed back to his warm bed, he went into the kitchen to get a drink of water. When he snapped on the light and went to the sink, he was startled to see a reflection in the window but... it was not his own. He took a couple steps backward shaking his head and when he dared look at the window again, he only saw himself, much to his relief.

At the same time on the other side of the forest, Jorden, Clare, and Veronica awoke just as startled as Sam. They raced around getting dressed and finding lights. They went outside and listened but could hear nothing different from the normal night sounds.

"What do you think that was?" Clare was the first to find her voice.

"I don't know but it sure sounded like a person," Jorden said, matter-of-factly.

"I agree with you," Veronica continued to stare into the trees. "That definitely was no animal."

They kept trying to speculate as to what it could have been.

———————————————

Leroy opened his eyes trying to focus. His head was sore, and he was a little disoriented. He managed to sit up and clear his head a little bit, but he didn't feel very good.

He finally stood and took stock of his surroundings. Then it hit him like a ton of bricks, Charlie! Charlie took Frank's truck! Who knows where he could be! Leroy was in full blown panic mode he had to do something.

He slipped into his boots, grabbed his coat and went out the door. He needed to get to a phone and the nearest one was a payphone a couple trailers away. He found it punched a few quarters in the slot and dialed the emergency number. Dispatch answered and contacted Deputy Riggs who was on his way. Leroy said he didn't know for sure where Charlie could be, but he had a pretty good idea.

When Deputy Riggs came to Sam's road he turned in. He didn't get vary far before he noticed Frank's truck parked in the trees to his right. Deputy Riggs got out of his cruiser to investigate. He shined his light inside the truck and saw it was empty.

He laid his hand on the hood and found it to be warm. Shining his light on the ground he could make out a set of boot prints heading into the woods. He notified dispatch as to his intentions and was in pursuit. A little way in he thought he heard something moving off to his right and he shined his light in that direction.

Laughter erupted on his left which startled him, and he pointed his beam in *that* direction. He felt odd like something was following him. Whatever it was moved fast. One moment it would be on his right the next he would hear it moving on his left... Sometimes it felt like it was behind him.

Deputy Riggs was plenty spooked; he even had his hand resting on his sidearm. And then the air grew heavy around him. So heavy that it was hard to breath. The treetops started swaying back and forth though Deputy Riggs was not aware of any wind. He looked up and saw darkness closing around him, he took out his gun, a nervous reaction, and back peddled but the darkness kept closing in. Slowly, its movement, clearly discernible against the half light of the night sky, undulated and changed shapes to the point where Deputy Riggs thought he might be sick. But then, it was gone. The air warmed, the trees no longer swayed against each other, and it was easier to take a breath, even though Deputy Riggs was breathing hard.

He turned his focus back the trail he'd been following. He was about to stumble onto to something that would haunt his dreams for a long time to come.

Just ahead, in the trees about fifty feet or so his light caught something he couldn't understand at first. He walked further, getting closer and still couldn't reason what he was seeing in his mind. Finally, he stood there with his light on what looked to be two arms and two legs only they didn't look right.

Deputy Riggs ventured closer walking around to the other side of the tree and was dumfounded by what he saw. There was Charlie wrapped around that tree backwards. As Deputy Riggs examined him in the round flashlight beam, he could clearly see the agony etched across his face when he looked closer Charlie opened his eyes and moaned causing deputy Riggs to fall backwards over a log.

He quickly sprang to his feet, pistol in hand, and shined his light at Charlie again. He reached for his radio and called it in. A sleepy voice answered.

"Sheriff, I-It's me, Deputy Riggs." Deputy Riggs was trying to keep his voice even, but it was a struggle.

"I recognize your voice Deputy," Sheriff Thompson sat up in bed. "What's got you calling me at this hour?"

"Sheriff, I got a call from Leroy. He said Charlie took Frank's truck..."

"Does this have a punchline, Deputy Riggs?"

"Yessir, Sheriff."

"Well, you mind letting me in on it?"

"No sir I-I mean yessir," Deputy Riggs caught his breath and proceeded. 'Sheriff, I'm out here in he woods around the Henning place and well, you're not gonna believe this."

"Try me," Sheriff Thompson was growing impatient.

"I-I found Charlie... he's in a real bad way. I never seen anything like it. He's wrapped around a tree." Deputy Riggs was very nervous and was shining his flashlight wherever he thought he saw movement or heard a noise.

"He's what?"

"He's wrapped around a damn tree... backwards. And Sheriff? He appears to be alive."

"Okay," Sheriff Thompson's mind jumped into action mode. "I'll get an ambulance over there pronto and I'm on my way."

"The truck and my car are just inside the trees at the beginning of Henning's road."

"You stay put Deputy we're on our way to your location."

"Okay Sheriff, we'll do. Oh Sheriff?" *Please hurry*, he thought to himself

"Deputy?"

"Aw nothing, never mind," He was going to mention the laughing but decided against it.

When Sherrif Thompson arrived he found both Deputy Riggs' and Frank's vehicles parked inside the trees. He got out and sniffed the cool night air then reached for his flashlight and headed into the trees.

He found Deputy Riggs easy enough.

"Over here sheriff," Riggs motioned with his flashlight beam.

"I'll be damned," Sheriff Thompson's breath hitched when he came around to where Deputy Riggs was standing.

"How the hell..." Sheriff Thompson shined his light on the unbelievable scene before him.

"I've never in my life..." Deputy Riggs' thoughts drifted off.

"Alright I want you to get back to the station and write a report while all this... whatever this is, is still fresh in your mind. You didn't see anybody else out here?"

"No, sir Sheriff. Nobody," he looked around nervously.

"Okay, Deputy better get a move on. Radio Melissa, on your way, have her get the ambulance rolling pronto."

"Will do Sheriff. Anything else?"

"I don't want Frank to know about any of this just yet."

"Will do Sheriff," Deputy Riggs took one last quick look at poor Charlie and faded into the night.

Sheriff Thompson watched his Deputy until he was out of sight then he turned his attention to the grisly scene in his light beam. He tried not to let it affect him in any way other than just another crime scene, only it wasn't not by any stretch of the imagination...

When Deputy Riggs walked into the Sheriff's Office he sat right down at his desk and started to scribble out his report. He glanced over at the cell that temporarily housed one Frank Dobbs who, thankfully was snoring away on his cot.

Sheriff Thompson came through the door a while later startling Deputy Riggs who was just finishing up his report.

"How'd it go Sheriff?"

"Well as can be expected, I guess," he hung his hat on the peg by the door and plopped down in his chair behind his desk. "How's our prisoner doing?"

"Sleeping like a baby," Riggs looked up and noticed the sun was coming in through the front window. "Geeze, what time is it anyway?"

"It's a little after seven," Sheriff Thompson had a form in front of him and a pen poised but, was having a hard time starting his report. The scene was just too unimaginable.

"How'd it go out there?"

"What's that Deputy?"

"I asked how'd it go? You know, out there?"

"Oh, yeah, well, it went... that's about all I can say for now," he scribbled down a couple quick notes then looked up. "Think I'll head on over to the Henning place. I'll be back in a while. Then you can go out on patrol. I need to talk to Frank when he ever wakes up."

"Will do Sheriff, I'll keep an eye on things till you get back."

"I shouldn't be that long," Sheriff Thompson grabbed his hat off the hook and was gone.

Deputy Riggs gave his report one last go over and put on the Sheriff's desk. He went over to check on Frank who was still out then found yesterday's paper and settled back to catch up on the news.

CHAPTER 41

Sam stood on his porch watching the lights flicker through the forest but was undecided as to whether he should go out and investigate. Suddenly red and blue lights filtered through the trees, and he decided to make some coffee. Even though he was sure they were on his property he opted for coffee because, as he was learning, tomorrow the news would be all over the place. After all it's a small town...

Sam held his warm mug between his hands as he listened to voices that raised just enough to hear every now and then but, he couldn't make out what they were saying. And once there was a horrendous scream causing Sam to spill hot coffee on his foot. He stomped around until the burn became an irritating sting then went inside for a refill.

When he went into the kitchen, he almost dropped his coffee mug. There, in the kitchen window was a very old dark face staring back at him and he let out an involuntary yelp.

"Shit!" Sam fell back into the kitchen table as he struggled to keep his balance. He got himself straightened up even managed not to spill the remaining coffee in his cup. When he looked back at the window, there was nothing...

The chimes began tinkling out on the front porch and there was a loud noise in the back yard. Sam was coming unglued. He never felt so frightened in his life. Even when he was... *no, no, no!* A voice screamed in his head, and he quickly focused on the fine steak he had for dinner, his awesome truck... anything to change his thoughts. Cancel the negative promote the positive. The chimes stopped which gave him some relief but that loud noise in the back yard...

Across the way the three sisters were awake and standing out in the cold grass watching the lights flicker in the woods and wondering what was happening.

"I hope Sam's alright," Clare said pulling her house coat tighter.

Veronica and Jorden stood silent as they watched, mesmerized by the flashing blue and red lights.

"It's an ambulance," Jorden declared. "I know it's an ambulance."

"I think you're right about that Jorden," Veronica agreed.

"Sheriff and Deputy Riggs cars are red only," Jorden couldn't take her eyes away from the lights as she speculated to herself what might be going on over in the Henning woods.

A cold heavy air settled over them at that moment and they shivered against it.

"What is this?" Clare wanted to know. As she watched a dark mass close in around them.

"I think it's," Veronica caught her breath watching darkness block out the sky overhead. "What took me to the tree the other night. It's…"

"Is it bad?" Clare was feeling kind of scared as a heavy chill settled around them, and she didn't scare easily. The dark mass suddenly lifted off the ground slowly moving away in a stop studder motion.

Laughter erupted close by startling the three women. They stood quietly, listening.

"What or who do you suppose that was?" Clare whispered to the others.

And there it was again, laughter, only it sounded a little farther away this time.

"I-I think it's the spirit of that little boy… the one in the blue bathing suit?" Something was definitely off. Veronica could feel another presence close by which sent a shiver through her body and Jorden noticed.

"Veronica? What is it?"

"I'm not sure but it's strong… and it's not good."

"I'm going inside," Jorden didn't wait for a reply.

"C'mon, Veronica," Clare had goosebumps racing over her body. "You feel something, what is it?"

"I don't know," Veronica scanned the area intently.

"What does it want with Sam do you think," Jorden called out of the kitchen window.

"It's tied to Sam's property and it's not... happy," She spread her arms out and started a slow spin as if trying to catch a stronger feeling of it.

"But, how do you know it's tied to Sam's place?" Clare was curious.

"I felt its presence there and told Sam about it. It felt much stronger over at Sam's place... I don't think he believed me..." Disappointment seasoned her words. "Shhh."

Something moved very fast over to their right, breaking off branches as it passed. Then there was laughter again but, closer, different, and the sound sent chills through the three sisters.

"I think we need to go back inside," Veronica was really shaking.

"Veronica what is it?" Clare took Veronica's arm. "You're shaking like a leaf. And you're cold," Clare wrapped her arms around her sister holding her tight. Jorden came out the back door to help.

"Okay, let's get her inside," Jorden took hold of Veronica's other arm, and they helped her inside the cabin. They sat her at the kitchen table and quickly put on some water to heat for tea. Once the water was hot Clare added one of her special herbal blends for a relaxing tea, and Jorden brought in a blanket which she wrapped Veronica with.

"Can you tell us what you felt out there?" Jorden asked after Veronica had a couple sips of tea.

"I-I don't know exactly what I was feeling but it was strong. I think it's trying to communicate with me but, I'm not sure why... exactly."

"You said it has something to do with Sam?" Clare took a seat next to her sister. "Why do you think it came here? To you?"

"I don't know Clare, I wish I did," she thought for a second. "That laugh? You both heard that laugh right?"

"Yes," Clare and Jorden answered.

"That laugh we heard tonight is not the same laugh we heard before. It was different... deeper... kind of... I don't know. Just different is all. I think it could be an imposter."

"An imposter?"

"A what?"

"An imposter. A mimic."

"But why?" Clare was having a hard time with the subject.

"Well," Jorden glanced out the kitchen widow. "Maybe we need to go out to our spot and do some clearings. Maybe it will come to us and communicate."

"The full moon is in two days," Veronica said feeling a little better. "I think we should try to summon whatever it is then."

"I think you're right, Veronica," Clare went to the stove, poured herself some tea and sat back down. "Are you sure you're up for this? I mean, you were pretty shaken up out there.

"I'm okay it just caught me off guard is all," she looked at her sisters to reassure them. "I'll be fine. We need to try to contact whatever's out there and find out what it wants."

CHAPTER 42

Susan awoke the next morning with a terrible headache. She groaned out of bed and shuffled into the kitchen where she put on a pot of water for coffee. She fell into a chair at the kitchen table and tried to get her eyes to focus. She almost lost it when she noticed the empty wine bottle in the other room. Didn't help her head any to see the awful proof.

Suddenly the pot issued a warning whistle before it escalated into an ear piercing high pitched shrill. Susan ran to the stove pleading with it to stop. When she slid it off the flame and it quieted down, she sighed with relief. She dropped a spoonful of instant coffee into her cup and filled it with hot water. When she turned for the kitchen table, she turned a little too fast and had to hang onto the counter till the room stopped spinning.

Once seated she held her face to the steamy mug and let it warm her. Her thoughts returned to the day before and Sam… She was so torn as to what she should do. She sipped her instant coffee while she tried to form a plan. Giving up on that idea she finished her coffee and took her cup to the sink. She needed to do something; it was her day off and she needed to take some kind of action.

Susan drove into town to get some breakfast but as soon as she walked through the door at Judy's she began to question her sanity. Her head was still throbbing, and she still had a tiny case of the whirlies so she slid into the booth closest to the door. The place was packed and buzzing. Only instead of everyone discussing their own topics, which would have been normal, everyone was only focused on one… Sam Henning, what he did and what he said. Sam Henning's name was moving through the restaurant faster than a grease fire.

"Good morning, Susan," Her thoughts were interrupted buy the waitress waiting patiently, order pad in hand. "Rough night darlin'?"

"Is it that obvious Grace?"

"Naw just don't make eye contact with anybody," she kidded but, Susan was slow on the pickup. "What can I getch'ya?"

"A cup of turbo coffee and some eggs, bacon…Oh hell, give the number three."

"I'm on it. Be right back with your coffee."

"Thanks Grace," Susan's ears were humming as she tried to sort out the conversations erupting all around her. It was so unusually loud, even for breakfast at Judy's. It was *Sam* this and *Sam* that but mostly the rest of the conversation just kept melting into each other. It was hard to make out what all was being said.

Their tone and their inflections were enough for her to get the gist of what the themes were.

"Here ya go hon, this ought to perk ya up some," Grace returned with a steaming mug of coffee. She noticed the look on Susan's face. "Pay no attention to that nonsense." She smiled and spun off in another direction.

As Susan slowly sipped, she noticed a few people gesturing in her direction which made her shift in her seat. What seemed like a good idea at the time was slowly becoming an uncomfortable situation. Even so Susan was hungry and that is what kept her focused on the plan… which she hadn't really figured out yet. But food first…

After she finished her breakfast paid and rose to leave. All eyes were upon her, their conversations quieted momentarily. Susan shrugged her shoulders and pushed out the door.

Susan stood just outside the front door warming in the morning sun. She looked up into the trees that lined the street and smelled the fresh pine scented air. She headed for her car and was met by Leroy who were leaning against her hood.

"Hey Leroy," Susan was not happy, and her expression let that be known. "Wanna get off my car?"

"Hey, is that any way to talk to someone who just wants to say hi to you?"

Susan was rapidly losing patience; it had already been a lopsided morning. "I'm kind of in a hurry so..."

"Yeah, okay Susan," Leroy stepped away from her car for which she was grateful.

Leroy jumped into Frank's truck and raced off in a cloud of blue smoke. He made a quick stop at The Springville Grocery Store for some much-needed beer an off he sped to the Lindsey Mobil Home Park.

CHAPTER 43

Sam finished his coffee, the last half had gone cold, and he downed it anyway. He was trying to focus on something constructive to tackle. Some easy around-the-house project. He went upstairs and got dressed then stood out on the porch scanning the yard. He finally decided to tackle the yard around the house. He went to the shed and remembered he needed the key.

Once the key was found he wiggled it into the lock, and it snapped open. He stood before the doors and was assailed by the weirdest feeling of regret. He took a step back and looked around as if getting his bearings, he felt lost even though he was in his own yard. It was an unsettling feeling to say the least.

He waited until the world around him stopped spinning then he looked at the shed doors again, weighing the odds of a good outcome. Taking a deep breath, he grabbed both door handles and pulled them open. The air that followed was heavy and oppressive and Sam had to take hold of the nearest tree for support.

What the hell's wrong with me? He thought to himself as he leaned against that tree. Sam stood and faced the open shed once more scolding himself for such foolish thoughts. Staring into the gloom he noticed there was a lot of old junk inside. He wasn't sure what to do so he noticed some tools laying on the ground and decided to start by hanging those back on the wall. When he was done, he looked at the rest of the stuff without much interest because it was all old stuff. He decided to leave the rest for another day.

Laughter erupted off to his left and he looked in that direction.

Suddenly his attention was diverted by the sound of an approaching vehicle. He watched as the Sheriff's cruiser pulled into his driveway. He walked around the side of the house to see what was going on.

"Morning, Sheriff," Sam tried on a smile. "What brings you out this way?"

"Mornin', Sam," Sheriff Thompson looked over at Sam. "Mind if we talk for a bit? Want to talk to you about some things."

"C'mon up Sheriff," Sam waved him lead the way up the steps and they each took a seat.

"What is it you wanted to talk to me about, Sheriff?"

"Sam, first off your face... think you should have Melissa take a look at that cut?"

"It looks worse than it is," Sam replied dully.

"If you say so, Sam. As you know I'm reopening the homicide investigation..." He let his words sink in.

"I wouldn't know anything about any homicide, Sheriff."

"Sam, I'm referring to the murder of your parents," he looked carefully at Sam's face but there was no reaction at all.

"Like I told you before, Sheriff..." Sam took a moment to compose himself. "I don't remember anything about my parents or my past. Nothing..."

"You sure you don't remember anything?"

Sheriff Thompson looked for any sign of a cover up, a lie... but all he got was a blank.

"I can't help you, Sheriff."

"You know, Sam. Not everything burned up in that fire. There was a metal file cabinet in another room that was untouched."

"I wouldn't know Sheriff," the line of discussion was rapidly losing interest for Sam. It was making him very uncomfortable though he didn't have any idea why it should.

"You have any idea what I found in that file cabinet?"

"Not really but I'm sure you're about to tell me."

"I have a record of your medical history while you were away. I read all kinds of things about you in that file. But your medical history is secondary to me."

"Oh?"

"There's this one problem I have with the whole thing," he took a moment to gather his words.

"Don't leave me in suspense Sheriff," Sam had about had enough.

"It's the presumed murder weapon; a knife to be exact… it was somehow lost?"

Sam shrugged his shoulders and made a face.

"Both Deputies, Green and Ellis had a knife in their reports, yet no knife was ever recovered. Don't you find that a little odd, Sam?"

"Like I said…"

"Yeah, you have no idea…" Sheriff Thompson finished his sentence. He stood, "well, Sam, I guess I'll leave you to your morning."

"Wish I could be more help Sheriff but…"

"If you do happen to recall anything… you know where to find me," he went down the steps to his cruiser.

"Have a good day, Sheriff."

"Oh, I almost forgot," Sheriff Thompson leaned on his open door. "You see anything or anyone suspicious around here last night?"

Oh, I've seen plenty of suspicious things!

"Nope… haven't seen anything, Sheriff."

CHAPTER 44

When Sheriff Thompson got back to the station, he found his Deputy engrossed in the newspaper and his prisoner wide awake.

"Okay Deputy you can head out on your rounds now. I'll take over here."

"Yessir, Sheriff," Deputy Riggs grabbed his hat off the hook and headed out the door.

Sheriff Thompson drug a chair over next to Frank's cell and sat down.

"I trust you had a good night sleep?"

"You makin' some kind a joke, Sheriff?"

"Maybe."

"What do you want? How long you gonna keep me locked up?"

"That depends."

"On what Sheriff?"

"It depends on how good you are."

"I haven't caused you any trouble, Sheriff."

"Oh, but you have Frank."

"Huh?"

"You keep after Sam like you have, we will continue to have trouble. Now, scoot your cot over a little closer I want to talk to you."

"I like it here just fine," Frank let put a low growling sound. "What would you have to talk to me about Sheriff," contempt seeped into his words.

"Soot yourself, Frank," Sheriff Thompson continued unfazed by Frank's poor attempt at intimidation "I'm reopening the homicide case."

"What homicide case Sheriff? I haven't killed anybody."

"The homicide case I'm referring to concerns the death of Sam's parents." Frank's expression was a lot different from the expression he saw on Sam's face.

Frank was smug about the news, but Sheriff Thompson saw he was stung by it, even if just a tiny bit.

"Why Sheriff," Frank stood and gripped the bars of his cell. "Everybody knows that fire took everything," he scowled down at the Sheriff daring him to say different.

"Not everything was consumed in the fire... Frank. Have a seat."

"I don't know why you think this concerns me, Sheriff. It was a long time ago. I just can't believe they let him out," Frank reached over and grabbed a pillow which he tucked behind his back. He was completely uninterested in the topic of conversation.

"It doesn't concern you overall, I don't believe at this time but... I just can't help wondering a couple of things. I'm hoping that maybe you can help me out," Sheriff Thompson went over to his desk and picked up a couple file folders. He picked one out and dropped the rest on the floor by his chair. He took a moment, turned a couple of pages but he wasn't reading... he wasn't looking for anything. He'd already read it over three times and knew exactly what he was looking for and it wasn't in the file folder he held in his hand; what he found was it was written on Frank's face and what he saw there was puzzling.

"So," Frank was growing impatient. "What you got there, Sheriff?"

"Frank..." he took his time, wanted to get the words to fit just right. "Why do you think your dad sent you away? Right after the murders?"

"How should I know," Frank stiffened ever so slightly, Sheriff Thompson made a mental note of it. "I was just a kid. How would I know."

"You were what? 15? What, do you think happened to your dad?"

"Shit Sheriff!" Frank got up again and paced the cell. He wheeled around and growled, "I don't like these questions and I'm not gonna answer."

"You really don't know? Frank?"

"Like I said," He stalked over to the Sheriff and grabbed a hold of the cell bars again and snarled. "I don't have to answer your questions... even if I could..." he sat back down on the cot and adjusted his pillow. "H-he died in the fire... everybody knows that... Sheriff..."

"Nobody ever told you what really happened, Frank?"

"Sheriff?" Frank folded his hands over his chest and appeared to be contemplating a nap. "Can you please get to the point."

"That's what I'm trying to do but where is it?" Sheriff Thompson closed the folder and let it drop on top of the others. "What was the point of murdering those people? What was the point of sending both you and Sam away right after? What was the point of the fire?" Sheriff Thompson shifted in his chair and looked squarely at Frank. "And what was the point of my friend, your father dying in that fire?"

Frank returned to his lumpy old cot and sat quietly, so did Sheriff Thompson. After a while Sheriff Thompson asked another question...

"Frank," Sheriff Thompson stood and slid his chair back over by his desk then he returned to Frank. "Do you know where we found your cousin?"

"Charlie?"

"Yeah, Charlie. My Deputy found him wrapped around a tree early this morning."

"Wait... What?"

"Your cousin Charlie, according to Leroy, took your truck out when he was asleep."

"Did he wreck my truck! When I get out'a here I'm gonna-

"Your truck's fine."

"You say he was wrapped around a tree?" only after Frank learned his truck was unharmed did, he act like he was concerned about his cousin.

"Backwards."

"Say that again, I didn't hear you right."

"I think you heard what I said the first time."

"Backwards huh? What would do a thing like that?"

"We don't know yet."

"Is he alive? I mean…"

"Yeah, he's alive alright. He's in a severe state of shock. Something scared him pretty bad out there."

"Witches," Frank mumbled.

"What's that Frank?"

"Witches, Sheriff. I bet it was those damn crazy witches."

"Witches, Frank? Seriously?"

"You don't know, Sheriff. Those three witches that live on the property next to Sam's? They hold all kind a weird stuff out in the woods."

"Hmmm."

"Wouldn't surprise me one bit they put some kind'a witchy spell on my cousin."

"I wouldn't know about that Frank…"

"So, how long you gonna keep me in here?" Frank was done with the conversation and wanted a nice cold beer, really wanted a nice cold beer.

"I'll turn you lose as soon as I'm convinced you won't make trouble with Sam or anyone else for that matter."

"What about my truck?"

"It's around back in impound," Sheriff sat at his desk shuffling some papers. "Let's see here. Gonna cost you sixty dollars and seventy-two cents to get it out."

"Damn Sheriff that's robbery!"

"However, you want to look at it it's still sixty dollars and seventy-two cents."

"Geeze Sheriff," Frank studied his hands.

"Oh, I also had a visit from Opal Lindsey?"

"Yeah, my landlady... why?"

"It appears she wants to be reimbursed for the destruction of some of her property last night."

"So, what, I didn't damage nothin' I was in here all night. Why the hell would she want me to pay for somethin' I didn't do?"

"It was your truck, Frank."

"But I wasn't drivin' it," Frank was becoming irritated all over again.

"Opal said fifty should cover it."

"How now I have to pay... what? A hundred an' ten bucks? For something I didn't do. That's crazy, Sheriff."

"Well, you can pay or walk... it's all up to you Frank."

"Hell, Sheriff," Frank stood and stretched. "I can get the money, but I don't have it on me right now."

"That's okay soon as you get it you can get your truck back."

Sheriff Thompson opened his desk drawer and pulled out a set of keys and strolled over to open the cell door.

"I'm letting you out on your best behavior, Frank," Sheriff Thompson swung the door open and stepped back. "Anymore trouble from you and your stay could be a lot longer."

"Wait til I see that damn good for nothin' cousin a mine," Frank swore under his breath as he stomped out of the Sheriff's Office.

"Might be a while, Frank your cousin isn't going to be seeing anybody for a while."

"I got time," with that he slammed the door and was gone.

CHAPTER 45

Susan was just heading out when she saw the Sheriff's white cruiser pull into her yard. She went out the front door to greet him.

"Why, Sheriff what brings you out this way?"

"Good day, Susan," he called as he walked up to her front steps. "I just stopped by hoping to ask you a couple questions. That is if you're not busy."

"Actually, it's my day off so, I think I can find the time for a couple of questions."

"Mind if I come up?"

"Oh sorry, of course c'mon up and have a seat."

"Thanks," Sheriff Thompson took the offered seat and started with the first question. "You know Sam Henning?"

"I do. What's this about Sheriff?"

"I'm reopening the homicide case concerning his parents deaths and if anything, his involvement."

"I wouldn't know anything about that Sheriff."

"But you both were very close from what I've gathered."

"That was a long time ago and we were very young."

"What about now?"

"Now?"

"How do you feel now that Sam has returned?"

"I don't know..." she sat back reflecting. "Sam doesn't know me."

"What do you mean he doesn't know you?"

"I mean just that. He has no idea who I am or for that matter who we were."

"I'm not sure I understand what you're saying."

"I'm not either. It's like his whole past has been erased from his memory."

"I can tell you he was committed to a hospital specializing in childhood trauma. Maybe that's where the doctors... I don't know. I'm just beginning to try and put things together."

"Why the sudden interest, Sheriff?"

"The dynamics have changed for one thing. Because not only has Sam come back but Frank has too. Frank had a deep infatuation for you as I've gathered. But you only liked Sam."

"Okay..."

"Also, and maybe the most important reason for me is Sheriff Dobbs was a good friend of mine. And I'd like to know what the heck really happened the night of the murders and why my good friend not only took his own life, but it would seem he also tried to destroy any evidence of that night in the process."

"I honestly wouldn't know."

"Is it true that Frank Dobbs still has feelings for you?"

"Whether he does or not is his problem. I have never much cared for Frank."

"But you did go out with him once when he got back. Is that right?"

"Oh yeah, it was more out of pity than anything else. It didn't mean anything."

"Maybe not to you. But to Frank it was a sign," he thought for a second then continued. "Do you really think it's a good idea to lead someone like Frank on?"

"First of all, Sheriff, I did not lead him on. I only agreed to go out with him that one time. I have no interest in Frank, at all."

"But he clearly has eyes for you though."

"Like I said that's his problem. I'm not interested."

"Okay, one more question, Susan. Why do you think Sheriff Dobbs sent his son away about the same time as Sam was sent away?"

"Honestly Sheriff, I haven't given it much thought. When Sam's parents were killed, and Sam went away I was heartbroken. I honestly thought that I would never see him again. And now…"

"Now?"

"I don't know. He doesn't remember anything about me or the past."

"Alright, Susan. Thanks for your time."

"Sorry I couldn't be of more help."

"That's okay you've shed light on some things," he got up and shook Susan's hand then headed down the steps to his cruiser. "If you think of anything or just have a theory on anything don't hesitate to contact me."

"Will do, Sheriff."

"Have a good day, Susan."

"You do the same, Sheriff."

CHAPTER 46

"Leroy," Frank yelled into the phone. "I need you to get over here to the impound lot with one-hundred and ten dollars, pronto!"

"Wait, what are you talking about Frank? You sound funny."

"I'm here at the impound lot..." Frank was really trying hard to slow down. "I need you to bring me that money asap."

"Okay, Frank, I can barely understand you. How do I get there?"

"You can damn well figure it out since you let Charlie take my truck in the first place!" Frank was fuming as he slammed the phone back in its cradle.

Leroy was able to thumb a ride into town and meet Frank at the impound lot where Frank reluctantly handed the money to the clerk behind the window and drove to the store for a much need beer run.

"You go in Leroy."

"Why me?"

"'Cause I don't want people to see me like this."

"Ya do look bad Frank. Can you see out of that eye?"

"Never mind," Frank was hyperventilating. "Just get the damn beer and hurry up, my head's about to explode."

"Alright let's get out a here," Leroy barely got in and off they went in a trail of blue smoke. When they pulled in beside their trailer, they noticed a note flapping on the door.

"The hell is this?" Frank ripped it off the doorknob and practically tore the note open to read it. His head was really throbbing.

"What's it say Frank?" Leroy was standing behind Frank with the twelve pack in his hand.

"That bitch!"

"Frank? What is it?"

"Says here," he took a breath. "That we owe our landlady *more* money for some broken lawn ornaments. Damn that Charlie now he's costing me serious money!" Frank was reaching full-blown pissed off and that always made Leroy nervous.

"Okay Frank let's just get in the house before we bother the neighbors."

"Dammit Leroy I don't give a shit about the neighbors," Frank pushed by Leroy, tossed the beers in the fridge but not before he grabbed one for himself and plopped down on the couch. He swallowed the first one and called for Leroy to throw him another one.

"Geeze Frank slow down a little will ya."

"Just throw me another beer and mind your business."

"Here ya go Frank," Leroy underhanded another beer to Frank who ripped off the tab and downed it just as fast as the first one.

"Hey Frank, mind if I have one?"

"Help yourself, Leroy." Frank finished his second and crushed the can before tossing it on the ever-growing pile in the kitchen corner. "Get me another one while you're at it."

"What are we gonna do now Frank?" Leroy balanced his beer on one knee.

"For one thing I'm not gonna leave my truck keys where Charlie can find 'em… that idiot!"

"I was asleep otherwise I would a never let him take your truck."

"He's damn lucky nothing happened to it," Frank crushed his beer can as if squeezing the last drop out of it.

CHAPTER 47

When Sheriff Thompson left Susan went into her house and stood at the kitchen window. She watched the trees sway in the light morning air, birds flited from branch to branch...

Susan was in a quandary, she couldn't decide what to do about just about anything, so she poured herself a glass of orange juice. As she sipped and watched the forest out her kitchen window, she concluded that she had to see Sam. She wasn't completely excited about the idea because of what happened the other day, but she felt it was the right thing to do. She grabbed her keys on the way out the door and before she knew it, she was pulling into Sam's driveway, where she stopped. *Was this really a good idea? She asked her inner self as she listened to the motor idle away.*

She took her foot off the break and rolled ahead. Her heart skipped a beat when Sam's house came into view. There was no turning back when she realized Sam was standing at the side of his house watching her. She was relieved when he stepped out of the shadows and smiled.

"Hey you," Susan called as she closed her car door. "What are you up to, oh geeze," she gasped when she saw his swollen face. "Damn, Sam you... are you okay?"

"Yeah," he touched the side of his face lightly. "It looks worse than it is."

"That's good... because it looks bad."

"C'mon up," Sam went up the front steps and arranged the chairs, even though they ended up in the same place they started, he was nervous. "Can I get you something to drink?"

"What do you have in mind?"

"Well, let's see," he was smiling even though it hurt a little. "Too early for wine or beers..."

"Is it?"

"I don't know, what time is it anyway?"

"Oh," she checked her watch. "It's a minute past eleven. But I'm sure it's much later somewhere else."

"So... wine or beer?"

"Oh, it's much too early for wine."

"But you just said that it's-

"I'll have a beer if it's not too much trouble," Susan took a seat and smiled up at Sam.

Sam could feel his face warm.

"Beer it is," he disappeared and reappeared with two cold ones. "Here ya go, nice cold beer."

"Thank you, kind sir."

"My pleasure," they both took a sip. "So, what brings you out this way?"

"Oh... I guess I..."

"You what?"

Susan hesitated; she wanted to tell him how she was feeling but... it wasn't easy. So, she stalled by taking another drink of her beer.

"Hey, c'mon," Sam looked at her; *damn she's beautiful!* He thought at that moment. "It's okay. You can tell me."

"I guess I thought it would all be different, is all."

"Different in what way?"

"I wasn't prepared for you not to remember me... I guess I'm just a hopeless romantic I shouldn't have expected anything at all. I mean why the heck should I? It's been fifteen years."

Sam didn't say anything just sipped beer and contemplated the circumstances that led them to be sitting together on this porch thinking about the many years that had drifted by.

"Earth to Sam? Are you there?"

"Huh? Oh yeah, I'm here. Sheriff Thompson stopped by this morning earlier."

"He came by to see me too, earlier. Must've gone to your place after he came here."

"I really didn't have anything to tell him," Sam finished his beer. "Like I've said I don't remember anything past fifteen years ago." He thought for a second. "I sure wish I did. *"Sometimes I get theses random images..."* he thought to himself. *"Should I tell her?"* Sam took a second then continued. "He mentioned reopening a homicide case, but I have no idea why he would ask me about it."

"He was asking me the same things but, I, we, were just little kids. I really had nothing to add."

"But... do you know anything about a homicide?"

"I've heard stories. But I believe they're just stories."

"Can I get you another beer?"

"Yes, I think that would be good, thanks."

"Here you go," Sam handed Susan another beer and stood at the rail looking out at the forest.

"So..." Susan started and stopped in one word.

"So? You were going to say?"

"I was going to say... About the other day..."

Sam's heart sank, he had a feeling what was coming. He really hated losing his temper...

"Hey I didn't-

"I know you didn't start that fight, everybody in town knows who did."

"Then what?"

"You scared me," she took a long sip of her beer and waited.

"I scared you. How?"

"I guess it was... part of it was how fast you kicked the crap   out   of   Frank   and   Charlie..."

"And?"

"It was the look on your face when you stopped hitting Frank and were walking away."

"The look on my face scared you?" Geeze he was starting to sound like a parrot. "I didn't even know you were there."

"I know, I don't think you saw anybody that day. Except Frank and his cousin, Charlie."

"Sorry, I was taken by surprise and everything happened so fast."

"You should a gotten stitches on that eye kiddo," she scolded good naturedly.

"It's not that bad," Sam raised his hand to his right eye self-consciously. It did hurt a little still.

"I don't know what the heck got into them to attack you like they did. You want another beer?" Susan took his empty and went for two more.

"Actually? I'm thinking of switching over to wine and taking a couple thick steaks out of the freezer."

"I like the way you're thinking. I'm game, where's the wine cellar?"

They went into the house and Sam pointed Susan toward the wine cellar which was a cabinet above the kitchen sink. She grabbed a bottle while Sam dug around in the freezer for the steaks.

"Wine opener?"

"Oh, in that drawer over there," Sam put the steaks on a plate to thaw and Susan popped the cork on the wine. "I got the glasses let's go back out on the porch."

"This is good wine," Susan smiled at Sam then caught herself and quickly looked away.

"Every once in a while, I get lucky," he felt his face flush and quickly added, "and find the right one," oh boy it wasn't coming out right he thought. "Wine, finding the right wine."

"Oh," Susan was enjoying his obvious discomfort. "Yes, the right wine can be hard to find sometimes."

"Yeah," Sam couldn't breathe so he sipped his wine instead waiting for his heart to stop thumping in his chest.

"So, where were we?" Susan was starting to relax letting the wine do its job.

"Were we talking about wine?" It was a lame question, but people say lame things when they're nervous.

"You do have a bad memory," Susan kidded. "We were talking about…" she caught herself still not sure how to proceed… what to say.

Just then the chimes started to tinkle providing a much needed if not disturbing distraction.

Sam jumped and Susan saw that he was not happy. Then they came to a stop and Sam relaxed again.

"Well, that was interesting," Susan made a face. "It's funny they started up and there's not even a puff of wind. Sam?"

"Yeah?" Sam pulled his gaze away from the troublesome chimes.

"What made them do that?"

"I wish I knew," He felt himself start to relax again and refilled their glasses. "There's a lot of things that happen around this place that I wish I knew."

"Well, that's why I'm here," She took a sip of wine, and it went down the wrong tube which sent her into a coughing fit.

"Hey, you're supposed to sip that wine not guzzle it," Sam was laughing which caused a chain reaction. And then an uncomfortable silence settled over them. They just sat together not saying a word until Sam broke the silence with a question.

"Susan?"

"Sam?"

"What," he caught himself for a second. "Why would the sheriff…" He was struggling to come up with the right words. So, he decided on simple. "What did the sheriff ask you about?"

"Well," Susan lost her voice momentarily. This was the big one. The package had arrived and has yet to be opened. You couldn't just tear it open. It had to be opened with great care for what was inside was very delicate. "He told me about a homicide that happened a long time ago."

"Yeah, he told me the same thing. Only, I had no idea what he was talking about," Sam topped off their glasses and set the empty bottle on the floor. "Do you know what he was talking about?"

"I was very young," she decided to try and keep it less personal.

"So, you do remember something... He said there was a murder. I have no idea..." his thoughts trailed off. "Are you gonna let me in on the big secret?"

"Hey, you think those steaks are thawed. I'm getting hungry." She just wasn't ready to go back to that place in the distant past. She wasn't sure how he would take it. She wasn't so sure how she was going to take it.

"Oh yeah, the steaks." Sam shot up out of his chair. "I'll start the BBQ and-

"I can season the steaks," Susan was up grateful for the break. She was already feeling better. It was getting very close to the truth of things, and she needed more time to sort out how to tell him.

"All the seasonings are in the cupboard to the left of the sink," Sam called.

"I'm on it," Susan grabbed the empty bottle and went inside. She found the steaks sitting on the counter and located the salt and pepper. She was salting the meat when something passed by the kitchen window. She didn't really see anything, but something went by the window. Must've been Sam she reasoned and went back to the steaks. She put them on a plate and was washing her hands when she heard what sounded like a child's voice in the backyard.

She quickly dried her hands while she listened. There it was again but the sound was different like a record played backwards. It definitely sounded like there was a child outside in the backyard. Susan went to the back door and paused, *is this one of those things that Sam was talking about earlier... One of the things he wished he knew.* Susan thought to herself. She opened the back door slowly. The light was starting to fade, and she realized that the day had almost slipped by unnoticed. She scanned the trees that surrounded the house back there and found nothing.

Sam came in and found Susan standing at the back door.

"Everything alright?"

"Huh? Oh yeah, I mean I guess," she was stumbling. "I just had the weirdest thing happen... or couple weird things happen."

"And?" Sam wanted to know but at the same time he felt he might already know.

"I thought I heard a child's voice out here," she didn't look back at Sam she stayed focused on the trees.

"A child's voice..." his heart didn't know whether to sink like a rock in his chest or beat with joy knowing someone else has heard.

"Sam? Have you heard the same thing? Is that what you were talking about earlier? One of the things you wish you knew?"

"Yes."

"Do you have any idea what it is?"

"I have seen it..."

"Sam, what does it look like? Is... it really a child?"

"It's a small boy wearing a blue bathing suit."

"Geeze," Susan got the chills all the sudden.

"Is he a..." she couldn't form the question.

"He's a spirit," Sam left it at that for now. "Hey, let's get those steaks going. I'm sure the BBQ is up to temp. Besides I don't know if you noticed but what the hell happened to the day? You have to work tomorrow?"

"Nope, I'm free as a bird for the next... well, today and tomorrow."

"Nice, c'mon let's get these steaks on."

After they finished their steaks, and the dishes were washed Sam located another bottle of wine in his vast wine cellar in the kitchen cabinet and they relocated out onto the front porch. The light had dropped from the sky and stars could be seen as tiny lanterns sprinkled across the night.

"Nice job on those steaks mister," Susan sipped her wine and settle into her chair. "Good wine too," she was feeling pretty good.

"Yeah, I'm stuffed," Sam pulled his chair closer to the rail so he cold prop his feet up. "So, I sure have had a good day, all things considered," Sam studied his wine glass feeling shy all the sudden.

"Me too, Sam," Susan felt her face flush and was thankful for the lack of light so Sam wouldn't notice. "I'm really glad I came over."

A loud bang suddenly ended the moment Sam was on his feet.

"What was that, Sam?"

"I'm not sure," it was a small lie, he didn't want to alarm her, but he was pretty sure what it was and he intended to investigate. "Wait here."

"Like hell I will," Susan declared. "I'm going with you."

Sam grabbed a flashlight and down the steps they went. Once they came around the corner of the house Sam's heart stopped. The shed doors were open.

"What is it, Sam?" Susan had a hold of his elbow.

"The shed... the shed doors are open," he let his flashlight illuminate the ground and it wasn't long before he found the lock. It was twisted out of shape and Sand picked it up. "Here's the lock."

"I don't think locks are supposed to look like that," Susan looked from the lock to the open shed and for the second time goose bumps raced over her body. The air even seemed to get cooler. "Do you feel how cool it is right now?"

"Yeah," Sam still held the lock loosely in his hand. He thought hard before he pointed his beam of light into the open shed. His light, as bright as it was, couldn't penetrate the darkness inside.

"What do you think did this," Susan marveled at how the beam of the flashlight got swallowed up by the darkness inside.

"It's happened before," Sam tossed the useless lock into the darkness of the shed. "Had Hank replace it the last time."

"Geeze," was all Susan could say. "Oh, sorry," she realized she had a death grip on Sam's elbow and released it.

"Let's go back on the porch," Sam led the way with the flashlight. When they got back on the porch, they discovered the bent lock sitting on the top rail of the porch.

"Sam," Susan was the first to spot it.

"I see it," Sam frowned at the lock, he grabbed it and hurled it into the woods.

"How do you suppose that got there?" Susan wanted to know.

"I can't begin to answer that question," he sat back in his chair and drained the remainder of his glass of wine.

"Sam," Susan had a question on her mind, heck she had a lot of questions on her mind who was she kidding?

"What is it, Susan?" Sam replenished his glass and topped off Susan's.

"Sam," she was stumbling on her words again, it was frustrating. "I was wondering… I mean it's getting late."

Sam's heart slammed against his sore ribcage as he waited for her to finish her sentence.

"Would you mind… how do I say this…"

"Just say what's on your mind."

"Would you mind if I stayed the night?" There it was her words flowed out like a flashflood, and she waited for his reply ready to go or stay.

"I have to think about that," he smiled.

"I don't mind sleeping on the couch," she offered.

"I got dibs on the couch you can have my bed."

"Are you sure?"

"Positive, I have an extra pair of pj's and the couch in the library is very comfortable."

"Alright then," she sat back in her chair much relieved. "Think I'll finish my wine and maybe you can show me where your bedroom is and those extra pj's."

"Sounds good," they settled back in their chairs enjoying the last of the evening.

"What is that?" Susan jumped out of her chair like it was electrified.

"What's the matter?" Sam was beside her in a heartbeat. "What do you..." His words trailed off like a puff of smoke, and his heart sank.

"That," Susan could feel her pulse racing through her body. "Right over there do you see it?"

There was a dark mass moving studder step through the trees not twenty feet away.

"I see it," Sam wasn't scared as much tired of the cat and mouse game. He wanted to know what it was... he wanted to know why people in town looked at him like they did... he wanted to know what the hell happened in his past and why the hell he couldn't remember a person like Susan who was supposedly very close to him in the past. It was aggravating.

"Sam. Have you seen this before?" she didn't look away from the shape in the trees that was darker than the night. "Have you Sam?"

"Yes," he answered in a voice that he'd never heard before. "I have seen it before but..." He paused mid-sentence as the dark mass dissipated. "I don't know what it is..." he wondered if he should tell her. "The women who live over that way. One of them seems to know what it is. Veronica, I think that's her name."

"I know Veronica, not well but I know her. What did she say?"

"She came over one day and said she felt unsettled spirits," Still didn't make much sense. As many times as he said it, it still didn't. Something was happening, that was for sure.

"Would it be alright," Susan took a gulp of wine. "I mean, I'm kind a spooked." She watched the dark mass disappear and felt somehow lighter.

"You were saying?" Sam looked at her though the light had pretty much left the day.

"I mean if we were wearing pj's..." Her words were playing hide an' seek and she was, at that moment, unable to find them. "Would it be alright if you slept with me instead of downstairs? I know I sound like a scaredy-cat and I'm not usually but... I sound crazy...I know," she gave up.

"I'm fine with that, Susan," he smiled over at her silhouette, "as long as you don't get any ideas."

They laughed, although a bit nervously. The mood had once again lightened. Sam fixed Susan up with a pair of pj's that weren't even close to fitting her, he put on his other ones, and they met back down in the kitchen for a cup of rosehip tea. They went back out onto the front porch to look at the stars.

"Sam?" Susan looked over her teacup. "Did you happen to notice when you shined your light into the shed... it didn't go in? I mean that flashlight of yours is bright, but it wouldn't shine past the doorway."

"I noticed," Sam sipped his tea carefully. "I've noticed it before."

"Why? Why doesn't it?"

"I wish I knew," Sam set his tea down at his feet. "Something is happening here, and I don't have a clue what it is except..." he paused when a shape ran through the trees. "Did you see that?"

"I missed it, what did you see?"

"A shadow... it ran off that way. It was fast. I've seen it before..." his voice trailed off.

"Did you say a shadow? How could you see a shadow at night?"

"That... whatever it is," he took a moment. He could take a hundred moments, and he still couldn't explain it. "Is darker than the night."

The chimes started to act up again. Lightly at first then they went wild like an invisible hand was knocking them around. Sam was first on his feet, Susan wasn't far behind. She stood close watching the chimes fly around on their hook. Both stood mesmerize by the frightening spectacle.

A loud bang brought them out of their stupor. It sounded like the shed doors were banging open and closed... open and closed.

"I'm going in the house," Susan declared. She was scared, more scared than she could remember ever being before. "You coming, Sam?"

"Yeah," Sam picked up his teacup and flung the remainder of his tea in the bushes. He went to the chimes which had stopped completely and ripped them off their hook he leaned over to see the shed doors coming to a halt and he tossed them into the shed.

As soon as they were both inside everything stopped. Even the light breeze had gone everything was strangely quiet all the sudden.

"I'm ready for bed," Sam was feeling drained.

"Me too, I'm not staying downstairs alone," she followed Sam up the stairs and into bed where they laid staring at the ceiling. "Veronica, she's a witch you know."

"Actually, she's a spirit talker," Sam put his hands behind his head.

"Okay I've heard that term before," Susan was getting sleepy and turned over on her side. "Good night, Sam."

"See you in the morning, Susan."

Sometime in the early morning hours the house started to tremble and then it shook.

"Was that an earthquake," Susan awoke blinking into the darkness. It happened quick like something slammed into the side of the house. They both sat up waiting and listening. Someone ran down the hallway and down the stairs. Sam was out of bed even before he realized he was out of bed.

"What was that?" Susan sat up straighter rubbing her eyes.

Sam didn't say a word he ran out of the bedroom and was gone. She heard him padding down the stairs then it got quiet. Not a sound, it was eerie. Goosebumps erupted all over Susan's body and she was shaking. Still, she waited for a sign. It had been a while since she heard anything and began to wonder if she should go check on Sam.

She stood and tiptoed to the bedroom door where she peeked around the corner to discover a dark empty hallway. Carefully and as quietly as she could she crept down the hallway.

She made it about halfway before the walls started to slant inward and outward like a pulse. The floor rippled under her bare feet causing her to jump. She tried reaching out to steady herself, but the walls were impossible to touch. She felt that she was losing her mind and started to scream. Then, it stopped leaving her with a wicked case of vertigo.

She made it the top of the stairs where she stood catching her breath and peered down into the gloom below. Nothing. Not a sound...

"Sam."

Silence...

"Sam?" she called in a voice almost a whisper. No answer. She slowly made her way down the stairs where she saw a shadow standing in the middle of the living room. Her hands scrambled to find the light switch on the wall next to her and when she flicked the switch, she saw Sam standing there; arms limp at his side. He was looking at the floor.

The house started to tremble again; ceiling lights swung, doors opened and slammed shut, a window suddenly shattered in the kitchen. The house was in the process of shaking itself to pieces. Susan and Sam stood frozen in the eye of chaos. Curtains lifted as if the windows were open and there was a strong wind coming in. Another window shattered.

Then it was over... The ceiling lights slowly swung to a stop the doors gently closed, and everything returned to the way it was. As if nothing had happened.

"Sam. Are you alright?" She stayed where she was because he didn't look right. Like he was in some kind of trance or something. "Sam," she whispered again, and he slowly turned her way.

"I saw it," he said more to himself than to Susan.

"What Sam. What did you see?"

"The..." he hesitated. "The body on the floor..."

"Sam let's go outside an get some air," the air inside the house had become heavy making it hard to breathe.

"Okay," he answered in a weak voice that broke Susan's heart. They went out onto the front porch just in time to see morning sun light up the forest with the first warming rays of a new day. Susan stood behind Sam with her arms wrapped around his muscular body, he was still trembling some, so she just held him.

After a long silence Susan spoke.

"Sam?"

"Yes," he exhaled slowly trying to calm the whirlwind in his head. He was enjoying Susan's warmth even though it was hurting his ribs a little.

"What do you think about talking to Veronica again?" She felt his body tense for a second then relax. "I mean it can't hurt to see what she thinks of… this."

"I don't know," Sam turned to look at Susan.

"I think she might be able to help you."

"How can she possibly help me? Can she help me remember what happened when I was young? Can she change the way people look at me when I'm in town? Can she tell me what I saw in there… on the floor?" He realized he was raising his voice. "I'm sorry Susan I didn't mean to take this out on you. I know you're trying to help. It's just that… I don't know maybe I am crazy."

"You're no such thing Sam Henning," she scolded. "You put that notion right out of your mind because you are not crazy."

"You're probably the only person who thinks that way."

"No. There are others who see things the way I do."

"I wish that was true," Sam went to the railing and looked out into the warming forest.

"It is true Sam," She went and stood beside him. "So… what do you think?"

"About what?"

"Hello… earth to Sam…" she smiled up at him. "What do you think about talking to Veronica?"

"I'll think about it."

"Okay, Sam you do that," She let the subject drop. "So, what are your plans for the day?"

"I haven't given it any thought," he answered trying to turn his mind to other things. "I was thinking of maybe putting some stuff together and we could go have a picnic somewhere."

Just then Susan's horn started honking. "Oh, geeze that's my phone," she went down the stairs and got in her car to answer it. When she came back, she wasn't smiling.

———————————————

Earlier that morning Sheriff Thompson received a call from the hospital. When he got there, he was met by the doctor in charge. He was led to an office where he was informed of recent developments.

"So, you're saying he died of..." he paused mid-sentence as he tried to formulate what he had just been told. "Are you sure he didn't die from his injuries? I mean he was in bad shape when we got to him."

"I am one hundred percent sure, Sheriff. This man died of fright."

CHAPTER 48

"What's the matter? Is everything alright?"

"Yes and no not really," she was back on the porch and slumped in one of the chairs.

"Well, what is it?"

"That was Daphne," Susan looked up at Sam. "She said that Charlie died last night. Everybody's talking about it."

"Are you okay?"

"I'm fine as can be, yes, I'm good. You?"

"Yeah, I'm good," He tried to keep the shake out of his voice when he answered.

"Well," Susan got up and stretched. "I have to do some errands… will you be okay here?" She looked over at Sam and smiled.

"I'll be fine," he got up and took their coffee cups inside then came back out.

"Well, I guess I'll be going then," Susan started for the stairs and Sam caught her arm. "What is it, Sam?"

"I…" he stammered for a second. "I'm really glad you came over… even though it was not much fun."

"Let's just say it was interesting."

"That's one way to put it," Sam looked into her green eyes and lost his train of thought.

"You were going to say something else?" Susan was holding her breath.

"Just have a great day, Susan." He could feel his face warming

"Hank should be here soon," they both stood there with so many thoughts racing through their minds that neither one could bring anything to voice. "Okay well, I should be going,"

"Susan wait," Sam called before she got all the way down the steps. His throat was dry, and his head was spinning a little. He went down and kissed her which surprised them both. "I'm sorry… I don't know what got into me."

"It's quite alright, Sam I've been waiting for you to do that."

"You have?"

"Almost the minute I saw you."

"Why didn't you say something?"

"I guess I was too shy to say anything."

"Sorry but you don't seem like the shy type to me."

"Kiss me again," Susan looked up into Sam's eyes and waited.

"How was that?" Sam stepped back after kissing her hard.

"Nice, a girl could get used to that," she laughed nervously like a high school girl on a first date. Her heart was flying around in her chest.

Just then they heard a car coming in the road and that drew their attention.

"That must be Hank," Sam said somewhat relieved for the distraction.

"Yep, that's Hank alright. Can't miss that old truck."

"Hey, what's wrong with old trucks?" Sam made a face and Susan laughed.

"Okay big guy," Susan gathered up her things. "Well, Sam, I should be going I have some things I have to do today."

"Me too. Are you're sure you're alright?"

"I'm positive," Susan smiled her best reassuring smile and hoped it was enough to convince Sam.

"I'll be seeing you around."

"It's a small town."

Sam watched from the front porch as Susan got into her car and waved as she disappeared down the road. *"She'll never come back..."* whispered a small voice inside his head, and it left him feeling a mixture of emotions that were impossible to sort out.

When he turned for the front door, he was assailed with a vision he saw through the front door window. It wasn't more than a flash, but it slammed him against the railing to the point he almost went over the side. In that flash of a second, he saw it again… laying on the living room floor… a body, unmoving…it was in shadow as before which rendered it unrecognizable. Then it was gone and so was Susan…

His thoughts were interrupted when Hank's truck swung into the driveway. Hank took a second to untangle himself from his seat belt. Sam could hear him swearing inside his truck. A flame erupted as Hank lit his cigarette. When he got out of the truck, he slammed the door and his right shoelace got trapped, he almost went down. He took a moment to steady himself while a whole new string of cussing painted the air. He managed to open his door and free his shoelace without further incident.

"Morning Hank, Thanks for coming so quickly," Sam was having a real hard time keeping a straight face.

"That's no problem I was in the area anyway. Ya say ya have a broken window?"

"Actually, I have two broken windows."

"Well, let's take a look and see what we got. Wait let me get my tape and something to write on," he went back to his truck and rummaged around in his glove box for a pencil and paper. He bumped his head on his way out which unleashed a string of particularly choice words.

Once he had everything, he needed he walked back to where Sam was.

"Okay show me those broken windows," he followed Sam into the house and into the kitchen where Hank stood scratching his head. "Ya must'a had yerself a hell of a mess in here."

"Actually… it broke from the inside out."

"Ya don' say," Hank inspected the opening where the window should be and whistled to himself. "Did a pan slip out'a yer hand or somthin'?"

"I didn't do it. I wasn't even in the same room when it happened."

Hank studied Sam for a good long second then he looked back at the broken window. "Alright well I'll take some measurements and be back in a day er two with the glass."

"Be great Hank thanks a lot," Sam took Hank into the study and showed him the other broken window, also broken from the inside out. Once he was finished, he got back in his truck and sputtered back down the road.

Not five minutes later Sheriff Thompson rolled into his driveway. Sam waited at the top of the steps until he got out of his cruiser.

"Morning, Sheriff," Sam could feel his pulse rise a little bit although there was no reason he should be apprehensive... about the sheriff coming to his house... bright and early. "What brings you to my house this morning?"

"Morning, Sam," Sheriff Thompson removed his hat and wiped his brow. "Gonna be a worm day, I believe. Mind if I come up for a talk?"

"Not at all Sheriff. Have you had coffee?"

"I could go a cup if it's no trouble," He climbed the stairs and took a seat on the porch.

Sam returned with two steaming cups. He set his on the top rail and handed the sheriff his.

"So, what's this all about, Sheriff?"

"Sam you must've heard that Charlie Case was attacked the other night?"

"Charlie Case? I Don't..."

"Frank's cousin, Charlie."

"I don't know his last name," Sam waited.

"He was attacked night before last," Sheriff Thompson looked hard at Sam for a reaction but there was none. "He was attacked over there in the woods not far from here. I think it was on your property."

"I woke up the other night and saw lights out there in that direction, but it looked like police lights, so I didn't go out there to check it out. I haven't heard what happened," he could tell he was about to find out by the look on the sheriff's face. "So? What does that have to do with why you're here?"

"You really haven't heard anything?"

"Sheriff I've been home since... well, since the other day."

"Sam," Sheriff Thompson set his cup down an took a breath. "Sam... Charlie was attacked the other night. Deputy Riggs found him wrapped around a tree."

"Sheriff?"

"He was wrapped around a damn tree backwards," Sheriff Thompson reached down to retrieve his coffee and took a sip.

"How... I mean backwards. Who or what could do such a thing?"

"Somebody who is very strong."

"Somebody? You say that like you have an idea who it might've been."

"Sam," Sheriff Thompson took a moment to look out into the forest. "Sam, you threatened Charlie and his cousin Frank after you beat the tar out of them. Too many people heard you say the words."

"Sheriff what exactly are you getting at here?"

"I got a call from the hospital early this morning... Charlie didn't make it."

"Shit... you don't think I had anything to do with that do you? I was home." Sheriff Thomson downed the last of his coffee and stood. "Doctor said he was scared to death," he answered flatly and headed toward his cruiser.

"Did you say scared to death, Sheriff?"

"Have a good day, Sam," with that he got into his cruiser and was back down the road.

Sam stood there looking down the road wondering who was next to be coming over. When no other car appeared, he went back inside and busied himself with covering the windows with tape and plastic.

CHAPTER 49

"So, what do you think of that?" asked Marten who was seated with Kyle at Judy's.

"Hell, what I think don't change nothin'. But I will tell you this I think there's more goin' on 'round here than we know." Kyle raised his hand to flag down the waitress for more coffee. When his cup was refilled, he looked over the small talkative crowd in the café. "I think," he leaned in closer like a conspirator unloading a top-secret plot. "I think Charlie had what came to him. He should have not gone out there. Do I think Sam had anything to do with it? No, I don't."

"I agree with you, Kyle. Sam has enough to think about what with coming back here and all. I think killing Charlie must be the least of his problems."

"He did threaten Frank we all heard that."

"But, the fact remains, the doc said Charlie was scared to death. Hell, Marten, haven't you ever said you wanted to kill somebody?"

"Well, sure I have but I never really meant it."

"My point exactly," Marten signaled the waitress for another round of coffee. "People tend to say things they don't mean in the heat of the moment."

"You're right about that but sometimes things are said that make you wonder though."

"That's for damn sure," Marten pushed his coffee cup away. "I had enough coffee I gotta get a move on. Got a call this mornin' from Sam."

"You don't say what is he up to?"

"Says he has a couple broken windows need something'. I gave Hank a jingle to see if he could take look."

"Well, how do you suppose they got broke?"

"How should I know, he just called to ask me if I'd seen Hank and to ask him to come over and take a look."

"Well, I got my own stuff to attend to, so I'll see you around."

"You will, see you later."

Both men paid their bill and left to their separate obligations.

CHAPTER 50

On the other side of town, the Sheriff had just finished up his last stop of the morning, over at the Lindsey Mobile Home Park where Frank was downing beers as he tried to process the fact his cousin had died.

"Damnit," Frank swore while crushing the beer can in his hand and throwing it hard onto the steadily growing pile in the corner. "He killed him!" Frank declared.

"But the doc said-

"I don't care what the damn doc said," Frank was really working himself into a frenzy and that made Leroy very nervous. "I tell you, Leroy, I feel it in my bones!"

"Okay, okay, let's just... try and keep our heads, Frank. I mean I don't like the way you're thinkin' right now," he grabbed a couple more beers and sat by Frank. "I know you Frank and I know what you're thinkin' on doin' but, you gotta settle down... Frank? You Hear me, Frank?" Frank was silent which made Leroy even more nervous. "Frank? Frank."

"What Leroy, what," Frank was barely able to contain his anger.

"Frank, promise me you won't do nothin' stupid, frank..."

"I'm not promisin' nothin'," Frank drained his beer and winged into the corner. "I don't know what I'm gonna do, but I'm not making any promises, Leroy."

"We need to get something' to eat Frank. I'm half plowed and it's only..." Leroy consulted the clock. "Hell, it's not even ten in the damn mornin'."

"I guess you're right," Frank deflated some.

"Let's go then," Leroy stood, a bit wobbly and grabbed his coat. Frank stood, just about as wobbly and grabbed his truck keys. They both got in the truck and Frank hit the gas.

"Whoa Frank, Slow down Judy's isn't going anywhere."

"Not goin' to Judy's," Frank said flatly as he swerved onto the hi-way.

"Well, where are we goin' then?"

"We're goin' to the hospital," Frank declared. "I wanna see my cousin."

"Frank, are you sure you want to do this? I mean what good will it do?"

"If you don't have the stomach for it you can get out right here."

"Then what? You just gonna leave me by the side of the road?"

"If you don't wanna go, yeah."

"That's cold Frank, even for you," Leroy turned his attention to the passing scenery.

When they got to the hospital they fell out of the truck and stumbled for the front entrance. Once inside they made their way to the reception desk where nurses were busy on phones and helping people.

"I wanna see the doc," Frank demanded leaning hard on the counter for effect.

"If you'll have a seat, we'll be right with you," A big woman with glasses that perched precariously on the end of her nose smiled up at frank who was not smiling.

"My name's Frank Dobbs and I'm here because my cousin is dead and I wanna know why," Frank was having a hard time focusing and decided to take a seat.

"We'll be right with you Mister Dobbs," the nurse kept her voice calm she was used to people being upset but he would just have to wait his turn like everyone else.

So, Frank and Leroy sat and waited. It didn't take long before the nurse called him back to the counter.

"Alright mister Dobbs, is it? What can we help you with today?"

"I'm here to see whoever the doctor was who saw my cousin, Charlie. He was brought here last night and now he's dead," Frank frowned down at the woman who consulted her logbook.

"That would be Doctor Bishop he was the doctor on duty. You're in luck he's just about to go off shift. I'll let him know you're here."

It wasn't long before Doctor Bishop came down the hallway.

"Mister Dobbs," he extended his hand and Frank squeeze it harder than necessary, which was his way of being the big man. Unfortunately for Frank the doctor met his grip with a strong grip of his own which deflated Frank just a little bit. "I was just leaving, come, let's go into my office where we can talk."

Frank and Leroy followed the doctor down the sterile hallway and into a small office where the walls were littered with diplomas and certificates. The doctor sat on the edge of his desk while Frank and Leroy took the offered seats.

"Now, what can I do for you gentlemen?"

"I'm here to see about my cousin, Charlie. He was brought in last night and I just found out from the sheriff that he's dead."

"Ah yes," he took a breath while he reached for a folder on his desk. "Your cousin was in vary bad shape when he was brought in. His injuries were very... shall we say unique."

"The hell's that mean?" Frank sat on the edge of his seat.

"He suffered from several injuries. Both shoulders were dislocated as were his hips."

"Geeze doc," Leroy stood. "What the heck would cause something like that?"

"That's a mystery to me as well. I have never come across anything like it." He consulted his notes. "Can I be candid with you, Frank, is it?"

"Whatever, I just want to know what in hell happened to him."

"Like I said I've never in all my years seen anything quite like it. Even as bad as your cousin's injuries were, they were not fatal."

"Well then, what killed him?" Frank got up to study the diplomas on the wall.

"Fright," the doctor answered simply without fanfare. "Your cousin was literally scared to death."

"I don't b'leive that!" Frank declared. "My cousin wasn't scared of nothin'."

"I'll have to take your word on that as I didn't know him, but the fact remains, something scared your cousin really bad."

Frank plopped down on a chair and tried to process what the doctor had told him. Hard as he tried nothing added up.

"Can I see him?"

"If you wish I can have someone, take you to where he is."

"Yeah, that would be great," Frank stood again but had to steady himself on the back of the chair.

An orderly came to the door and Frank and Leroy followed him back down the hallway into a room that had tables of covered bodies. The orderly walked over to one of the tables and lifted a tag attached to a toe and motioned for Frank to come closer.

"Are you ready?" He asked and lifted the sheet.

"What'r all those bruises there?" Frank pointed to Charlie's shoulders.

"Those are from the trauma inflicted on him. From being dislocated."

"Geeze, Frank," was all Leroy could come up with he had never seen a dead body before.

"I can't b'lieve he was scared like he was," Frank just couldn't wrap his head around that disturbing fact.

"I'm sorry," the orderly said. "That's what the report says right here."

"Well, that report's wrong," Frank had seen enough, and he needed to get the hell out of there. "C'mon Leroy, let's get out'a here."

They stormed out of the hospital and flew down the road to the store where Frank bought a twenty-four pack of beer, and they made their way back to the Lindsay Trailor Home Park.

Once inside Leroy made the observation that they still hadn't eaten.

"Well, hell, Leroy why didn't you get something when we were at the store?"

"We were in and out so fast I forgot," Leroy popped a beer and fell into the chair. "So, what are we gonna do now, Frank?"

"I don't know about you Leroy, but I'm gonna get nice an' drunk," Frank squeezed the last drop of beer out of the can and tossed it.

———————

After taking a long drive Susan rolled into her driveway and sat there looking up at her house. She willed herself to move barely making it to her front porch where she fell into her favorite chair. She was shaking so bad she thought her bones were rattling loose. She felt so cold, yet the sun was drenching the porch in warmth. Her mind was racing all over the place as she tried to piece together just what happened last night or early this morning or... she went blank all the sudden... her car phone blared, and she almost fell over backward out of her chair. It took her a second to get herself together enough to answer it.

"Hello?"

"Susan, geeze I've been trying to get a hold of you." The excited voice on the other end belonged to her best friend Joan. "Where the heck have you been? Susan? Hey, are you okay?"

"I'm... I don't know... I..." Susan's voice trailed off. She was shaking so bad she could hardly hold the phone.

"Are you home?"

"I just got here," her answer sounded like she had just arrived at a place she'd never been to before.

"Okay you stay put I'm coming over," Joan commanded.

"I, I'm fine Joan it's alright."

"Yeah, you could say that to anybody else and they would probably believe you, but I don't. I'm coming over. Are you hungry? I could stop at Judy's and grab something."

"No, really. I'm okay I'm not hungry."

"Okay hang tight," and just like that Joan was off the phone leaving Susan holding the receiver in her shaking hand.

It took a couple tries before Susan was successful in returning the receiver to its cradle and she had to sit for a second... *"I've got to pull myself together!"* She scolded herself for being so ridiculous. After checking herself in her rear-view mirror, a thing she rarely does, she pulled herself free of the car and climbed back up the short path and the couple stairs to the front porch. She once again threw herself into her comfy porch chair and waited...

CHAPTER 51

Sam needed some air and decided to hop in his truck a just drive somewhere. The roar of the engine when he started it up gave him a great sense of gratification. He shifted into reverse cranked the wheel and would have been gone had Hank not chosen that time to come over to repair the windows.

"Hey, Hank," Sam called as he got out of his truck. "I was just on my way out."

"You don't need ta stand aroun' an' watch me young man," Hank snubbed out his cigarette and promptly lit another one which was giving him a little trouble and caused a short burst of swearing for which Hank sheepishly apologized for.

"Well then if you don't need my help…"

"Nope."

"I'll be on my way then. Thanks Hank."

"Don't mention it glad ta do it," he went into a coughing fit as he struggled to get his ladder out.

Sam headed out and onto the hi-way. He rolled his window down all the way he needed as much air blowing in his face as possible and still stay on the road. When he topped the divide, he slowed to look back at the valley that held the town he now called home. He drove on for a little while longer until he came to a nice turnout with a view. He pulled in and got out to stretch which was a little painful.

———————————

Back at Sam's place Hank was finally able to get all his tools organized and his ladder up to work on the first window. He was halfway up the ladder when he thought he heard something... behind the shed. He ignored it and climbed to where he could work and suddenly his ladder started to shake. He swore as he held on and looked around below to find nothing there. He quickly climbed down and fired up a cigarette which he almost inhaled in one shot. He leaned against the ladder and caught his breath while his eyes continued to jump all over the place.

Once he felt it was just the wind he went back up and continue working. That's when one of the shed doors flew open. He turned hanging on to the ladder just as the door swung back. Hank let out a string of words that would make a seasoned sailor blush. Then someone was laughing and that's when Hank decided it would be a good idea to climb down off the ladder.

He was having a hard time getting his cigarette lit his hands were shaking so bad. The chimes on the front porch started up and Hank jumped. He slowly walked around to the front porch and looked up at the chimes that were dancing all over the place even though there was no wind.

Hank swore again, ignored whatever it was and was able to finish the first window without further interruption. It was when he started on the second window by the library that things got bad...

The shed doors started to bang open and shut out of control. Somewhere out in the woods someone was giggling, and it sounded like a little boy. Trees started bending this way and that but there was little to no wind. Hank, swearing a blue streak hurriedly finished installing the other window and literally ran to his truck, leaving his tools and ladder where they lay. He sped out of there in a thick cloud of dust and smoke.

Hank didn't let off the gas until he was safely parked in front of the Dusty Rose Bar where he intended to have himself a stiff drink... or maybe two.

CHAPTER 52

It didn't take long before Susan was aware of a car coming up her road. She had no doubt who it could be but wasn't sure what she should say or even how much she should tell her friend. She knew one thing for sure there was no hiding anything from Joan.

Susan stood up when Joan rolled in.

"I got here as fast as I could," Joan was already breathless with anticipation.

"You didn't need to hurry, Joan," Susan was quickly embraced in a fierce hug. "I'm fine, really."

"Yeah, you don't look fine to me," she held Susan at arm's length. "I know when you look fine and when you don't. Right now... you don't look so fine."

"Can I get you something?" Susan was trying to stall the inevitable. "Are you thirsty?"

"The only thing I need right now is to know what's going on. Did you hear about-

"Yes, I have heard," Susan sat back down, and Joan pulled up a chair to sit beside her, "Sheriff Thompson has already stopped by."

"So..."

"So, he told me," Susan heaved a big sigh.

"Where were you last night I tried to call you."

"I guess my phone wasn't working," it was a lame excuse but that's all she had.

"Okay so tell me," Joan sat with her arms folded.

"Geeze," Susan was blushing.

"Come on Susan out with it. You know I will bother you till you tell me."

"Okay, okay, I give up."

"That's more like it. Now give."

"Alright... I went to see Sam. To make sure he was alright."

"Okay, now we're getting somewhere."

"I ended up spending the night."

"You what? Can you say that again? Only slower."

"I stayed the night at Sam's place. Don't look at me like that. We had pajamas on, I mean I was wearing his."

"Oh… my… God… are you serious? I mean really?"

"Nothing happened if that's what you're thinking."

"Sure, you expect me to believe that?"

"It's true, I swear," Susan got up and went inside to get herself a drink. She needed something to help her get through what was coming next. Joan followed her.

"If you're pouring wine I'll have a glass," Joan smiled conspiratorially.

They returned to their respective chairs on the front porch and sipped their wine in momentary silence.

"Tell me Susan."

"I don't know how to explain it."

"Try."

"Well, like I said I spent the night at Sam's last night…"

"And… c'mon quite teasing me already."

"I'm not. It's just not easy to tell you is all."

"Okay, just go slow, I don't need to be anywhere."

"It was weird, I mean the night started out okay but then…" She was having a really hard time sorting it out herself let alone having to explain it to some one else. "Things started to happen."

"What things? You're making me crazy."

"Things like, noises… and oh boy crazy things. There was somebody running down the hall and down the stairs and… Sam got up to see what it was and… When I was in the hallway… the walls…"

"The walls?"

"They were moving, in and out like they were breathing or something."

"Wow," was all Joan could say.

"Yeah, it was very creepy."

"Is that it? I mean there must be more. I can tell by the tone of your voice when we talked earlier it was… not your own. I can see you're still shaking."

"I got scared, Joan. I've never felt so scared in my life. I don't know what the heck it was, but it was… frightening."

"Shit, what the hell. Great now I'm talking like Hank," Joan gulped down the rest of her wine. "You got anymore of this stuff?" She held her glass up.

"Sure, I'll get the bottle."

"Good idea."

Susan returned with the bottle and topped off their glasses. Then she tried as best as she could to explain the events of last night. The day slipped by and the two women sat quietly with their own thoughts until Joan got up and stretched.

"I've never seen you like this," Joan brushed a lock of hair from her face. "Are you sure you're going to be okay? I mean I can stay if you want me to."

"I'm feeling better now, thanks for…"

"Hey, anything for my best friend. If you need to talk some more, you just let me know."

"Thanks," they hugged again. "I… would appreciate it if you didn't mention this to anybody. Not yet at least."

"What is said between us is nobody's business."

———————————————

Sam sat back against a boulder and watched the sky turn colors. He was trying to process what happened earlier that morning and what exactly he saw there on the living room floor. His thoughts were still filled with shadows, and he wondered what he was going to find when he got back home.

He didn't really feel afraid so to speak, just concerned. Concerned because there were so many things that didn't even come close to making any sense. When color finally drained from the sky and the light began to fail, he decided it was time to face whatever awaits at home... So, he climbed into his truck and headed down the road.

When his road came into view he pulled over and took a second. He rolled down his window and the forest smelled good; it was a comforting smell. *"Alright,"* he said to no one in particular. *"Can't sit here all night."* With that he rolled on down is road watching the shadows form and retreat before his bright headlights. Around the last bend he felt his pulse rate ratchet up a little. For the briefest of moments, he thought he saw someone standing in front of his house. But there was nothing. He left his headlights on and went up the front steps to turn on the porch light then went into the house turned the living room light.

When he went back outside to turn off the truck lights, he stopped dead in his tracks. The truck lights were off. He stood there staring out into the darkness. He was starting to get spooked, and it wasn't a very good feeling. When he was able to get his feet moving again, he went to his truck and retrieved his keys, but they were gone. Now he didn't feel good at all...

CHAPTER 53

"Okay Hank," Ron the bartender was walking over to where Hank was sitting and informed him that he had had enough.

"Young man," Hanks words were starting to slur together and his swearing sounded like gibberish which was just as well.

"It's time to go Hank," Ron was collecting glasses and snagged Hanks as he walked by.

"One more for the road," Hank was trying to focus on Ron and not having the best of luck.

"Gotta close out my register for the next shift, Hank. It's late."

"It's not that late," Hank was swearing but fortunately his words were hard to make out.

"Hank," Ron turned to consult the clock behind him. "You been here all afternoon, Hank. It's time to go."

"All right if that's the way you want to be."

"That's the way I want to be, Hank," he smiled because he genuinely liked the old man.

Hank walked out to his truck, if you can call it walking, it looked more like he was balancing on a beam, but he made it, though not without a string of cussing that was completely unintelligible. Somehow, he was able to get the key in the ignition on the third try. He rolled out of the parking lot and onto a deserted street.

He was humming to himself as he drove trying desperately to drown out the effect of what he experienced at the Henning place. Halfway home things were mostly under control that is until he noticed he had a passenger. He swerved to the side of the road nearly missing a tree and slammed on his breaks which caused a major cloud of dust. He scrambled out of his truck once he was able to free himself from the damnable seat belt. He lit a cigarette and puffed on it like it was his life support.

He swore into the darkness until his voice cracked from the abuse. Once he sucked down that cigarette, he ventured a glance inside his truck. At first, he didn't trust his eyes, so he took a step closer. Still not believing what he was seeing he stepped closer and pulled open the driver's side door and what he saw made his knees buckle. There on the passenger seat... was nothing...He shook his head trying to clear his eyesight and when he looked again, he saw a shadow figure sitting there. It didn't seem like it was aware Hank was even there it looked like it was staring straight ahead, waiting...

It's funny that just a short time ago he was really feeling the effects of a long afternoon of drinking and now... he was stone cold sober, and he was not happy about it.

"Git the hell out'a my truck, whatever the hell you are," he was yelling not because he felt he wasn't being heard but because for the second time that day he was genuinely scared which brought out a whole new string of vulgarity. But the thing or whatever it was just sat there like it hadn't heard a word. Hank took a step back and lit another cigarette while he contemplated his next move.

As he smoked, he watched the thing in his truck get bigger and bigger until it overfilled the cab. Hank took longer puffs as he watched in horror as the thing spilled out of his truck and formed, like a black cloud, over him. Suddenly he stopped sucking on his smoke letting it slip from his fingers to fall at his feet.

The air had turned sour, and it was hard to breath. Hank felt lightheaded almost to the point of passing out, so he grabbed the door handle and held on for dear life. He took in great gulps of air but didn't feel like he was able to draw a breath.

Just when he felt his sanity slipping, he had this sensation of falling. Suddenly, the thing dissipated right there and then and the air became breathable once again. He hastily lit another cigarette while his eyes jumped all over the place. He was so shaken that he was having a hard time keeping his hand steady enough to take a pull on his burning smoke.

The night had grown cool. The forest all around him was quiet and still, it was an eerie feeling. One that made his stomach lurch. For a second, he thought he was going to be sick, so he sat down on the running board of his truck trying to settle down.

It took some time and several cigarettes before he was able to regain control of himself. He stood, kind of wobbly, and took a good look inside his truck. He didn't see anything so he cautiously opened his door and slid behind the wheel. He didn't have to fumble with the key this time as it was already in the ignition. The engine roared to life, and he wasted no time getting back on the road.

CHAPTER 54

The morning sun was a box of light slowly creeping across the bedroom floor. It climbed up the foot of the bed drenching it in morning sun. Finally, it reached Sam who covered his face with his arm.

He gave up on the notion of sleeping in and swung out of bed. Sitting on the edge he rolled his shoulders and felt his face. He was still sore from the attack the other day and he groaned to stand.

When he was dressed, he padded downstairs and put on some water for coffee. He noticed that the kitchen window was replaced, and he was glad.

While the water was heating up, he wandered into the den and saw that window too had been repaired. He looked out the window which afforded him a view of the shed and surrounding forest.

He noticed that there was a ladder leaning against the outside wall of the house, but it didn't look right. He didn't have time to really look at it as his water started hissing on the stove.

He ran into the kitchen and took the pot off the stove right before it boiled over. Coffee in hand he went outside to inspect the ladder he saw leaning against the side of his house. When he rounded the corner, he stopped. The ladder he saw was in fact there against the wall, but it was bent, almost to the point of breaking.

He stood there for a long time trying to think what the heck could bend a ladder like that. And then he thought about Charlie, and how he was bent around that tree. For a second he felt sick but it quicky passed. He studied that ladder while he sipped his coffee and wondered if Hank was okay. Sam decided to call him and see, but after his coffee.

Laughter erupted somewhere in the trees behind the shed, and he spilled coffee burning his hand some. At this point what's another injury? He set his cup on the ground and walked into the woods to see where the laughter was coming from. He found himself surrounded by thick forest and stood listening. Birds flitted through the branches over his head and a slight breeze kicked up causing some of the trees to saw against each other.

He caught movement out of the corner of his eye and looked in that direction. The laughing started again only it was off to his right, not where he thought he saw movement.

Goose bumps raced over his body as he searched through the forest for the source. The laughter was slightly nauseating, and Sam felt it would be a good idea to leave the area.

Well, his path led him back to the broken ladder which reminded him to try to get in touch with Hank to make sure he's okay and to thank him for fixing the windows. He picked up his coffee cup and headed back inside. He set his cup in the sink; he was a little to wound up to be drinking more coffee. The phone started to ring, and he went into the study to get it.

When Sam sat down and grabbed the receiver there was only static on the other line, so he hung up thinking it was a bad connection. Whoever it was will call back. Breakfast, that's what he needed, something to eat. After searching through his cupboards, he decided to go out and get something to eat. It wasn't because there was no food he just didn't feel like cooking.

The phone started to ring again, and he went back in the den to answer it. He picked up the receiver and got the same static only this time he could have sworn he heard a voice…

He listened for a while, there was a voice, but the static was so bad he couldn't make out what it was saying. Then it stopped and a loud electronic ring replaced it. It was so loud Sam slammed the receiver back in its cradle.

He stood and stared down at the phone, but it remained silent. His stomach growled reminding him he needed to eat something. He left the den, grabbed his truck keys off the hook by the front door and headed out.

When he reached the end of his driveway he hesitated. He was having second thoughts about his decision. He was still pretty banged up though his face wasn't as swollen it was discolored. He scolded himself and turned for town and a nice breakfast.

It wasn't long before he saw the sign announcing Ida's Café on the corner to the right. Sam found a place to park which was no problem as many of the breakfast crowd had gone. There were a couple of people sitting in the booths and when he walked in, he could feel their eyes fall on him. He tried to ignore the side glances and took a stool at the counter.

Ida came out of the kitchen and took Sam's order. She was a big woman and called everyone hon or dear. She smiled at Sam, took his order and returned to the kitchen to cook it. While Sam sat there, he thought about that bent ladder and felt bad that he didn't call Hank before he left.

Before he got too deep in thought Ida returned with his breakfast and he dug in like a starved animal until he realized he might be making a scene, and he slowed down. He took a breath and looked around everyone he saw turned their stares away quickly. He made a face and went back to his breakfast. When he finished, he thanked Ida, paid his bill and left.

He decided to drive on over to the emporium and get a new flashlight his old one wasn't reliable anymore.

_____

On the other side of town back at the house where the three 'spirit talkers' lived they were just cleaning up the morning dishes when their phone rang. Veronica was closest so she grabbed it. When she put the phone to her ear all she heard was static and something else she couldn't make out, so she figured it was a bad connection and hung up.

"Who was that?" Clare wanted to know.

"Don't know, it was a bad connection," she answered slightly bothered by the call though she had no idea why she would be. They went back to what they were doing until the phone rang again. Veronica picked up and heard the same static except this time there was a voice underlying the noise.

"Who is it, Veronica?" This time it was Jorden who was asking.

"I don't know," Veronica was trying to hear a voice that could barely be heard through the static interference.

"Help me," the barely audible voice said.

"Who is this?"

Now both Clare and Jorden were standing close to Veronica.

"I need help," the voice sounded strange like it was struggling to speak.

"Tell me who this is?" Veronica was trying to keep her voice calm but the sound of the voice on the other end… It just didn't sound right for some reason. "I can't help you unless you tell me who you are."

Jorden and Clare turned their questioning expressions to Veronica who only shrugged her shoulders letting them know she still had no answers. The static was almost deafening now, and it was very hard for Veronica to stay on the line.

Veronica's ears were starting ache with the attempt to understand.

"I'm only going to ask you one more time to tell me who you are or I'm going to hang up," she was a little scared though she didn't have a clue as to why she should be. The static scratched on, and Veronica couldn't take it any longer. "Are you still there? Answer me. Tell me who you are and maybe I can help you."

The static was unbearable, and Veronica had had enough. She was returning the receiver to its cradle when she heard the voice again. "Help me…" More static.

"Your name," Veronica was shouting now.

Static… "My name's… Sam…" Static drowned out any more chance of conversation until the voice came through. "Sam… Home… Help me…" The static stopped abruptly leaving Veronica's ears ringing big time. Veronica slowly returned the receiver to it's cradle and sat down at the kitchen table rubbing her temples.

Clare and Jorden took seats on either side of Veronica and waited.

"Well?" Who was that?" Clare couldn't stand the suspense and had to ask.

"I-it was Sam or someone claiming to be Sam."

"What's that supposed to mean?" Jorden wanted to know.

"How should I know," Veronica was experiencing the first throb of an oncoming headache.

"You said it was Sam," Clare moved her chair closer. "Why do you sound like it might not be him?"

"I have to go!" Veronica was suddenly all motion as she grabbed her car keys and headed for the front door.

"Wait!" Clare and Jorden shouted at the same time.

"You're just going to run off like this?" Clare asked following her to the door.

"Geeze, Veronica what are you doing?" Jorden had joined Clare at the door as Veronica went down the front steps.

"We all agreed that if Sam needed help, we would help him," Veronica opened the door of her VW bug. "He's asked for help," She leaned on the car door for a second. "I'm just going to check things out. I'll call you from his phone when I get there," she was trying to reassure her sisters. She waved to them and slid into the driver's seat.

"You better call us or we're coming over!" Clare called after her sister, who was already driving away.

———————

Sam pulled into an empty spot in front of the Emporium and walked through the front door. As always it took him a second to take in the size of the place. He headed for the stairs and was met by Daphne who just so happened to be heading in the same direction.

"Hi Sam," Daphne beamed up at him. First, she had a smile on her face but that quickly changed when she got a good look at *his* face. "Oh my, Sam you... are you all right?" She made a face gritting her teeth as if someone stomped on her foot. "Your fa-," she stopped cold.

"I'm fine, just need to pick up a flashlight," he continued and so did Daphne.

"I heard what Frank, and his cousin did to you the other day and they deserved to get themselves arrested," she was matching his strides hopeful of some tidbit she could call her own...

"Yeah well, I'm just making a quick stop before heading back home."

"Are you going to press charges? I would," she was relentless.

Sam smiled down at Daphne and stopped at sporting goods.

"Have a good day Daphne," he changed course leaving her standing there staring after him.

"You too," she whispered to herself.

When Sam walked up the cashier which, as luck would have it was Daphne. He set his flashlight on the counter.

"So, we meet again," She batted her big eyes and smiled. "Will this be all for you today?"

It was a loaded question and Sam ignored it.

"Is Susan off today I didn't see her where she normally works," he took his flashlight and the change.

His question made her feel like she just had a bucket of cold water poured over her. "She's supposed to be working today but, I heard she never called in sick or anything..."

Sam pocketed his change and left without comment. When he reached his truck, he got in and sat behind the wheel thinking. He was thinking about Susan and worried about… what? Was he overreacting? Was he about to make a thing out of nothing? He was starting to get a bad feeling and that solved his problem about what to do. Even though he wasn't a hundred percent sure what he was going to do was the right thing to do…

Veronica pulled up to Sam's and noticed his truck wasn't there. That gave her a slight pause. She opened her inner spirit to try and get a feeling of things even though she was already getting some pretty hard hits as she drove in. She got out of her car and walked halfway to the front porch.

She spread her arms to intercept energy pulses and as soon as she did that her fingertips got tingly. She began a slow circle turn and was seriously getting shockwaves that traveled up her arms and through her body. It was like being in an electrical storm when static electricity is charged through the air. Her hair was sparkling with electricity she was getting the strongest reading she had ever experienced.

She stopped and lowered her arms; she was drained and a little nervous. Laughter erupted suddenly and it took her out of trancelike state. It sounded like it was coming from somewhere around the side of the house… but it didn't quite sound like the laughter she had heard before. This time the laughing was a little darker somehow, even sinister maybe, and she hesitated to investigate.

As the laughing continued the chimes on the front porch went off. At first, they were doing what they would do in a slight breeze, but there was no breeze. Not even a breath of air was moving. Then they went wild, and Veronica was sure they were about to fly off the hook. The laughter started up not wanting to be outdone and the hairs on the back of her neck prickled.

Taking a big gulp of air and calling on all her protectors she slowly made her way around the house to find out the source. As she rounded the corner of the house the chimes stopped as suddenly as if someone had grabbed a hold of them.

She saw that there was a somewhat dilapidated old shed in the back with a wood pile stacked against one wall. As she stood in front of the shed, she felt a strong presence. She was drawn to the structure and it puzzled her, then the shed doors slowly opened with a squeal of rusty hardware.

Veronica stood mesmerized by the sight. She ventured closer to look inside and saw only blackness. Not darkness like a building with no windows, blackness... Without warning she was propelled into the shed and slammed against the back wall where she slumped to the dirt floor. Stars erupted and floated before her eyes. When she was able to clear her head enough to see she saw a young boy standing in the light just outside, he had no face just like the ghost boy she saw before only this was different; it stood different, kind of crooked.

Veronica willed herself to get up and out. She rose to her feet and made for the sunshine but before she could get there the doors slammed shut and she was enveloped in total darkness darker than anything she had ever experienced. An unseen force catapulted her back against the wall where she again slumped to the dirt floor.

Something or someone started knocking on the outside wall of the shed. It was not much at first just a soft thumping. Then the knocking grew louder and soon there was rapid hard knocking coming from all four walls at the same time.

A tiny twister erupted inside the shed throwing loose debris and dirt so that she had to cover her face with her hands. As the little wind churned it created havoc in that small space. Veronica was aware of a movie starting up in her mind it made clicking sounds as the film played through the old projector. It was an old movie but that wasn't the odd part. It was playing backwards at a faster rate than normal speed while the wind kept up its relentless pressure.

Between the violence of the twister and the horrible knocking Veronica was having a hard time keeping from screaming into the darkness.

The movie was without credits or cast names and it started with her sitting in the darkness of the shed and quickly changed scenes to two boys chasing each other through the woods and around a lake. There were family pictures captured right out of a family album.

Then the movie went to a dark room where there were only unidentifiable shapes which scared her some, as if she wasn't a little shaken already. Again, it changed scenes, both audio and video were backwards which added to the confusing environment she was trapped in. Each time it showed a house it was the same house different people. The wind stopped and Veronica blinked the dust out of her eyes. The whole time she chanted and called on her protectors. As the movie clicked to a halt, the lose end of the film slapped the projector.

Veronica placed her hands on the ground to try and steady herself. She was suddenly aware of a warm feeling under her left hand. She could feel something under there but was reluctant to investigate further. It was a strange feeling because the dirt under her right hand was cool to the touch.

The last frame of the movie hung like a wet towel on the line it showed an old man sitting in a chair on the front porch... He was dead... The knocking came to a halt...

———————————————————

Sam felt kind of silly driving up to Susan's house especially since it looked like she had company. It was too late he was already there. He would only stop in to say hi and go he didn't want to impose. He was getting out of his truck when the front door opened and outstepped Susan and a friend.

"Hey, Sam," Susan smiled down at her new arrival. "What brings you out to this neck of the woods?"

"Good morning, Susan," he looked to her friend. "I was at the Emporium and Daphne said you hadn't showed up for work."

"Oh," Susan remembering her manners introduced her friend. "I'm sorry this is my friend, Joan."

"Hi, Sam," she smiled down at him. "I've heard a lot about you."

"Oh..." he frowned for a second. "I hope it wasn't all bad."

"Actually, most of it was good," she turned to Susan. "Okay you I must hit the trail. If you need anything you call me, you hear."

"I will. And thanks for coming by, I feel much better now."

With that Joan skipped down the steps brushed by Sam with a big smile and was down the road.

"Wanna come in?"

"Actually, I have to get back, I just stopped by to check on you," that didn't sound right. "To make sure you're alright."

"Well, that's very nice of you mister," she smiled feeling her face warm. "I'm fine thanks. You sure you don't wanna come up?"

"I'll take a rain check if that's okay."

"I'll mark it down," she teased.

"All right, I guess I'll head back to the ranch. I'll talk to you later."

"I look forward to it."

Sam pulled up in front of his house and was puzzled to see a robin's egg blue VW bug sitting in his driveway. He figured it belonged to Veronica; she was driving it when she first came to his house. He didn't see her but figured she must be around some place. He got out of his truck and went up on the front porch. He stood there scanning the surrounding forest and listening.

A woman's voice barely heard sounded like it was coming from behind the house. He listened for a moment longer to be sure his ears weren't playing tricks on him. There it was again a muffled voice. He went down the steps and around to the side of the house where the sound of a woman's voice was unmistakable. Sam rounded the corner, and a chill ran through his body as he realized that the woman's voice was coming from inside the shed.

He went to the closed doors and tried to open them, but they were closed tight. He tried to pull with all his strength, but they would not budge.

"Hello?" Sam called.

Veronica was awakened from her dreamlike state by a familiar voice.

"Sam?" She answered hoping it really was Sam. "I'm in here. I can't get out."

"Hang on I'll get something to open the doors with." He looked around and saw there was a shovel leaning against the other side of the shed, so he grabbed it. He tried wedging it between the doors, but they were too tight. He went over to the chopping block and retrieved the axe. Just as he was about to swing at the doors when they slowly creaked open. Inside it was very dark and at first, he couldn't see anything.

Then out of the darkness Veronica appeared. She stumbled toward him and she was a mess. Her hair was all over the place with bits of debris tangled in it. Her face was a muddy mask except for the furrows down her cheeks where tears had traveled. Sam rushed in and took her by the arm. He helped her out of the shed and held her steady while she stood gasping for air.

"Are you alright? What happened?" Too many questions too soon.

He helped her over to the chopping block and she sat down still breathing hard, drenched in sweat.

"What the hell happened?" Sam was trying to understand what he just came home to.

"I-I don't know exactly," she answered after a bit, she was still trying to get her breath back. "I got a phone call, I thought it was you, but it didn't quite sound right. I decided to come over to make sure."

"Wait here I'll get you some water," when Sam turned, he saw the ladder again and it took his breath away. The ladder was still there bent in the middle. For the first time he noticed there were deep furrows down the side of the house made from the ladder as it slid down the wall. "Damn," he said to himself. "I'll be right back, you gonna be, okay?"

"Would you mind if I came with you?"

"Not at all c'mon," he helped her to her feet, and they went up onto the front porch where Veronica fell into one of the chairs. "I'll be right out," Sam went inside and came out with two glasses of water.

"Thanks," Veronica took the glass and practically gulped the contents in one swoop.

"Easy there," he said. "I have more where that came from."

Veronica relaxed and sat quietly; Sam sat quietly next to her he would have to wait till she was ready to tell him what happened to her. The ladder thing would have to be another time.

"Here let me get you another glass of water, ice?"

"Yes please," she closed her eyes while Sam went inside.

He handed her glass back and sat down. He waited, he was in no hurry and glad she was safe. When she drank half the glass, she set it on the floor beside her and looked out into the forest. It wasn't long before she told him what happened, to the best of her knowledge.

"Holy crap," he whistled low and shook his head. "You said something about a phone call? And that the voice sounded like me?"

"It was hard to tell for sure because there was so much static. I thought it was a bad connection. But, yeah, the voice on the other end said it was you and that you needed help, so I came over. The next thing I knew is you were helping me out of the shed.

"Wow, I don't know what to say except I'm glad you're okay... are you okay?"

"Whatever that was in there is very powerful. I think I know what it is, I think. It's very possible, and I'm not exactly sure myself, but I think it's a mimic."

"A mimic... What exactly is a mimic? I mean I think I have an idea but, for the heck of it what do you think a mimic is?"

"It's an entity that copies voices... sometimes it can take on the form of someone..."

"Yeah, okay, that doesn't sound too good."

"Sometimes they're just trying to communicate with us. But..." her words trailed off and she reached for her glass of water.

"But?"

"Mimics are also tricksters and that sometimes makes them..."

"Take your time Veronica," Sam took another sip of water his mouth was awful dry.

"I have had experience with this once before. A spirit was trying to communicate with a family member. To do so it mimicked certain members of this family. It turned out that it was the spirit of one of the families' dead relatives."

"So, what did it want? This spirit."

"It couldn't cross over for some reason and was reaching out. It was quite unsettling."

"I can't imagine," Sam was way out of his comfort zone on this topic. But, considering recent events, he was curious.

"It turned out that it was a grandfather, and he was stuck in between worlds."

"Between worlds…"

"Yes, he was stuck between the world of the living and the world of the departed."

"How exactly does something like that happen," Sam wanted to know.

"Something interrupted the transition. It could be anything. I saw an old man sitting on a porch… This porch," she looked at Sam for the first time.

"Okay, what does that have to do with anything here?"

"He was sitting on *this* porch, Sam."

CHAPTER 55

When Veronica reached home, she tried as best as she could to explain what happened to her at Sam's. It was getting late, and she was extremely tired, so she excused herself and went to bed. Clare and Jorden were wide awake discussing options of what, if anything, could be done.

"I think," Clare said between sips of tea. "I think we need to do the ceremony."

"Are you sure?" Jorden was suddenly nervous. "I mean we haven't done it in a long time and the last time we almost lost you."

"Well, Jorden, I can't think of any other way to do this. Veronica mentioned an old man who, she thinks, is stuck in between worlds. I mean, what else can we do?"

"Let's not rush into this," Jorden, the ever cautious one of the three. "Let's see what tomorrow brings, we'll have much clearer heads in the morning."

On the other side of town there was only one light on, except for the yard light at the entrance to the Lindsey Mobil Home Park. That single light was illuminating the office of Sheriff Thompson who was hunched over looking at the spread of papers on his desk.

He must've read through those reports fifty times at least. And still two things gave him a headache. The first and most obvious one was what really happened the night his friend, the former Sheriff, died in the fire that took his office? And secondly, and this one was most perplexing… What happened to the murder weapon?

Both Deputies, Green and Ellis wrote in their reports that they saw a knife. They both entered into their reports that they believed the knife was the murder weapon being both parties were stabbed to death. And the boy was standing there holding it when they entered the house. It was both of their judgments that the boy had murdered his parents.

Their reports clearly and consistently state that the boy, Sam Henning was holding a knife and was covered in blood. Sheriff Dobbs' report said the boy had a bad, half-moon shaped cut on his left forehead just below the hairline. Could've gotten it in the struggle Sheriff Thompson surmised.

Sheriff Thompson took out the crime scene pictures again and flipped through the deputy's reports until he matched their observations with that of the pictures taken. The bloody handprint on the wall to the right of the kitchen door leading to the back yard. Blood on the doorknob...

And yet the boy claimed he never went outside. So, who went out the back door? Besides as Deputy Green pointed out in his report, the handprint on the wall was too big to be the boy's, the detective assigned to the case agreed though the print was too smudged to answer any questions. And still no motive, nothing was stolen. And no damn weapon. He lost a good friend shortly after the murders and he wondered if it was connected in some way. The former Sheriff's son, Frank, who was fifteen at the time, was sent away almost immediately after the murders, as was Sam.

Sam to a mental institution in, he shuffled a couple papers, France. Well, his family is very wealthy. It says he had a little anger management problem. Reading further they started a boxing program for the more 'aggressive' boys and the report goes on to say he was very good at fighting. A natural they said.

After they determined he wasn't a threat to society he was released on a work program so he could learn a trade. He got a job, and everything was fine no further reports of violence. He was never late for work. He was actually free to g back to the United States, but he stayed... Until three weeks ago.

Frank on the other hand was put into a school for troubled boys. Apparently, according to the school records, his friend, Leroy was placed there a year before. Evidently, his parents could no longer control him. Very interesting but, doesn't answer any of the million questions swirling around Sheriff Thompson's sore head.

The last and most aggravating question of all hit him again as he reached over to turn out the light. Where, in this small town full of everybody knowing everybody else's business, does a murder weapon hide?

No, there was one other thing... If Sheriff Dobbs was trying to hide or cover up something, like about half the people in town believed, especially some of the old-timers, then why wouldn't he make sure the reports burned with everything else? And then, he was too tired for anymore and then's but then... there was that strange call from Hank...He stood in the dark staring out the front window where there was only more darkness...

He hoped, as he locked up, that he would be hearing from Judge Crane over in Centerville. He had sent him a petition to reopen a cold case, the murder of, Andy and Lynn Henning, two prominent and well-liked people in the community. He sent copies of everything he had now, it was all up to the Judge. He also requested an arrest warrant for Sam Henning...

CHAPTER 56

Sam awoke the next morning feeling refreshed from a solid night's sleep. There had been no more disturbances after Veronica left for which he was extremely grateful. Once his mug was filled with steaming coffee, he went out to sit on the front porch to watch another day come out of the shadows.

As the morning warmed the forest the pleasant smell of pine filled the air. He wasn't thinking of anything in particular which was surprising considering what happened yesterday, he was even amazed. Nope, he was going to enjoy his cup of go juice and that was it. Well, it lasted about as long as it took to drink his first cup because down the road came Sheriff Thompson...

Sam stood, set his empty cup on the top rail and waited.

"Morning Sam," the Sheriff called when he got out of his cruiser.

"Morning yourself, Sheriff. What can I do for you?"

"Mind if I come up?"

"No not at all, C'mon up," Sam wondered what was on his mind as he climbed up the steps. "Cup of coffee?"

"Yeah, sure I could use a cup, thanks."

"No problem I was just having some, there's enough for the both of us."

"Great."

Sam returned with a fresh cup for himself and one for his surprise visitor. They both took a seat.

"So, Sheriff," Sam took a sip and waited.

"Coffee tastes real good," Sheriff Thompson took his time enjoying the bitter liquid. After an agonizing moment he balanced his cup on his knee and looked at Sam's battered face. "Those boys sure roughed you up, didn't they? You still of a mind not to press charges? Really should've had stitches for that cut over your eye."

"I'm fine, Sheriff," Sam didn't want to be rude but...

"Oh well, what's another scar, right? We all have a few scars."

"Sheriff," Sam took one more sip before setting his cup down by his feet. "I'm not exactly following you."

"I was referring to that other scar on your forehead there. Looks like a half-moon. How'd you get that?"

"I don't remember. Why?" Sam was starting to feel uncomfortable. Maybe he was still a little undone from yesterday, he tried to shrug it off.

"Oh, no reason in particular," he stood and downed the last of his coffee. "Thanks for the coffee, Sam I'm glad you're doing okay." He headed down the steps.

"You're welcome, Sheriff," He was relieved the awkward visit was at an end. "Thanks for stopping by." But before Sheriff Thompson got to his cruiser, he had one last thing.

"You have Hank doing some work for you the last day or two?"

"Yeah," Sam stood on the top step frowning down at the Sheriff. "He was fixing some windows, why."

"I don't know, on the phone he sounded shook up. It's probably nothing he tends to have a few drinks during the day."

Hank had been to Sam's House a couple of times and he didn't seem like the alcoholic type. He wasn't about to comment one way or another thinking about that bent ladder in his back yard.

When Sam didn't react, he gave it up. "Well, like I said most likely nothing." He gave a half salute, slid in behind the wheel and just like that he was gone.

Sam sat down in his chair and watched the dust of his passing settle to the ground. The image of the ladder snuck in; he had to look at again because ladders don't normally bend very easily.

————————————

"Good morning, Veronica, you're up early," Jorden strolled sleepy-eyed into the kitchen as Veronica was pouring herself a cup of tea.

"Hey, you two early birds good morning," Clare shuffled in. "That tea smells fabulous."

"Grab a cup it's ready," Veronica turned off the fire and moved the pot off the stove. Clare poured herself a cup and melted into a chair at the kitchen table holding her face over the steam.

"You, alright, Clare?" Veronica sat across from her and was joined by Jorden.

"Huh? Oh yeah, I'm fine just didn't sleep that great," she bent over her cup again.

"How about you, Jorden? Did you not sleep either?"

"Not really... maybe a little bit here and there. You slept alright though?"

"I slept soundly. Why are you two looking at me like that?"

"For one thing you were in pretty bad shape when you came home from Sam's," Clare was quick to point out. "You were exhausted and..."

"Dirty," Jorden stepped into the fray. "Your hair is a mess, full of who knows what. Your face was, is like you had mud on your face."

"You need to hop in the shower, Veronica. Lucky the store is closed today," Clare gave her sister one of her patented looks like, *boy, if we had to go to work today...* shaking her head slightly for emphasis.

"Have you looked in the mirror," Jorden offered one of her own patented looks.

"I don't normally look at myself in the mirror first thing in the morning," she felt her hair and it *was* stiff, with... she felt around. Her hair was indeed messed up. She glanced at her sisters and without another word headed for the shower.

"Okay, Clare so now what," Jorden wanted to know. "I mean, does she not remember last night?"

"I don't know, Jorden," Clare stopped steaming her face and drank some of her tea. "What I do know is she was in bad shape. There are things happening, we've all seen them or felt them."

Jorden nodded. "I saw that little boy, but only for a second. Why do you think his face is blurred? I mean you saw him too, right?"

"I have no idea, but it definitely has some meaning. Look, we have to talk to Veronica about doing the ceremony, when she gets back."

"I agree. We have to make a plan," Clare emptied her cup and rinsed it on the sink. "I'm gonna go get dressed."

"Me too," and off to their respective bedrooms they went.

Veronica was busy trying to untangle her hair when she realized the water had risen considerably. She looked down and saw there was a logjam of the things she pulled out of her hair blocking the drain. She bent down, grabbed a handful brushed the rest aside so the water could drain.

She turned off the water and slid the shower curtain back to throw the junk in her hand away. There was a moment, a split millisecond where she saw a dark shape standing by the bathroom door. She stumbled a little but there was nothing there, trick of the light she reasoned…

She wrapped a towel around herself and headed to her room to get dressed. By the time she came back into the kitchen Clare and Jorden were sitting at the table dressed and waiting.

Veronica stopped mid step, "What?"

"Come sit down, Veronica," Clare smiled up at her. "C'mon we have to talk."

Veronica stood there gauging her sister's expressions. She decided her best move was to sit.

"That's better," Clare leaned on her elbows. "You sure do look a lot better."

"That's for sure," Jorden chimed in. "You do remember yesterday, right?"

"I remember yesterday very clearly," she got up and poured herself another cup of tea while Clare and Jorden exchanged questioning looks. When she sat back down, she had a hard time trying to explain it.

It took a while, and her sisters were more than patient as she sorted it all out. Once everything was on the table the three of them sat quietly, not a word could be found between them, they just sat there...

"So," Clare broke through the silence first. "You actually saw a ladder bent in half?"

"There were deep furrows down the wall like something heavy jumped on it."

"Veronica," Clare moved her chair closer. "Jorden and I were up half the night wondering what it is we should do. And we kept coming up with the same conclusion. We must perform the ceremony."

"The ceremony?"

"It's the only way, Veronica," Jorden looked hard at her sister.

"But we haven't done one in a long time," Veronica was suddenly feeling nervous. "What happens if I can't remember the whole thing? What if something bad happens? I mean really bad... What happens-

"Okay, Veronica what's the matter?"

"Are you kidding me right now?" Veronica was on the defensive. "After what I just told you guys?"

"Veronica... we can only do the ceremony on a full moon, right?"

"Yeah, it has to be a full moon, sure."

"We have to do it at Sam's, he must be part of this. Besides that's where the energy lives."

"I'm aware of that but-

"The next full moon is in three days."

CHAPTER 57

Sam rolled out of bed with a groan his face though not as swollen was still tender. His side was the worst and he was sure he had a cracked rib or two. He shuffled downstairs and put on some water for much needed coffee. While that was getting hot, he went back upstairs and got dressed. He made it back down just as the kettle started to hiss.

Once he had his perfect cup of coffee he went out onto the front porch. He sat there for a long time with his perfect cup slowly cooling on his knee. He was replaying yesterday in his mind and it puzzled him, what happened anyway? She was a real mess. He hoped Veronica was alright he couldn't help but wonder why she was there in the first place. And still his perfect cup of untouched coffee sat cooling on his knee while he contemplated that.

"We have to go see Sam," Clare said as they were cleaning up the breakfast dishes.

Jorden nodded but Veronica was still a little hesitant.

"Veronica? We don't have any time to waste."

"I know," she was pouring herself a glass of water. "You're both right."

"Today, Veronica," Clare rinsed the last cup and put it on the strainer.

"Okay, I got it. I'm ready when you guys are."

They were relieved to find Sam's truck out front as they rolled into his driveway. Clare went up and knocked on the door while Jorden and Veronica climbed out of the VW. When she received no answer, she ventured a look inside. Nice cozy place she thought.

Without warning a dark mass blocked her view and she fell back against the porch railing. She gritted her teeth against the sharp pain in her back. She caught her breath and saw only her reflection in the front window.

"Clare!" Veronica and Jorden called in unison.

Clare waved her hand to signal she was okay.

Veronica and Jorden stood at the bottom of the steps squinting up at Clare who was rubbing her back.

"What happened, Clare," Veronica was feeling a slight electrical charge on the souls of her feet. She wondered where Sam was.

"Something blocked out the window."

"Wait, what?" Jorden was feeling goose-bumps race over her body. She climbed the steps and looked in the window. She saw a nice comfortable room. Then she had a flash of darkness... not complete darkness because she could see into the room. There stood a young boy and on the floor was a body... flashing blue and red lights flooded the room...

"Jorden?" Clare took her sister by the shoulders and gently turned her away from the window. "Let's see where Sam is," Clare marched down the steps followed by Jorden and the three sisters walked around the side of the house. Veronica started to shake a little when the shed came into view.

"Sam?" Clare called out.

Veronica was feeling the electricity start to surge through her body almost incapacitating her.

They heard something and they all tensed. When they were passing the shed about to round the corner to the backyard they ran into Sam. They couldn't help being startled a little bit, they were pretty wound up, but Sam was also startled when he ran into the girls.

"Whoa!" Sam put his hands out defensively. "What's going on here?"

Once they all composed themselves, they reconvened on the front porch. Sam even put some water on for tea. With tea in hands and a beautiful day burning through the pines Clare started the conversation. But Veronica cut in.

"Sam…" she stared into her cup as if her next words were floating around in there. "We need to perform a ceremony. After being… in that shed out back and seeing what I saw…" her train of thought just left the station without her.

"Sam there is a powerful presence here," Jorden picked it up. "When I saw my sister last night, well, I was honestly frightened," she was trying to keep her voice level. The last thing they need was a panic situation.

"Okay, give me a second," he fidgeted in his chair trying to get in that comfortable spot… but he was stalling.

"Sam, I saw things in that shed. I felt things…" Veronica took a gulp of water and promptly chocked. Clare patted her on the back until she stopped coughing. "I felt things when I was here the first time… I am feeling something right now. It's strong…" she shivered. "It's hard to describe. It's like a weight pressing in. An electrical current is buzzing me."

Sam gulped; he had a quick flashback just then. One which found him as a young boy, strapped to a bed, surrounded by people in white coats hovering over him with note pads, pencils scribbling away.

He was no stranger to the feeling of electrical current pulsing through his body. The doctors would take him to this room with lightboards and switches and colored lines that they hooked up to him… *But he never got to play with the other kids…* He always wondered where they went during the day…

"Okay, so…" he took a deep breath while he cleared the remnants of distant nightmares from his thoughts. He rummaged around for the right words. He smiled at the thought. What exactly were the right words in a situation like this? "You were saying?"

"We have to do a ceremony," Clare Leaned forward resting her elbows on her knees. "We don't have much time."

"What exactly do you mean by that?" Sam was very uncomfortable with this conversation. "I'm not quite following you."

"It has to be done in a full moon," Veronica picked up the explanation.

"Okay," Sam was still not really getting what the girls were trying to convey to him.

"It's getting stronger. It needs to transition out of this world into the world of the departed," Veronica could plainly see that it wasn't getting through to Sam.

"What's getting stronger? I'm sorry I just don't understand what it is you're getting at," Sam stood and looked out into the forest.

"Sam," Veronica stood next to him. "This thing, this entity is stuck between worlds. I-I have seen it I know what it is."

"Okay, what is it?" Sam was growing impatient. "Just tell me straight out."

"Alright, Sam, here it is…" Veronica cleared her throat and explained. "This entity is the spirit of an old man. He lived in this house a long time ago he…" The chimes suddenly sparkled to life at the end of the porch startling all of them.

"That's what we're trying to tell you," Clare walked over to the chimes and staired at them as they tinkled lightly then stopped. "There are two here, one is stuck, and one is a warning. A sort of barrier between you and this old spirit."

"Why would I need a barrier? How can you tell which is which?" Sam asked looking over at the now still chimes

"It's the way they present themselves."

"Yeah, uh, I'm getting more confused," Sam sat back down. "You say it's the way they present themselves… How?"

"There is a boy," Veronica continued. "A boy in a swimsuit? He has no face, or he does but it's always blurred. Have you seen this boy?"

Sam took a deep breath and let it out slowly. "I have seen a boy... And the other..."

"Yes," Clare was happy that they were finally getting somewhere. The boy and the other. "We believe that the boy is the spirit that is trying to warn you. The boy is the barrier. The other is trying to make you pay for it being stuck here."

"I have no idea who that is. I mean why would this..."

"Entity," Clare helped him out.

"Okay entity spirit... whatever what does all this have to do with me?"

"Sam," Veronica sighed. "This entity wants to attach itself to you."

"Oh boy, I'm just not understanding any of this."

"It's okay, Sam," Clare said in a calm voice. "We do. We can help it make the transition and clear it from doing any more harm."

"But," Jorden found her voice and added, "we don't have much time to do this. The full moon is in three days, and we have to prepare for the ceremony."

"Sam, you have to trust us."

"Okay, what should I do?" Sam wondered.

"First of all, keep your mind clear of negative thoughts."

"That shouldn't be a problem," He smiled.

"Good... that's good," Clare was trying to be reassuring.

"I was kidding."

"Oh, okay," Clare frowned. "Sam, you have to take this very seriously. If you don't, Sam look at me. If you don't the entity will eventually be able to lock onto you."

"Happy thoughts... I'm trying to have happy thoughts," But what he was being told did not contribute to his positive thoughts.

"The entity will latch onto you, Sam. It will take over your body," Veronica realized what she was saying must be crazy to hear.

"Define 'latch onto'."

"Steal," Clare always the blunt one. "The entity will steal your body. In doing so it will have essentially traded places with you."

"And I'm somehow supposed to stay positive."

"If you take this seriously and listen to what we are saying to you," Veronica looked at her sisters then back at Sam. "We can perform this special ceremony and open a sort of porthole for it to pass from this world into the next."

"Sounds a little dangerous," Sam stood. "Would anybody like a beer? Glass of wine? I'm having a beer," he announced and went for the front door. Before he had his hand on the doorknob Veronica said she would like a beer. "Very good, that's two beers coming up," he looked at the other two women got nothing so two beers it was.

"Veronica," Jorden looked hard at her sister. "A beer? Seriously?"

"Yes, a beer."

"Here we are," he handed Veronica her beer, the faces the other two were making was not lost on him.

"Thanks, that feels good," Veronica held the bottle to her forehead. She took a sip and set it down on the floor beside her.

"Okay," Sam was still standing. "You ladies want anything?" Clare and Jorden shook their heads no so Sam plopped back down in his chair.

"Sam," Clare cleared her throat. "We need to do the ceremony here, at your house."

"Oh, I was wondering where this was supposed to happen."

"It absolutely *has* to be here. The energy is strongest here. It will take us a full two days to gather everything we need and prepare ourselves."

"Sam, you have to want us to do this," Veronica had to have him say it. "You have to really want us to do this."

"Okay."

"Sam, you have to say the words," Clare instructed. "It's meaningless for us to do this thing just because we feel it necessary. It doesn't work that way."

"Alright..." he studied the three expectant faces before him. "I... I want you to come over to my house and help me..." Three heads nodded in unison. "To help me get rid-

"No," Veronica stopped him. "You can't say it like that. You shouldn't say get rid. We're helping it to pass over."

Sam took a good gulp of his beer, gazed at the three women, cleared his throat and tried again.

"I want you to come over to-

"Wait," It was Jorden this time. "Instead of want shouldn't it be more like want to ask?"

Sam took another swig of beer, squared his shoulders and started again...

"I want to *ask* you if you *could* come over and help this entity? Cross over... and finally be at peace," he finished his beer and smiled.

"Okay, that's very nice of you to ask," Veronica picked up her beer in salute and gulped the rest of it down. When she finished, she let out a long satisfying burp and glowered at her sisters who were not happy with her behavior.

"Alright then," Veronica stood and stretched. "We have a lot to do in a very short time so, thanks for the beer and we'll see you in a couple of days."

"Sounds good, thank you," he stood on the porch watching the little bug drive away. He went into the house and grabbed himself another beer then returned to his chair on the front porch.

CHAPTER 58

"Hey Frank, Frank," Leroy went over and shook Frank by the shoulder.

"W-what are you doin'? Leroy back off a me," Frank growled to a sitting position, his face said it all, he was in bad shape from the beat down he suffered, and he wasn't at all happy about it either.

"Let's go get some breakfast, Frank we got nothin' to eat here."

"Why don't you go get us something to eat and I'll stay here."

"C'mon Frank," Leroy, sat down on the couch looking dejected.

"Alright, Leroy," Frank grumbled. "Give me a second to wake up, will ya?"

"Sure thing, Frank," Leroy switched on the TV and waited.

When the Frank and Leroy show arrived at Ida's there was quite a crowd parked in the lot. Frank had to park across the street which didn't add to his humor. They pushed through the doors and just like in the movies everybody stopped talking and turned their way. Frank glowered back with little effect, so they took the last two stools at the bar.

Slowly the conversations continued although not as loud as before.

"Mornin' boys what can I getch'ya?" The waitress stood ready while, true to form, Leroy couldn't decide.

"C'mon Leroy," Frank nudged him. "Lady's waitin'.

"I'll have the number three over easy with crispy bacon."

"Would you boys like some coffee while you wait?"

"Sure, two please, black."

"Frank why did you order both our coffees black? You know I like a little cream in mine."

"You can tell that to the waitress when she comes back."

As they were eating and trying to ignore the stares a man came by. He stopped next to Frank on the way out.

"Say," he leaned conspiratorially. "You heard Sheriff is reopening the murder case?"

"What murder case old man?" Frank asked with a full mouth of pancakes.

"Why, the Henning murders," he went, paid his tab and walked out the door as Frank and Leroy stared after him.

"D'you hear that, Frank?" Leroy was wide-eyed. His Face was threatening to quiver.

"I hope they get the son-of-a-bitch," Frank forked in another bite of pancakes and washed it down with some coffee.

"Geeze, Frank," Leroy stopped eating. "Do ya really think they'll catch 'em?"

"He's right here under everybody's nose," Frank motioned for more coffee.

"W-what do ya mean right here... u-under everybody's nose, Frank?" Leroy was suddenly very tense.

"Sam," Frank had a mouthful and was not interested in talking any more.

"Oh, yeah, Sam," Leroy relaxed and started in on his crispy bacon. "Well, he did it for sure."

"Hey, Joyce, how's the Judge doing with my petition?"

"Can I put you on hold for a second Sheriff while I check?"

"No problem," Sheriff Thompson put his feet up on his desk careful not to disturb the pile of papers.

"Hello, Sheriff?"

"Yes, I'm here."

"I just spoke briefly with the Judge, he said he should be finished looking over your request and have your warrants in a couple of days."

"That's great I'll send my Deputy over as soon as we hear back. Thanks, have a good day."

"You bet Sheriff. You'll be hearing form this office very soon. Good day to you."

Sheriff Thompson set the receiver back in its cradle, leaned back in his chair and closed his eyes. Until his door opened.

"Hey, Sheriff," Deputy Riggs walked through the door with a wide smile plastered across his face.

"Well good morning, Deputy. What's got you all smiley face this morning?"

"Oh, nothing," he went over to his little desk and sat down. "I was over at Ida's for breakfast and I gotta tell you the place is buzzin'".

"I figured it wouldn't take long before everybody in the county find out."

"Have you talked to the Judge?"

"Right before you stormed in."

"Well, what did he say? Or can't you tell me."

"There are not secrets here. His secretary informed me that I will have the warrants in the next couple a days."

"Oh, boy," Deputy Riggs let out a low whistle. "You know this is gonna turn this town into a circus, 'specially when the media finds out."

"There's nothing I can do about that. But when I get the call, I'm sending you up to retrieve the warrants. There will be two; one is an arrest warrant the other is a search warrant. Make sure that you look them over good before you leave the courthouse."

"Will do Sheriff," Deputy Riggs busied himself with his daily report which wasn't a whole lot different from the day before and probably won't change much from tomorrow... But when he brings those warrants back?

———————————————

Susan was busily stocking fishing supplies when Daphne walked up and surprised her.

"Hey, Susan," Daphne had this grin on her face that Susan had seen before, it was the look of someone with a very important secret to share, you know the look the *I know something you don't* look? That was it.

"Hey, Daphne, what's up?"

"Oh nothing."

Alright Susan had the feeling that Daphne wasn't going to just bust out and tell her. She would make Susan wait.

"So, I know you want to tell me something. I'm really busy so if you don't mind. I have to get this section done today," Susan kept stocking shelves while Daphne watched. "C'mon Daphne what is it?"

"Well, since you're probably the only one in town that hasn't heard…"

"Geeze, Daphne what's with all the drama?"

"Alright," Daphne took her time she wanted to watch Susan squirm a little. She could be very mean that way. "Sheriff Thompson… well it's all over town…"

"Daphne you're supposed to be downstairs minding the check out."

"I know, I know but I thought you might like to know that Sheriff Thompson is reopening the homicide case of Sam's parents."

"Wait what are you saying?"

"Sheriff has petitioned Judge Crane up in Centerville to reopen the case. I'm surprised you haven't heard."

"I've been busy, and I don't pay much attention to town gossip."

"Susan this isn't your average town gossip. This is real and according to Deputy Riggs the Judge is getting the paperwork in a couple of days."

It took everything Susan had not to react to this disturbing bit of information. She was not going to give Daphne the satisfaction. "Okay, Daphne well, I have to get back to work," just like that she dismissed Daphne who was left stunned that Susan hadn't acted like she thought she was going to.

"I just thought that you should know is all, Susan," she was disappointed and just went back downstairs to the cashier area and sulked.

Susan on the other hand was having a very hard time concentrating on what she was doing. Her mind was racing with what if's though she couldn't venture any guesses one way or another. She well knew the story as did everyone in Springville. But she'd be damned if she would let Daphne make her feel uncomfortable in any way.

Only problem with that theory was... she did. She had the very strong feeling that she should go see Sam after work. Her mind was cluttered with possibilities. None were good... And... this is a biggie with fries, what about that house?

By the end of the day Susan was mentally drained. She went into the employee locker room grabbed her sweater, her car keys and bolted for the door before anymore encounters with the town gossip.

She got in her car and turned the key, the engine roared to life startling her. After calming down she switched the radio on and headed for the liquor store and a fresh bottle of wine. When she got there, she wondered if she should get the wine and go home... or get the wine and go see Sam. It was a quandary for sure.

Oh heck, she scolded herself for being so contrary and went for the wine. Once back in her car the same nagging questions filled her head. She decided to go see Sam, what could it hurt? As for the house... she'd just take that as it came and hope it doesn't do what it did the other night.

She rolled onto Sam's road and slowed down. It was still early afternoon, so she scanned the forest that loomed in on both sides. She loved this time of day as the light changes to more muted colors.

Something ran in front of her, and she stepped on the brake pedal with both feet creating a suffocating dust cloud. She frantically rolled her window up while she coughed her head off. When the dust settled, she slowly rolled her window back down and looked around. It was long gone whatever it was, but it was fast, really fast.

Susan took her feet off the brake and continued down the short dirt road. When she rounded the last little bend her heart skipped a beat. Sam was out at his BBQ. Smoke was in his face, but she could see he was smiling. She pulled in and got out before he noticed her.

"Hey you," Sam waved with his tongs. "What brings you out this way?"

"Well," Susan walked over to Sam and his smoking grill. "Found this bottle of wine and was wondering if you'd like to have some with me."

"I would never turn down an offer like that. I have a steak on and it's big enough we can split it if you want."

"I definitely would never turn down an offer like that," she grinned up at him and handed him the wine bottle.

"I'll be right back, keep an eye on that steak."

While he was gone, she couldn't help looking around at the trees that surrounded his house. She saw nothing unusual for which she was grateful.

"Alright we have wine," Sam announced as he descended the steps. "Here you go pretty lady." He handed her a glass and sipped from his own. "So, to what do I owe the pleasure?"

"Oh," Sheriff Thompson jumped into her thoughts just then but, she wasn't quite ready for that conversation. "I just thought I'd stop by. Does a girl always have to have a reason for visiting her friend?"

"I guess not," he smiled at her forwardness. He admired it. "How do you like your steak?"

"On my plate," she laughed into her glass.

"Oh, a wise guy huh?" Sam returned to his sizzling steak nudging it around on the grill.

"Okay, let's take this beauty inside and put it on our plates," Sam carefully removed the steak from the fire placing it on a plate and headed for the front steps.

"Sam? Sam," Susan stood frozen to the spot as she tried to process what exactly she was seeing. Sam was halfway up the steps before he stopped and turned around. He didn't like the look on her face, it was a mask of fear.

"What is it Sus- Sam looked in the direction she was staring, and his heart sank. There at the corner of the house stood a small boy in a blue bathing suit...

Sam set the plate of steak carefully on the top rail and went down to Susan.

"I-I think it's okay," *did he just say that with a straight face?* Was it *okay* that a young boy, in a blue bathing suit, was standing at the corner of his house? And to top it all off he had no face, it was a blurry ball resting on his shoulders.

Then he was gone, like poof disappeared as if he was never there to begin with.

"Okay, let's eat! I'm starving," he was trying like hell to sound upbeat but inside he was anything but.

"Yeah," Susan was still staring at the spot where the boy was. "I could use some more wine." She took the steps a little too fast and almost went down on the top step.

"Are you okay?"

"If you are then I guess I am," her words fell flat, and she knew it, though Sam didn't let on.

"C'mon in, let's get this steak cut up and eat," he held the door while he balanced the steak plate.

"Oh, this steak is heaven," Susan proclaimed with a mouthful.

"Slowdown, enjoy it," Sam smiled. He felt good in Susan's company, comfortable. "How was your day?"

"It was long today," she forked another bite and made a purring sound as she chewed it. Sheriff Thompson's voice invaded her thoughts just then and she stopped chewing for a second.

"You, okay?"

"Yeah, what was that out there anyway? I mean you act like you've seen it before."

"I have," how do you even begin to explain that the boy… naw, he wasn't ready, maybe it will all become clear when the girls do their thing. For now, he was willing to let that one ride.

"Well, are you going to keep me in suspense?"

"Honestly, Susan, I'm not exactly sure what it is. It knows my name," boom there it was, and he was being truthful.

"It what," she stared choking. It got so bad Sam got up and patted her on the back until she could catch her breath. She quickly finished chewing and took a swig of wine. "I'm fine now, thanks," she stared down at her plate. "You… did you just say it knows your name?"

"I know how crazy it must sound," his words left him hanging in the wind.

"After the other night?" She took a sip. "Why would I think anything sounds crazy that… what is it, he, it?"

"I was told by Veronica; she's one of the-

"I know Veronica, well I don't really know her, but I've seen her around a few times. What does she have to do with all of this?" She gasped, hoping *she* didn't sound like some jealous girlfriend.

"She visited me a while ago, I don't know, it wasn't that long ago. Anyway, she saw him too," he took a moment to measure Susan's reaction. She itched her nose but that was the extent of it. So, he carried on. "She said that he was a spirit. She said he was a warning and a…barrier that it's close to me. Geeze, more wine?"

"Why don't you just bring the bottle out."

"Great idea, save my place."

When Sam returned, he had another bottle of wine as they had almost finished the one Susan brought. He poured without spilling any and took his seat.

"Uh, earth to Sam."

"Oh, sorry I was thinking of what else she said," he took a deep breath of the pines. "She said… there is another one," He was really having a hard time talking about this, but it was too late to stop now. "She told me the other one is an old spirit, it's a mimic," he was out of breath and his injuries started making themselves known.

"Sam? You okay, buddy?" She noticed he winced a little bit. He was still pretty beat up. The swelling in his face had gone down but the bruising was showing up in dark patches on his cheek and jawline.

"Yeah, guess I'm still a little sore."

"A mimic?"

"Huh?"

"You said the other one is a mimic. I mean I think I know what it means but, what does it mean?"

"It's a shapeshifter."

"Shit!"

"That's what I said," he took a drink of wine, because men don't sip, and continued. "Veronica and her sisters are coming over here day after tomorrow," he paused unable to believe what he heard himself saying. "They're going to perform some kind of ceremony, to… I'm not sure I understand it but, this ceremony is supposed to help these 'spirits' move on to wherever they move on to, I guess."

"Wow, you know… refill please. Thanks, when I heard you were back in town-

"Back in town?" He gritted his teeth in frustration. Why couldn't he remember.

"Sam," she took his hand. "Sam, I don't know any other way to tell you this, so I'm just going to say it. Sheriff has reopened a murder case that happened a long time ago…"

"He told me."

"I heard from a fairly reliable source, or I wouldn't even bring it up. Sam, Sheriff Thompson has petitioned an arrest warrant from the Judge up in Centerville."

"So... what does that have too do with me?" He was truly baffled by the turn of conversation.

"They're arrest warrants. For *your* arrest, Sam," Susan took a long sip of her wine, she set her empty glass on the top rail. "I-I really thought hard about this information and what I should do with it, I'm sorry Sam."

"Well," he had no words.

"You really have no idea about any of your past?"

"I remember the hospital... and the room they kept me in..." those memories, memories of a never-ending nightmare flooded his thoughts. "Nothing before that, if that's what you mean. I don't remember my parents, this town, you..." his emotions were running too close to the surface, and he had to get control of them. Now was not the time to break down, as if any time really was.

"It must've been awful," Susan tried to imagine the unimaginable. "You say they kept you in a room? What kind of room."

"I was locked in it, the room," Sam closed his eyes and held onto Susan's hand. "It had a big window, and I used to watch the other kids who were sleeping in beds all along the walls. They would all leave during the day and come back in the afternoon. I always wondered where they went... and why I had to be locked up in my room. I watched the other kids, they never looked right. They rolled their heads, some clawed at the air..."

"Oh, Sam," she squeezed his hand. "I can't imagine, I don't want to imagine."

"Do you know how long it will be?"

"What?"

"The Sheriff, how long before he gets the warrant?"

"It's hard to say, I don't know," she felt like a deflating balloon.

"Susan, I didn't kill anyone. Why would he arrest me?" Then it all started to make sense. "Is this why people look at me the way they do? Damn everybody knows me except *me* why the hell can't I remember?"

Everything got eerily quiet all the sudden, so quiet it made their ears ring. Then the chimes slowly came to life and the laughing...

CHAPTER 59

The next couple of days were busy times for the three sisters. There were a lot of things to gather and prepare and everything had to be exactly right nothing could be forgotten or fast-tracked.

When the day finally came to face the darkness, they were as ready as they would ever be. It was early, just after two in the afternoon when they made their final preparation, they would go into a deep meditation to clear any negative thoughts from their minds.

———————————————

Sheriff Thompson waited anxiously at his desk for Deputy Riggs to get back from Centerville. He got up and paced around his small office occasionally looking out the front window. The day was slipping by.

Finally, Deputy Riggs pulled up in front of the station and got out, but he wasn't smiling. He entered the office looking like a kid who had his lunch money stolen.

"What is it, Deputy?" Sheriff Thompson took the offered folder and went to his desk.

"Well, the Judge wasn't all that convinced. You'll see his notes right on top there. He told me in no uncertain terms that, 'your Sheriff better be damn sure about this,' "he said," 'what about the handprint on the back door in the kitchen? What about the murder weapon?' "Hell, Sheriff it's right there on top," He plopped down at his own desk exhausted by the lecture he received up in Centerville. Deputy Riggs sat quietly and waited to hear what the Sheriff had to say about all that.

After he looked over the comments and the warrants he stood and reached for his hat and keys.

"Sheriff?" Deputy Riggs rose from his chair.

"Time to go Deputy," Sheriff Thompson held the door while his Deputy slipped by.

Sheriff Thompson and Deputy Riggs arrived at Sam's a minute before the girls got there. When they saw the two police cruisers sitting in front of Sam's they paused a second before they drove in. Sheriff Thompson was walking up the steps when they got out of their car. They said hi to Deputy Riggs who remained standing by his cruiser.

"Deputy," Clare was concerned by their presence. "What's going on here?"

"You all need to stay back," he was visibly nervous, but he also had a job to do and that was to keep everyone on scene safe and to block any interference in police business.

"Is Sam being arrested?" Veronica walked up and asked Deputy Riggs.

"Yes, we are arresting Sam Henning. Now please stay where you are."

"You can't arrest him now," Clare protested. "Now is exactly the wrong time."

Jorden was starting to panic. "What were they going to do?" They needed Sam for the ceremony. This was not happening.

CHAPTER 60

Back in town people were already buzzing with the news of the arrest. Clevus Monroe walked into the McKandless Emporium and sought out Susan whom he had known since she was born, he was her uncle. When he spotted her, he went to her and took her by the elbow.

"Susan," He whispered as he looked around for anyone eavesdropping on their conversation. "Susan, Sheriff Thompson and Deputy Riggs just drove out to Sam's place," he paused and took a breath.

"Why? What for?"

"You must've heard that Sheriff Thompson reopened the Henning murder case?"

"Yes but-

"They got the warrants a little bit ago and are going out there to arrest him for the murder of his parents. I'm sorry to be the one to have to tell you but I figured you'd rather hear it from me than some loose mouthed town gossip."

"I appreciate you telling me." She was looking around trying to decide what to do. "I have to go. I have to go see Sam," with that she hurried to the employee locker room, pulled her stuff out of her locker and raced out to her car.

By the time she reached Sam's she was stunned to see him walking out with his hands behind his back led by the Sheriff. The three sisters were there looking just as shocked by the events. She watched Sam's face as he was led to the cruiser and placed in the back.

His face was a mask of confusion and, there was something else she saw in his face, something she had seen before; the day he was jumped by Frank and his cousin. It was a look of pure coldness.

He didn't look at Susan or the three sisters who were standing with her in the sun-drenched yard. They stood there; mouths open but no words were said. They stared after the cruisers as they drove away.

"What are we gonna do now?" Jorden was the first to find her voice.

"What do you mean?" Susan came out of her shock. "What's happening?"

"We're going... or were going to do a ceremony to rid this house of the trapped spirit. But now..." She looked to her sisters who were shaking their heads.

Susan looked around half expecting to see the boy with no face, but the area was empty except for the four of them. And it was quiet almost too quiet. "So, what happens now?" Susan was curious.

"The only way we can do the ceremony is with Sam..." Jorden was very disappointed with the turn of events as were her sisters.

"Wait," Veronica became animated all the sudden. "We can still do the ceremony."

"How?" Jorden wondered.

"How do you figure we can still do it without Sam here?" Clare also wanted to know.

"We just need someone who is close to him," at that moment three pairs of eyes bore into Susan who took an involuntary step back.

"Oh no," she put her hands up. "I don't think that's such a good idea."

"Susan you're the only one in this town who is close to him. You guys have a history," Veronica wasn't taking no for an answer.

"Yeah, a history that he has absolutely no memory of."

"It has to be you," Clare reasoned.

"There's no one else Susan," Veronica added.

"I have to sit down," Susan suddenly felt her legs were about to buckle. So, she went up to the front porch and fell into one of the chairs. The sisters followed her up and sat down with her. For a while nobody said a word until the chimes started to tinkle.

"It's here," Veronica looked at the chimes. While goose bumps raced over Susan's body.

"What is it, exactly?" Susan rubbed her arms she felt cold all the sudden.

"It's a spirit. The spirit of an old man who lived here before Sam's family lived here," Veronica answered. "It's trapped in this world unable to make the transition into the next. It's not happy either."

"Why… why would it wait so long to…" She didn't have any idea how to ask that question, so she just let it kind of drift away.

"Because Sam's back…"

"I saw that… boy or whatever it is…" Susan said watching the chimes tinkling even though there wasn't any wind to make them do that. Now she had goose bumps on top of goose bumps.

"Yeah, we've seen him also he has an important purpose is in all this."

Veronica walked over to the chimes and held her hands out cupping them but not touching them. She got a jolt of freezing cold that caused her to shiver, and she backed away.

"Veronica? Are you-

"I'm okay but, we don't have much time," she looked back at her sisters. "We still have things to do to prepare and it's getting late.

"Alright I guess I'll be going and let you do whatever it is you're about to do." She stood testing her legs and started for the stairs.

"Susan wait," Veronica gently took her arm, and she felt Susan flinch.

"I really can't stay. I have to work tomorrow and…" a movie of the other night played in her head making her shake a little.

"Susan please," Veronica could feel her trembling. "I'm not sure you fully understand what has to happen here."

"That would be an understatement."

"This spirit has been basically dormant all this time. It was Sam's energy that woke it up. The longer it stays trapped in our world the stronger and more dangerous it will become."

An arctic blast of air swept down the porch startling everyone and yet the chimes remained still...

CHAPTER 61

"Frank! Frank!" Leroy burst into their trailer swinging a twenty-four pack.

"Geezus Leroy!" Frank shot up from the couch where he was having himself a little nap. "What the hell is it?"

"They got 'em, Frank! They got 'em!"

"Will ya quit your damn yellin' I'm right here for…" He sucked in a breath and rubbed the sleep from his eyes. "What the hell time is it anyway?"

"It's beer thirty brother," Leroy sat down in the chair and proceeded to tear open the box of beers.

"Don't call me brother! What the hell's wrong with you?"

"While you were sleepin' Sheriff Thompson and Deputy Riggs went over and arrested Sam."

"What? Slow down and hand me one of them bruskies."

"I was sayin' that while you were-

"Skip that part," Frank popped his beer and took a swig. "Get to the last part again."

"Okay, as I was-

"Dammit Leroy."

"Okay, okay," Leroy popped his own beer and took drink, he looked over at Frank.

"Leroy," Frank crushed his beer can and heaved it onto the pile in the corner. "If you don't get right to it and I mean right to it I'm liable to strangle you."

"Whoa there, Frank," Leroy hurried his next drink and coughed. "They arrested Sam just a little while ago, Frank. They caught the murderer."

"Well, I'll be," Frank sat back and contemplated that bit of news for a second. And the way his mind processed it came down to one thing… Susan.

"Toss me another one of those, Leroy." He had a ridiculous smile plastered across his swollen, bruised face. "Tell it to me one more time, slowly."

———————————

Sam sat down on the thin hard bed completely devoid of thought. Sheriff Thompson was on the phone with Judge Crane up in Centerville. The light had left the country an hour ago and Sheriff Thompson sent his Deputy home.

"You read the notes I sent along with your Deluty?" The Judge asked.

"I did, Judge," Sheriff Thompson looked over at his prisoner who was sitting quietly in his cell. "I have the same concerns."

"Then am I to understand that we are on the same page here, Sheriff?"

"We are sir," Sheriff Thompson was looking at the clock.

"I have set a preliminary hearing for the tenth. That's in two days."

"That's awfully soon judge."

"I have assigned Howard Pamplen to the case he's our Prosecuting Attorney here in the capital courthouse. I have spoken with him, and he has everything you gave me. Unless there's something else?"

"No Judge that's everything."

"I have also contacted both Deputies Green and Ellis who were first on the scene as was your friend Sheriff Dobbs. They have declined to be present, and both have conveyed to me that anything they had to say was in their reports. They both sited reasons of distress and I agreed to let their reports speak for them."

"I think that's kind of you Judge. I heard they were pretty shaken up by the event."

"The whole town was, Sheriff."

"As was I Judge, Sheriff Dobbs was a good friend of mine."

"That's the other thing I want to discuss with you Sheriff."

"What's that Judge."

"Is that why you decided to open this wound, Sheriff?"

"I want to know the truth Judge, that's all."

"Very well, Sheriff, I will see you at nine o'clock sharp two days from now."

"I won't be late Judge," the line on the other end clicked off and Sheriff Thompson set his phone in its cradle. He went back to his reports pouring over them until his eyes went buggy and he had to call it a night.

He stood, stretched and grabbed his hat off the peg behind him. He glanced over at his prisoner who hadn't moved or made a sound the whole time. Sheriff Thompson locked the door behind him and drove home for some much-needed sleep.

CHAPTER 62

"Okay, Susan?" Veronica stood next to her in the living room.

"I'm okay as I'll ever be all things considered," truth be told she was very nervous.

"One last thing has to be done before we start," she lit a tied bundle of sage and handed it to Susan who refused it.

"Why do I have to do this? I don't even know what's going on... mostly."

"We'll be right with you the whole way but it's you who must do this last part. What you will be doing is basically clearing the area."

"See, that's what bothers me," Susan looked out the window and only saw their reflections. It was dark out there.

"We're just going to walk around the house, inside and out, even the shed and hit it with sage. Then we're going to come back in here and get started with the final part."

"You make it sound so easy, nothing to it right?"

"Wrong," Clare stepped next to her sister. "There's nothing easy about any of this. And to be honest?"

"Do you have to be?"

"Not if you don't want me to be."

"Okay be honest," she said louder than she had intended. "If it's going to help Sam... This *will* help Sam right?"

"We sincerely hope so, Susan. But we need to get going."

Once they finished the rounds in the house they went outside. From the moment they closed the front door they could feel a distinct temperature change. The change wasn't due to the time of year, it was summertime. No, this kind of temperature change comes from something else, something that's not supposed to be here...

They walked down the porch going slowly around the chimes which were still. They went down the front steps and darkness closed in around them. Clare, Veronica, and Jorden were holding lit candles, but their flickering light wasn't near enough to pierce the darkness. Susan held the stick of sage out in front of her it's orange glow was somehow comforting.

It wasn't until they rounded the corner of the house that things took a turn. Something blew on the stick of sage sending sparks into the night air. Susan almost dropped it and would have if Clare hadn't stepped up behind her and held her by the shoulders.

"What was that?" Susan looked back at Clare.

"Let's just keep going. We're almost there."

Veronica was buzzing with electrical currents that were running through her body just then. Jorden sensed her sister's unease and grabbed her arm. When they began walking again there was an immediate feeling that someone or something was watching them, they huddled closer together.

The moon was lighting the forest now casting sharp shadows across the ground. Up ahead was the grey image of a small building.

"That's the shed," Veronica whispered, and the little party came to a halt.

"Is this where-

"Yes, this is where it happened," Veronica straightened herself, she had to absolutely have no doubt about anything tonight.

"What? Where what happened?" Susan turned to face the three candle lit faces.

"Something pulled me into that shed and I couldn't get out until…" Veronica thought she heard something moving off to their left.

"What is it Veronica," Jorden was spooked. "Did you hear something?"

Four pairs of startled eyes scanned the surrounding trees and came up empty.

"It was nothing I guess," Veronica composed herself. "We have to keep moving."

When everybody got turned back around and headed in the right direction the shed doors burst open causing one of them to fly off its hinges and shatter against the nearest tree. An icy cold wind hit them just then extinguishing the candles while sparks from the sage glittered in the night air, then it was gone.

"Yeah, so, I'm about done with this," Susan brushed at a tiny ember that found her sweater.

"No, no you have to stay," Veronica pleaded. "Once we started this ceremony we can't stop."

Clare gently spun Susan around so she could see her. "I know what you must feel like right now but, we need to continue. To stop now would... well it wouldn't be good."

"You're sure not making me feel any better," Susan studied the face in front of her. It appeared relaxed but she also saw just a hint of, *oh shit* in her eyes.

"Let's, we have to stay together and keep moving," they passed the open shed like people pass a major traffic accident; not wanting to look but looking anyway.

When they reached the last side of the house Susan was beginning to feel somewhat relieved, soon they would be inside. *Okay around the last corner all good. There's the front steps,* the front steps looked like a jagged tongue in the moon light. *Okay, up the stairs door opening...* a cold hand that felt stiff and sharp, like bone clutched Susan as she was about to close the door.

Sam was completely lost in the semi-darkness of his cell. His mind wasn't functioning. He got up and walked the short way to a window stepping over the barred shadow that stretched across the floor...

The window was up high on the wall but, he was tall enough to reach the cold bars and strong enough to pull himself up and stay there. He looked out onto a weed strewn patch of property that no one seems to see any potential in. It looked about as lonely out there as he felt, at that moment. He couldn't see much out that small window, there wasn't all that much to see anyway. A quiet town where everyone went to bed early and rolled out of bed early. The moon was almost straight up shrinking shadows when he dropped back down to the floor. He went over to the cot, took off his boots and lay down to study a ceiling he could barely see.

What am I doing here? He asked the ceiling. *Why, am I here in this place of ghosts and lost memories?* Sam rolled over and closed his eyes he was done with questions that had no answers for one day.

CHAPTER 63

"Okay everybody ready?" Veronica surveyed the faces in their little circle. Susan was able to find half a smile and Veronica was just going to have to leave it at that. "Remember, whatever happens we absolutely cannot let go of each other's hands."

Candles had been placed in the center of the table. They had carried the kitchen table into the den so they could make a fire in the fireplace. The ambient warmth helped to relax everyone. Sage filled the small cozy room. Veronica opened her book and began read and as she read things changed.

Wind, mild at first was now livelier. Small bits of forest debris tapped at the window and rattled the eaves. Veronica was unfazed almost trans-like as she read the ancient words meant only for occasions like this one. Half the words Susan couldn't begin to make out, she didn't need to. All she had to do was hold onto the hands on either side of her. That's all she had to do.

Susan was hanging on pretty well considering... until the moaning started. It was low and persistent, sinister in its tone. It sounded like it was on the front porch. Susan opened her eyes just long enough to look at the others. Veronica was concentrating on her reading, Clare and Jorden were looking around the room as if expecting something. She closed her eyes quickly and hung onto the hands for dear life.

A light puff fluttered the candle flames, the wind continued to assert itself outside, and still Veronica read. Time was lost somewhere, it ceased to matter. Then the candles went out casting the room in a warm orange glow. It was startling but it wasn't dark, everyone was still visible.

The room, even though there was a nice fire in the fireplace, turned cold. Grips tightened around the table as it started to vibrate. It was tapping the floor with wooden legs that jumped up and down like bare feet on a hot surface. Then, just as suddenly as it started it stopped. *That was startling*.

The front door crashed open and though everybody jumped no one lost their hold. Wind filled the rooms of the house. It entered the den with a vengeance swirled around picking up anything that was light.

Papers flew around, the light on the stand over by the easy chair began to rock back and forth. There was an almost audible voice centered in it all. The wind stopped. A funny thought hit Susan just then, the chimes, she didn't recall hearing the chimes through it all and that was a little disturbing.

Veronica stopped reading and looked at the others, her face was ashen. She had a strange look, everyone's hair was tossed about their shoulders.

"He's here," Veronica whispered in a voice made husky from the long reading. "Don't anybody move, no talking. Only me." Everyone nodded.

"I know who you are," She spoke to the emptiness. "I have seen you. We are here to help you make the journey you so much want to take."

Something fell in the kitchen and shattered on the floor. A book flew across the room smacking the wall. Then another and another until it stopped.

"We are not here to bring you harm. We can help you." The candles raised off the table and ended up in the fireplace where they melted in a sputtering fire. Veronica flipped a couple pages and began reading again even though her voice was almost gone.

The entity in the room perched itself, in the form of a black mass, on the ceiling over their heads. It undulated like thick smoke but stayed in one spot; it did not dissipate. Veronica read until her voice was gone. She pushed the book over to Clare without breaking her grip and Clare took it up.

As Clare read the walls slowly moved in and out as if they were breathing. The floor buckled slightly under their feet and still Clare read and still they held hands in the firelit room. The dark cloud was moving down the opposite wall now pooling on the floor. Clare did not look she kept reading and they all kept holding hands.

"The man who now lives here knows nothing about you. He means you no harm but, he does want you to move on and that's why we are here tonight."

The dark pool on the floor was taking shape. It was moving all over the place as if struggling to create form out of nothing. Then, it stood before them; a dark shadow of a man no features just a dark shape standing quietly.

Clare called to it, "Take the portal we have opened for you to pass through, leave this house. It does not belong to you anymore. You don't belong here anymore."

The house shuttered and shook until they until they were sure it was going to come apart. It was loud and incredibly frightening. There was a long terrible moan that shook the women to their foundations and still Clare spoke to it the way a fireman would talk to someone on a ledge, nice and easy. The moaning was reaching deafening proportions and Clare rallied her troops.

"Don't break the circle!" she cried. As the volume of the voice intensified Susan heard herself scream, she couldn't help it she was being pushed way past her limits.

The ceiling bowed and Susan was sure it was about to cave in on them. Clare continued speaking and the moaning continued to elevate. Everything and everyone were nearing their breaking point. Veronica was exhausted and crying as was Jorden it was all so impossible... and then it was over. The dark shape vanished along with that awful moaning, the wind stopped, and the room settled.

A new day was making its presence known shooting a warm box of morning light into the room. Four exhausted women sat quietly at the table still holding hands. Until one by one they let go. A blue jay hopped onto the window ledge and tapped on the glass. Birds could be heard warming up their morning songs. The air grew light.

Susan was up and stretching with a groan. The house was a complete disaster, but it was quiet, and it felt peaceful.

"What do we do now?" she asked looking around at the mess.

"There's nothing left to do, Susan," Clare smiled brushing a runaway hair out of her face. "We did it, the spirit has passed on and there will be no more problems here."

"We need to clean up this house, but I'm way too tired to think about that right now," Veronica held her arms out doing a slow spin and smiled. There was only a slight sign of a presence, she thought she knew what it was.

"I need some fresh air," Susan declared and went for the front door. The others followed until they were all leaning on the top rail gulping for air.

CHAPTER 64

Two days later, you could've driven down any street in Springville and you would have found them deserted. It was like a ghost town. News travels at light speed in a small town like Springville the people donned their Sunday best and left for Centerville in a stampede.

The courtroom was filled to maximum capacity. People were lined along the walls and out the door. Judge Crane entered the courtroom and stood for a moment smiling at the crowd that had mostly quieted down.

"Order in this court," the Deputy called. "The honorable Judge Crane presiding."

Judge Crane took his seat behind his massive bench and banged his gavel.

"You may be seated," the Deputy instructed and those that could, did.

"Let me remind you all," he grabbed his gavel and brought it down with force. "You people in the back. If you can't hold your conversations until we are through here today, I will have you removed." He waited and they complied.

"That goes for the rest of you. I will not tolerate any distractions in my courtroom. I want to remind you this is a preliminary hearing. We are merely here to discover whether this case continues, or it doesn't." He leaned back in his chair which the prosecution took as a signal to begin.

"Your Honor," Howard Pamplin, the Prosecuting Attorney stood and addressed the bench. He laid out the facts as they were presented to him and it seemed like an open and shut case until the Judge turned his attention to the defense table where Sam sat handcuffed and alone except for the deputy standing behind him.

"Sir, please stand and state your name for the record."

"Sam Henning," he answered simply.

"Sam Henning," the Judge consulted his notes. "Do you know why it is that you are in my court today?"

Sam didn't reply. Susan was in the front row heart pounding in her chest.

"Did you not hear the question posed to you Mister Henning?"

"I heard."

"What do you have to say, Mister Henning?"

The crowd held their collective breath and waited. Susan squirmed in her seat. And still Sam had not answered.

"Young man right now you are getting awful close to being slapped with a contempt of court. Do you understand?"

"No, I don't understand."

"I have been informed that you passed on the offer of a court appointed lawyer."

"I have, your Honor."

"Then we are to assume that you will be defending yourself in this most serious matter."

"I have always defended myself, your Honor."

"Very well, do you have any questions for this court before we proceed?"

"I wouldn't know what to ask."

"Did Sheriff Thompson inform you of the charges against you upon your arrest?"

"He mentioned a murder, but I have no idea what he's talking about. I never killed anyone in my life. I don't know the people he mentioned even though he said they were my parents."

"Please, take a seat up here on the witness stand."

Sam walked over to take the seat but before he could the Deputy had to swear him in. He held out a bible and instructed Sam to put his right hand on it and swear the truth. Sam looked down at the bible but did not make an effort to place his hand on it.

"I do not need to place my hand on your bible to tell the truth, Judge."

"Very well, Mister Henning. Let the court record show that Mister Henning is combative."

"Now, again, Mister Henning do you have anything to say?"

"I have no idea what *to* say."

"Mister Pamplin, would you like to proceed with your opening remarks?"

"Yes, your Honor," he stood adjusted his tie and approached Sam who watched him closely.

Susan couldn't breathe. She was silently praying that Sam would stay calm. She kept her eyes on him the whole time. Sam sat there quietly gritting his teeth she could see his jaw flexing.

The Frank and Leroy show were occupying a place by the side wall. The room was completely silent, all eyes on Sam and the Prosecuting Attorney. He approached Sam with a smoothness born of just this sort of thing and he was very good at what he did. If you were to ask him, he would tell you the same. Other familiar faces from around town were there but, Sam didn't see anyone except for the man who stood before him.

"On the night of February, the," He held up a paper he was holding and squinted at it. "12th. Sheriff Dobbs formally of the Springville Police Department entered the Henning house followed by Deputies Green and Ellis. What they found and later described was straight out of one of those horror movies.

Nobody in the audience moved, some were afraid to even take a breath.

Susan was concentrating so hard on Sam she was getting a slight headache. She was the only one, out of all the people that were there, to know the truth that Sam absolutely had no idea what was going on.

What thoughts must be chasing around in his head, she wondered. She looked around the courtroom and couldn't help but notice that neither Veronica, Clare, nor Jorden weren't there. Probably outside somewhere.

The Prosecutor faced the crowd, he had a definite flair for the dramatic, you could hear the people gasp.

"What they saw would lead to the requested transfers of both Deputies Green and Ellis to another post. We believe, and intend to prove, that this terrible act of violence had a connection to the death of then Sheriff Dobbs."

People shifted in their seats and looked at the person next to them. The Prosecutor gazed at the people with the air of someone used to being in a position of authority which didn't exactly sit well with some of the more fisty old-timers who were not impressed.

"The evidence will prove beyond a shadow of doubt, who murdered those fine upstanding citizens," He waved the folder around for effect. "It's all within these three eyewitness accounts. They tell of the *gruesome* tale of a *bloody* murder. Two people dead... Two prominent citizens of Springville... Two friends... And perhaps the most *horrifying* fact of all..." He let his words hang in the air for a moment before he continued.

"The most..." he lost his words for a second and paced the floor. "The thing that *most* troubles me and any other person in this room *today*," he said pointing at the crowd. "It's the *sad* fact is... they were also *parents*, mom and dad..."

"What the Sheriff and his Deputies walked into that night was unlike anything they'd *ever* seen before... It's right *here* in these reports I hold in my hand. What they found was a small *boy* standing over his *father* there was blood *everywhere*.

"This... little boy, ten years old. Ten *years* old! When Deputy Ellis came down from the upstairs bedroom having finished his sweep, he reported that the wife was upstairs...*dead* in her bed...

"Getting back to the boy... he was holding a *very* nasty knife in his hand and both parents had been stabbed *multiple* times."

By the time the Prosecuting Attorney finished even Susan had her doubts which made her feel awful inside.

The people waited as the Judge deliberated. Nobody left their spot for fear of losing it. And then he returned and took his seat behind the bench. He took off his glasses and asked Sam to stand.

"Sam, while it is true this crime is the worst I've ever come across, there are a few points that I'm not sure of. That being said, and though this happened a long time ago... I want to *you* to understand that there are *no* statutes of limitations on murder. It is hereby my discission-

"Wait!" A voice from the back had everyone's immediate attention. Veronica followed by her two sisters were making their way to the front. Veronica was carrying something wrapped in a towel.

"What is the meaning of this interruption?! Identify yourselves to this court!"

"My names is Veronica and these are my sisters, Clare and Jorden we-

"Your Honor this is highly out of order."

"I will say what is out of order and what isn't Mister Pamplin."

"Of course, your Honor, my apologies," he sat down.

"Your Honor? Judge? We found it," Veronica was panting with excitement. Her sisters were behind her smiling.

"Alright, since you have already interrupted these proceedings, for which there will be consequences, humor me. What on God's green earth have you found?"

"I object! This is turning into a circus!" The Prosecutor protested. His plea for normalcy went out the window.

"We found this in the shed behind Sam's house," Veronica handed a wrapped object to the Deputy who unwrapped it and handed it to the Judge who took his time examining it.

"You say you found this in a shed behind Sam's house? Young lady there were detectives and forensic officers all over that place," He looked down at the three sisters assessing the strange situation. "How did you happen to find what professionals could not?"

"A ghost showed it to me," simple question, simple answer."

"Young lady you don't know how close you are to-

"Look at the butt of the handle."

The Judge put his glasses back on and saw something that made him almost bite his tongue. He remembered seeing in the reports there was a bloody handprint on the wall by the back door. Green and Ellis even said it was too big for the boy to make.

"Well, I'm inclined to swear about now, but I will refrain," he looked out into the faces of the people and found the one he was looking for. He waved his Deputy over to the bench and said something to him his Deputy motioned the other two Deputies stationed at the back.

"Mister Dobbs, would you make your way to the bench sir," Judge Crane adjusted his glasses and watched Frank make his way through the sea of bodies, he wasn't hard to miss as big as he was. When Frank pushed through the batwing doors to stand before the Judge, he was not happy.

"State your name for the record."

"Why? I didn't do nothin'!"

"Son, I will only warn only you once... do not raise your voice to me again. Do we understand each other?"

Frank made a face.

"Good now please state your full name for the record."

"Frank Dobbs," he growled.

"Your father was the Sheriff of Springville at the time of the murders was he not?"

"He was."

"Judge, if I may come up?"

"Why not pretty soon we'll have the whole town up here. Come up, state your name and speak your piece but, be quick."

"Judge?" Susan smiled up at the Judge who peered down at her. "My name is Susan White. Sam and I... well when were kids we..." She glanced back at Sam.

"We were close friends."

Someone yelled, "We all thought they were gonna get married!"

"Order!" The gavel came down hard. "Next outburst and I swear you will all be held in contempt of this court. Now settle down!"

"The honest truth is that Sam, he doesn't have any memory of his childhood. When we first met, when he just came back... he had absolutely no idea who I was. He didn't even know who's house it was that he'd inherited. That's why when you asked if he had anything to say he honestly didn't know what to say.

"Judge Sam has a scare on the left side of his forehead," Vernica wasn't used to public speaking, and she was feeling light-headed.

"Judge Crane, this is highly irregular. I must insist we stop whatever it is we're doing here," again his words fell on the floor to be swept up later.

"You need to explain yourself very quickly," the Judge warned.

"I think," Veronica had a hard swallow. "That scar was made by the butt of that knife, Judge."

"And how do you intend to prove such a notion."

"I don't have to stand here and listen to this garbage," Frank was feeling cornered.

"You do and you will," Judge Crane waved for his Deputy. "Restrain this young man, Deputy."

"Hey, git your hands off'a me," Frank squirmed but he was caught, and he gave up.

"If you will come down, I think I can show you."

"Now is not the time to doubt yourself young lady either you can, or you can't. Which is it?"

"I can," her heart was banging against her ribcage. She hoped desperately that no one else could hear it within the tight, stifling confines of that over-crowded room.

"Alright you have my undivided attention. Don't waste my time further."

The Judge stood eyed the people and came down off his bench adjusting his glasses.

"Sam, can you lean forward a little bit? Look." She placed the butt of the knife against Sam's forehead, and it lined up exactly with his care. "See?"

"Here, let me try," Judge Crane took the knife and sure enough the evidence was beyond the shadow of a doubt. That explained the handprint. The original report stated the possibility that the wife hit her assailant with the phone receiver because it was found to be broken but forensics wasn't buying it. The receiver is a blunt object and the cut on Sam's head was made with something that had a sharp edge like the knife he now held.

"Thank you, Susan, ladies. I was about to send, what I now believe to be, the wrong person to prison. Deputy remand mister Dobbs to our fine jail facility as a prime suspect in the murder of Mister Andy Henning and his wife Lynn."

"Wait a damn minute! I haven't done nothin' what the hell is this?" Frank put up a good fight for about two seconds, but the beer and cigarettes had taken their toll. Plus, there were a couple very big Deputies laying on top of him.

"Deputy, remove Mister Dobbs from my courtroom please."

The deputy stood Frank up and took by the arm. He was just ushering him out a side door when the back of the room erupted.

People were yelling and pushing back there.

"Now what? What is all that ruckus back there?"

"He didn't do it Judge," a nervous voice split the courtroom air.

"Who the hell are you? Identify yourself and you better be quick about it, I'm damn near out of patience!"

"M-my name's Leroy." He shouted to be overheard.

"Well, Leroy, do you have a last name, or do we have to guess?"

Leroy laughed at that, but the Judge was not laughing.

"That was not meant as a joke sir, get on with it."

"Frank… H-he never killed those people, Judge."

"And how do you come by this fact if you don't mind sharing."

"I know who did." The room was like a tomb, suddenly all eyes and ears pointed at Leroy whose face was all over the place as he tried to speak.

"We are all waiting…"

"Frank, h-he loved Susan, Susan White a-and so did Sam. A-and so did I…" he paused feeling the weight of the room press in on him. His life was passing before him. "I-I knew I didn't stand a-a chance with Susan, so I-I wanted Sam to leave her alone…"

A murmur passed among the people who were glued to the spot.

"Order!"

"It's a little late for that Judge," the Prosecutor stood, hands on the table he surveyed the room.

"Your sarcasm, at this time, is greatly unappreciated, sir. Sit down."

"I only wanted to scare him…" Leroy's voice once again brought the room to silence.

"Leroy, what in hell are you talking about?" Frank was clueless.

"I-I only wanted to scare 'im I-I swear. But his ol' man he heard me and chased me downstairs where we fell to the floor, he was on me, and I was scared. I stabbed him before I even knew I did. And I kept stabbing him until he let me go."

The crowd gasped and the Judge raised his gavel as a warning, and they took it seriously.

"W-when I stood up, I was crazy… I-I saw Sam standing there and… I-I hit him hard with the butt of that knife you got there in your hand. I-I heard his ol' lady upstairs and it sounded like she was calling the Sheriff… I-I ran back upstairs, and she attacked me… "So I stabbed her until she quit then I ran back downstairs and put the knife in Sam's hand and went out… the… back door… I-I did it… not Frank. Me I-I killed those people… I-I'm sorry, Frank."

"Leroy?" Was all Frank could say he was out of breath and completely caught off guard by this whole thing.

CHAPTER 65

Well, Leroy went to spend the rest of his natural life in the Washington State Prison. Frank he wasn't the same after that, he mellowed some. He and Sam crossed paths a time or two with no trouble. Frank had no desire to tangle with Sam ever again, he could *have* Susan for all he cared.

As the days melted one into another the town of Springville went back to being a nice little town to live in. One morning while Sam was out on the front porch enjoying his first cup of coffee, he heard someone coming down his road. He stood balancing his cup on the top rail.

Arriving in a cloud of dust and smoke was Hank the town handyman. He swung out of his truck and promptly closed the tail of his jacket in the door. He opened it again and pulled his jacket free, closed it, and lit a cigarette.

"Hey there young man! Good mornin" to ya," he walked up to the steps and smiled up at Sam. "How's it feel ta be a free man?"

"Why, Hank I've always been a free man." *Except when I was in that room...*

"Sure, and for certain, Sam."

"What brings you out and about this fine morning?"

"Oh, I thought I'd swing by and get my busted-up ladder out of your way."

"I'll help you get it loaded up, Hank."

"I appreciate that, I truly do."

They walked back around the house and Hank let out a whistle when he saw his ladder.

"Well, I guess it's time to invest in a new ladder."

"Yeah, this one's about had it I think," Sam smiled. They carried the ladder around and loaded it onto Hank's truck. When they were done Hank leaned against his truck and lit another cigarette. "Hard to figure people idn't it Sam?"

"That's a fact," Sam thought for a second then said with a big smile sneaking across his bruised face. "You know, Hank it has just occurred to me…"

"And what is that?"

"You've been here for, what, about half an hour now? And we've been talking… and it just hit me. You haven't sworn once. Not even close."

"Huh, imagine that." He snubbed out his cigarette and lit another, he climbed into his truck and leaned out the window. "Sam, if ya need anything, anything at all don't hesitate to call."

"Thanks Hank, have a great day."

"Same to you Sam, I'll be seein' ya," he fired up his truck and drove back down the road.

"It's a small town, Hank," Sam called after him.

Just as Hank's rumbling truck faded into the distance it was replaced by the sound of another vehicle. Sam took a sip of his cold coffee, frowned and dumped it in the bushes. Into his yard came the most incredible person he had ever known. A person he hardly knew who had literally saved his life. A person he wanted to spend the rest of his life getting to know, again. She came to a stop in the yard, got out and waved to Sam, and he waved back.

"Feel like having company?"

"I would love to have some company. Got anybody in mind?"

Susan made a face and reached into her car. She pulled out a paper bag and held it up.

"Nice I can always use paper bags," he laughed, and it felt good.

"It's what's inside it smartass," she took to the front steps and stood looking up into Sam's bruised face. "I Have in here a nice cold bottle of champaign do you think we could pop the cork and fill some glasses?"

"I think that sounds like an excellent idea have a seat, I'll be right back."

"Don't be too long I'm thirsty and I feel like celebrating!"

She kicked off her shoes wiggling her toes in the warm sun.

There was a pop and the sound of a cork bouncing off the ceiling then Sam was back out with two glasses of bubbly.

A little boy in blue swim trunks stepped out from behind a tree not far away and waved. Susan set her glass down. She looked at him then at Sam who was smiling. The boy had a face, a nice smiling face.

"Sam?"

"I see him."

"Do you know him now?" Susan was smiling so hard her cheeks hurt.

"He's my brother... Pete," Sam was at peace suddenly... finally.

As they watched, Pete waved then disappeared into thin air.

Sam took a second to recover then held his glass up, "What shall we drink to," He asked. He felt a great weight had been lifted off him.

"Let's drink to you and me," Susan said. They clinked glasses and settled back to enjoy the beginning of a new day and a new life.

A short film played in Sam's mind just then. Two young love-struck kids splashing and laughing while the sun shimmered on the surface of the cool waters around them...

"I sure do miss you and me swimming in the lake..." He looked at Susan who had tears in her eyes.

"Me too, Sam," she rested her head on his shoulder and smiled.

"I could sure get used to drinking champaign on a Sunday morning," he held his glass in the sun and watched the thin trails of bubbles march to the surface. He took Susan's hand and looked out into the forest.

"Me too, Sam," she squeezed his big hand tightly. "Me too."

The End

About the Author

Mike Taylor left his life in Montana to live on the island of Hawai'i. There at a local theatre, where he volunteered and eventually became Technical Director for many years, he met his wife, Marion. They eventually settled in the southern district of Ka'u.